The fairie Sinnan stood behind Dylan on
the horse's back and whispered in his ear . . .

"Who was it that saved your life and returned you to your own time when you were mortally wounded? And who was it sent you back to the battle once you were all stitched together again by your wondrous future surgeons? It would be well for ye to listen to me, laddie. What will ye do once you're in Edinburgh? I suppose when you find Ramsey's house you'll simply march right in and take your Cait away from him?"

"I'm crazy, not stupid, Tink." Dylan sighed. "But all I want to do right now is see Cait. And my son. I've got to see my son. . . ."

DON'T MISS J. ARDIAN LEE'S TIMELESS DEBUT:
SON OF THE SWORD

"From Highland Games to highland hills, Lee takes us on an entertaining— and ultimately Scottish—journey as a witness to the making of a legend."
—Jennifer Roberson,
national bestselling author of *Lady of the Glen*

"A good historical fantasy."   —*Science Fiction Chronicle*

Ace Books by J. Ardian Lee

SON OF THE SWORD

OUTLAW SWORD

OUTLAW SWORD

J. ARDIAN LEE

ACE BOOKS, NEW YORK

OUTLAW SWORD

An Ace Book / published by arrangement with the author

PRINTING HISTORY
Ace trade paperback edition / July 2002

Copyright © 2002 by Julianne Lee.
Cover art by Dan Craig.

Visit our website at
www.penguinputnam.com
Check out the ACE Science Fiction & Fantasy newsletter!

Library of Congress Cataloging-in-Publication Data

Lee, J. Ardian.
Outlaw sword / J. Ardian Lee.
p. cm.
ISBN 0-441-00935-2 (alk. paper)
1. Scotland—History—18th century—Fiction. 2. Outlaws—Fiction. I. Title.

PS3562.E326 098 2002
813'.6—dc21

2002019042

ACE®
Ace Books are published by The Berkley Publishing Group, a division of Penguin Putnam Inc., 375 Hudson Street, New York, New York 10014.
ACE and the "A" design are trademarks belonging to Penguin Putnam Inc.

PRINTED IN THE UNITED STATES OF AMERICA

10 9 8 7 6 5 4 3 2 1

For
Travis and Nicole

ACKNOWLEDGMENTS

The following have my heartfelt gratitude for aiding and abetting: my agent, Russell Galen; swordmaster F. Braun McAsh; fight consultant Rev. HyeonSik Hong; Russell Handelman of the Philipsburg Manor Upper Mills, Sleepy Hollow, New York; Ernie O'Dell and the Green River Writers of Louisville, Kentucky; Gaelic language instructor John Ross; the Fort William, Scotland, Public Library; native guides Gail Montrose and Duncan MacFarlane of Glenfinnan, Scotland; Teri McLaren; Sarah Stegall; Trisha Mundy; Michael LaMarche; Julie Bolt; Betsy Vera; Diana Diaz; Jenni Bohn; Dale Lee; and, as ever, Ginjer Buchanan.

Author's Note

Though this story is loosely based on historical fact, the fictional characters are not actual people, and any resemblance to historical or contemporary persons is coincidental. Glen Ciorram and its people are imaginary, and no fictional character is meant to represent a historical member of the Matheson, Bedford, or Ramsay families.

However, the nonfictional characters and events are as true as possible to what is known about them.

On spelling: In the early eighteenth century, spelling was a dodgy affair any way one looks at it. Standardized spelling in English didn't come along for another century at least, and for Gaelic it didn't happen until the latter part of the twentieth century. The spellings for Gaelic words in this book are from *MacLennan's Dictionary*, which tends to the archaic and therefore lends itself to the period. All other words are either English or dialect words used by English-speaking Scots, and for the sake of internal consistency are spelled according to American usage.

E-mail J. Ardian Lee at ardian@sff.net, or visit *www.sff.net/people/ardian/*.

CHAPTER 1

"Ye'll get yourself killed, riding in the open as you are."

"I'm not in the mood to take the long way around." Dylan's flush of gratitude was wearing thin with the nagging. The Irish faerie was getting on his nerves once again, the way she had for the entire two years he'd been stuck in the eighteenth century.

It was only a day since the defeat at Sheriffmuir, but now he wanted to put the uprising behind him, the same way nearly the rest of the stripped and demoralized Jacobite army was doing that day. Never mind he was riding an English cavalry horse, and never mind that the countryside was crawling with Hanoverians looking for rebels, his only wish now was to reach Edinburgh and find Cait. And his son. He continued along the trail that threaded its way among wooded hills, and the horse's hooves thumped the ground with a steady beat.

"You willnae get there at all if George's men find you with this horse." Sinann Eire sat on the rump of his stolen horse, her thin legs stretched across it and her feet dangling. One toe played with the cropped tail, and the horse snorted at the indignity of it. She leaned against Dylan's back, and he pressed back against her to compensate.

The pre-winter frost crusted the ground and bit his nose. He huddled into the plaid he wrapped around himself, wishing he'd also been able to liberate his coat from those thieving English soldiers. Keeping his blue cap would have been nice, too, but it was somewhere back on the battlefield, probably trampled into the mud or taken by one of King George's men for a trophy.

"Don't worry, Tink, I'm going to sell it." He'd already dumped the saddle and bright red blanket into a gorse thicket not far from Dunblane. "But I'll sell it in Edinburgh where, firstly, I'll have a shot at being just another face in the crowd and, secondly, I'll also have a shot at getting more than a Scottish threepence for it."

"For a certainty, laddie, it's but another face you'll be in that filthy kilt you've got on."

Dylan urged the animal into a trot just to bounce Sinann from her seat and shut her up. The ends of the piece of cloth he'd tied around his cut arm for a bandage fluttered as he rode.

Tossed into the air, Sinann flew to catch up and, once Dylan had settled back into a walk, stood behind him on the horse's back. She squatted, held his shoulders for balance, and said into his ear, "A bit rough, aren't you, laddie? Who was it saved your life and returned you to your own time when you were mortally wounded?" Dylan tugged his plaid higher on his neck and declined to reply, but she continued, "And who was it sent you back to the battle once you were all stitched together again by your wondrous future surgeons?"

"Will. You *will* send me back from the future. November, 2000. Remember that. You haven't done it yet." His fingers went to the fresh scar just below his rib cage, where he'd lost a kidney and his spleen after being run through by an English cavalry sword. Sinann had returned him to his own time, where his life was saved by modern surgery. After six weeks of recovery, she returned him to the moment of his near death. The entrance and exit wounds still ached. At each step the horse took, his entire left side throbbed with a dull thud.

"Be that as it may, it would be well for ye to listen to me. What will ye do once you're in Edinburgh? I suppose when you find Ramsay's house, you'll simply march right in and take her away from him, and he'll be saying, 'Och, but I dinnae know! By all means, take her and be happy, the both of ye!' "

Dylan sighed. "I'm crazy, not stupid, Tink. Not that I don't think she would come with me, but I *know* she's married. I *know* she can't leave him without causing a big enough stink to make us both miserable for the rest of whatever." His voice took on a thick sarcasm. "I *even* know that as an outlaw I'm more of a liability than a protection to her and the boy. I'm not going to let them get hurt."

"They will if you dinnae leave her there."

Dylan shook his head. "No way. You heard him last summer. He beats her, and thinks it's his right. He thinks she cheated him."

"And did she not? She went to him already with child. I daresay that could be called cheating."

"Whose side are you on, anyway?"

Sinann's voice took on an irritating tone of anticipated triumph. "Deny it. I'm listening, lad."

Anger rose, warming his cheeks against the frosty air. "It was her father who deceived Ramsay, not her. In a business deal, for God's sake. He made her marry that Whig pansy to cover his political ass. Furthermore, I *daresay* the only reason Ramsay married her was to cover his own butt in case the Jacobites won and James took the throne. Which, for that, I could have saved him the trouble and told him the cause was doomed. Which means, Tinker*bell*, now that the Jacobites have lost for the time being, he'll treat her worse than ever. For all I know about that sleazebag, he might find a way to get rid of her so he can marry someone else. For all either of us knows, her life might be in danger right now. Besides, it wasn't her fault. She was supposed to marry me."

"You were arrested."

"I didn't do it."

"The *Sassunach* Major surely does not care whether ye did or dinnae, as eager as he was to cut you to ribbons with a whip in spite of knowing you were innocent. You cannae win this one, Dylan Matheson. Ye're a marked man as long as George of Hanover has the throne."

Dylan's jaw clenched. "I don't want to hear any more talk about what happened. It's done, and what I want now is to see Cait and Ciaran. That's all I want right now, and I'll figure out the rest later. I've got to see my son." Dylan's gut tightened, and he pressed the heel of his hand to the sore muscles. "He's damn near a year old, and I've never seen him. I just want to see my son." He tried to picture the boy, but of course had no idea what he looked like. Was he happy? Healthy? How was he affected by Ramsay's hatred for him? Was he being taught Ramsay was his father?

Sinann slipped down behind him to straddle the horse and fell silent, her face pressed to his back. Dylan rode on, to the thudding of hoofbeats on the trail and the jingle of the bit as the horse fidgeted it in its mouth.

After a while, she lifted her head and began fiddling with something behind Dylan. He glanced back, and found her untying a string she'd worn around her wrist for over a year. It was a red braid that reminded him of the friendship bracelets he sometimes had seen on kids in his kung fu classes back home. This was a long one and, tied around Sinann's tiny wrist, the ends dangled several inches. She said, "Give me your arm."

"Why? What's that, more of the craft?"

"Aye. Give me your hand. It's a talisman, for strength."

Dylan figured he could use as much of that as he could get, so he reached back to let her tie the string around his left wrist. Even though his wrist was much larger than hers, the ends dangled some and lifted in the cold wind as he rode. Several knots had been tied along it, and he counted seven of them. He'd learned enough of the craft to know that seven was a magic number. "You made this?"

"Aye. I made it for you, and have carried it a long while. It's time you carried it yourself."

"Your powers being wonky and all, you're sure it works?"

There was a short hesitation, then she said, "Aye. It'll work. It must." Then she said, "Ye'll be needing to learn more of the craft, you know."

"Yeah." He knew that. She'd already taught him some things, and he'd come to realize the advantage of knowing useful tricks. "What's on your mind now?"

"Astrology."

Dylan blurted a bark of a laugh. "Been there, done that."

"Ye dinnae say?"

"Well, enough to know that I'm a Taurus/Gemini cusp, born on May 22, 1970." He took a deep breath and recited in a singsong voice, "I'm loyal, a lover of beauty, and I'm somewhat ambidextrous, which means that though I'm right-handed, I can fight with both hands. That's all true, but so what? Astrology's a parlor game. Nothing really useful. Take it from one who knows, knowing the future is completely overrated. And how come a maiden of the *Tuatha De Danann* knows that stuff, anyway?"

"What, ye think I've lived in a cave all my life? Astrology, in fact, is often used by priests hereabouts, and dinnae think it hasnae been a bone of contention for the past few centuries. I, myself, have been familiar with the teachings since the coming of the priests."

Dylan chuckled. "You can believe in the influence of planets, but you don't believe in God?"

"*Och*, I wouldnae say that, now. I've been around quite long enough to know I dinnae know everything."

"Which means . . . ?"

"Which means I dinnae *not* believe in your Yahweh." Dylan's eyebrows raised, and he turned to stare at her, but she gave his chin a shove to make him face front. "Ye needn't look at me like I've gone daft. I'm a great deal older than yourself, and know a great deal more."

"Yeah, like you knew the uprising would fail."

"*Och!*" She was silent, sulking, for a few minutes. Dylan's mind drifted to Cait, pulling together a picture of her in his memory. Then Sinann said, "What time of day were ye born?"

"Huh?" Dylan returned to the discussion reluctantly.

"What time of day?"

His eyes narrowed as he tried to remember his birth certificate. "Um . . . 5:30 a.m., I think. Something like that. Central Daylight Savings Time. Six hours earlier than here."

There was only a moment's pause, then, "Taurus rising. You're far more than just loyal, laddie. You're the one to stand by your guns and your people until death."

Dylan grunted. "You didn't need to know my chart to figure that. I've come close enough to death more than once." He shrugged one shoulder and felt one of the scars on his back tighten.

"Nevertheless, with a nativity such as yours, ye're in great danger this day. I beg you to get bloody hell off this track. Please. For the night, in any case."

Dylan pulled up his horse and turned to peer at Sinann's face. Begging? She was serious. He bit the inside corner of his mouth and then sighed. What the heck, the sun was setting and the bitter night cold would be on them soon. "All right." He threw a leg over the horse's neck and slid to the ground, then drew the animal off the trail and into the loamy forest. Sinann flew behind, scattering leaves over the track they made. He went downhill to find a burn trickling and falling over rocks among reeds and bracken ferns, then followed that to find a dry, level spot to stop for the night.

He didn't dare light a fire, and ate the last of his army ration of oatmeal cold from his hand, wetted by water from the burn and mashed into sticky globs he then picked out with his fingers. *Drammach*, it was called, and he'd eaten a lot of it over the past year. Then he washed his hands and face in the burn. Once the horse was hidden and hobbled in a stand of birches, he lay in the dirt and rolled into his plaid for sleep. Sinann perched on the rump of the horse and folded her wings around herself.

He went unconscious quickly, a habit he'd developed soon after coming to this century. The ability to sleep on demand while cold and wet sometimes meant the difference between survival and death, for a fuzzy head from lack of sleep could weaken a man before his enemies.

Dylan didn't know how long he'd slept, but the pain of awakening in a hurry told him it wasn't long. There had been a noise, he would swear it, but though he strained to hear, he couldn't tell what it had been. Dylan peered into the darkness.

The wind made the trees sigh, the sound like voices of the spirits. Branches reached out to each other, then retreated, the tall pines in conference over Dylan's resting place. Then, carried on the wind, he heard it: a distant jingling sound. He tensed as it approached, and discerned the sound of horses' bridles on the trail above.

As they approached, hoofbeats grew louder. Soldiers? Probably. It didn't matter much, since just about everyone this side of Glen Dochart was on the lookout for scattered Jacobites. He glanced up at Sinann, who was alert in the moonlight, listening. There were no voices among the riders, which struck Dylan as strange. In fact, soldiers on the trail after dark was also very weird. He and Sinann waited as the large party passed above. When the hoofbeats receded, Dylan whispered to Sinann, "How did you know?"

She snorted. "Surely even you have lived long enough to know you dinnae know everything, lad."

The next morning Dylan shook frost and dirt from his hair as he rose from the ground and draped his plaid around himself. It was a struggle not to shiver as he arranged the plaid over his shoulder and tucked it into his belt. He rubbed his face to restore the circulation to his nose, for a moment afraid the numbness might be frostbite. But soon feeling returned, and he began to scratch his itchy beard stubble. He debated letting it grow, but decided to shave in the cold burn as he remembered there were still English soldiers out to arrest him who knew his face as bearded. The skill of shaving with his *sgian dubh* was like riding a bicycle. He quickly dispatched the stubble in spite of having no fire and no hot water.

Down the trail a bit, he came upon a harvested oat field between two hills and let his mount graze on the stubble. He pulled his large dirk from the scabbard strapped to his right legging. He'd named the dirk Brigid when he'd consecrated her by fire years ago, after a pagan goddess turned Catholic saint. He spun her in the air and caught her by the hilt, then began to warm up with some light stretching. Once he was loosened, he eased into a formal kung fu exercise. Wielding Brigid, he made wide swaths in the air and worked to hone his focus till he sweated in spite of the cold. It was good to stretch, after weeks of inactivity.

It was a struggle to clear his mind and focus. His thoughts kept drifting to Cait, causing him to tense up. He shook his head and blinked, determined to think only of the exercise at hand. Slowly the tension drained from him and his mind calmed.

Martial art and swordsmanship were nearly lifelong interests that had led to his vocation back home as an instructor of kung fu and European fencing, and there had been a time when he was as skilled a fighter as anyone he knew. But the wound and surgery had wrecked his stamina. Eighteenth-century Scotland wasn't a place where the average man could coddle himself and live. So, while his empty stomach grumbled and the November air found its way under his kilt and into his sark, he stretched the damaged muscles of his side and back until they ached and sweat trickled from his hair down his shaven jaw. Then, properly warmed and loosened, he mounted the cavalry horse and went on his way. His left hand absently pressed to his side as if still trying to hold in his guts, the way it had the day he was wounded.

It was not long at all that morning before he and Sinann emerged from a patch of forest and caught sight of Edinburgh. In the distance, across open, rolling ground, the castle was visible, perched on a rock just apart from a cluster of buildings that huddled on the length of that rock. Dylan cursed the lack of cover.

Sinann's voice was without sympathy. "Show me a town or village in this entire kingdom to be approached by stealth on horseback in daylight. Ye'll need to get rid of this horse, lad."

"No, I'm going to bluff it." He urged his mount forward again. Stray snowflakes began to drift by in the wind: big, fluffy ones that didn't stick, but they'd be followed by others that would.

Sinann muttered something in Gaelic he didn't quite catch, and buried her face against his back.

Dylan rode at a walk, as if he didn't give a damn who saw him. The road was not deserted, and he encountered several people who peered at the horse and at the costly double bit in its mouth. As he neared town and the castle grew larger in the distance, there were one or two thatched stone houses to be seen along the road, and Sinann urged him to try selling the horse at one of those. He didn't reply, lest anyone along the road think he was talking to himself, and rode on. By midmorning they were on the street that circled to the south of the castle.

The hill ended in cliffs, and the stone buildings of the castle seemed to grow from it like stalagmites. Awe struck him as he rode through the Grassmarket. He realized this place had once been the abode of Robert the Bruce and the birthplace of King James VI and I. Much of the history he'd read of Scotland had taken place within those walls. Then he circled the hill to where the battery of cannon covered the approach to the port-cullis on the northeast side. Funny, it didn't look quite right to him. He'd seen photos, and would swear he'd seen ones taken from this side, but it just didn't seem right.

Then it clicked. The entire Esplanade was . . . different. The approach was nothing more than a dirt track flanked by low heather and thistles. The paved Esplanade and the portcullis bearing statues of William Wallace and Robert the Bruce hadn't been built yet.

Dylan gawked like a tourist, until he spotted a Redcoat on guard at the old portcullis to the north of the battery. More Redcoats rode toward the castle along the track on the hill above him, and he quickly looked away to mind his own business. He should have known there would be Redcoats: since the construction of Holyrood Palace at the other end of the city, the castle was no longer a royal residence. In Hanoverian-occupied Edinburgh it was now being used to garrison English soldiers.

Soon Dylan was able to duck among the tall buildings of the city, climbing the rock on which it stood, and his mind slipped away from the soldiers. Cait was here. Somewhere in this mess of crowded, stinking stone and wood was the house where she lived, and perhaps she was thinking of him.

The wynde by which he reached the High Street was steep and

crooked, and the climb was relentless until they crested the long, narrow summit. To the left the castle was just visible between tall stone buildings, and on down to the right the main road sloped gradually to the tail of Edinburgh's rock. Shops and tenement houses, all seemed to lean on each other for support, some with turrets reaching out over the street for whatever space could be had.

The smell was appalling. Dylan had thought his time in this century had taught him not to be bothered by stench, but here the street itself was a sewer that made his eyes water from ammonia and methane. At the side of the street, a cart full of the stinking mud stood by while a woman with her skirts tied up between her legs shoveled muck into it from the ground. Probably she would sell it for fertilizer out in the countryside, and thank God for that, or else the city must be buried in excrement. He muttered to Sinann, "I'm not so sure any more I want to sell the horse. I'll have to walk in that."

"You're a fool if you think a cell in a tolbooth would smell prettier."

Dylan grunted and began looking for a sign that might indicate a buyer of horses. By the standards of eighteenth-century Scotland, Edinburgh was a big place, but it still didn't take long to find a stable. Several were tucked into the foot of the hill near Cowgate. Dylan was able to sell the horse for fifteen shillings in good, cold English cash.

"Ye could have gotten an entire pound, at least," said Sinann, who hovered over the filthy street so as not to walk in it. Before answering, Dylan stopped at the window of a baker's shop and bought a wheaten loaf to eat, half of which he wolfed in two bites. It was warm and delicious, heaven after having eaten nothing but two handfuls of oatmeal in two days. He moved on, wending his way between pedestrians and riders, back up a narrow wynde to High Street.

When he swallowed, he finally replied to Sinann, "No, I couldn't have gotten an entire pound. The man guessed the horse was stolen. Which is good, since he'll know not to let it be seen by those who would care."

"And if he turns you in?"

Dylan peered at Sinann. "Where's the profit in that? They'd confiscate his horse and he'd be out fifteen shillings. No, if he was going to do that, he would have refused to buy."

"Probably."

He sighed and looked around at the crowds. "Yeah, well, if they find me, they find me. Meanwhile, I've got to find Ramsay."

"You could ask after him."

He chuckled. "What, just go up to someone and say, *Pardon me, but I'm a fugitive Jacobite and former raider for Rob Roy, and though I'm wanted by the Crown for treason and murder, I'm really a nice guy and I swear I didn't do those horrible things they say I did—well, not all of them anyway—and I'm looking for the man who married my sweetheart so I can kill him. Would you care to help me out here?*"

Sinann perked up. "Ye're set to kill him, then?"

"I would have done it already if I was."

"You dinnae do it because I stopped you."

Dylan opened his mouth for a stinging reply, but a rough, young voice piped up from behind him, "Are ye out to kill someone? With that there sword? Can I watch?"

Dylan spun to find a runny-nosed boy in a raggedy coat, with mud on his legs almost reaching the hems of his breeches, a perfect Dickensian picture a century before Charles Dickens would be born. The coat was old, faded red, and of a man's size in the military style. Even without insignia or other bric-a-brac, Dylan figured it must have been stolen off a dead soldier. He shook his head. "I was just kid . . . uh, joking.

Sinann said, "Ask the lad. He'll know where to find Ramsay."

Dylan said to the boy, "Can you help me find someone? He promised me a job, and so I want to work for him."

The kid frowned, not fooled. Sinann said, "Dinnae lie."

Dylan glanced at Sinann, then back to the boy. "No, really. I want to work for him." He addressed the boy, but his words were meant for both him and the faerie who was not visible to anyone but himself. "You know, get to learn all the ins and outs of his business. Really be *indispensable* to him. Maybe even get to know his *family*." He cut a glance at Sinann.

Understanding lit her eyes, but the boy was still mystified. He gave a gurgling sniff that did nothing for the glob of green snot under his nose. "All right, sir, if you say so, sir. Where is it ye need to get to?"

"I need to find the offices of a merchant named Connor Ramsay."

"Right. A thruppence for it." Dylan fished in his purse and handed the boy a silver coin. "This way." The boy was off like a shot, hurrying through the crowded High Street. He ducked under the head of a horse pulling a cart, and Dylan had to wait for the cartload of leather goods to pass by before he could cross. Sinann fluttering after, he caught up at the next block down the street and followed the boy through a narrow archway and down a steep wynde slippery with mud of suspicious origin. The weak northern sun nearly disappeared this deep among the towering stone buildings, and moss grew in thick patches over everything. The path leveled out at a tiny close, planted with rose bushes and surrounded on all sides by wrought iron. The boy pointed to a narrow wooden door on which was mounted an iron plaque that said in raised lettering, *Ramsay, Ltd.*

Dylan thanked him and the guide was about to dash off, but Dylan said, "*Wait.* Here." Another threepence piece was pressed into the boy's grubby hand. "You never saw me." The boy nodded eagerly, but as he tried to dash off again, Dylan grabbed his arm. "Be assured I have friends, madmen from the Highlands, who will hold you to that." This time the boy's eyes darkened and there was a pause before he gave a heavy, rolling sniff and nodded slowly. Then Dylan let him scurry back up the wynde.

He then faced the door, ran his fingers through his shaggy hair to get it off his face, and told Sinann, "Well, Tink, here goes nothing."

CHAPTER 2

The door was small but doubled, each side a narrow slab of wood not as wide as his own shoulders, and came to a gothic point overhead. The wall in which it was set was curved, and as Dylan looked up, he realized what it was. "It's a stairwell."

"Aye. The spiral stairs are the first line of defense. This one would be built deiseil, to the advantage of the right-handed defender. You can see by the way the windows are set in it." Sinann pointed upward, and Dylan saw. There were pairs of windows between the landings, each pair with one window slightly higher than the other, indicating the risers inside ran clockwise. "Left-handed folk build them widdershins. It's a narrow door and narrow stairs ye're looking at." She pointed to a small window near the ground, which would be high ventilation for a basement floor. "The stairs go down as well. Try not to get yerself trapped. Having to rescue you at every turn has become a wee bit tedious."

Dylan cut a sideways glance at her, rapped on the wood, and whispered to the faerie, "Or maybe I'll just ask to see Ramsay."

"Draw your dirk, at least."

"No." One side of the door opened almost immediately, and a man with one bleary eye and an empty socket looked out. His beard was a growth of two or three days and his coat was a greasy, torn mess, but he looked Dylan up and down as if he found Dylan's kilt an appalling fashion faux pas. He said in English, "We got nae work fer wanderers! Off with ye!" He slammed the door in Dylan's face.

"Huh." Dylan bit the inside corner of his mouth and gazed blandly at Sinann. "That boy don't know me very well. Ya think?"

"You can take him." Sinann was remarkably bloodthirsty today.

Dylan shook his head. "There's a better way." He knocked again, and when the door opened, before the one-eyed man could utter a word, Dylan burst forth with a big smile and a flurry of cheerful greeting in an affected highbrow English accent. "Right," he said, and offered a friendly hand. "Dear chap, we seem to have gotten off to a bit of an awkward start. I'm Charles Emerson Winchester III, at your service. I wonder if I might have a word with your employer."

The bewildered man took Dylan's hand on reflex, upon which Dylan dropped the accent and the spiel, grabbed the man's hand in both of his and tilted the wrist up. The man gasped and stood on his toes in an effort to straighten the wrist, which was not made to bend in that particular direction, but Dylan kept the pressure on simply by turning the hand farther. Still smiling, he said in his native suburban Tennessee drawl, "Now, take me to Ramsay."

The man backed into the stairwell and headed downstairs, cringing at the pain in his wrist. "Upstairs," Dylan commanded, and pointed with his chin the other direction. "You first. Up." Sinann giggled.

The man obeyed, backing up and around the stone steps ranged in a tight spiral. His eyes bugged out with pain and the fear that Dylan might break his wrist. Around and around they went, up four or five flights. Finally at one of the landings the man backed through a door painted in gleaming black enamel, and into a whitewashed office that smelled of dust, ink, and old paper.

A young man at a heavy oak desk leaped up when he saw the doorman dancing on his toes, walking backward before Dylan. "Good God!"

Dylan said, "I'm here to see Ramsay."

The fellow was slender and wispy, with a voice to match and a forehead high with a prematurely receding hairline. "You'll see hell first! How did you get in here?"

Sinann commented, "He's the brave little puppy, that one."

Across the room was a door Dylan guessed led to an inner office. He shoved the doorman toward it, away from himself, then pulled Brigid and held the dirk extended in his left hand, his right hand on the hilt of his scabbarded sword. He wouldn't draw the longer weapon unless he had to, for the room was only about ten feet across, too small to use it to full advantage.

The young secretary reached into a drawer and pulled out an etched steel flintlock pistol. Before he could aim it, Dylan drew his sword and with a slight tap of the blade tip parried the single-shot gun. It deflected the aim just enough to miss him as it went off with a puff of powder and a deafening roar.

Dylan bit back anger and said through clenched teeth as gun smoke stung his nose, "Tell Ramsay that Dilean Mac a'Chlaidheimh is here to collect a debt." The doorman staggered against the back wall, holding his sore wrist as if it were broken, and stared hard at Dylan's broadsword.

The young man sputtered, "I don't expect the likes of you could be owed anything by Mr. Ramsay."

"I saved his life."

"Indeed?"

Ramsay's lazy voice came from behind the door. "Show him in, Felix. And in the future please refrain from putting holes in the walls."

The young man's jaw dropped and he turned toward the door, forgetting his back. "Sir?"

The Lowland accent behind the door became clipped, impatient. "I said, show him in. Without *too* much delay, if you please, Felix."

Dylan scabbarded his sword and transferred Brigid to his right. Felix, making an attempt at saving face, said, "Leave the weapons." Dylan ignored the request as he strode past Felix and into Ramsay's office. He closed the door behind him.

Behind a large, cluttered desk the wealthy merchant lounged in a huge carved chair that was more throne than furniture. Shelves filled with ledgers lined all four walls, leaving room only for one window and the door. As tall as Dylan, but thin and languid, he looked Dylan over with pale blue eyes. He said, "You are, of course, insane. I should have you arrested."

"I want a job."

Ramsay shifted in his seat and crossed his legs. "So naturally you thought of me. How considerate of you to offer your indispensable services to undeserving me. As it happens, I have nae need . . ."

"You do." Dylan stood hipshot, Brigid in his fist by his side, as if he didn't care how Ramsay might protest.

Ramsay considered that for a moment, then said, "Would this be more blackmail from Mr. MacGregor? It isn't enough you and the rest of his men kidnapped me last August?"

"Rob has nothing to do with this, but call it what you like. You need me to work for you. Your life is in great danger from those who know some of your sympathies do not lie with the Crown. Not to mention I got in here past your doorman and secretary, without spilling so much as a drop of blood. There is not the slightest mark on your guard, who, had he been the sort of man you need, would never have let this happen. You need me."

Ramsay's eyes narrowed, but he said nothing.

Dylan went on. "Remember, I saved your life. I spoiled Alasdair Roy's aim when he fired at you. Alasdair is a dead shot. If not for me, he'd have put a bullet in your head as easy as pissing in a pot. I let you escape."

Another light came into Ramsay's eyes and an edge to his voice. "Yes. And just why did you do that?"

Dylan took a deep breath. He couldn't tell the truth—that he was in love with Ramsay's wife and the man's death would have left Cait shamed and destitute. He said, "I need a job. Raiding cattle with Rob Roy MacGregor isn't a career with a future. Especially now the men have disbanded."

Ramsay grunted and fingered one of the papers on his desk. "He's off fighting Argyll."

"No, just about now he's ducking and running, like the rest of the Jacobite army. The uprising is almost over. The ones who can are going home for the winter, and they won't be back."

A frown creased Ramsay's brow. "And you know they won't be back because . . ."

Dylan bit his lip and mentally cursed himself for forgetting his current place in the time line. He took a step toward the desk and said, "Two days ago there was a battle near Dunblane. The Earl of Mar thinks he won, but his army has dispersed. Last time I saw them, they were most of them headed north, going back home because they're demoralized, they have responsibilities to their families, and their kilts and baggage were captured by Argyll's Hanoverians. They're all pretty pi . . . they're very angry at Mar for his poor leadership. Mar waited too long for King James to come, and the chance of success in taking the crown from King George has passed."

A smile curled Ramsay's lips, which alarmed Dylan. Perhaps he had underestimated Ramsay's position with the Hanoverian government, in which case he held nothing that would influence the rich merchant. If Ramsay's position was solid enough, his marriage to the daughter of Iain Matheson could be weathered, and a spin might be put on his Jacobite activities so they would be seen as double espionage and therefore in Hanoverian interest. However, Dylan forged ahead. "I have friends in need of jobs. Men who would consider themselves beholden to an employer in this time of economic uncertainty and who would be quick to protect the reputation of said employer." He paused to emphasize his next words. "No matter what they may have known of him in the past."

Ramsay tensed. "MacGregor's men. I've done no business with him."

"The MacGregors have done business with Matheson of Ciorram. You've received cattle from Iain Mór, reived from the MacDonells, have you not?"

Ramsay's nostrils flared, and his eyes took on a metallic chill. Satisfaction settled in Dylan's heart as he knew he'd struck fear in Ramsay's. He raised his chin and continued, "I have three men loyal to me who, I assure you, are best kept loyal."

Sinann said, unheard by Ramsay, "And who might they be? Ye liar." Dylan ignored her as she continued, "*Och*, it's a slippery character you have become, Dylan Robert Matheson."

Ramsay rose from his chair and said, "Very well, Mac a'Chlaidheimh. You've got yourself a job, and your men as well. Come, I'll show you the building." He narrowed his eyes at Brigid and said, "You can put that away now."

Dylan slipped the silver-hilted dirk into the scabbard strapped to his legging, and followed Ramsay from the office. In the anteroom, Ramsay addressed the one-eyed doorman as if he were not entirely there, in a voice that held a tough edge Dylan wouldn't have suspected in him. "Mr. Simpson, you are dismissed for letting this man past the door. Felix will pay you off. Do not return." He gave an imperious roll to the "r" in "return."

The man sputtered and protested, but Ramsay acted as if he didn't hear. He gestured to Dylan, who followed him from the room to the spiral stairwell and up to the next floor. Dylan couldn't resist a glance at Simpson, whose one eye glittered with fury. Dylan ignored him and proceeded on his way.

Ramsay walked with a fluid motion, his hands making languid gestures to match his voice. The effect was puzzling, for it was apparent the man beneath the lace and silk was devoid of the sensitivity his dress suggested. This was a man who had once joked to Dylan about beating his wife and disinheriting her and her baby so that on his death they would be left with nothing and the boy revealed as illegitimate. Ramsay was a Jacobite spy who functioned publicly as a Whig, and nobody, not even his father-in-law, was entirely certain of his true sympathies. Dylan despised everything about him, but followed his new employer on a tour of the premises he was now bound to protect.

CHAPTER 3

Cody Marshall pushed her glasses up onto her nose as she paged through yet another book about the Jacobite uprising of 1715. Hope was not high, but she missed Dylan and just couldn't bring herself to give up searching. She leaned back in the library chair to stretch her arms, yawned like a cat, and blew out her cheeks. College students wandered past on rubber soles made silent by thick carpet, and a homeless man slouched discreetly in a corner, lending a urinary tang to the ambience.

Cody's husband had made it clear he thought spending afternoons in the Nashville library was a waste of time, and she couldn't blame him. Poor Raymond didn't know why she was suddenly a history buff with a particular obsession for one of the less significant British wars. She sure couldn't tell him why, either. She loved Raymond—they'd been married for four years now—but the man had no imagination and would never understand what had happened to Dylan.

She barely understood it herself. If it hadn't been for those scars that had appeared miraculously on Dylan's back, fully healed in less than a week, she might have thought his story of being abducted to the past by an Irish faerie and her enchanted sword was the product of a crazed mind. As it was, she'd wondered for a while if *she'd* gone nuts. But now, what with Dylan disappearing so completely and mysteriously after bequeathing his car to her, she had to know what had happened to him.

In any case, she figured this was a harmless pastime that took no more of her attention than had the fencing lessons she was no longer taking from Dylan.

Certainly he was dead, but Cody also figured he hadn't died at the early age everyone thought. The Glen Ciorram police had found no body, only his rental car with some blood on the seat and his passport on the floor. They'd also found Dylan's clothes and a gym bag nearby. His cash and credit cards were missing, so the Scottish authorities had ruled robbery and homicide. But Cody hoped Dylan had found a way back to the past to see his son.

"Dylan, where are you?" She snapped back to alertness. This happened a lot these days. Often she drifted off, thinking about him—about where he'd gone. Her fervent hope he'd lived to a very old age was what held grief at bay, and she needed to find proof he had.

She rubbed her face and sighed. To find mention of him, any mention at all, would enable her to be at peace with this. But there was nothing of "Black Dylan," nor Dylan Robert Matheson. It had taken weeks, but she'd read everything in the library about Scotland in the eighteenth century, even books covering dates that must have been later than Dylan's best life expectancy.

Using the interlibrary loan system now, she was searching down books from all over the country. No matter how arcane or obscure the information, no matter how dry and dusty, she wanted to find out whatever she could about that period in history. From the extensive libraries in Los Angeles and New York, she received some books with lists of names, which she now pored through with care, on the lookout for any sort of misspelled version of Dylan's name. Still she found nothing. Mathesons she found in small sprinklings here and there, for, according to this book, the several branches of the clan had apparently been divided on the issue of King James VIII. At Culloden in 1745 she found mention of a John Matheson, James Edward Matheson, Ciaran Robert Matheson, and Eoìn Eòin Matheson.

Whoa. Back up. *Ciaran Robert Matheson.* Wasn't that Dylan's son's name? Cody shut her eyes to think, and replayed the phone conversation she'd had with Dylan the night he'd told her about his two years in the eighteenth century. The child had been born in January, the year of the first uprising of that century. The mother was Caitrionagh, and the son was Ciaran. Yes, she was sure of it. Ciaran Matheson was the name of Dylan's son. He would have been thirty-one at the time of that battle, and Dylan's own middle name was Robert.

She read carefully the quick, tantalizing reference from a diary written by a Jacobite officer. "The famished army foraged unsuccessfully, and many were absent on the morning of the battle, looking for food. I ordered Ciaran Robert Matheson to lead a contingent of men to round up stray soldiers." That was all. No mention of whether he returned to the battle in time to face the English cannon. No clue as to whether he lived or died.

Cody groaned and frantically grabbed another book about the final Jacobite uprising, but though she spent the rest of the afternoon and most of the evening searching, there were no other references to Ciaran. Finally she had to give up the search and go home, for it was almost dark out.

Raymond was in a snarly mood by the time she got there. "I've been home for an hour," he said, as if that were enough to explain the anger in his voice. He slouched in the green leather recliner in front of the TV and didn't look up when she crossed the living room to the kitchen. He piled on the guilt as he informed her, "You spend more time in that library than you spend on your real obligations. You know what? When I got married, I never thought I'd have to compete with a dead guy for the attention of my wife."

She hung the car keys on the brass hook behind the kitchen door, set her purse on the chair next to the toaster, hung her coat on the back of that chair, and rolled up her sleeves. The words to tell him to make his own damn supper rose to her lips, but she swallowed them. He was trying to make the library an issue, and she couldn't let him. So she needed to keep quiet and fix dinner, and hope the anger would blow over. She let the snarky remarks go over her head while she pulled a package of chicken from the refrigerator and a glass baking pan from the cabinet under the stove.

Arguing with him would be pointless, and mentioning Dylan's name would be suicide. Dylan had never been a threat to their marriage—Dylan had never wanted to marry *anyone*, let alone her—but convincing Ray of that was hopeless. She and Dylan had grown up together and had been best friends their entire lives, but she couldn't communicate to Ray what that meant and why the fact that she couldn't just let go of Dylan didn't mean she wanted to let go of her husband. In silence she set the chicken pieces in the pan and covered them with Italian salad dressing before shoving it all into the oven.

Silently she blinked back the tear that tried to sneak from her eye. She missed Dylan in a way she just couldn't explain. She puttered with other things while the chicken baked, rather than go back to the living room and endure the guilt.

Supper was silent until Ray said, "Chicken's good." That was Ray-speak for "I'm sorry."

"Thank you," she replied, Codyspeak for "Apology accepted." Ray helped her with the dishes, a rare enough thing, so she spent the evening in front of the TV with him, without putting her nose in a book. Tit for tat. It was the way things were negotiated between them; all fair in love. The next day she planned to be occupied. Raymond would just have to be patient, for there was one other source of information she hadn't yet tried.

Dylan's mother lived on the other side of Drake's Creek, in the upscale area settled in recent years by country music stars and others with a good bit of money. The Mathesons were an old family here, able to trace back past the Civil War to the early Tennessee settlers, and beyond. In addition, Mrs. Matheson was a Brosnahan with solid roots of her own. Though Cody had grown up in that neighborhood back when it was all farmland, and still lived in the same town, she liked to joke she now lived on the right side of the tracks but on the wrong side of the creek. Ray hated when she did that. Cody, though, liked to tease him with it and thought it was funny. He took it as criticism of his paycheck. She shrugged and told him she didn't care enough about rich folks' money to give a damn.

Nevertheless, she felt very small as she climbed the steps to the porch of the white antebellum mansion owned by Dylan's parents, and knocked on the door.

She looked around as she waited, at the thin blanket of snow on the ground, and huddled into her leather jacket. She'd played in this yard often as a child. Back then the area hadn't been nearly this built up, and open fields and forests had surrounded the house. Now tract houses for the upwardly mobile were clustered all around, looking like miniature brick mansions, set in artfully arranged lots and surrounded by mature maple trees. The rickety farmhouse she'd grown up in had been demolished while she was in college, and the land developed. Her parents had retired on the money and now lived in a condo in Louisville. She sighed. Sometimes she wished the world would stand still and time could just stop.

There was no answer at the door, but she knocked again and waited. Dead, brown leaves from fall sheltered beneath a green, wooden glider that hadn't been sat in for years. Its paint curled up in spots, and a thick coat of dust covered it. The stone porch was free of any other ornamentation. February cold crept in on her, and she turned up her collar. She knew Mrs. Matheson was home, for the hunter green SUV was in the circle drive. Dylan's father was surely at work at this time of day. She knocked again.

Finally the door opened a few inches. "Yes?"

Cody peered inside, and her heart sank. Even through the narrow opening she could see the ugly shadows on Mrs. Matheson's face. One entire side was purple, and that eye was swollen shut. "Mrs. Matheson? It's me. May I come in?"

"Cody . . . I don't know. . . ."

"Mrs. Matheson, it's about . . ." She was going to say it was about Dylan, but remembered in time that Dylan's mother didn't know where he'd gone, and thought her son had died at the hands of robbers in Scotland. Cody said instead, "I'm doing some research on Dylan's ancestry . . . it was something we talked about before . . . well, we talked about it the last time I saw him. I wonder if I could ask some questions that might help me find what I'm looking for."

"I'm not. . . ."

"It's all right. I mean, I used to feel like I was family. I hope I still am."

There was a bit of silence, then Mrs. Matheson opened the door wide for Cody to enter. She wore pink sweats, and though her hair was combed she wore no makeup, not even to cover her bruises. Cody had seen this before, and had always known why Dylan had never wanted to go home in the evenings when they were kids. He'd talked Cody's mom into letting him stay for supper more often than he ate at home.

Cody wanted to talk to Mrs. Matheson, to tell her she didn't need to live like this, but instead kept shut. It wouldn't do to upset the poor woman further. Cody pretended not to see the bruises, and followed Dylan's mother into the living room, where she took off her jacket and laid it over the arm of the sofa. The house was in perfect order, as always, and tastefully decorated. A new living room suite had been bought since her last visit. Not a speck of dust anywhere; the room was as perfect as the window in a furniture store. The television was silent, a huge expanse of black against the far wall. She could hear the wooden tock-tock of a grandfather clock in another room, also added since the last time she'd been here.

She sat on the couch, perched on the edge of the cushion, leaning toward Mrs. Matheson, and went straight to the point. "Before he left for Scotland, Dylan told me some stuff about someone called Black Dylan."

Mrs. Matheson nodded. "That was a story Kenneth's father used to tell, about a Scottish highwayman a few centuries back. Black Dylan wasn't a direct ancestor, I don't think, but was a member of the same branch of Mathesons as Kenneth's people. A cousin, I believe. Can I get you something to drink? Some fruit tea? Perhaps some hot tea. Would you like some hot tea?"

Cody nodded. It was cold outside, her fingers were numb, and she could use something warm to drink. Also, she knew Mrs. Matheson would feel better to be doing something. Cody tagged along to the kitchen, saying, "A highwayman? How does one find out that sort of thing? History books don't generally tell the names of outlaws." Unless they were hanged or beheaded in some spectacular manner. She'd read enough of those histories to know. She hoped Dylan hadn't been hanged, or worse, beheaded.

"No, not in history books." Mrs. Matheson took mugs from a cabinet and tea bags from a canister on the counter. "It was an oral tradition handed down among the Mathesons in Scotland. We only heard it because Kenneth's father became friendly with an RAF officer while serving in England during World War II. They found out they both had the same name, James Matheson, and when they got to talking, they found out they were also both descended from the same branch of Mathesons in the Western Highlands. Except, of course, the Scottish fellow was actually *from* the Highlands. He had a lot of stories to tell of the clan history, and that was one of the stories Dad Matheson heard. He brought it back with him, and when Dylan was born . . ." Her voice failed her for a moment, and Cody waited as she composed herself. Mrs. Matheson continued, "When Dylan was born, we decided we liked the name." A trembling smile touched the corners of her mouth and she added with a little laugh, "Though we preferred to ignore the highwayman aspect of it. We certainly didn't want him to grow up to rob people."

Cody felt herself pale, for she knew Dylan had done exactly that. She said, "But he must have ended up better than just a robber. For people to remember him centuries later, I mean."

Mrs. Matheson shrugged. "I really don't know. He was a colorful figure, I do know that. And Dad Matheson felt he was viewed as a hero. I can't say why." Cody knew why. Dylan had worked for Rob Roy, who was an even more colorful and more historical figure. "I only liked the name because at the time I was a big Bob Dylan fan. I never paid much attention to the story."

Cody swallowed her disappointment and picked up the steaming teapot to pour water into the cups Mrs. Matheson had set out with tea bags.

Dylan's mother made a noise, almost of surprise, and a distant look came to her eyes. "He said before he left . . ."—her eyes misted up as she remembered her son's last visit—". . . he said something about wanting me to look for that Black Dylan fellow. In history books, I think. Also, I should look for the name in Gaelic . . . but I can't remember what he said that was. Dylan . . . Doo . . . I don't know. Doo?"

Cody didn't know much Gaelic, but just enough that she knew there were a lot of silent consonants in it. A word pronounced "doo" might be spelled any number of ways. All she knew for sure was that it must start with *Du*. "It was the Gaelic for Black Dylan? So *Doo* is Gaelic for black. I could look that up."

Mrs. Matheson stared into her cup and bit her lip. Cody sipped her tea and waited, but Dylan's mother's nose began to turn red and her mouth trembled. Finally she said, "He wanted me to leave Kenneth. That was the last thing he said before he left." Tears fell and she wiped them away, but there was no stopping them. She sniffled and continued, "I haven't even been able to bring myself to go to his karate gym. I know he wanted me to live there, but I can't. Kenneth wanted me to sell it to Dylan's assistant, but I can't do that, either."

"Is Ronnie taking care of things there?"

Mrs. Matheson nodded. "He was quite shocked when he inherited ten percent of the business. He's keeping it going just as Dylan requested in his will. But the apartment hasn't been touched, and Dylan's things are still in it. I couldn't bear to go there."

Cody's voice went very soft. "He wanted you to be safe. He gave you a place to go so you can be. He loved you."

Dylan's mother set her tea down and pressed her palms to her face as sobs shook her. Cody set down her own tea and went to put an arm around her shoulders. Her heart ached to tell what she knew, but even that wouldn't be much comfort. Though Dylan had not died at thirty, he was dead nevertheless, and wasn't coming back.

CHAPTER 4

The offices of Ramsay, Ltd. were five floors of hirelings up to their elbows in paperwork, fingers filthy with ink but their clothing smart and well cared for. They wore breeches, for that was the fashion south of the Highland line. No self-respecting Lowlander would dress like a heathen Highlander, and the men at their writing desks warily eyed Dylan and his kilt. Their coats were wool, but nicely styled and of conservative colors, which gave Dylan to believe Ramsay's employees were well paid for their skills with words and numbers. None seemed much pleased to see Dylan, but each paid the respect due their employer as long as Ramsay was present and showing around the new security chief. They nodded unsmiling greetings to Dylan. Once he and Ramsay moved on, Dylan was sure he was forgotten.

Ramsay then donned his overcoat and rapier, which hung on pegs in his office, and directed Dylan to follow him outside and up the wynde to the High Street. They turned right, toward the castle. The merchant strolled like a fop, slowly and not entirely in a straight line. He greeted men he knew with a smile and a nod, or sometimes with a handshake and a short chat. Dylan walked behind and kept an eye on the street crowded with peddlers, carriages, single riders, and children running in and out between pedestrians. Awareness of more than just his immediate surroundings was a habit Dylan had learned soon after coming to this century, for most everyone carried an edged weapon of some sort. Even a man whose sword was left at home certainly had a dirk or *sgian dubh* secreted about his body. Though there were more people here than any place he'd been in Scotland, he quickly sized up everyone who came near.

Ramsay fell back with Dylan and explained, "I have a meeting at the coffeehouse in Lawnmarket Street. Once I've done with that, we shall go to the docks. I've two warehouses there, for mine is the largest operation in Edinburgh. I handle everything: wool both raw and spun, linen cloth, grain, sugar from Madeira and America, oils, ironware I buy up from blacksmiths all over the Lowlands, gold and silver, spices, everything."

"What, no slaves?" Dylan had meant it as a dry joke, but apparently hit a nerve.

Ramsay cut a sideways glance at him and thought a moment. "I told you, everything. That is, I have involvement in shipments of slaves. They're quite profitable, and the demand for them in the Americas is high."

"You don't care that you're selling people?"

Ramsay's laugh had an edge, and he stopped walking to peer at Dylan. His limpid eyes held a chill that almost made Dylan shudder. "You're an impudent lad. Should I suppose you spoke to your previous employer that way?"

Dylan's eyes narrowed. "I apologize. I was impertinent." Ramsay's tone was infuriating, but anger would accomplish nothing more than getting him fired or arrested, and in any case would be bad strategy. He bit his lip and looked down at the street.

Ramsay thought that over, then continued on his way and said with a light tone and a casual gesture of dismissal, "I don't get the slaves for nothing, you realize. They're bought from other Africans. So I don't make them slaves, do I? I merely move them from one place to another so their value will increase. Did I not, they surely would still be slaves in Africa. Or dead, I expect. Perhaps if you colonials weren't so eager to buy them, there wouldn't be so many made available."

Dylan only grunted, then replied, "Aye, sir," and pretended interest in a window filled with brightly colored wool. It was true his American ancestors, both the Mathesons and the Brosnahans, as well as a couple other branches of his tree, had owned slaves right up until the Civil War.

As much as it turned his stomach to feign agreement with Ramsay, Dylan could hardly claim the moral high ground and still pass as one of his own ancestors.

Ramsay continued, "I assure you, there is no race on earth that will not sell its own into slavery, given the opportunity." Dylan still didn't reply, so Ramsay said, "At any rate, I'll be expecting a great deal from you and your men. During the business day and when I travel, you'll be my bodyguard, and I will require a guard on my warehouses. You'll be responsible for the safety of my goods and my life. Do you think you're up to the task?"

Dylan nodded. "Aye, sir."

Sinann, hovering nearby, sneered into Ramsay's face, though he could neither see nor hear, "If he doesnae kill ye himself." Dylan glanced at her and gave her a minute frown. But she fluttered over and addressed Dylan, flying backward in front of him as he walked. "It doesnae appear he's intending to take you home to meet the wife, laddie."

Dylan wished he could take a swipe at the little nuisance. He said to Ramsay, "It will take me a week or two to send for my men. How much can I promise them in wages?"

A smile curled Ramsay's lip and he said expansively, "I daresay I can afford to lure a man away from the Jacobite army."

"But can you afford to lure him away from Rob Roy?"

The smile died, but then reappeared in a twinkling. "All right, sixpence for each man you deem necessary. And one shilling and threepence per day for yourself."

Sinann whistled low. "*Och*, it's a handsome wage he's offering you. An entire shilling more than the army gave ye."

Dylan agreed. It was nearly twice what Iain Mór had paid him, and from that he'd been able to stash five guineas which still awaited him in Ciorram. But he said, "Seven pence a day for the men." The sixpence was adequate, and happened to be what Rob Roy had paid for reiving cattle, but the men would have to be enticed to leave the Highlands and he knew Ramsay would go higher.

He was right. After a show of irritation, Ramsay nodded. "Done." Then his smile returned. "Ah, here we are," said Ramsay as he stepped through a narrow door and removed his hat. Dylan followed.

The coffeehouse was small and dark and smelled of strong coffee, wood smoke, and greasy food. Several wooden tables stood about, where clusters of men talked, some in whispers and some in loud, boasting voices. The hum of conversation was irregular and oppressive in the stone enclosure, in spite of the high ceiling and tall, paned windows. The walls were darkened by grease and smoke. Dylan followed Ramsay between the tables to one that stood near the enormous stone hearth on the far side. A large iron pot hung over the fire, and something in it smelled quite enticing. A stew of some sort, it seemed. Dylan's mouth watered, and he swallowed hard.

Off to the side of the room was a large, wooden booth with a polished bar across the front, attended by a man in a tall, dirty wig and brown coat. He hurried back and forth, filling orders for drink and food, handing them off, taking money and making change from a wooden box, then cleaning up after himself whenever there was a moment to spare. Refreshments were served from the booth and taken by customers to their tables. A boy scurried about, waiting tables and keeping customers' change from payment as tips.

Ramsay approached a man who was already seated, his befeathered hat resting on the table and an earthenware mug in his hands. When he saw Ramsay, he rose for what seemed to Dylan a short bowing ceremony. Ruffles fluttered from coat sleeves for a moment while brief greetings were murmured, then it was over and the two sat at the table. Ramsay tossed a coin to Dylan, which he snatched from the air without really looking. "Fetch me a coffee."

Dylan bowed his head slightly, and his jaw clenched as he went to the bar on his errand.

Sinann, fluttering behind, informed him, "You requested he hire you. And he's paying you handsomely. More than you made working for Cait's father." It was true. He'd sold his services, so he should have no complaint of Ramsay's behavior. Besides, his goal was to have far more than just the man's money.

Dylan brought the coffee to Ramsay and tried to hand back the farthing and a half in change, but was waved off with an air that said the merchant wanted nothing to do with such small and bothersome coins. Dylan was just as pleased to slip them into his sporran for some ale later on.

Ramsay then gestured to a chair against the wall nearby for Dylan to sit. Not part of the conversation, but within earshot, Dylan kicked back against the wall. He pulled Brigid to clean his fingernails, and listened carefully to all that was said while tendrils of tobacco smoke stung his nose.

It was apparent the two men in conference believed Dylan too ignorant to understand what he overheard. Kilted as he was, they probably took him for an illiterate, rural Highlander unschooled in the ways of big business. What they couldn't know was that Dylan was a man from the twentieth century, with a business degree from Vanderbilt University in Nashville, Tennessee. Though the specifics of commerce would change over the next three centuries, the theories were immutable, and Dylan followed almost every word of the discussion.

Today the subject at hand was wine. Ramsay and his friend spoke of prices in Le Havre, Champagne, Burgundy, and Nancy, and soon Dylan had a fair grasp of the current markets for those wines in London and Glasgow. At the same time, he learned three of Ramsay's ships were *Dover*, *Sea Lion* and *Marietta*, and the hold capacity of each; that the first two were shipping wine to New York; and that the third was headed for France with a load of muscovado from Prince's Island, whatever "muscovado" was. The conversation was utterly boring and had no relevance to his goal of finding Cait, but he filed the information anyway.

Also, Dylan was not surprised to note, the men spoke of Amsterdam as if it were a sort of financial mecca. Dylan already knew Dutch commerce was a huge influence in Europe, the British Empire not yet having risen to world financial domination. Now he learned Ramsay was putting out feelers for agents familiar with the Amsterdam Exchange who would work on his behalf, for a commission. The man at the table was an Englishman who partnered with Ramsay in the London Exchange, and he made disparaging noises about Amsterdam. "Too difficult," he said, with an air that suggested *not worth it*. Ramsay pretended to accept the verdict, but Dylan could see he was still determined to find an agent in Amsterdam and had merely accepted it wouldn't be through this guy.

Though Dylan's stomach gurgled as the afternoon wore on, he stayed in his seat rather than go to the serving booth to buy a meal and risk missing the thread of conversation. Sinann curled up for a nap on the floor at his feet.

While listening, Dylan gazed about the room. He was, after all, Ramsay's bodyguard and needed at least to appear to care about the safety of his employer's person. Everyone in the room seemed engrossed in his own business or diversions. A couple of well-dressed drunks sitting at a table laughed loudly, accompanied by two women of questionable virtue whose hair dangled from loose pins, and whose bosoms were falling from their bodices. The girls were dirty, loud, and extremely drunk. Dylan watched, amusing himself to see whether a breast or two might come completely out of the dresses. One of the men at a table near the door pulled the younger girl onto his lap and began to squeeze her breast. The girl took his hand and guided it through an opening at the side of her overdress skirt, whereupon the man growled like a large cat as he groped her.

When Dylan realized this was what awaited Cait if he couldn't get her out of Ramsay's house before her husband finally kicked her out, he broke out in a cold sweat and looked away, no longer interested in the silly spectacle.

The Englishman told Ramsay in a chiding voice, ". . . and His Majesty's Navy is hard after the *Spirit*, I'm told."

There was a moment of silence, and the Englishman awaited Ramsay's response. The Lowlander finally said, "Indeed? And what should that have to do with me?"

The southerner's head tilted and he said, "Were she captured, would your purse not squeal?"

Ramsay laughed. Dylan's ears perked to hear an edge in his voice as he said, "I've not the first idea what you mean, Charles. The *Spirit* isnae more mine than is His Majesty's flagship. All my dealings are legitimate, and there's naught in the least legal about that sort of slavery."

The Englishman wore a smirk and said, "As you say, Connor." But nobody was convinced of anything, and it was apparent Ramsay was only asking that the subject be dropped. It was dropped, and Ramsay brought the meeting to an end. The two rose and another bowing ceremony took place, then Ramsay took his leave of the Englishman, gesturing to Dylan he should follow.

Dylan shoved Sinann with his boot to awaken her, then followed Ramsay onto the street. The merchant hired a carriage to take them down to the docks, where Dylan was shown the two large buildings for which he was now responsible. Descending from the cab, Ramsay said, "Your men, when they come, may sleep here. There are a mattress and a chamber pot in each building, where in the past I have had the occasional watchman." He waved a languid hand at the nearest warehouse. "Here is where your predecessor used to live, so I'm certain your men will do well here. You will take a room in Edinburgh."

"Perhaps I should stay closer to you at night if I'm to do my job correctly. Is there a spare bed in your house?"

Ramsay grunted. "There is not." He proceeded toward the door of the nearest warehouse.

Dylan persisted as he hurried to follow. "You have servants' quarters, surely. Or else I could claim a corner of the kitchen?" *Anything, just to be inside the house.*

"Nonsense. A hired room in Edinburgh will do. I value my privacy."

"You need privacy from a watchdog?"

Ramsay stopped walking and threw him a glance. Dylan skidded to a halt on pavement stones slick with mud. Ramsay said, "Take a room at the Hogshead Inn. You can afford it now."

Dylan nodded, and let the issue go. To insist further would appear suspicious in the worst way.

Ramsay took him into the nearest warehouse. Dylan looked around. The building was of wood, unlike everything else around Edinburgh, and was filled with merchandise of every description. Sacks of oats, barley, and wheat were stacked higher than Dylan could reach, all the more strange for there being no pallets, and of course no forklifts. All of it had been stacked by hand. Crates stood everywhere. Hides of mink from Russia stank of tanning and were tied in bundles, stacked like the crates. Moving down an aisle, he saw wines from France, spices from the Middle East, bolts of silk from Asia. Dylan was not surprised so much by the volume of goods as by the variety. In two years of living in the Highlands during this century, he'd never seen anything like this. Not even at the tryst in Crieff, where drovers brought their cattle to sell and small merchants came from all over to trade for the drovers' silver as soon as the stock was sold, had he seen such lavish amounts of merchandise. These luxuries would have astonished even Iain Mór, who was Laird over several glens.

Staring at a stack of cloth bags filled with grain, he remarked, "There are folks up north who could use some of this over the winter."

"They can wish for it, but if they've got nothing to trade, then wishing is all they'll do."

Dylan knew he should keep shut, but he couldn't help saying, "You'd let them starve?"

Ramsay laughed. "If they're starving, then they should come down out of their barren mountains and work. But they're stubborn. They expect the land to support too many people, and they don't produce things I can sell elsewhere. That's why they starve."

Dylan hated that he was right. Many of the clans, clinging to traditions that had held them together and safe from outsiders for centuries, couldn't comprehend the new ideas of capitalism and industry. And they wouldn't understand until huge numbers of people were forced from their ancestral lands. Even worse, there would be two more uprisings and much suffering before the last glimmer of hope of saving the feudal clan system would finally die with Bonnie Prince Charlie in about seventy years.

When Ramsay returned him to the High Street in Edinburgh, then rode away in the hired carriage, Dylan waited until it was out of earshot, then muttered to Sinann, "Pig."

"Aye," she replied.

Dylan blinked and turned toward her. "Oh, you're agreeing with me now?"

She shrugged. "As it happens, this time you're right."

He stared up the street as the carriage made its way west and said, "I wonder what Iain Matheson, Laird of the Glen Ciorram Mathesons and Master of *Tigh a' Mhadaidh Bhàin*, would say if he knew he'd married his daughter off to the very sort of flaming capitalist who would happily take his land, boot out his clan, and turn the entire glen into a huge sheep farm. 'Cause you know that's what's going to happen. In about thirty years, after the last Jacobite uprising is defeated at Culloden, the English and the Lowlanders are going to be crawling all over the Highlands, evicting people. The lucky ones will be shipped off to America or join the English Army. The unlucky ones will be imprisoned or hung for treason. All of them will leave behind weeping relatives. Not to mention they will leave a hole in the labor force that will take generations to fill." He took a look around, then headed down a wynde, looking for a sign with a hog's head on it.

Sinann followed, walking two steps to his one and occasionally fluttering into the air to catch up. "Nae, they will not. For you are here and you will prevent it. You will be the Cuchulain of modern times, who will save our people from invasion."

Dylan sighed and said nothing more. It was no use arguing with that faerie.

The sun was almost down, and Dylan nearly missed the sign of the

Hogshead Inn at the far end of the loch, at the north foot of the rock on which Edinburgh huddled, tucked into a crook of the wynde. It seemed modest but welcoming, so he went inside to ask after accommodations. A room and the meal he bought to take up to that room cost him more silver than he thought fair, but he didn't care to wander around Edinburgh all night. He paid without comment, and climbed the four flights of spiral stairs to his room, carrying the wooden plate filled with cold mutton and bread, and a horn tumbler of ale.

The room was small in addition to being expensive. The width was exactly the length of the bed and the depth was just enough for the bed and a table on which rested a candle and an earthenware bowl of water under a linen towel. There was no ewer from which to refresh the water. The stink of feces in the closed space choked him as he looked around.

"Good God!" He set his supper on the table next to the bowl, lifted his baldric over his head to lean his sword against the wall, and knelt to find the chamber pot under the bed. The previous occupant of the room had left it half full. Dylan leaned over the bed and reached for the window, but Sinann stopped him.

"No! Ye cannae toss it yet!"

Dylan frowned and held the pot as far at arm's length as he could. "Why not? Oh, I suppose you want to savor it for a while, then."

"Ye must wait until ten o'clock. When the drums sound, then it may be gotten rid of. Otherwise, there might be an unsuspecting fellow below. You wouldnae wish to have people empty their pots on your head while you were on the street. Aye?"

He looked at the pot, then around the tiny room. A hearth near the head of the bed held a couple of peats that had dwindled to mostly ashes, and a stack of five dried peats stood ready for the fire. There didn't seem to be anything he could put over the top of the pot. He looked to Sinann and said, "Wave your hand, or something."

She obliged, and with a snap of her fingers the contents of the pot dried to a black, wrinkled lump and yellow crystals. Another snap removed even the dried matter, and the pot jerked in Dylan's hand. "*Och!*" she said. Inside the pot, a gouge had been taken from the metal on the bottom.

Dylan peered at it and held it up to the waning light from the window. "Don't be putting a hole in it, Tink. I'll need to use this in the morning." He slid it back under the bed, then reached for the window and opened it. The air outside was fresh by comparison, and Dylan ignored the cold as he aired out the room. Then he put a peat on the fire to keep it from dying, and knelt to gently blow the embers into flame. When the peat caught he lit the candle from it.

Then he went to the table, untied his black sealskin sporran from his belt, set it aside, rolled up his sleeves, and plunged his hands into the bowl of water to wash. The water being warmer than that of the burn he'd washed in earlier, he was able to do a more thorough job of it than before and dug his fingers into his hair to scrub his scalp, which was itchy with filth.

The wash water turned rusty brown with blood from Sheriffmuir as he rinsed his neck and ran wet fingers through his hair a few times so it would lie straight. His nose crinkled in disgust at the bloody water, for it always gave him the creeps to wash someone else's blood from himself. But that was a good thing all in all, he figured. Being covered in blood wasn't something he ever wanted to be used to.

He wiped his face with the towel, then ate his supper at the wide sill of the window, sitting on the bed's lumpy straw mattress and looking out over the nearby buildings. Exhaustion was zooming in on him, having been at bay since the battle two days before. The mutton and the ale conspired to make his eyes want to roll back in his head, and he leaned heavily on the sill as he ate. Sinann perched on the headboard of the narrow bunk. The meat was a mite strong, and Dylan peered at it to detect any discoloration. When he found none, he stuffed the meat into the bread and ate both at once to cover the taste. He washed it all down with the last of the ale, then shuddered and made a noise of disgust.

Sinann said, "Ye've eaten worse before and not minded it, lad."

"I always mind it. It's like playing Russian roulette every time I put something in my mouth." He picked with his thumbnail at a shred of meat stuck in his lower teeth, and wished he had a willow twig in his sporran.

"I dinnae know what Russian roulette might mean, nor do I think I care to."

He shrugged. "It just means gambling with my life. I mean, I take a chance of poisoning myself with bad meat or wormy bread when that's all there is to eat. Or maybe I could pick up a disease from someone else who handled the food. I never know."

Sinann snorted. "You cannae receive disease from a body by eating food they touched."

"Oh, yes, you can. Trust me on this one. You can get food poisoning from someone who handles a chamber pot then handles the food without washing. You can get malaria if you're bitten by a mosquito, or plague if bitten by a flea. You can get a cold by touching a doorknob that was touched by someone with a cold."

"You believe this?"

"I know this. Where I come from, lives are saved every day by knowing this."

Sinann considered that for a moment, then said, "It may be true. But you asked to return, did you not?"

Dylan closed the window and got up from the bed to undress. His belt fell to the floor and he unwound his kilt from himself, then dropped it on the bed as additional cover. "Tink, you should know that by coming back, I've cut my life expectancy by at least ten years, if not twenty, or even thirty if I end up in the next uprising. Which, incidentally, is in . . ."—he hesitated a moment to recall—". . . about three or four years." He sat to remove his sheepskin leggings and took Brigid from her sheath to slip her under his pillow. "Furthermore, even if I don't die in battle, I'm still unlikely to keep many of my teeth very long. I'll probably lose them all by the time I'm fifty, and that's still allowing for thirty years of fluoridated water and the fact that I know how to take care of them. Before I came here, I never went a day without eating, but since coming here I have stayed hungry many a day. And there are a lot of people around here far hungrier than I. In this century, just keeping alive is sometimes a struggle; keeping healthy is next to impossible."

Sinann shrugged, "*Och*, you're making me regret you came back, I'm so dead sorry for you."

Dylan cut a glance at her and continued readying for bed. The paper bag he'd slipped under the straps of one legging just before his return to this century was now tattered and soaked through, but the items inside were intact. He slipped the glass bottle of aspirin into his sporran—later he would find a cork to replace the plastic top—but the cellophane bag of cinnamon jawbreakers presented a problem. He held the bag, turning it over in his hands, thinking. The candies were wrapped individually, and the clear plastic would attract attention, but he'd been soaked to the skin far too many times to think he could keep them for long if he unwrapped them to carry them in his sporran. So he emptied the bag onto his green silk kerchief and tied them all inside. All but one, which he squeezed from its wrapper into his mouth. The spicy candy stung his tongue, and he shoved it into his cheek as he pulled his sark over his head and dropped it on the bed.

The jawbreaker rattled against his teeth and his distended cheek hollowed out his voice as he continued, "Back home, Sinann, I never had a scar larger than a small cut." He indicated a tiny, white line on his left index finger that had been made by a razor blade he'd used to open a cardboard box when he was seventeen. Then he pointed to each injury as he continued, "but now I have a knife wound on my arm; a nick in my ear; great, honking, big whip scars all over my back; a musket ball hole in my leg; and I'm missing a kidney and my spleen from having been run through with an English cavalry sword." A finger traced the red surgery scar on his belly, which still ached. "Twice I have been knocked unconscious by blows to the head, and it's a wonder I haven't died from concussion." He removed the *sgian dubh* from under his left arm and set it on the table next to the washbowl.

"In addition, I've taken my last hot shower, eaten my last french fry, heard my last electric guitar, taken my last drive in a car, made my last telephone call, and . . ." His voice failed and his heart sank. He had to take a deep breath. ". . . and I've said good-bye to my mother. Forever. That's a lot to get over, Tink."

"But you returned to save your people from the English." She said it with a confidence and pride that made him wish he didn't have to disabuse her. But he couldn't let her go on thinking he could change anything.

"Sinann, I came to save my son from the history I know is coming." He scratched his chin as he sat on the bed, and said, "I've come to save two people. Only two. Cait and Ciaran. I'm no hero, Tink. I'm not your Cuchulain. With all I know about what's going to happen, I can't change it. I couldn't change the outcome at Sheriffmuir, and I can't prevent the Highland Clearances."

Sinann's voice was soft. "Perhaps it's a more modest goal for which the claymore brought you here."

Dylan peered at her. "Like what?"

She shrugged her thin shoulders. "I know not, exactly. But think on it."

He swallowed hard. "All right, Tink." Then he blew out the candle before slipping into bed. Though the mattress was unforgiving straw and as hilly as the Highlands themselves, he moved around until he found the position other bodies had impressed on it and settled in. The linens were clean, at least, and the smallness of the room made the fire's heat adequate. The room spun as drowsiness swept in on him.

Sinann then said, "And think on this, lad. Ramsay has gone home, and ye're still speaking English."

Dylan frowned, irritated that she was right. He grunted and muttered, "*Mar sin leat, a Shinann.*"

Sinann giggled at that. "Goodbye yerself, lad." Then he dropped off to sleep like a rock.

The following day Dylan made his way to Ramsay's office, zigzagging up the wyndes and closes along the north side of town, and came out on the High Street too far east. "Damn," he muttered as he realized he'd gotten lost, and turned back on the High Street toward the wynde that led to Ramsay's office. But he was stopped short by the sight of a Redcoat dragoon on guard at the entrance to that wynde. His step faltered as his mind raced.

Sinann shoved his back and hissed at him, "Keep going. If he sees you avoid him, he'll stop you and ask questions you're ill-equipped to answer believably. Keep going!"

Dylan hesitated for only a second, and realized the faerie was right. He strolled up as if he owned the entire street, smiled his most ingenuous "cute teacher" smile, and greeted the guard with "*Dia dhuit.*"

He blinked when the round-faced guard replied, "*Sibh fhein,*" but remembered even the deeply bigoted Major Bedford had some Gaelic. Certainly enough to answer "God be with you" with "And yourself." The surprising thing was that the soldier would have given such a pleasant reply, or even a reply at all.

Dylan strolled on up the street and ducked into the next wynde. Halfway down the hill a close opened up, and Dylan cut back toward Ramsay's office. Another tiny alley took him to the wynde in which Ramsay's offices stood, and he stopped to peek around the corner of the building. Standing in the alley at the low end of the offices, below the level of the entrance door, he could see through a wrought-iron fence at shoulder height, up the wynde, to Ramsay's door. On up the hill, through the stone archway at the High Street, he caught a glimpse of the back of the Redcoat's uniform. Ramsay's door opened and Dylan ducked back, obscured by a rose bush. An English officer hurried from the building, followed by an escort of a third soldier.

Dylan's blood ran cold as he recognized Major Bedford securing the chin strap of his hat. The blond aristocrat strode up the hill in a businesslike hurry, his short uniform jacket bright in the shadows of the buildings and his riding boots gleaming in the scant light. He took his dark gloves from under his arm and pulled them on.

Dylan's knuckles turned white as he gripped the wrought iron before him. He tensed to spring toward the wynde and an Anglo-Saxon vulgarism rose in this throat. "Ffffffffff . . ."

Sinann yanked him back by the collar, hard. His sark tore and he grabbed at her, but she yanked again and, wings beating furiously, succeeded in pulling him back behind the corner of Ramsay's building. There she shoved him against the stone, fluttering just above his head, and clapped both her hands over his mouth. "Quiet, ye fool!" He tried to shake her loose, but she held on and pressed her hands harder. "*Quiet!*"

Dylan put his hands down and glared at her until she let up. By that time Bedford was gone up the High Street. Dylan hissed at her, "That was him! That was the sonofabitch who ordered *this*!" He jerked a thumb at the flogging scars on his back.

"And what were you to do about it, laddie? Shout rude words at him to give his men an excuse to cut ye down for good? Or perhaps it was a sword duel you wanted? As if you werenae in enough trouble already!"

Dylan calmed down enough to think, and realized what a stupid thing he'd almost done. He took a deep breath, wondered why Bedford had been there, and said, "It's a trap. Ramsay told him to come get me."

Sinann shook her head. "I think not. He wouldnae have come here, were it that. The whole business would have been arranged elsewhere, and they would not have let Bedford be seen here until it had been sprung. Besides, Bedford is the last man Ramsay would summon for your arrest, since it's Bedford who is looking for Jacobite spies in Edinburgh and Ramsay kens you are far too familiar with his doings. It would be better for Ramsay to have ye done away with by unofficial means, were that his intent, than to let you be arrested and questioned. Nae, this is something else."

"What, then?"

She shrugged. "I dinnae ken. But what I am sure of is that ye dare not let him see you. Else Ramsay will learn who you are, and who you are to Cait."

CHAPTER 5

Inside the building, Dylan didn't go straight into Ramsay's office but instead requested paper, quill, and ink from Felix in the front office. The pursed-lipped secretary provided them without a word, and handed over a stick of sealing wax as well. Then he went back to his own work.

"Is Himself in yet?"

Felix finally looked up, disdain plain on his face. "If by that you mean Mr. Ramsay, the answer is yes. He's arrived." Then the clerk returned to his work.

Dylan twirled the sealing wax in his fingers and caught it. He turned, looking for a place to write, and said to Felix in an exaggerated hick voice, "Seumas don't read, or nothing, but I can draw pretty good."

Felix was not interested enough to even look up, and Dylan stood at a bookshelf in the corner to write his letter on a tiny space he claimed by shoving aside a clock and a candlestick. Seumas Glas couldn't read, but he could understand a drawing of a crown and a castle, a drawing of seven pennies and the sun, and an accurate representation of Dylan's aging Scottish broadsword with its heart-shaped hilt of pierced steel. Seumas, like everyone else he'd met since his escape from Fort William, knew him as Dilean Mac a'Chlaidheimh, Gaelic for Dylan, Son of the Sword, and would know who was offering seven pence a day in Edinburgh. Carefully, lest the quill drop a blob of ink on his only sheet of paper, at the bottom he drew a hog's head. Given the primitive writing tool and his absolute lack of drawing talent, it was a miracle he produced a passable copy of the sign outside the Hogshead Inn.

Once the ink was dried, Dylan folded the paper into an envelope-sized packet and lifted the candle from its holder on the shelf to melt a bit of sealing wax onto it. A good glob of red wax ran onto the paper, and he returned the candle to the holder to press his thumb to the seal. It stung like a bastard, but borrowing Ramsay's seal to press the wax to the paper would have been a mistake. Seumas would never come then. He put the tip of his sore thumb in his mouth and handed the letter to Sinann. She slipped it inside her dress.

He whispered, "Find Seumas Glas. See that he brings two men with him."

"Where . . . ?"

"Try Glen Dochart first. He talked last summer about marrying a local girl there. Also, he's a MacGregor. He may have stayed with Rob or he might be among Gregor Ghlun Dhubh's main force. Go. Fly."

She snapped her fingers and blinked out of the room.

During the next week Dylan did his job, following Ramsay around like a faithful hound. Much time was spent in the coffeehouse, in meetings with various businessmen, but Ramsay also frequented a house where he wouldn't let Dylan follow him inside. It was far down the slope toward Holyrood Palace, in a tiny close near the Canongate Tolbooth.

Dylan was told to wait outside in the cold, so he loitered among the street folk and tried to figure out the floor plan of the house by examining the windows. It was something to do, and knowledge was power. But that game waned quickly, and he began looking around for something to keep him occupied.

A woman street vendor in a ragged red dress, pushing a handcart piled with used clothing, happened by, so he bought a coat from her to replace the one he'd left behind on the battlefield. Though he could afford to have one made, this was the third coat he'd bought in two years and he was fed up with losing the costly clothing. This one was nice enough; it was hardly worn, of a plain cut and sturdy fabric, and had a silk lining. It was the best fit of all her coats, but was still a mite large on him. The thick wool took the edge off the winter chill that cut through his linen sark as if it weren't there, and would keep him from having to huddle inside his plaid all the time. Unlike his other coats, this one was short and enabled him to drape his plaid over his back on the outside of it. This way he still had use of it while wearing the coat.

He fooled with the heavy length of wool, trying to figure out where to put it on the outside of his coat, and wished he could use the crest brooch in his sporran. But Sinann had enchanted it, turning it into a talisman of invisibility, and he didn't care to disappear from human sight every time he stood still. In the back of his head he heard Sinann's usual deprecating tone, for he knew what she would say. *If you had let me teach you the craft sooner, you'd now be powerful enough to control the talisman without taking it on and off.* Great—he couldn't get rid of her even when she was gone.

But since he couldn't control the magic, there was nothing for him to do but sigh and address the lady with the cart. "Have you a brooch for sale?"

A wicked smile crossed her face, and she said, "I've far more than that fer a handsome lad such as yerself." Her tongue touched her lip, which was full and red and tempting for a man who had been without sex for a year and a half. But Dylan knew better than to accept such an offer in this place where even the simplest venereal disease was as incurable as AIDS, and often as deadly.

He shook his head. "Thank you, just the brooch, please."

She stuffed a lock of jet black hair into her kerchief, then brought out a wooden box from under a pile of kerchiefs and rummaged through a jumbled mess of buttons, buckles, and other items of base metal. A plain steel brooch was found, nothing more than a circle four inches in diameter with a thick pin hinged to it. "I've this. Four pence."

His eyes narrowed and he snorted. "In your dreams. Three farthings."

Her response was to throw the brooch back into the box.

"All right, one penny. No more, 'cause I don't need it that bad. I bet there's a nail in that there fence ready to fall out." He pointed with his chin to a row of gray wooden slats down the alley, some of which had already rotted to pieces. He could pull a nail from the soft boards and use it like a straight pin until an affordable brooch would come along.

After a moment's consideration, she handed over the brooch and he paid her a single silver coin. He wandered away from the vendor as she continued on her way, crying her wares in a screechy voice that pierced the other street noises as well as his ears.

Draped over his shoulder as he'd always worn his plaid, with some of the weight hanging in back, the cloth end brushed his knees in front. So he held it at his shoulder and threw the end of it back over his shoulder, then shoved a wad of rust-red plaid and black coat wool through the steel ring. He stuck the hinged pin through the layers of cloth, then let it all fall back so the tip of the pin lay against the steel ring. The end of the plaid now reached the middle of his back.

Dylan shot his cuffs. The coat cuff buttons were of ivory, yellowed only slightly with age, two of them decorating each sleeve. If he wished, he could open them and turn back the sleeves to show off the sark cuffs beneath. For a moment he longed for the nice white sark Cait had sewn and embroidered for him almost two years before, which had been left behind at the castle in Glen Ciorram. For now he kept the sleeves buttoned over the plain cuffs of this unbleached sark he'd brought from the future. So far he hadn't needed to field any commentary about the unnaturally perfect stitching, and didn't care to. Around here, future technology would too easily be confused with witchcraft, so it was best the cuffs stayed covered.

He sat on a mounting block to await his employer, and turtled his neck into the black wool of the high coat collar. Once more he wished he hadn't lost his blue cap on the Sheriffmuir battlefield, but not enough to buy another at Edinburgh prices.

When Ramsay emerged after his tryst to return to the offices, Dylan followed silently.

In the evenings, Dylan made his way to his room at the inn alone, to eat, sleep, then rise to face another day in the service of a man he despised.

Toward the end of the week, as the days shortened toward the solstice, his walk to the inn was in the dark. He encountered few people on the street during the chilly pause between day traffic and the emergence of night folk with less savory business at hand. The tavern at the crook of the wynde was gearing up, and a lively jig on a fiddle drifted onto the street. Though the cold bit his knees and his face, he hoped for a hard freeze that would kill the noxious stench of Edinburgh's streets.

As he approached the Hogshead Inn, the harsh scrape of boot on stone behind made him turn, and he caught a movement in shadow just in time to drop in a squat and avoid a rapier thrust to his heart. From his legging scabbard Dylan pulled Brigid, spun in a crouch, and in one motion made a sweep of his assailant's legs. The man cried out with a curse as the blade embedded in his thigh, and Dylan tore a long gash yanking it out. He stayed crouched and parried high as the rapier made a return slash, then stood, gave a hard shove to the unknown man, and backed up to gain room.

Though bleeding hard from his thigh, the assailant ignored the wound and came at Dylan again. From this angle, with a full moon overhead, Dylan could see it was Simpson, Ramsay's one-eyed former doorman. Dylan backed up some more, headed downhill toward level ground by the loch. One-Eye should have attacked fast to keep him from it, but instead merely followed him, looking for an opening and feinting, which kept Dylan guessing. Dylan switched Brigid to his left hand and drew his broadsword. He said, "You deserved to be fired, you slug."

Simpson said nothing, and Dylan knew he had a long way to go before this one would lose his temper. This was a cold attack, and though the opponent was a mediocre swordsman, he was also calculating. Dylan bit his lip and wondered why Simpson was letting him back down the hill. It was plain the man knew something Dylan did not, which meant downhill was not where he should go. Dylan let out a roar and charged the rapier, hacking hard and pushing Simpson uphill. Having the lower ground and the larger, slower blade, it took huge strength and a measure of bluff to force his attacker back. Steel clanged and echoed from the surrounding stone. Dylan growled as he fought, and bared his teeth. He succeeded in making his opponent retreat in fear.

The steely zing of a sword being drawn came from behind. Dylan parried a low attack of the rapier with Brigid, and at the same time spun to catch a glimpse of flashing steel. He was barely able to parry with his sword. He spun again to parry Simpson, then took a step toward the new opponent, who was on the downward slope. One snap kick sent the man toppling and rolling.

Yet again he spun, to just catch Simpson's sword with Brigid and toss off the blade. He then ran across the street and up, circling. Simpson followed, but with his injured leg wasn't fast enough, and found himself with the lower ground. Dylan faced him off and mulinetted furiously to both sides, his sword in motion like a windmill gone mad. One-Eye glanced back and discovered his compatriot had run, not having the stomach for a real fight, and he hesitated. He looked down at the blood soaking his breeches, and backed off to run at a limp. Dylan stood down, gasping for the icy air, his breath spouting huge plumes in the moonlight. He could have followed and finished off Simpson, but decided he preferred not to kill tonight, and let him go. He let his assailants get well away before continuing toward the inn.

Turning several times as he moved on down the hill, to be sure there was nobody else to try his sword, he wiped the blood from Brigid onto his kilt and scabbarded her, and his sword, then turned and made his way to his room. His mind tumbled with what the assault could mean, and who the second attacker might have been, but there were no ready answers. He bought his supper, then climbed the stairs to his room, deep in thought.

The next day Ramsay visited his mistress again, the second visit to the mystery house in three days. This time Dylan had a glimpse of the woman who answered at Ramsay's knock. She was very thin in a gangly, youthful way, dressed in bright blue silk. Her jet black hair was decorated with jewels, and her smile shone white even from where Dylan stood. She gazed on Ramsay with dewy eyes that made Dylan certain his boss was having a dalliance with this woman. Dylan wondered if she was married, but doubted it. Ramsay was far too indiscreet, visiting at the front door in daylight, for the woman to be anything other than a widely known whore. An extremely young, expensive, and well-kept one, but obviously not anyone's wife.

Today, while waiting, Dylan bought a chunk of scrap hardwood from a cabinetmaker who had a shop nearby, and brought out his *sgian dubh* to whittle and pass the time while his boss got laid. It was a struggle not to think of Cait, who was married to that . . . *apple squire*, as they called such men these days. Thinking of Cait would only put him in a frame of mind not conducive to accomplishing his job, or to his goal of finding a way to take her away.

The days passed in this manner. By day Dylan guarded his employer's life, accompanying Ramsay to meetings and liaisons, and at night he returned to the inn, where he ate, then slept hard. One morning Felix peered at him as he entered the offices, and slipped from the high stool in front of his writing desk. "You'll be interested to know your predecessor is dead."

Dylan stopped short. Felix spoke so seldom, especially to him, it was a shock to be addressed at all. Besides, Simpson's death wasn't particularly good news, even if the man had asked for it. Dylan blinked, expressionless, then said, "I'm sorry to hear that. How did he die?"

Felix's eyes narrowed. "He bled to death, three days ago." The angry demeanor made Dylan wonder why Felix was making such a point of telling him this.

He straightened, raised his chin, and tugged the hem of his coat over the wide belt that held up his kilt. "Went to the doctor with a cold, did he? One leech too many?"

"He was stabbed. In a street fight." An edge sharpened in Felix's voice.

Dylan thought back to that night and dredged his memory for what he had glimpsed of the second assailant. He'd not seen the face, but now he realized the frame could have matched Felix's. Dylan's voice took on an edge as well. "Then dear Simpson should have picked his fight more carefully." Leaning into Felix, he forced the young man to lean back onto the writing desk as he continued in a low, dangerous voice, "Good advice for any man." Then he straightened, tugged on his coat again, and went on into Ramsay's office.

A week after Dylan had sent her, Sinann popped back from nowhere. He was in his room at the inn, eating, his plate on the sill as usual, for there was no other place to set it. "I found them!" she crowed.

His hand was at the dirk under his pillow before he realized it was the faerie who spoke next to his ear. Then he drew a deep breath, relaxed, and took another bite of the salmon he'd bought in the fish market and had the innkeeper cook for him downstairs. "Good. When can I expect them?"

A knock on the door gave him his answer, and Sinann grinned and fluttered as she gestured to it. "I saw them here safely myself."

Dylan leapt from the bed, wiped his fingers and mouth on his wash towel, and threw the door open. Seumas Glas MacGregor stood in the corridor, a skeptical look on his face until he saw Dylan. In an instant the look fled and he broke out in a wide grin. "Mac a'Chlaidheimh!" He stepped into the room and took Dylan in a bear hug, then slapped his shoulder, hard. "I knew it must be you!"

Behind him was Alasdair Og, who had also been part of Rob Roy's Glen Dochart crew, and who no longer looked so young as his nickname suggested. "It's true," said Alasdair. "He told us that, and it's also true we wouldnae have come, except to work for Dilean Dubh." With a grin he said, "Be glad you are Himself." The uprising and battle had put lines on his face and shadows in his eyes, and he seemed to have aged about ten years in the past few months.

Another man Dylan didn't recognize stood behind Alasdair, eyeing Dylan with the same skepticism Seumas'd had. Dylan reached into the corridor to shake hands with them both, also greeting Alasdair with a pat on the shoulder. The new man was introduced as Keith Rómach. "Shaggy Keith" lived up to his name, with the most unruly mop of hair and beard Dylan had ever seen in this place of few combs. He figured if Keith's hair were ever brought under control, it might fall to the middle of his back, and the beard was so thick there was no telling what the face underneath might be like. The eyes, though, were watchful and his demeanor was of stillness.

The men crowded the rest of the way into the room, and Dylan gestured to the bed for them to sit. Alasdair sat, Dylan leaned against the corner by the hearth, and Keith stood by the door like a sentry. Seumas began, as he plopped heavily onto the bunk next to Alasdair. "Murchadh Dubh would be with us, except he has died." Dylan frowned, and Seumas continued, "The French pox ruined his mind, ye ken, and of late he had fallen more deeply into the madness. The day after the battle he went at Alasdair Roy with his dirk. Who promptly shot him, of course." He patted Keith's shoulder and said with cheer and enthusiasm, "Keith, though, is as good a man as any in Glen Dochart, and I can vouch for the lad. He's a Campbell, cousin to my wife. . . ."

"Your wife?" Dylan leaned down to look Seumas in the face. "Your *wife*? You married that girl in the glen?"

Seumas now wore a hard smile that puzzled Dylan. "Aye! We married soon after you went to march with Balhaldie's men, before Sheriffmuir."

Dylan was speechless for a moment, for the question that rose to his lips was why Seumas was in Edinburgh if he had a pretty, new wife in Glen Dochart, to whom he'd been married less than a month. But Seumas had been Rob's second-best swordsman and was a valuable asset to Dylan in the new job. Dylan didn't want to look a gift horse in the mouth, so he didn't ask.

Alasdair quickly jumped into the silence. "So Keith is here to make the three."

Dylan welcomed him with a nod. "Keith."

Seumas said, "Seven pence a day, you say? Doing what? Who are we to rob?"

Alasdair laughed, and Dylan replied, "No stealing. It's a perfectly legitimate job, and if anyone is caught stealing they'll be given the boot, if not my sword. In fact, gentlemen . . ."—that brought the expected chuckles—". . . we're to *prevent* theft. I want to hire the three of you to guard warehouses on the docks. You'll need to buy pistols if you don't already have them. . . ." He looked at Keith. "Do you know how to load and fire a gun?"

Keith nodded, and Dylan continued, "You'll all carry pistols and swords. You're to keep away pilferers. It's seven pence per day for each of you, and a bed for sleeping. Are you men interested?"

Seumas grunted. "Seven pence daily is four pence more than the army ever paid, and it's seven pence more than they've paid since Sheriffmuir. George's army is hard in pursuit, and Rob is harrying them with only a small contingent. So you can be sure seven pence a day is enough to make us come all this way, to a place crawling with English soldiers, on the strength of a piece of paper delivered from thin air."

"Dinnae forget the voices," said Alasdair.

"Oh, aye, the voices." Seumas nodded. "Dylan, lad, have ye faeries in yer service? Every time I tried to throw away and ignore that silly paper, it ended up flattened back out before me. When I ate, when I laid myself down to sleep, there it was. And if all was quiet, I could hear a sweet voice telling me it was you who sent the pictures and that I should bring two men. We had to come, or face the wrath of the wee folk, for a certainty."

Dylan bit hard on the inside corner of his mouth to keep the smirk from his face, for he knew it wasn't a joke to Seumas, who believed heartily in faeries and apparently was afraid of them. But he nodded. "Aye. It's the faeries on my side. I send them where I like, and they go. Obedient as dogs, they are."

That brought a laugh, and Dylan was happy to let the issue of faeries drop with that.

Then Seumas asked, "Who might our new employer be?"

Dylan's urge to smile died, and he coughed. "Well, we're working for Connor Ramsay."

Seumas blurted a vulgarism, then cursed. "The hell, ye say! Did we not hold the man for ransom some months ago?"

Dylan nodded.

"And did you not help him escape and make us look like fools?" Seumas's brow furrowed and his eyes glittered with anger.

Again, Dylan nodded.

"And did you not then tell us his wife's child was your own son?"

Dylan bit his lip, and again nodded.

There was a tense silence as Dylan waited. Seumas stuck out his lower lip and his eyes narrowed at Dylan, then his mouth curled into a smile and he let go a loud, rolling guffaw, joined by a round of laughter from Alasdair and Keith. When he could breathe again, Seumas sighed and said, "It's iron balls you've got, man! Does he have an inkling?"

Dylan shook his head.

"Then you're hoping to get on the good side of King George, working for a Whig?"

Seumas and the others didn't know, and Dylan wasn't about to tell them, that Ramsay was a Jacobite spy. Dylan nodded.

The three were each assigned shifts in the warehouses, rotating at twelve hours, with one man off duty at any given time. Dylan showed them around the buildings. One of the warehouses had emptied over the past week, but the other was still half full of beaver pelts from the vast American wilderness, a place the Indians called *kan-tuk-ee*.

The men settled in and Dylan left them, secure in the knowledge they would discharge their duty loyally. He had no concern they might steal, for the sort of theft they had once done had been carefully circumscribed by tradition. To them, reiving cattle from a rival clan who could afford the loss wasn't stealing, but taking an employer's merchandise they'd been hired to protect would be the worst sort of betrayal. Not to mention it was Dylan they would be betraying, not Ramsay. These particular men wouldn't have that sort of evil in them. And if they somehow found it in themselves, such betrayal would earn them a taste of Dylan's sword. None of them would try Rob Roy's best swordsman, not even Seumas.

Dylan went to Ramsay's offices.

Entering without knocking, as had become his habit, he settled into a wooden armchair near the door, his accustomed post. Ramsay was reading some mail, a deep frown on his face. Dylan's presence wasn't acknowledged, so he pulled out his whittling from his sporran and drew his *sgian dubh* from under his arm. The wood block had somehow begun to morph into a jet airplane, which he knew would one day cause him grief when people would ask what it was, but for now he amused himself with this touchstone to his own past and the world's future. The swept-back wings and the domed cockpit reminded him of long ago when he had played war with his best friend, Cody, in the sandbox behind his parents' house.

It had been an awfully long time since he'd thought much about his childhood. Those years had been memorable only for the terror he'd had of his father, whose drunken railing was the only communication Dylan had ever known from him. Once grown, leaving home had been the best move of Dylan's life, and he'd gone back to visit only for the sake of his mother.

He leaned back in the chair and thought of his mother now as he smoothed the trailing edge of one wing with the dirk he kept sharpened for shaving. He'd hated to leave her with that abusive sonofabitch. If it weren't for Cait . . .

Ramsay spoke, and almost startled him. Alarm rose that he'd been so deep in thought he'd lost track of his surroundings. Ramsay had said something about the chess game.

Dylan looked over at the board and its squat figures of walrus ivory Ramsay kept on a stand next to the wall. It was a game the merchant was playing by mail with a friend in London, and Dylan had studied the board several days before. Nothing had moved recently, since mail from London was slow, but now Ramsay's opponent had moved a knight to queen's knight five and thereby freed his queen to move. "What do you think?" Ramsay said.

Dylan considered the situation for a moment, but not awfully long, then went back to scraping his jet with the edge of his dirk. He shrugged. "Your knight is vulnerable and your king might be trapped if you don't get that rook out of there."

Ramsay's face was impassive, but he said, "And where should it go?"

"Not far. You've castled already, and moving the rook too far would defeat the purpose. Just up to king's bishop two, I think."

"And checkmate in . . . ?"

Dylan chuckled and shrugged again. "Danged if I know. I figure, though, you're going to lose both knights before it's over."

"Par for the course, I'd say. Do you play chess often?"

Dylan stifled a smile. "Not as often as I'd like." Back home, by the time he'd finished college, nobody he knew would play against him any more. But more recently there had been a few games in Glen Ciorram where he'd taken some judicious losses among his distant cousins at the castle. Losing wasn't as much fun as winning, so he'd played fewer games there than he might have.

Ramsay moved his king's rook to bishop two, then turned his attention back to his correspondence.

Dylan said, "Incidentally, my men are posted at the warehouses, as of this morning."

Ramsay grunted. "I'll have Felix put them on the payroll. You're to take their wages to them each week. Collect their money with your own."

"Aye, sir." Dylan went back to his whittling.

"Dylan . . ."

He looked up, but Ramsay was engrossed with his work and in any case was not in the habit of calling him by his first name. A glance around the room revealed nobody else, but Dylan was certain he'd heard someone say his name. Discreetly he leaned back and took his Goddess Stone from his sporran, glanced at Ramsay to be sure he wouldn't notice, then put it to his eye like a monocle. Another glance around the room through the hole in the small gray stone told him Sinann wasn't lurking invisibly. She was probably off giving grief to random folks just for fun. It was her favorite amusement to watch people slip and fall in the filthy streets, and she screamed with laughter whenever anyone who seemed a bit too self-important found his feet tangled and landed on his ass. Dylan slipped the stone back into his sporran and peered around the room. No Sinann here.

The voice had seemed like a woman's. Could it have been Cait? He shut his eyes to concentrate. It had been so long since he'd seen her and heard her speak. Was she thinking of him? Perhaps, even, trying to communicate with him? She'd done it before. He leaned forward on his elbows, carving detail on his jet, and tried to open his mind for Cait to come. But the voice was gone. Cait wasn't there; she was trapped in Ramsay's home. Dylan looked over at Ramsay and decided it was time he learned where the man lived.

"Find Ramsay's house."

"It'll do ye nae good." Sinann perched on Dylan's headboard as he lay down to sleep.

"I don't care. I've got to know where he lives. She's somewhere in Edinburgh. Him I found within an hour of arriving here, but I've been here two weeks and I still don't know where she is. This place just isn't that big. I want to know where he's got her. Tomorrow I want you to follow him home after he leaves the office."

She cocked her head at him. "And what will ye do when I find her? Is it a kidnapping ye have in mind? *Och*, I see, ye'll go marching into the house, throw her over one shoulder and the bairn under your arm, then make a run for it into the Highlands with Ramsay after ye, and as many of King George's men as can be summoned."

"I've got to know where they are. I can't stand it any longer, not knowing." Dylan stared out the window at the tiny square of black, starry sky visible between the nearby buildings, blurred by the uneven glass.

"Dyl. . . ."

"I mean it."

Sinann sighed. "Very well."

Late the following evening Sinann led Dylan up High Street to the Lawnmarket, almost to the end where it overlooked the castle. Dylan paused and stood looking at the imposing structure across the narrow dip the road took on the approach to the battlement. Its cannonade covered a 180-degree expanse, including the entire approach. Torches dotted the walls, and there were so many candles behind the colored glass windows of the royal apartments he could almost see the designs glowing yellow and blue in the night.

Sinann said, "When I followed Ramsay, it was a long journey here, for he came home the roundabout way to stop for a dram of spirits. If someone were out to kill him, it would be a simple matter in his wanderings to slip a dirk into him."

Dylan stopped gawking at the castle and frowned at Sinann. "I'm not going to murder him, Tink."

"Aye. I ken it." But he knew she wished he would.

He ducked into the close where Sinann gestured him onward. Ramsay's house was off Lawnmarket Street at the west end of the High Street, in a close above Bank Street, which ran along the shore of the small loch below the city to the north.

Ramsay's house was a magnificent stone structure. Dylan stopped just inside the archway that led to the close where it stood, hidden by darkness lest anyone look out. The stone edifice was gray, and a pair of leaded glass windows along the courtyard stood two stories high. A third story was above that, and low windows along the cobbled paving of the close probably were for the kitchen and servants' rooms. He leaned against the building next to him and stared hard at the large windows. Heavy drapes let out only slivers of light, but he perked each time a shadow passed one of them. Could it be Cait? He tried to will her to look out, and whispered to Sinann, "Make her look out. I've got to see her." It was a year and a half since he'd been taken from her. The ache to see her was monstrous.

The faerie's voice was low and soft. "Would you have me put an enchantment on her? Are ye certain ye wish it?"

He groaned. As much as he wanted to gaze on Cait's face, he couldn't ask Sinann to place an enchantment she wouldn't be able to remove. He shook his head and stared hard. His imagination tortured him with images of Cait walking, smiling, laughing. She was just over there, only a few yards from where he stood, but he still couldn't see her. Couldn't touch her skin or smell her hair. Couldn't taste her lips.

Also just over there was his son. Dylan huddled into his coat and pressed his back hard against the stone behind him, to keep from charging into the house to claim his family and take them to safety. He couldn't, because there would be no place safe to go until he was free of the charges against him.

But every fiber of him demanded he do something. *Anything.* The culture of turn-of-the-twenty-first-century America, bred into him for the first three decades of his life, looked with disgust and impatience on absentee fathers and deadbeat dads. Before, when he'd thought of one day having children, he'd always assumed his life as a father would be filled with pride and involvement, with Little League, Boy Scouts, parent-teacher meetings, and school plays, not this unbearable powerlessness. Shame gripped his heart. "Tell me they're all right, Sinann. You looked inside, didn't you? Tell me they're safe."

Sinann didn't speak for a long moment, then she said, "The bairn is too wee yet to ken. Your Cait keeps him safe."

"And who keeps her safe?"

"There will be a way, Dylan. Ye must find a way to take her from here. She's a sturdy lass, but she needs you."

He swallowed hard. For a long time he stood there watching, shivering in the winter night, until the last candle inside had been extinguished. Then he retreated and made his way back to his room.

CHAPTER 6

"Dylan . . ."

Dylan jerked awake and sat up in the dark. The fire was embers that threw no light, and he peered around. "Cait?"

Then he heard it again. A woman's voice, but not in the room. Faint, as from a distance. It was in his head. "Cait?" He couldn't understand what she was saying. Only his name came clearly, and that but once more. Then the voice stopped. "Cait!"

Sinann's sleepy voice came from the darkness at the foot of his bed. "It isnae yer Cait."

"How do you know?"

There was a pause, then the faerie said, "I dinnae ken. But I sense it's nae Herself."

"Can you hear what she's saying?"

"Nae, but I can hear her."

Dylan frowned and slipped from the bed to put another peat on the fire. He blew on the embers to make it catch, then hurried back under his blanket and plaid where it was warm. In the new light he looked at Sinann. "Ramsay didn't hear it," he said.

"You've heard her before?"

He nodded. "I thought it was Cait. But if it isn't, then who is it?"

"I surely cannae tell ye."

Dylan huddled under his blanket and stared at the burning peat as his mind tumbled with questions.

Christmas was lonely and dreary, just another workday for Presbyterian Edinburgh, where the holiday was discouraged as "pagan." Rain came hard, and as Dylan ate breakfast by his window, he looked out on grayness: gray stone washed with gray rain, the North Loch seen in patches between the few buildings north of the inn, and the slightly darker gray of the hills of Fife beyond. The upside was that the streets were washed clean by all that rain and the walk to Ramsay's offices was less disgusting than usual. Though a workday, it was a slow one and Dylan spent the quiet hours in his chair by Ramsay's desk while his boss wrote letters.

On New Year's Eve, Dylan bought a jug of whiskey from his landlord to take down to the docks and share with his men. Seumas and Keith were to be found in one building, huddled around a small fire that sent a thin trickle of smoke into the rafters. They'd brought in a second mattress, and lying about the fire were remains of meals, as well as a sack of oatmeal for future meals. The men greeted him with enthusiasm, for they hadn't seen him more than occasionally since their hiring: on payday, and the brief times Ramsay was on site and Dylan stood behind, mute and alert like a Secret Service agent.

"Cud's bobs!" said Seumas in an incredibly bad English accent, then continued in Gaelic, "But it's a filthy, crowded place, Edinburgh."

Dylan nodded and sat by the fire pit they'd scraped in the dirt floor. "I'll be happy when things have blown over and we can go home." He missed the Highlands, and wished he weren't talking through his hat that he might one day return to Glen Ciorram. As much as he wanted to leave this city, he knew he might never shake the charges against him.

Keith said, "It's overly crowded here. A man cannae breathe with so many people about."

Dylan and Seumas nodded agreement. "*Och*, aye."

Dylan uncorked the jug and handed it to Keith. "Take a drink, then go fetch Alasdair."

Keith happily obeyed and took a large pull from the jug, swallowing the raw whiskey as if it were water. Then he handed back the jug. Puzzled,

Dylan took it and sniffed at the mouth, but the spirit was as potent as when he'd bought it that day. Keith belched, then with a grin ran off to fetch Alasdair.

The others watched him go. Seumas said, "He has a cast-iron stomach, that one."

Dylan chuckled and wiped the mouth of the jug. He raised it to Seumas and said, "To peace and prosperity." However, he knew neither was in the cards for Scotland during their lifetimes. He drank, then offered the jug to Seumas, who also drank happily.

Seumas raised the jug and said, "To the one true King, James VIII." He drank, then passed the jug.

Dylan hesitated. He knew from his old history books that James had just that week landed in Scotland, though the news had not yet reached Edinburgh. But the rising had already petered out and there was nothing for James to do but pack it in and retreat to Rome for another four years. Dylan hated knowing the future. He wished to share Seumas's passion for the cause—wanted something to believe in that would strengthen his soul and make his heart soar with hope. He hated Bedford, and all the English Army stood for, but even that wasn't enough to keep his heart for a cause he knew was doomed. He sighed. Nevertheless, though it was a lost cause as well as a treasonous act punishable by hanging, he drank to James VIII. Then he said a silent prayer for Seumas's life.

There was a long silence, then Dylan raised the jug again. "To your new wife." He put the jug to his mouth, but before he could drink, Seumas blanched to the grayness of death. Dylan set the jug down. "What?"

Seumas's lips pressed together till a white line surrounded his mouth. He'd stopped breathing as well as talking. Dylan thought his friend might pass out, and was ready to slap his back when Seumas finally gasped, then took a deep breath and spoke. "They killed her."

Dylan waited for Seumas to continue, which he did in a choked voice that was barely a whisper.

"It was the day after the battle. The *Sassunaich* entered the glen and commenced to questioning people. Asking after the whereabouts of Rob and the rest of us. I wasnae there; we were still following Mar at the time, before I finally gave up and lit out for Glen Dochart. Someone among the Grays doing the questioning knew we'd been married, and so my wife was taken for examination. She was unwilling to go, and let her feelings be known." A thin smile crossed his face and his gaze lost focus. "She was a feisty one. Took guff from nae man, not even me."

Dylan had an unclear memory of the girl, but nodded in agreement, for it was true she'd had a reputation for stubbornness, even among people widely known for it.

Seumas continued, "When the soldiers insisted she go with them, she balled up her fist and hit one." Dylan raised his eyebrows in surprise, and Seumas chuckled. "Aye. Like a man, with a closed fist, right on the chin, I'm told. Then she ran. And they . . ."—he looked down into the fire that reflected in his eyes as orange flickers—". . . they fired upon her. Killed her on the spot."

A long silence spun out, until Dylan cleared his throat and said, "She didn't suffer, then, as she would have under interrogation." He shuddered at the memory of his own experience of questioning by Redcoats.

"Nae, she dinnae suffer. That's for me." Seumas was silent for a moment, then took the jug and raised it high. He spoke in a weighty tone, and Dylan recognized he was quoting the Declaration of Arbroath of 1320, written during the struggle of Robert the Bruce against King Edward I, *"As long as only one hundred of us remain alive, we will never on any conditions be bowed beneath the yoke of English domination; for it is not for glory, nor riches, nor honors that we fight, but for freedom alone, that which no man of worth yields up, save with his life."* Then he drank, and handed the jug off to Dylan, who considered for a moment.

Finally he nodded, and murmured in English, *"When in the course of human events . . . ,"* then drank also.

Keith and Alasdair came to join the drinking, and Seumas straightened, blinking and wiping his eyes on his sleeve. Dylan passed the jug to Alasdair.

Keith peered at Seumas, then at Dylan, and was about to say something when Seumas told him, "We were speaking of Herself."

That was explanation enough for Keith, who nodded, then sat on the dirt floor and reached for the jug. "Sodding *Sassunaich*," he muttered in a mixture of English and Gaelic that seemed extraordinarily appropriate.

The whiskey went down hard, a powerful swill distilled from malted barley in a back room of the inn, and aged not at all. It warmed Dylan's gut, and as the night proceeded, the artificial sense of well-being crept outward from his stomach until the world almost looked rosy.

He reached into his sporran and squeezed one of his cinnamon jawbreakers from its wrapper, then popped it into his mouth. The fire on his tongue was delicious, and a smile crept across his face.

"What ye got there, laddie?" Seumas peered at Dylan as if trying to see into his mouth.

"A jawbreaker. Want one?"

Seumas and the other two laughed. He said, "I dinnae think I care to have my jaw broken, thank you."

Dylan laughed. "No, it's candy. Tastes good. Sugar and cinnamon. They're called jawbreakers because they're hard."

Alasdair said, "I've tasted cinnamon. It tickled my tongue."

"This'll do more than just tickle your tongue." He reached into the sporran again and squeezed more jawbreakers from their wrappers to give to the other three, who looked over the bright red candies. "Careful, though." He stuck out his tongue to show them it had turned blood red. "They're not for the weak."

Alasdair handed his back, but Keith and Seumas put theirs in their mouths. For a moment all was well and they seemed to enjoy the sweetness. But as the spice kicked in, Dylan could see the unaccustomed strength singe them both. Seumas's eyes went wide, and Keith's eyelids drooped. Both of them appeared in pain.

"Too much for you?" Dylan couldn't help chuckling.

Seumas shook his head, though his nostrils flared and he breathed through his mouth. "*Och*, but it's a tasty thing." He rolled it around with his tongue so it rattled against his teeth. Keith suffered in silence.

Sinann, sitting on a crate nearby, said, "I've never before seen the cruel side of ye, lad." Dylan *hee-heed* to himself.

Once the first wave of flavor had passed from the candies, the men settled in to suck on the lumps of sugar. Keith went cross-eyed to see how red his tongue had become, which sent Dylan into a fit of inebriated laughter. He leaned on one elbow in the dirt and reached again for the jug, which was more than half empty now.

Toasting this, that, and the other, they descended into silliness and began drinking to things they found lying around or to things they *wished* they would find lying around. A smile began to curl the edges of his mouth. He could live like this forever. No pain. Blitzed like his father.

He blinked, then sat up. No, not like his father. Never like the old man. Dylan had never been out of control. He would never be out of control. He shook his head to clear it. Damn. He didn't want to be like his father. He stood and excused himself. "Gotta pee." *Gotta get out of here and clear my head.* The others ignored him as he went unsteadily outside to the dock.

"Stay away from the edge," said Sinann.

"Lemme 'lone, Tink." Dylan strolled about halfway to the end of the pier before swerving toward the edge. He steadied himself against a piling to lift his kilt and the tail of his sark beneath. Dark water lapped at the pilings below, smelling salty and dank.

"Ye'll fall."

"I said . . ." Dylan turned to address her, tottered, and nearly fell, but grabbed the piling and hung on. Sinann held his collar and pulled, wings beating hard, until he was balanced on the dock again. Then he shrugged her off to reach for his kilt again and take aim beyond his boots and into the water. "Tink," he said, "do ya think it's possible to decide what you're going to be in life?"

She laughed. "Nae. Were that possible, I'm certain ye would have decided to be born in Scotland."

"No, I mean . . ." His brain struggled to think, though the whiskey made his head feel packed with sludge. He shook himself off, dropped his kilt, then sat on the dock and let his feet dangle. "What do I mean? I mean, I want to know how much control I have over my own life."

There was another chuckle from behind. "I've told ye what ye're meant for. Dinnae try to dodge it."

"Well, that's your opinion, Tink. What if I'm not meant for that? What if I'm doomed to something . . . else? What if . . ."—he leaned forward to stare at the pitch-black water below—". . . what if I'm fated to, say ferinstance, fall into that water and drown? What if . . ."

"Ye're drunk. Ye're daft when ye're drunk."

"What if I don't sober up? What if I just stay this way, so I don't care about anything? Huh? What then? What if I just stop caring about anything and just let the whole sodding world go to hell? I mean . . . I mean . . ." He took a deep breath as he saw where he was going with this. "My father was an alcoholic. Is. Will be. Lots a times if your parent is a drunk, you'll be a drunk. My dad . . . you know, I can't remember my dad being sober even one day. Not one."

Sinann commented, "I've seen you sober many a day. A wee bit too sober at times, is my opinion."

"*Right*. And I never hit a woman. *Never*. Not even Cody, even when she didn't play fair. Hitting girls . . . women . . . is for cowards."

"This is another thing yer father did which you would prefer not to?"

Dylan nodded, and the world spun. "Last time I saw him, I damn near killed him because he took a swing at my mom in front of me. That was when I knew I had to get out of there. I knew I was gonna kill him one day if I didn't, and I couldn't stand that." He peered into the darkness to focus on the faerie. "But what if I end up like him? What if, deep down, I'm just as chickenshit as he is?"

Sinann made a disparaging noise. "Nae, young Dylan, your Yahweh dinnae make ye so. Ye're meant for other things. Drowning, either in whiskey or in water, is not for you. I'll wager if you leapt from this dock, you would float like a cork until someone fished you out."

Dylan sighed and looked down between his boots at the surging, black water. He groaned. "I suppose you're right, Tink. I swim like Flipper."

A commotion came from the shore end of the pier, the dull thundering of horses pulling a wagon or carriage, but muffled as if Dylan's hearing were faulty. Dylan stood to look, still clutching the piling. The huge shadow hung no lanterns. The horses came slowly, with as much stealth as was possible for horses and wheels, and soon Dylan could see the hooves and the wagon's wheels were covered with thick padding to deaden the sound. Sodden as he was, he just stared dumbly as the thing came nearer. Sinann said, "Quick, the brooch."

Dylan reached into his sporran for the Matheson crest brooch, but his fingers fumbled as he pinned it on his coat. Sinann helped him, and as the wagon approached, he stood perfectly still, for the invisibility charm of the talisman was worthless if he moved. Only his eyes turned as he watched the wagon pass. A large man was at the reins, and there were people huddled in the back of the wagon. All were silent.

The wagon proceeded on down the pier, and Dylan followed at a discreet distance, stopping at each piling to hold himself up. Deep gulps of night air helped clear his head, but he knew he was hopelessly inebriated. Not to mention his sword was left back in the warehouse. He reached down for Brigid, though, and hoped he wouldn't need to use the dirk.

The wagon stopped at the very end of the pier, as Dylan approached on silent, rubber soles, still keeping his distance, for he was visible now. He could hear oars thumping in the locks of a dinghy below. The driver leapt from his seat, and another man stood at the end of the wagon. Dylan stopped where he stood, to watch, unmoving. The two men spoke to the others in the wagon, who then began to move to the tailgate, where they were lifted down to the pier boards one by one. They were women, dirty and holding their ragged skirts in fists, and some equally ragged children. No men, except for the two who were herding the rest. Soft weeping reached Dylan's ears, and there was a loud clanking of chains. One of the women suggested the weepers "shut the hell up," but it did no good. The crying became louder, and one of the children began to wail in response.

One of the men smacked the crying boy across the back of his head, hard enough to knock the kid to his knees. Dylan tensed to step forward, but Sinann yanked his collar and he kept still. He wasn't likely to help anything in his condition. The boy quieted to snuffling and climbed to his feet again. The men directed the group to a ladder, where they descended one by one to the boat below. One of the men followed, and the other climbed back into the wagon to turn it around. Dylan stepped toward one of the pilings, then was still once more as the wagon passed on its way to the shore. He watched it go, wondering if he should follow, but Sinann said, "There. On the water."

He turned back and went to the end of the pier. The firth was dark and the moon only a warning sliver, but Dylan could discern shadows here and there. Ships anchored in the bay glowed with lanterns on deck. Below, one long shadow pulled away from the pier, and the sound of oars was discreet but audible. Dylan extrapolated its trajectory out to sea, to find a large shadow that seemed to perch on the horizon between sea and stars. It hung no lanterns, and no lights were visible through portholes.

"Can you see anything, Tink?"

"My eyes are nae better than yours."

"What's the name of the ship? Fly out there."

"*Och*, ask the salmon. They'll ken more than I can tell from looking only."

Dylan blinked, certain he was even more drunk than he'd thought and knowing he couldn't possibly have heard right. "Huh? Which?"

"Call to the salmon. They'll ken. Get yerself down the ladder to the water, and repeat what I tell ye." Dylan just stared stupidly at her. "Go! Do as I tell ye!

He obeyed, descending the ladder until the unutterably cold firth lapped at his boots. He hooked an elbow around a rung of the ladder, against the excellent chance of falling in. Sinann hovered beside him and said into his ear, "By Lir, God of the Sea . . ."

Dylan repeated, "By Lir, God of the Sea . . ."

"By Brigid, daughter of Dugall the Brown . . ."

He repeated.

"Deep in the trough of the whirlpool, in ocean and narrow, in loch and burn, on their protection, come the *Sidhe*."

Dylan uttered the incantation, and waited. It seemed a long time he waited. He adjusted his weight on his elbow and muttered, "It's not working, Tinkerbell." His stomach began to turn, and he wondered whether the jawbreaker with all that whiskey had been a mistake.

"Patience," was all she said.

Finally there was a fluttering in the surface of the water and Dylan gripped hard the wooden rail of the ladder. A large, silvery flash slipped past, just below the surface, then there was a splash. The thing flashed past again, then a shadow emerged from the water below, triangular and gleaming in the moonlight. A low, gurgling voice said, "Who wishes my counsel?"

Sinann poked Dylan's shoulder. "Introduce yerself, ye goof. Dinnae stand there a-gawping."

Dylan said, feeling stupid for talking to a fish, "I'm Dylan. Uh . . . Matheson."

"And who is Dylan Matheson, that I should be concerned?"

Dylan said, "I come from . . ." Sinann poked him again, so he said only, "America."

The salmon gurgled, a sound of disgust. "Even less that I should take note of ye."

Sinann's voice took on an edge, "Dinnae be so cheeky, ye fish. It's the Novice of the Granddaughter of Lir ye're addressing now."

The voice of the fish suddenly took on a tone of respect as the salmon finned backward in the water. "*Och.* My apologies, Novice Dylan Matheson. In what way may I be of help to a student of the Granddaughter of Lir?"

Dylan gestured toward the shadow on the horizon. "Do you know the name of that ship? The dark one."

The fish quivered in the water, and laughed. Dylan blinked at the queer sound of a laughing fish. "For a certainty I do," said the salmon. "That there is the *Spirit.* A slaver bound for the Orient."

"Those weren't slaves. They were white."

The fish laughed again. "*Och,* there's slavery, and there's slavery, lad." The voice rose, and the fish said, "So, Granddaughter of Lir, how is it ye can teach him anything if he knows so little of the world?"

"Not to worry, fish, he knows of things we cannae yet imagine. I'll teach him of the world."

"A daunting task, Granddaughter of Lir. Overly daunting for me, I'll say. And good luck with it to ye." Then the fish leapt from the water and disappeared under it with hardly a splash.

Dylan blinked, thinking hard through the fog of whiskey. "What did he mean? Slavery?"

Sinann's voice was subdued, and Dylan thought there might be a note of dread in it. "Do ye not remember what Ramsay said about there being not a race in the entire world that wouldnae sell its own? And are ye nae aware of the poor folk of the cities, with nae families to look after them? An enterprising and unscrupulous man could turn a handsome profit by transporting such people so their value will increase, were he able to capture them and hide them away to await shipment. It would seem yon *Spirit* has just been loaded with slaves bound for a place where whites are not considered people. There they will be put to work in brothels and such until they die. Which will be soon if your Yahweh would have pity on them."

As this sank in, Dylan remembered Ramsay's conversation with the Englishman in the coffeehouse. Realization struck. "Ramsay owns that ship. Or at least is connected with it."

There was a long silence, then Sinann said, "I think it best ye get yer Cait out of his house at the earliest opportunity."

CHAPTER 7

"I've an errand for you." Ramsay barely glanced up from his desk. Dylan's jaw clenched, and he stifled a groan as his head throbbed and his boss continued. "You're to convey something for me to Perth, and transact some business there." When Dylan didn't reply, Ramsay looked up and said, "Well, you might at least appear a bit more flattered than that, Mac a'Chlaidheimh. For the sake of form, at least. It's not every man I would trust with this much of my money."

Dylan swallowed hard, in an attempt to budge the aspirin he'd dry-swallowed earlier, and said slowly, "With all due respect, I'm accustomed to being trusted with money, and were anyone—anyone at all—to suggest any amount could turn me, I would take deep offense and require satisfaction on the issue." He tilted his head. "If the implication were ever made."

Ramsay peered at him a moment, then went on, "You're to take one of your men with you—the big, smiling fellow, I think. There are two mounts awaiting you at David's stable in Cowgate. When you get to Perth, there are two things you are to accomplish. One is to take this gold"—he produced a green silk purse from a box at his elbow and set it before him—"and turn it over to a man who will approach you with the words,

Glamis hath murdered sleep, and therefore Cawdor shall sleep no more. Whereupon, you will reply, *Lay on, MacDuff.*"

Dylan nodded, as if he did this sort of cloak-and-dagger nonsense all the time. If Ramsay wanted to play M to his Bond, he was welcome to it.

"The other errand," Ramsay continued, "will keep you occupied in Perth until such time as you are approached. Go to the Dog and Bull, where you will meet a man who goes by Polonius Wingham." At Dylan's raised eyebrow Ramsay leaned back in his chair and said, "Possibly an alias, but not necessarily. Men in his profession operate in full view of the authorities, given the authorities make nearly as much from the trade as those who ply it. In any case, he is a tall Welshman, with a rather prominent nose, and can hardly be missed by his speech." Never having heard a Welsh accent in his life, Dylan wasn't so sure. "You are to do as he asks, and bring back to Edinburgh what he turns over to you. I wish you to proceed with all discretion"—here he lowered his chin and his voice became pointed—"as you once did for Rob Roy."

Dylan was familiar with Perth, and had once been to the inn to which he was being sent. "Dog and Bull. Wingham is a smuggler, then." Dylan weighed the purse in one hand and felt of the coins through the cloth. Thirty guineas, if it was a farthing. A fortune. His mind strayed to the five gold coins he'd hidden in Glen Ciorram. He said, "I get the feeling this trip isn't entirely on the up-and-up."

Ramsay blinked. "I beg your pardon?"

Dylan slipped the purse into his sporran. "That is, it's not strictly legal."

Ramsay snorted. "It's not the least bit legal, but I'm sure that won't cause you any loss of sleep. Be sure you and your man are well armed, and watch your backs, for one never knows when the excise men could become greedy. I'll expect your return within the fortnight, possibly within the week. Whatever you do, do not let Wingham learn of the other business at hand."

Dylan nodded, then opened his mouth to segue the conversation toward the thing he'd seen the night before, but Ramsay waved him off and said, "Haste, Mac a'Chlaidheimh. You have your orders, now carry them out." There was nothing for it but to go.

Out on the street, Dylan hawked up the remains of his aspirin and reswallowed the bitter mess.

David was the fellow in Cowgate who had bought Dylan's stolen cavalry horse, and Dylan was amused to learn that horse was one of the two Ramsay had hired for this trip. Dylan mounted and chuckled. As he picked up the lead for the other horse and urged his into motion, he muttered, "Come on, you limey nag."

Fortunately, it was a civilian saddle this time. When he'd first leapt onto this horse at Sheriffmuir, the hard cavalry saddle of wooden slats and long, centered stirrups had nearly unmanned him in his kilt. This civilian saddle, with shorter stirrups set more forward, allowed him to sit rather than straddle so his weight rested on more appropriate parts of his anatomy.

With the horses at a walk up the steep hill toward the High Street, Sinann settled into her accustomed spot behind Dylan, but he said, "Uh-uh. You're not going."

"The hell, ye say!"

"You're not. You're going to stay here and watch Cait and Ciaran."

"And what of watching you?"

"I'm a big boy and can take care of myself."

"Oh, aye, like you did the last time you told me to watch Cait. How close to dying were you when I found you then?"

"You're still not going. I can't just leave them here alone with him. Not after what we saw last night."

There was a long hesitation. Dylan pressed, "You know she and the baby are not safe here. It wouldn't take much to piss him off enough to put them on a boat and claim she'd run off and taken Ciaran with her."

"But you know I cannae . . ."

"If there's any danger, if he tries to hurt her or even *thinks* about hurting the boy, you just bust out all his windows. That ought to distract him, especially if you break those really big, really *expensive* ones in the front." Sinann giggled, and he knew he'd struck a chord. After more than two years, he knew where all her best buttons were. "In fact, all that glass should look right pretty, flying every which way. It'll at least give Cait and Ciaran time to get away."

There was another long hesitation.

"Do it, Tink."

The faerie sighed, leapt from the horse, and flew away in the direction of Ramsay's house. Dylan also sighed, feeling fewer qualms, now, about leaving Edinburgh. He urged the horses into motion and headed toward the docks to collect Seumas for the trip to Perth.

Dylan and Seumas traveled well into the night, not stopping until the cold and fatigue forced them to dismount and build a fire. They ate bread and cheese, then rolled up in their plaids by the small fire to sleep until the sun would rise and take the edge from the cold. Both of them dropped off immediately.

Sleep was deep when Dylan snapped awake. He ached from the sudden alertness, and struggled to shake off grogginess and cold as he looked around for what he'd heard. Almost as an afterthought, he reached for Brigid. The sky was still dark, the sun not even having begun to color the night. Dylan peered into impenetrable shadows, listening. Seumas lay on the other side of the dying fire, still unconscious. The night was unnaturally silent, but there was something out there in the darkness. Dylan could almost smell it, and the hair stiffened at the back of his neck. He rose and turned, Brigid at the ready.

"Seumas."

The sleeping man didn't stir.

"Seumas, wake up." Dylan went to poke Seumas with his boot, but his friend slept on, his breaths soft in the quiet night. This was deeply wrong. Seumas was as alert a man as Dylan had ever known. He would awaken at the slightest sound.

A low growl came from deep in the shadows, and Dylan turned to face it. Two yellow eyes gleamed in the darkness, unblinking. There was almost a sense of relief as the unknown threat became known. Though by the eighteenth century wolves were extinct in Scotland, there was no denying the existence of this animal. He shrugged off the oddity and readied for a fight.

The wolf sprang and Dylan swept the dirk before him, but the leap had been only a feint. The animal was fighting like a man. It dodged the dirk and leapt again. Its jaw clamped onto Dylan's knife arm, teeth cutting through wool with ease. Dylan growled, as well as his attacker. He took Brigid in his left, and thrust as the wolf tore at his arm. The long blade caught the animal's right eye. With a yelp of pain, the wolf let go of Dylan's arm and fled.

Dylan snapped awake, panting. The sky was purpling and the fire was dying embers. "Seumas," he said.

"What is it?" Seumas was sitting up in an instant, his dirk at the ready, looking around.

Blinking and also looking around, Dylan wondered *what* as well. He said, "Did you hear something?"

Peering into the darkness, Seumas said in a low voice, "Nae. I heard naught."

Dylan rose to look for signs of the wolf, but there were no prints. No blood from its wound, and no signs of a scuffle. Brigid was in her scabbard, though he didn't remember replacing her. He didn't remember lying back down, either.

"What's troubling ye, lad?"

"Nothing." Dylan shook his head. "Just a dream, I guess."

Seumas chuckled. "Ye poor sod, dreaming of sounds in the night. Myself, I was enjoying a romp in a bed of feathers with a comely and obliging lass."

"Sorry for disturbing you. It's almost day. Go back to sleep."

Seumas rolled himself in his plaid and did exactly that.

As Dylan lay down also, he noticed a soreness in his right arm. He felt of his coat sleeve for tears, but there were none. However, when he slipped off the coat and unbuttoned his right cuff to roll it up, he found four small, round marks in his skin. Fang punctures: two on each side of his forearm, oozing blood. He slipped his coat back on and lay down, unable to sleep after that.

Dylan and Seumas resumed their journey at dawn. The sun was nearly set as they made their way to the Dog and Bull, a bustling little inn near the River Tay, just within sight of the quay where a small ship stood by the dock.

Dylan had been here before, but it had been only briefly while Rob conducted business with a guest in one of the rooms during the dead of night. The common room was much like Ramsay's favorite coffeehouse in Edinburgh, scattered with tables and fitted with a booth near the hearth, where food and drink could be bought and taken to the tables in earthenware bowls and cups. The stone walls were plastered white, and one broad expanse of wall was painted with a mural of a sailing ship on high, white-capped seas. Dylan had learned on his last visit the mural was a signal that "free traders" were welcome and safe, and his reaction had been to wonder why they needed it. Smuggling was nearly the town industry in Perth.

Dylan scanned the room, Seumas standing patiently to his right and slightly to the rear. A woman in a ragged red dress accented with dirty lace at neck and sleeves sat at a small table near the door, appearing too drunk to move. Three men were clustered at another table, deep in intense discussion, over plates of food and horn tumblers of ale. Nobody in the room matched the description Ramsay had given: all were far too short, and none of the noses he saw struck him as "prominent."

A small man with not a hair on his head entered from another room. Dylan recognized the innkeeper, who approached them with care if not outright suspicion. "May I ask what ye're in need of?"

"We're to ask after a man named Wingham. Polonius Wingham." Though Dylan kept his voice low, he noticed the group of three men at the corner table stopped talking at mention of Wingham's name. One of them shifted in his seat.

"And what would you say to this famous Mr. Wingham, were I to procure him for ye? Or, even, were he to exist?" He ran trembling fingers over his shiny pate.

Dylan's gaze went past the innkeeper, checking the doorway for lurkers and watching for movement among the table of guests. "I would say, 'We're to ask after you.' "

Seumas snickered. The nervous little man was not amused, and tossed them both a sour look.

The restless one at the table stood to step over his bench, and made his way quickly toward the door. From the corner of his eye, Dylan watched him go as the other two men arose from the table and sauntered over. One of them said, "We couldnae help but overhear. . . ."

Dylan overrode him. "Then you must hear like a bat. I'm in awe." He made a slight bow of his head.

"What business have you with Polonius?" He was belligerent, and stuck his chest out so Dylan would know who was in charge.

Dylan ignored the posturing. "Produce him, and find out." Dylan kept his hands away from his weapons, but his focus was on the other man's eyes. He flexed the fingers of his right hand to attract the other's attention.

The chest puffed out some more. "Well, now, I cannae just let anyone stroll in here and have an audience with Himself, ye see." As he spoke, his hand went to the dirk at his belt. "I'll need to . . ." By the time the blade cleared the scabbard, Dylan's left hand had snaked out to grab the other man's hand by the thumb. He yanked the man off balance, bending the thumb backward until Mr. Puffy Chest was on his knees in pain. Dylan's right hand caught the dirk as it fell from the loosened grasp.

Seumas emitted a gleeful giggle and leaned down, nodding into the man's grimacing face, "Hurts, doesn't it?" It was the voice of experience.

Dylan relaxed his own body while keeping his opponent's thumb taut, then set the tip of the man's own blade precisely against the carotid artery, which made its location obvious by its panicky throbbing. He said in an utterly calm voice, "Now, where is Wingham?"

"I'm here."

The voice came from behind. Seumas spun, his dirk out. Dylan threw him a look, and Seumas reddened at having let down the rear guard.

Dylan put his boot against the chest of his humbled opponent and shoved him backward onto the floor, then turned to face the voice. Seumas turned to protect Dylan's back from fresh assault by the man on the floor.

Wingham was possibly the tallest man Dylan had seen in this century, and must have stood six foot two or so. He lounged against the doorway, wearing well-tailored breeches and a wine-red velvet coat. His large nose was offset by a long jaw, making for an imposing countenance more dig-nified than his chosen profession might warrant. Yet, even in the dim candlelight there seemed to be a twinkle in his eyes and a tiny smile touched the corners of his mouth.

"Bravo. Congratulations on putting George in his place. He often steps over boundaries just to see if he can. You'd be surprised at how often he gets away with it." Dylan found Wingham's Welsh accent low and growly, but not as Celtic as he'd expected. The closest to it he'd ever heard was the way the Liverpudlian Beatles talked. Wingham addressed the man on his knees. "Go outside, George, and take the others with you." Dylan let go of George, and Wingham waited until the three had passed through the door before pushing off from the door frame and sauntering over to a table. "Come. Sit. Eat and drink while we wait for the moon to set. We've work to do tonight." When Dylan and Seumas didn't move, he shifted his weight and held up his palms. "Unless you'd prefer to stand there like blocks of wood until it's time to go."

Dylan shrugged, then went to sit. Seumas followed. Dylan said to Wingham, "I'm Dilean Dubh, and this here is Seumas Glas."

Wingham eyed their kilts. "You're both Highlanders."

"Nothing gets past you."

Wingham gave a small shake of his head and shrugged. "I'm merely surprised." That was all he said on it. He called to the bald little man,

"How about some supper over here? And some ale, perhaps? All around, if you please." The innkeeper hurried to comply, carving mutton pieces from a carcass spitted in the hearth. It caught Dylan's attention that this fellow carried enough weight the innkeeper himself was waiting on him. Wingham returned his attention to Dylan and Seumas. "How many horses have you brought?"

"Just the two."

"Damn!" He sat back, looked around as if entreating heaven for an explanation, then leaned forward again. "Did he not get my message?"

If that was a rhetorical question, Dylan didn't think it sounded like one. In any case, he wasn't going to answer it because he didn't care to sound as clueless as he was. "Regardless of whether or not the message made it there, we're here with the two horses. How many more will we need?"

"At least four; five would be better. Unless you want to take it all in a wagon. But horses and men could scatter and not be such a target on the road."

Dylan was puzzled now. "Or a wagon pulled by two horses could look a bit less like a smuggler's train. What in the world are we picking up?"

Wingham blinked. "You don't know?" Dylan shrugged. "Sherry. Twenty-five casks."

Dylan blew out his cheeks. "Holy moley."

Wingham sent one of his men to obtain a cargo wagon, then over the next half-hour, while they ate, went over the details of the pickup with Dylan. He waved his dirk for emphasis as he said, ". . . and tell your employer I'm holding back a cask in payment for the wagon." Dylan was certain he would have a few words for Ramsay on his return, for sending him into this situation without adequate preparation. For a fleeting moment, he wondered if James Bond ever had snafus like this.

The sherry had been hidden in a kirk near the river. Once the moon had set, Wingham and his men guided Dylan and Seumas to it in their wagon, and they were met outside by the pastor, who was well camouflaged in clerical black. Dylan wondered at the religious man with the criminal life, but the pastor didn't seem much perturbed by the idea of cheating the Crown of its outrageous tariffs.

Even this early in the century, duties on some imports ran as much as 112 percent of the value of goods. Not many of King George's subjects were willing, or even able, to pay those prices, and the high profits in

smuggling made it a community activity in which everyone either participated or looked the other way. When Wingham's money guy handed
over payment to the pastor for storing the contraband, the man of God
grinned, clinked the coins together in his hand, and proudly declared he
would buy a bell for the church.

Dylan looked at the ground for a moment to hide his amazement.
Whatever.

The fellow handling the money was a small, contained fellow who
dressed more plainly than Wingham but spoke with the same accent. He
seemed to know everything, but didn't control much. Dylan thought he
might be a second-in-command of sorts, but he was awfully small for a
smuggler. Certainly such a short man wasn't the sort Dylan would want
guarding his own back in a fight, but Wingham seemed to trust him fully.
While the three of them watched Seumas help Wingham's men load casks
onto the wagon, Dylan said to the money man, in idle chatter, "You're
Welsh, too?"

A tiny smile crossed his face. "Somewhat."

Dylan had to chuckle. "Can one be *somewhat* Welsh?"

The money man shrugged. "With a name like Gilman, it's apparent
to all I have relatives on the continent."

Dylan perked. "Dutch?"

Gilman nodded. In the dark it was impossible to read his face, but his
voice seemed to carry a note of amusement. "Possibly. Or German, nobody
is entirely certain. At least, when I'm in Amsterdam I let them all *think*
it's Dutch. It's good for business."

"You know the Exchange there?"

Gilman nodded again, never taking his eyes off the shadowy men
carrying the casks. It was plain he was taking a running count as he talked
to Dylan. "There is much money to be made in Amsterdam by men with
much money to risk."

"Aye." And Dylan knew a man with money who was itching to risk
it in Amsterdam.

"Well," said Wingham as the last of the casks was loaded onto the
wagon and the load draped with canvas that might have once been a ship's
sail, "we're off. Dylan Dubh, tell your employer it's a pleasure doing
business with him, and I hope we shall do so again in the future. Cheerio."
He paused, then said, "Or is it *mar sin leat?*"

"*Tha. Mar sin leat.*" Dylan climbed onto the back of the wagon, letting

Seumas take the reins up front. The end of a wooden sherry cask made a less than comfortable seat, but someone had to watch the rear and Dylan had no experience driving a wagon. As the church building receded into the darkness behind them, he began to wonder what he was going to tell Ramsay about the guy who never showed up for his thirty guineas. Dylan was feeling less and less like an agent in Her Majesty's Secret Service. He teetered on the cask as the wagon bumped and trundled, and wondered how his butt was going to make the trip.

As soon as they'd left the town, a shadow came at them from the side of the road. One moment it wasn't there, and the next a shadow on horseback rode alongside the wagon. Dylan stood on the casks and drew his sword, but the shadow said, "*Glamis hath murdered sleep, and therefore Cawdor shall sleep no more.*"

Dylan nearly followed through to take the fool's head, for in that instant he recognized the voice as Major Bedford. It was all he could do to stay his own hand. His mind flew to decide whether to kill the Redcoat, run, or bluff it through. Killing him would be disadvantageous in the long run if Dylan wanted to get Cait safely out of Ramsay's house, for at the very least it would put Dylan on Ramsay's bad side. Running would be even worse, for it would give him away and leave Bedford alive, and again Dylan would be on Ramsay's bad side. The only course was to bluff it through and hope to remain anonymous in the dark. He affected a Lowland accent, like Ramsay's but lower class. "*Lay on, MacDuff.* It's about time you showed yersel'!" He spoke low, hoping Bedford wouldn't hear him well. Contrary to his response code, his sword went back into its scabbard, and he sat back down on the casks as Bedford rode alongside. By the silhouette, Dylan could see the Major was in civilian attire.

"I couldn't show myself to those smugglers, could I? Not that I haven't made my own silver from these very casks, but I could hardly let them know what *our* business is. Could I?"

"I suppose not," said Dylan, with no clue exactly what that business was, and particularly intrigued that it was illicit enough to require a clandestine meeting, yet was unrelated to the smuggling. He pulled Brigid from her scabbard and began cleaning the already clean blade, preferring to have her handy in case it became necessary to kill the Major.

Bedford continued, showing no indication he recognized Dylan's voice, "I expect your presence means the *Spirit* took on her cargo without incident?"

Dylan's attention perked. What did Bedford know about the white slaver? He wanted to look straight at him, to read him, but instead kept his chin buried in his coat collar. Most of his face was covered by the standing wool. "Aye. Night before last. Headed for . . . China, I think."

"Singapore, actually. They simply can't get enough white women there. And boys. They eat up the boys at a rate that makes it a bit difficult to keep up with demand, and therefore makes them the most profitable cargo afloat. I suppose a woman is always a woman, but boys don't remain boys very long." His seat was perfect, and his back perfectly straight as he rode. His chin held high, he might have been viewing troops rather than skulking about the countryside after money from the sale of human beings.

Dylan shuddered at the casual chatter about the shelf life of small boys.

He chewed the inside corner of his mouth, then said, "Not enough widows and orphans from the uprising landing in the custody of the state?"

"Precisely so. Not to mention the monstrous risk involved. Smuggling is one thing; smuggling women and children is . . . well, it's kidnapping, actually. Even if they are Scots." Then his voice brightened as he said, "At any rate, you've got something owed me, young fellow."

Dylan was sure he had, and some gold as well. He reached into his sporran for the green purse and held it out to Bedford. The Major took it, and Dylan felt a quiver of revulsion at the touch of his hand. He said, "Tell me, what happens to those women and children once they get to Singapore?"

Bedford hefted the purse, then stuffed it inside his jacket. "I haven't the faintest idea. Nor the slightest concern. Adieu."

The Major turned his horse back the other way, and immense relief washed over Dylan. Once Bedford was out of earshot, Dylan returned Brigid to her scabbard, and let out a sigh accompanied by a string of expletives disparaging Ramsay's entire life and heritage for at least three generations.

A laugh came from the front of the wagon. "Ramsay's associate knows something about ye you dinnae care to have known, then?" Seumas had undoubtedly heard Dylan's fake accent.

"The sonofabitch knows my real name."

Seumas whistled low. Even he didn't know Dylan's real name.

A shout went up from the left. Dylan was on his feet in an instant, sword drawn and slashing at attackers. Four men rushed the wagon and were climbing the side rails, shouting and cursing. Seumas whipped the horses to a gallop, and with one hand reached with his dirk to sweep behind him.

Dylan parried furiously, barely able to see flashing steel under the stars. One man was caught in the gut by Seumas's dirk, and fell from the wagon, clutching at the sides as he went over. The wagon lurched as a rear wheel ran over him, and he cried out. Dylan rode the tottering casks like a surfer.

The other attackers gained the cargo bed, and Dylan was forced to the opposite side. He nearly went over. One attacker was short and fat, but had a bright, quick sword that glinted in the scarce starlight. Dylan could do little more than keep himself alive and on the wagon. Another of the attackers had a wooden leg, which he used to parry low attacks. The jolting of the wheels flying over the narrow, rutted track worked both for Dylan and against him, for the attackers' swords missed their marks as much as his did. It was a flurry of poorly aimed steel, and the attackers stabbed with their rapiers while he slashed with his broadsword. Dylan refrained from shouting, in order to keep them guessing his position as he dodged. The fat man was tossed from the wagon by a bad bump, leaving two raiders. Dylan roared at the hot pain of a stab through his right biceps. His sword dropped, and clattered from the wagon.

"Shit!" Brigid was all he had left, and though he could still move his right arm, he continued to parry with his uninjured left. In the darkness he was able to fake out Wooden Leg, grab the knuckle guard of his hilt, and yank him off-balance to topple him over the side. That left one opponent, the smart one who had hung back, saving his strength. The last raider put another shallow slice in Dylan's left shoulder before Dylan could feint, duck, and come up under the sword to bury his dirk in the man's gut. The raider bellowed, a note of disappointment in his voice at this turn of events, then fell over the side.

Dylan didn't bother trying to see if the raiders were following. He urged Seumas to keep the horses galloping, hoping they could see the road better than their driver, until he figured enough distance had been covered. Even then he didn't let Seumas stop completely until well past dawn.

"It was Bedford, I tell you." Dylan leaned over Ramsay's desk, his teeth clenched in anger. His right arm was stiff, but functional, and the cut on his left shoulder, little more than a scratch, had stopped bleeding almost immediately. The injuries were less aggravation than having to sew the holes in his coat and sark.

"Impossible. More likely you were followed from Perth."

Dylan didn't care who it really was; he wanted Ramsay to think his buddy the Major had betrayed him. But the subversive attempt failed. "Damn straight, we were followed. It must have been a fucking parade, there were so many men behind us. And whoever sent those men after us was someone who knew not to attack until *after* Bedford got his money. That lets out Wingham, and anyone else from Perth who knew only about the casks."

Ramsay frowned, thinking hard on that point.

Sinann wasn't helping anything. She hovered near the ceiling, making snarky comments to Dylan. "See what happens when you send me away? I could have followed them for you. Gotten proof, perhaps. Discovered their identities. *Och*, it's an idiot I've brought to save the Scots from the English! Just as well to hand over the country, and every last one of us get on a boat for the American wilderness!"

Dylan ignored her, and continued to Ramsay, "Bedford wasn't just lucky to have been missed by those raiders, whoever they were."

"You don't know but that he could very well have simply been lucky." Ramsay was right.

But Dylan knew in his heart the raid had been set by someone who knew Bedford would be there and had an interest in making sure the Major got his money. Besides, Dylan's interest in ruining Ramsay's business relationship with the Major was strong. He said, "You should *hope* it was not Wingham, because he might be able to lead you to a man who could represent you in Amsterdam."

Ramsay leaned back, his eyes wide with bald surprise. "I beg your pardon?"

Dylan straightened. "You're looking for a liaison to represent you in the Amsterdam Exchange. Wingham knows someone who might be willing to work with you. His name is Gilman, a Welshman of Germanic ancestry. He says he knows the Exchange."

"You spoke to him of this?"

Dylan shrugged. "It came up in conversation. He handles Wingham's money; he might be interested in going legit . . . I mean, working legitimately. Aboveboard." He snorted. "More or less."

There was a long pause while wheels turned in Ramsay's head. "You listen mighty close for an illiterate Highland highwayman."

"I never claimed to be stupid, and you assumed I was illiterate without asking. I suppose you could have found Gilman on your own. In a decade or so." Dylan turned away from the desk with another snort of disgust, and went to sit in his chair.

"I'll investigate this possibility."

"You hire him, I want a finder's fee."

Ramsay grunted. "You'll get what you deserve; count on it."

Dylan flexed his sore right arm and peered at his boss as Ramsay involved himself with his work, then said, "May I be excused for a short while? It seems I've lost my sword, and I've got to buy a new one." Ramsay waved him out of the office, and he rose to hurry onto the street.

Sinann came to hover. "So, I've been a-thinking this morning. You say Bedford is handing over to Ramsay the women and children who are then shipped to the Far East, eh?"

Dylan only grunted. There were people around, and it didn't take much aberrant behavior to be accused of talking to faeries. Part of him longed for the days when talking to oneself could be shrugged off as eccentricity, and heresy would no longer be a capital crime.

Sinann continued, "Do ye think revealing Bedford's nefarious occupation to the Crown might be a chance at pardon?"

Dylan stopped in his tracks and looked up at her, his eyes wide with sudden hope. A white grin lit up his face. But it died and he said in a low voice as he continued on his way, "Not if the Crown catches me first. Who am I going to surrender to? Bedford? How about one of his fellow officers? Even if they don't hold with what he does, they won't be falling all over each other to pardon me for bringing them the news one of their own is a white slaver."

Her shoulders slumped. "Aye."

There was a swordsmith's shop on the High Street, near the Edinburgh Tolbooth and St. Giles Cathedral, in which Dylan had seen, in passing, a few swords he admired. Most of them he couldn't begin to afford; he was in fact deeply annoyed at having to replace even the worn weapon he'd used for the past two years. Keeping a room while working for Ramsay was expensive, and having to buy a sword was going to cut his savings in half, even after selling his empty scabbard. He steeled himself for the cost and entered the shop.

The fire heated the place almost beyond endurance, in spite of the winter cold outside. The smelter bent over his work, shirtless under his apron, sweating mightily over the heated metal. Near the wall a large wheel was turned by an apprentice which, by pulleys, spun the stone on which a new sword was being sharpened by another apprentice. A craftsman sat with a blade held between his knees as he slipped the tang of it into a brass hilt. All around the shop, hung on pegs along a wooden rail, were swords for sale, some new and some not. Dylan browsed them all and wished he had a lot more money.

After a long while yearning for the beautiful weapons in gilt and silver, then a brief moment crinkling his nose at the more plain and affordable steel hilts, he tried a few that were good quality but moderately priced. In the end he settled on a broadsword with a cast-brass hilt and a wire-covered grip. It had only a single knuckle guard and one short quillon, which made him absently flex the scarred fingers of his right hand where he'd once been cut up for lack of protection, but this was the best he could afford. On the plus side, the pommel was decorated with the image of a dancing lady, and the sword was new. A step up from the one he'd lost.

He handed over his shillings, then put the new, leather-covered scabbard into the frog of his well-worn baldric and slipped the sword into it, then out, then in again. It was a nice, smooth fit, again better than his old sword. Tonight he would find space in a close somewhere to work out, and become accustomed to his new weapon. Then he muttered dryly to Sinann, "Come on, Tink. Ramsay is unprotected, and God knows what might happen to him."

She followed him from the shop. "Do ye suppose he may have been attacked in his own office and murdered by a band of renegade clerks?"

Dylan chuckled. "I'm not that lucky."

Winter wind cut through Dylan's coat as he leaned against a stone wall inside the wynde that emerged on the close where Ramsay's house stood. Directly across the small courtyard the leaded windows rose like a facing of glass, the glow of many candles inside boasting the prosperity of the owner. Since his return from Perth, Dylan had come every night. He always kept to the shadows in this unfrequented alley, hoping for a glimpse of Cait and puzzling over the layout inside. He thought there might be bedrooms at either end of the second floor, but the great room with the tall windows took up most of both the first and second floors. The third floor had a few small windows, which were usually still lit long after the rest of the house was dark. Sometimes he heard a woman's laughter and hoped it was Cait, though it stung that she could be so happy without him.

"Perhaps she doesn't need me?" he whispered to Sinann. His talisman was pinned to his coat, and so he was as invisible as she.

She was drowsing at his feet, leaned against the wall, and snapped awake. "Beg pardon?"

"She sounds happy. Maybe she's all right here."

Sinann listened to the laughter for a moment, then shook her head. "That isnae Cait. It's Ramsay's whore."

Dylan took his eyes from the window to peer at the faerie. "Say, what?"

"His whore. He keeps a woman in his apartments on the third floor. I told ye that."

"You didn't. Is it the same one he goes to in Canongate?"

Sinann shook her head. "He spreads himself thin, that one. And if they knew, they would scratch each other's eyes out."

"What for, if they both know he's married?"

She chuckled. "The salmon was right. There is much of the world you do not know. Sure, they dinnae care he's married. They care only of who is in his favor. They both know his wife is not and never will be. That is the way of things."

Dylan pressed his lips together and returned to watching the house.

There was a shout inside, and Dylan perked to attention. Something crashed, and a woman screamed. One end of the first floor darkened, and Ramsay's voice shouted obscenities while loud, thumping noises emanated. "What's going on, Tink? Is it Cait?" But he didn't wait for an answer. The screaming turned to cries of pain. The woman was being beaten. It no longer mattered who it was he heard, he had to make it stop. Dylan unpinned his talisman and slipped it in his pocket, then drew his sword and took off across the close toward the front stairwell door.

"No!" cried Sinann. She flew after him and yanked on his coat collar. But he shook her loose and threw himself against the wooden door studded with iron, attempting the latch.

It was locked and barred. He pounded on it and shouted, "Ramsay! *Ramsay!*"

Sinann hissed in his ear, "And what're you to say when your employer opens that door? How will you explain yerself?"

Dylan's fist thudded against the door. "Open up!" Inside the house, the screaming stopped. Dylan called again, "Ramsay!" After a long moment, the bar thudded inside and the iron latch clattered.

Ramsay himself opened the door, his face flushed and his wig not quite straight. His eyes went wide when he saw Dylan and his sword. "Mac a'Chlaidheimh! What on God's earth are you doing here?"

Dylan strained to see past him without looking like he was trying to see past him, but there was nothing to see. As in nearly every other building in town, the door opened onto a spiral stair and the inside of the house was beyond view. Thinking fast, he scabbarded his sword and said, breathless, as if he'd just run a distance, "I came to see if you were all right. I heard the noises and thought you were in danger. A boy from whom I buy information came to tell me a man was out to murder you tonight."

Ramsay fluttered, but didn't seem to think the news surprising. "Who is this man?"

The only candidate that leapt readily to Dylan's mind was "Simpson." That brought a blink.

Sinann hissed, "He's dead, ye goof!"

Dylan suppressed a curse and urgently pressed, hoping Ramsay was unaware of that. He put his hand against the door lest Ramsay try to close it. "I think I should stay to guard the house tonight. Just in case he attempts it by stealth."

Ramsay thought a moment, then nodded. "Come." Dylan stepped through the door, which was closed and bolted behind him, then followed Ramsay up the stone spiral, lit by candles in sconces at each quarter-turn.

The entry from the stairwell was to the largest room, the one with the tall windows. Before an enormous hearth stood a dining table large enough to seat a dozen or so people. It took up half the room, but was set with the remains of only one supper. Great chandeliers hung from the ceiling, and though they were dark on this evening without guests, the elaborate crystals glittered with reflections from the lit candelabras on the table and the brace of single candlesticks on the mantle.

At the far end of the room, just beyond an archway, was a smaller, darkened sitting room lit only by its hearth. To his left was a windowed landing, furnished with a small love seat upholstered in burgundy satin, and beyond that a hallway led off behind a narrow stairwell. That stairwell apparently led to the balcony, the dark, wooden rail of which ran along one entire side of the great room and curved at one end toward the door that led to the spiral stairwell at the front of the house.

This was an amazing wealth of space for Edinburgh, especially in these times of restricted new construction and partitioned tenements the length and breadth of the rock on which the city perched.

Ramsay was saying to Dylan, "I'll have a pallet made up for you in the kitchen downstairs."

Dylan nodded, but said nothing. His mind quickly slipped away from the luxury of the place, for it smelled of Cait. She lived here, and her scent filled his head. For a moment he was transported to the castle at Glen Ciorram, to the nights reading poetry with her and months anticipating the day they would marry. He wanted to search the house for her, but took deep breaths instead and didn't move.

"Cait!" Ramsay turned and swayed as he called to the dark sitting room. A whiff of alcohol let Dylan know why Ramsay was unsteady on his feet. "Caitrionagh, get over here, you cunt!"

Dylan's cheeks warmed, and his hand ached to pull Brigid and teach this fool not to treat Cait like that. But rather than cause a bloody scene, he looked past Ramsay and searched the shadows for her. There was a stirring on a chair in that room, and a figure rose. Her cap had come off, and the freed locks dangling from their pins gleamed before he even saw her face.

When he did, he drew a deep, shocked breath through his teeth. She held the cloth of her folded kerchief cap to her nose, and spots of blood soaked through it. Her left eye was just purpling and would soon be black. Her dress was heavy wool, dyed green and in the English style, the bodice rigid with stays that narrowed even her slender waist to a ridiculous point and mashed her breasts almost flat, pushing them very high, just under her chin. A ruffled lace collar adorned her neck, just touching the edge of her jaw, as if her head rested lightly on the dainty fabric. She stared at the floor as she approached, her eyes nearly closed, looking at neither Ramsay nor Dylan. She stopped before them and curtsied, still not looking up.

"Cait, this is Mac a'Chlaidheimh, my bodyguard. You will make him comfortable among the servants for tonight. I cannot tell how long he'll be staying. See that he's fed."

She curtsied again to Dylan, her gaze never leaving the floor. "Mac a'Chlaidheimh."

He reached for her free hand and bowed over it in the Continental manner. "*A Chaitrionagh.*"

Her fingers suddenly gripped his with white knuckles. Trembling. He covered the hand with his left, lest Ramsay see, and looked up to find her face pale. Her wide, blue eyes searched his and began to swim with tears. He gave a tiny frown and a barely perceptible shake of his head that she shouldn't blurt his real name, nor give any indication she knew him. She bit her lip, hard. Her grip on his hand tightened, and his in return. It was all he could do not to take her in his arms right there, and to hell with Ramsay.

CHAPTER 8

Ramsay's attention was on his own reflection in the hall mirror nearby as he straightened his wig. Addressing Dylan, he said, "You may wait in the sitting room until your pallet is prepared. The clumsy bitch knocked over the candelabra in there, and I was forced to stamp the candles out lest the entire house burn to the ground. You may relight any ones you find that are whole."

Cait said to Dylan in Gaelic, "Have you eaten?"

Ramsay spun and took a backhanded swing at her, which she dodged expertly. "Stop that barbaric mumbling!"

Dylan stepped between them, fed up beyond endurance now. "I'll thank you to not do that while I'm here."

Cait's husband peered at him from under lowered lids. "And what have you to say about how I keep discipline in my own home?"

Dylan pressed his lips together, knowing he might blow his job and his very thin welcome in the house by this, but he couldn't just stand by and watch Ramsay clobber Cait. "Nothing, sir. But I don't believe in hitting women under any circumstances, and can't let it continue. I must ask you to not strike her in my presence." He swallowed and glanced at Cait, sorry he had to say this. He continued, "What you do while I'm not here is none of my business, but if I witness it, I must put a stop to it and can do naught else."

Ramsay's eyes narrowed. "You're not a bloody Puritan, are you?"

Dylan blinked. "*Och,* no. I'm a . . ." He hesitated and fingered his sark. He could feel the ebony and silver crucifix around his neck beneath it, and wasn't sure what to admit to. He'd been raised Methodist, but that denomination wouldn't exist for another several decades, and his life in Catholic Glen Ciorram had quite taken the edge from his Protestantism. He had no idea where Ramsay's religious convictions lay, beyond the fact that he seemed to dislike Puritans, so Dylan stuck with what Cait knew of him. "I'm Catholic."

Ramsay grunted. "Aye, another bloody papist. God save me from the bead rattlers."

Dylan's cheeks burned, but he kept his voice level. "I stand by my statement, sir. I won't allow a woman to be struck in my presence. If you can't abide by that and must send me away tonight, then so be it. But I will remind you there is a man with murderous intent abroad."

Sinann, hovering overhead near the chandelier, commented dryly, "And he's standing right in front of you, ye Lowland scum!"

"You don't believe in hitting women?" Ramsay chuckled. "God help you if you ever marry, then! You'll be a cuckold for a certainty!"

Again Sinann piped up, "It's not helped you any, has it?" Dylan shot her a glance, glad Ramsay couldn't hear her.

The master of the house tidied up his shirt, tucking it into his breeches where it had pulled out, then said airily, "I'm off. Take care I'm not disturbed, woman."

"Aye, my husband." But she raised her chin and said, "I'll need to put Mr. Mac a'Chlaidheimh in the guest room. There isnae room in the kitchen for a pallet."

He frowned and waved a languid hand. "Can they not shove aside some meal sacks, or something? Perhaps he could sleep *on* the meal sacks?"

"The kitchen is quite full, and Nellie is down with a fever besides. Mr. Mac a'Chlaidheimh being younger than she, she might pass it to him. You wouldn't want to lose your sentry with that madman out and about." There was a brief pause, and she caught her breath a little. "Or, perhaps, it would be even better if Mr. Mac a'Chlaidheimh would make a pallet on the floor of *your* chamber."

Ramsay's eyes narrowed. "You'd like that, wouldn't you?"

"I merely think that if your life is in danger . . ."

"No, ready the guest room for him. That is my final word." He said it as if it had been his original idea. Then without further discussion, nor even a by-your-leave, he went up the stairs to the balcony, across, then up the next flight to the third floor. Dylan and Cait watched him go, neither moving nor speaking.

As soon as Ramsay was gone and the echoing footsteps retreated into the upper stairwell, Dylan leaned over and for one precious moment touched his lips to Cait's. She quickly kissed him in return, then pulled away and glanced around as she took his hand and drew him toward the darkened sitting room. She held both his hands and whispered, "I thought you were dead! God help me, I thought they'd killed you!" New tears sprang to her eyes, and words tumbled over each other, "*A Dhilein, m'annsachd.* Beloved, they told me you'd died on the way to Fort William!" She then lapsed entirely into Gaelic, and her voice cracked with tears, "How is it you are here? How did you escape? How did—"

Dylan put a finger to her lips and whispered, also in Gaelic, "I escaped, but I couldn't come here. They will hang me if they find me, because I had to kill a soldier, and almost killed Major Bedford, to save my own life. Robin Innis told me about the baby. I couldn't stay away any longer."

At the mention of the baby her face lit up through the tears. "You should see him! He's healthy and strong, and he's the most beautiful child on earth! I've named him Ciaran Robert. Let me get him, he's upstairs." She turned to dash away, then turned back to take his hands again. "Dylan, dinnae leave us. Take us away from here. I dinnae care how we live, just so it's away from here."

Her desperation broke his heart. He couldn't reply, knowing that living as an outlaw would be death for Ciaran, no matter how healthy he might be now. In this century, the infant mortality rate was just too high to take the risk. She couldn't mean what she said. Rather than disappoint her with the only reply possible, he kissed her again and said, "Bring him here. I want to see my son." *Ciaran Robert.* She'd given the boy his own middle name.

As she smiled and hurried away toward the stairwell, a maid emerged from the stairs to the kitchen below to gather the supper dishes on the dining table. As the old woman worked, she watched Cait scurry with her skirts in her fists, then peered at Dylan, who struggled to compose himself for the stranger. She was a thin woman, with a deep crease over her nose from habitual frowning. After a moment, watching Cait cross the balcony to the nursery near the spiral stairs, she sniffed and said, "I ain't never seen the Missus so chipper."

Dylan peered at the maid and wondered if he and Cait had been successful in hiding anything from this woman. He replied, "Maybe she's just glad Ramsay has stopped hitting her for the evening?"

The maid threw a sour look toward the balcony. "She brings it on herself, with her back talk and all."

His eyes narrowed and his voice lowered. "Better her than you, eh?" The look on the woman's face suggested he'd struck a nerve. Ramsay had probably stopped beating the help only when he married Cait. He said, "Perhaps you're right. Smacking around a woman who talks too much just might be the thing to do. Now, I'm thinking you might ought to be careful of your own mouth, then. How about it?"

She blinked and her eyes narrowed, as if trying to read his face in the dark sitting room. Then her back straightened and she hurried on her way to the stairs with her tray of dirty dishes.

While he waited for Cait's return, Dylan searched the floor for dropped candles and salvaged the ones in large enough pieces, then began lighting them from the fire in the hearth. He put the lit candles into the candelabra. Soon there was a nice glow to the room and he could see his surroundings. An arched window looked out to the north, where, though at this time of night there was nothing to see in that direction but uninterrupted darkness, Dylan knew in the daytime one would see the North Loch, and beyond that the Firth of Forth. Beneath the window was a short sofa, and a few wooden armchairs stood about the room, but the smallness of the room and the openness of the arches made the spot little more than a wide eddy in the flow of house traffic.

With a start, he remembered the wooden jet plane in his sporran, and reached inside for it. Then he drew his *sgian dubh* from under his sark and in three quick strokes lopped the nose and wing points from it, dropping the shavings into the fire. With a little more care, he curved the trailing corners of the stabilizer and rudder. Then he returned the dirk to its scabbard. The plane wasn't a bad representation, though one wing was a mite shorter than the other. He moved it through the air and made a jet engine noise. A gentle smile touched his mouth.

His name on Cait's tongue behind him made him turn. His pulse surged, and then for a moment his heart stopped. Cait stood in the archway, and on her hip she carried a tiny, dark-haired boy wearing a linen nightshirt. The baby looked around the room and rubbed his face, apparently unaccustomed to being awakened in the evenings. The little, pink mouth opened in a yawn so wide his entire body shook as it finished, then his mouth shut and he leaned against his mother's breast. Dylan stared, unable to speak.

Sinann, perched on the sofa back, was awed as well. "*Och*, he's the image of ye, laddie."

It was true. Seeing Ciaran was like looking at an old baby picture of himself. The blue eyes and fuzzy, dark hair . . . "Nobody thinks he belongs to Ramsay," he said. It wasn't a question. By no stretch of the imagination, even in this century before genetic inheritance was fully understood, could anyone think blond, pale Ramsay had fathered this boy with blonde Cait.

She shook her head.

Dylan started toward her, but she held up a palm. "Wait. Watch." Then she knelt and set Ciaran on his pudgy little feet. Dylan went to one knee and waited as Cait steadied the boy. A frown of concentration creased the baby's forehead, and he carefully took a step. Then another, and he was away from his mother and walking toward his father.

Five steps, and Dylan grabbed him up. He thought his heart would burst as he hugged his son and set him on his knee. "Good boy," he whispered before his voice failed and he was reduced to ruffling the head of soft, black fuzz.

Ciaran smiled and made wet, drooly, sputtering noises as he kicked his feet and grabbed Dylan's lower lip. Two infinitesimal white teeth were coming in on Ciaran's lower jaw, gleaming and perfect in the pink gums. The eyes, of course, were blue. Matheson eyes, inescapable since he was a Matheson on both sides. Dylan gently freed his lip and handed over the wooden toy, which went straight into the boy's mouth. After a moment of chewing, Ciaran waved the toy aimlessly in the air and made the sputtering noise again. Dylan had to grin, it sounded so much like an engine, though even Ciaran would never live to hear one. He finally found his voice and said, "He's . . . amazing."

Cait, with a big, white smile, came to sit in the chair next to them. "He's my life." She sobered and said, "He's all that keeps me alive in this evil, hateful place. For so long, I thought he was all I would ever have of you." She fluffed the nearly black baby hair. "I prayed he would be born strong, and my prayer was answered. Every day I look at him and see you. I thank God you're still alive." She laid a palm against Dylan's cheek, and he turned to kiss her hand. For one brief moment the world was perfect, and all that mattered was that he, Cait, and Ciaran were together at last.

A step was heard on the kitchen stairs, and Cait took the baby from Dylan's arms to stand, ready for the approach of a servant. Dylan stood and turned toward the mantel over the hearth and cocked his head as if appraising the painting on that wall. It was a portrait of someone resembling Ramsay, in Elizabethan dress, and Dylan wondered if it was an actual ancestor or just Ramsay himself being a poseur.

The voice of the skinny maid came from behind. "You've awakened the child." It was an accusation.

Cait ignored the comment, and switched back to English to address the maid. "Nellie, please find some supper for Mr. Mac a'Chlaidheimh, per orders from Mr. Ramsay."

"Get it yerself."

Dylan turned, stunned. Obviously Cait's position was not supported by her husband, and the help took advantage. He said, "I wonder what Mr. Ramsay would say if I took to carrying out discipline around here."

Nellie threw him a sour look. "He'd dismiss ye for certain, master swordsman or no."

"Aye, but it might be too late, then, for you to keep the few teeth you have left. I won't stand by and allow disrespect toward my employer's wife."

Nellie's eyes narrowed, and after a long moment of thought she said, "We've naught but one cold game bird left from supper."

"That will be fine." She turned to leave, and he said, "And Nellie . . ." She halted in her retreat. "Make up the guest room. I'll be sleeping in there tonight."

She pressed her lips together, threw an evil look at Cait, and went back down the stairs.

Cait stared after her, the color high on her cheeks and her eyes glittering with anger.

Dylan whispered in Gaelic, "Miss Nellie doesn't seem so feverish to me." At that moment, a solid, rhythmic thudding noise began somewhere above the Great Room. Cait ignored it. Dylan stared at the high ceiling, puzzled, until he realized it was the headboard of a large bed banging a wall. Then he looked away, avoiding Cait's eyes.

She replied to him in Gaelic, "Connor neither knows nor cares what goes on in the servants' quarters." She continued to stare after the maid. "You may guess there is plenty of room for a pallet before the kitchen grate, as well. But I'll not have you sleeping on the floor. Not in my house." She shifted Ciaran's weight on her hip and said, "Nor will I have you spied on by the servants." She turned to Dylan, stepped close, and lowered her voice. "Come to me tonight. Come to my chamber." She raised her face to indicate the room directly above, then looked at him.

Finally he let his eyes meet hers, and he found them pleading. She knew the danger—that Ramsay would kill them both if they were discovered together. He would be perfectly justified by law as well if he did. Dylan knew enough about the world to understand at least that much about this century, that men were expected to answer cuckoldry with deadly violence. But the risk didn't matter. Dylan needed her too much, and for too long, to deny her. He nodded.

Quickly, before Nellie could return with Dylan's supper, Cait hurried up the stairs to the nursery.

Nellie appeared with a pewter ewer of water inside a matching bowl, and a folded towel, and over her arm was draped a dark green silk garment. She was accompanied by a young girl carrying a tray that bore a pewter plate covered with pieces of a roasted bird and a chunk of wheaten bread, a napkin, and a pewter tumbler he guessed would be filled with ale. A silver knife and fork weighted the napkin, and Dylan's eyebrows raised. This seemed an emphatically English household, even by the standards of cosmopolitan Edinburgh. Dylan followed the maids through the landing and the back hallway to the guest room. The silence was stiff.

The guest room was the first door off the hallway, a small room, relative to the rest of the house, but still large compared to that hole he'd rented at the Hogshead Inn. The hearth mantel was carved and the windows were tall, and a comfortable-looking bed dominated. An armoire stood against the wall near the door, and a table next to the bed. That table received the bowl, ewer, and towel. The supper tray was set on the foot of the bed. Nellie then hung the green silk garment, which turned out to be a robe, in the otherwise empty armoire, and both maids left. Sinann perched on the headboard of the bed, according to her habit.

Dylan sighed as he closed the door behind the servants, and hoped to shut out the incessant banging upstairs. It was no good. He threw a disgusted look toward that corner of the house as he lifted his baldric off and leaned his sword against the armoire. "There must be something wrong with him that he takes so long. I mean, stamina is one thing, but that there borders on impotence."

"Be assured, laddie, you would rather not know what's going on up there."

Dylan's imagination wandered into kinkier areas, then returned with a visual that made him flinch. He shook his head to clear it. No, he didn't want to go there. Didn't want to know who was banging whom or with what. He shut out the noise from his mind and went to wash.

He stripped quickly, unbuckling his belt and letting it, his sporran, and his kilt fall. Then he pulled his sark over his head and let it also drop to the floor. He pulled Brigid and her scabbard from his right legging and slipped them under the bed pillow, then the *sgian dubh* was set on the table. His leggings came off as quickly as he could untie the straps and let them drop. He kicked off the rubber-soled, loose-laced chukka boots he'd brought from his own century, then he peeled his socks from his feet. Finally, he lifted the crucifix from his neck and placed it, still hung with Cait's gold wedding ring, on the table next to the bowl.

The fire was new and high, making this the warmest he'd ever been in Scotland, so he took advantage of the opportunity for a thorough wash. He poured water into the bowl, wet the towel, and began with his face, running wet hands through his hair until it dripped water down his back and made him shudder. He scrubbed crusted dirt from around his ankles, worked his way up, and finished with the last of his water by paying particular attention to areas that rarely saw soap or sunshine. He stood by the fire for a moment to dry, then took a look at the robe Nellie had put in the armoire.

It was a green brocade dressing gown. Heavy and rich, but it was also very worn, fuzzy and frayed at the edges and deeply comfortable. Though he didn't much miss the fine clothing of his wealthy childhood, he was human and very much enjoyed the feel of silk against his skin. Huddled into the robe, he then sat on the bed to eat his supper while he waited out Ramsay's fun time upstairs. The rhythm changed often in speed and force, and sometimes stopped for a moment, but always resumed.

Sinann, who had been remarkably less talkative than usual, said, "You're going, then."

He looked over at the faerie and whispered, "Of course, I'm going. You didn't expect me to do any different, did you?"

"And if ye're caught?"

Dylan shrugged. "Then the cat will be out of the bag, I suppose."

"He'll kill you."

"He'll try."

"And if you succeed in killing him?"

"I won't kill him."

"Nevertheless, if he discovers the two of ye, there will be few choices of action. You could either take Herself and the lad with you, which would mean death for him and possibly also for her. Or you could leave them here to face the consequences of it. The likelihood would be you would never see either of them again."

Dylan stared into the fire for a long moment, thinking. The risk was high, and for something that might seem not worth it. But he was too near Cait now. "I've got to see her. I can't stay in this room, knowing she's just upstairs, and not go see her."

"But . . ."

"I don't know if I'll ever come this close again. If I don't go tonight, and never have another chance, I'll regret it for the rest of my life. However short that might be, I don't want to spend it regretting the one night I could have had with Cait and didn't."

She sighed and shook her head. "No. I dinnae expect so."

Dylan addressed his supper. He tore open the bread lengthways, like a hot dog bun, then began pulling shreds of meat from the game bird until he'd stuffed all of it into the bread, then wiped his fingers on the napkin. He wished for some mayonnaise or mustard, but at least this meat seemed fresh and the bread wasn't buggy. A miracle, in January. The drink turned out to be wine rather than ale. He was no expert on the stuff, but it was dark and a bit sweet. A burgundy, perhaps. He sure didn't know what wine was appropriate with a dry chicken sandwich, and didn't care much, either. He drank it and enjoyed it. Halfway through his supper, the noises upstairs quit and didn't resume.

For a long moment he listened, but there was no further banging. He stuffed the remainder of his sandwich into his mouth, then went to the door of his room to see if Ramsay would wander from his rooms after his completion, but there was no sound. Dylan swallowed and said to Sinann, "You wait here."

She chuckled. "*Och,* your privacy, from me at least, is assured on this night, laddie. There are few things I'm less likely to witness. However, I'm nae wanting to stay here, since lingering outside the chamber where yer Cait sleeps, alert for unwanted visitors, would be a far better use of my time."

Dylan nodded, with a thankful smile. Then he downed the rest of his wine and wiped his fingers and mouth with the napkin before slipping into the hallway to shut the door behind him. The candles on the hall table had been extinguished, and all was dark except for thin, silvery outlines cast by moonlight through the windows at the landing. He felt the candles and found them cold. The servants had gone downstairs a while ago.

Silently he felt his way through the dimness to the landing. All the candles in the Great Room and sitting room had been extinguished as well. As far as he could tell, the entire house was dark. He proceeded up the stone stairwell. The passage was so narrow his shoulders almost touched on either side, and pitch black this deep in the house. The steps were steep and cold under his bare feet, centuries old and worn in the middle so they sagged as if they were wooden. They spiraled a quarter-turn at the top to exit at the end of the balcony overlooking the Great Room. Directly across from him was the door to the bedroom above the sitting room. Cait's room. The nursery was on the other side of the house, at the opposite end of the balcony.

The door before him was open a crack, and light flickered through it from a high fire in the hearth inside. Dylan pushed on the door, and it opened on silent hinges. Cait, wearing a linen nightgown and blue silk robe, was seated on the floor in front of the hearth, and stood at the whisper of her name. He stepped in and shut the door behind him. It was a small room containing little more than a narrow bed and a trunk. A Persian carpet covered the floor in rich red, blue, and gold. The hearth was large, the fire well stoked, and the room was warm. Cait put a hand on the post at the foot of her bed, and held out her other hand to him. "*M'annsachd,*" she said. *My most dearly beloved one.*

Suddenly, he hated this. For two years all he'd wanted was to be a husband to Cait, to make a place where they wouldn't have to sneak around and pretend they weren't in love. He'd dreamed of the day everyone in the glen would know she was his, and that day should have come by now. Lurking was adolescent. During the first six months it had been a game, thrilling in its promise. But back then the game had been one where the ending was supposed to have been marriage and legitimacy, not this shameful skulking. This was no longer fun; this was adultery.

His hesitation brought the pleading to Cait's eyes. She whispered as her hand dropped to her side, "Nae, Dylan. I couldnae bear to know you were downstairs tonight and not be with you. I couldnae bear to know you were in the *world* and not be with you."

His hand on the doorknob, he tried to imagine turning it, opening the door, and returning to the guest room alone. But he failed. His body just wouldn't do what his conscience demanded. He let go of the door, and that was all it took. In three strides he crossed the small room, took her in his arms, and kissed her. She hugged his neck and pressed his head as he held her soft body to his. Tongues tasted, mouths opened as far as they would go, low sounds came from their throats. He wanted to press her straight into his flesh, to make her a part of him forever. It had been so long . . . so terribly long. . . .

They descended to the carpet, no longer able to stand. He leaned over her on one elbow, his mouth playing with hers and his hands entwined in her hair. His body ached with more than a year of yearning for her. He wanted to savor this time with her, for he knew the moments were fleeting and precious, but it was impossible. His muscles trembled as his skin jumped at her touch. He couldn't bear to wait. She unbuttoned the front of her nightgown, all the way down. There must have been a hundred tiny, cloth-covered buttons, but her fingers flicked each open expertly.

Inside the gown, her skin under his hands was warm, but he was shocked at how thin she was—far too thin for health in these times. But there was no chance to dwell on that, for she tugged the sash of his robe to open it, and a low moan rumbled in his throat as his thoughts scrambled. Her hands stroked his belly, lower and lower, until it was no longer his belly she was stroking.

He couldn't stand it a moment longer, and she didn't seem to want him to. He settled between her thighs and she drew him inside, receiving him with warmth and caresses and one leg tight around his waist. He moved hard against her. Her back arched and she took her mouth from his to hold him. Quick, deep breaths broke against his neck. They moved together, opposite but in tandem, as a single being. Gasps rose in her until she shuddered in his arms, then he knew nothing but joy. The world was gone, leaving only himself and his beloved, together in the eternity of one moment.

He pressed against her, panting and still, then moved again, slowly. She lay beneath him, a smile of utter peace on her lips. He looked into her eyes as he moved, and his heart swelled to see the adoration he remembered from before. It was the look he'd carried in his memory during the long months away from her. She hadn't forgotten him, either, had always loved him, just as he had continued to love her. He kissed her soft, swollen mouth and pressed himself to her. Then, ever so lightly, he kissed the eye Ramsay had blackened earlier.

When moving became pointless, he lay next to her on the carpet and rested his head, propped on his elbow. Her hair clung to the sweat on her forehead, and he moved the strands away from her face. He couldn't take his eyes from her. "Caitrionagh," he whispered. "*A Chaitrionagh, tha thu m'annsachd.*" She smiled and kissed him. Then he kissed her neck. He still wanted her, though he couldn't do anything more about it just then. By the flickering of the fire high in the hearth he gazed, fascinated at the way the light danced on her pale skin, warm and golden. He brushed aside the linen of her nightdress to see her breasts. Their size surprised him. He stroked them, her belly, her hip, fascinated with the changes since he'd last seen her. Some dark, pink marks made a row, like ragged pickets, across her lower belly. Stretch marks, from the baby. He ran his fingers across them, in awe of what had happened to her. He wished he'd been with her while she was pregnant. Wished he could have seen the baby grow in her, watched her fill with it.

Her whisper interrupted his thoughts. "What is it ye see?"

Hypnotized by her body, he said, "You are most . . . fetching." When he touched a nipple, it rose quickly and produced a single, white drop. The smile that touched his mouth grew wider.

"You're still nursing," he whispered.

"Aye." She sounded surprised he would think she might not be. "Connor wanted to engage a wet nurse, but I wouldnae have it. It embarrasses him for me to nurse the baby, as if people think he cannae afford one, but I'm sure I dinnae care what his Whig friends think of him. I'll not let my son suck a strange woman's teat, and that's the long and the short of it."

He chuckled at her vehemence, then laid a kiss between her breasts and murmured, "Would you let a man who is not your son suck yours?" Her anger at Ramsay dissolved as a puzzled look crossed her face. He took that for a "yes." His tongue flicked out to the nipple, which rose again eagerly. When she didn't object, he licked it and took it into his mouth to give it a good, steady pull. Several thin streams hit the roof of his mouth and he swallowed. He smiled. "Sweet. You're very sweet. But I knew that." He kissed her mouth and hoped she could taste the sweetness of herself on his.

Her hands slipped inside his robe once more, and down his flank. He began to harden again and leaned up over her as she stroked the back of his thigh, then ran her hand over his buttock. She gasped. He groaned and put his hand over hers as he realized what she'd found.

"What is that?" But she must have known.

He removed her hand, lay back down on his side, and held her hand in front of him to keep it from exploring. "Nothing. It's just a scar."

"It's a great, knotted gash!" With her other hand she tried to reach behind his back to feel, but he kept her from it.

"No. Don't."

She stopped, and shoved hair away from his face to look into his eyes. "Dylan, there's nae need to hide it. Let me see."

He didn't want her to see. Nobody should see those scars. He wished he could forget they existed, but he felt them whenever he moved or stretched the muscles of his back. One gash had been so deep he'd lost some range of movement turning at the waist to his right. He shook his head.

But she sat up and laid a palm against his cheek. "Please. Never hide anything from me. I couldnae bear for you to hide yourself from me."

After a long moment, he decided she wasn't going to let him not show her. He sat up and turned away from her, sitting cross-legged. She pulled his robe from his shoulders and let it drop behind to hang from his elbows. He listened for a gasp, but there was none. She made no sound as she gazed on the damage. He waited a long time, impatient to put the robe back on but willing to let her stare as long as she wanted. Then he would restore the robe and nobody would ever see his back again.

But then she kissed one of the scars and he was the one who gasped. The memory of the pain inflicted returned, and he knew it was the deepest wound she'd chosen—the one that had taken longest to heal. Then she kissed another one, and the memories began an avalanche. She kissed more. His back flinched with each touch of her lips. His chest tightened. He wanted to shout for her to stop, but he couldn't even whisper.

Soon, though, the pain began to fade. As she continued pressing her lips to the places that had been most injured, the memories crumbled. She kissed them all, and traced each long, white stripe with her fingers, from his shoulders to his waist. Much feeling had been destroyed by the whip, but not all, and his skin warmed at her touch. When she was finished, she pressed herself against his back and hugged him. He whispered, "Why did you do that?"

Her voice murmured into his ear, "They're nae pretty, but they're a part of you. I can do naught but love them as I love you."

A knot somewhere inside loosened, one that had been there since his escape from the garrison. He felt whole again, for the first time in nearly two years.

She hugged him again, and ran her hands over his shoulders, tracing for a moment the scabbed-over cut on his left shoulder, then his arms. When her soothing hands reached his wrists, she stopped short and looked over his shoulder at his left wrist. "What have ye there?"

He looked at the knotted string Sinann had tied to him, and held it up to the light. "It's . . ." He thought back to what Sinann had said. "It's a talisman. For strength."

She fingered it. "How long ago did you do this?" There was a strange note in her voice. Obviously this string held a significance that was lost on him.

He frowned, then said, "A while. A long time, I think. Give or take."

"It was you, then." The strangeness in her voice changed to excitement. Maybe even triumph. "You kept me alive."

"Huh?" For the first time in ages, he wished Sinann were there to explain things to him. "Start from the beginning and tell me what you mean."

There was a long pause while she gathered her thoughts, and he turned toward her to wait. He fiddled with a lock of her hair, then she began, " 'Twas on our wedding night." Dylan pressed his lips together, certain he didn't want to hear about the wedding night, but he said nothing. She continued, "He came to me, and I was prepared to fulfill my obligation to him. . . ." Dylan's interest perked, for this didn't sound like it was going where he'd assumed it would. ". . . but then I saw it."

"It?"

"He had sores. On his member. I knew it must be the French pox, so I wouldnae let him touch me. I screamed and made him get dressed and leave."

Dylan chuckled. "You screamed?"

The memory seemed to upset her, for she spoke faster and her voice rose. "I dinnae dare let him near me. I dinnae wish my bairn to be still-born." Dylan shushed her, lest she be overheard. She lowered her voice to a whisper again, and continued, "Also, I would prefer not to go mad and die myself. I'd rather have been sent back to my father in shame than to have lost my son. I've seen it. Men who went to Edinburgh with the herds, then came back with the sores. They would give it to their wives, and then both die. Their unborn bairns, as well. It's happened even in Glen Ciorram." At the last, her voice lowered almost to inaudibility, for she was surely telling the ugliest secret she knew about her father's people.

"But you knew you were expecting. You knew if you refused Ramsay, he would know the baby wasn't his."

She looked at him as if he'd said something unutterably stupid. "As I said, I wished for Ciaran to live. At all costs. And besides, Connor would have known regardless. The bairn came far too soon, and a blind man would never mistake a son of yours for one fathered by him."

Dylan had to smile. There was something to that.

"And this," she held the ends of the red braided string around his wrist, "is what gave me the strength these eighteen months to keep him away. Many a time I feared I might surrender, but something kept me from it. This talisman."

Dylan smiled. Sinann was up to her old tricks, but this time he couldn't quarrel with her magic. Then a thought made him blink with surprise, and it seemed the world went sideways as his mind flew and excitement rose. "Wait a minute. You've never slept with Ramsay."

"Aye. He's not been to my bed, though I have had to fight him off many a time and taken heavy beatings for it." She touched the purpling around her eye.

"You've never consummated the marriage."

"Nae. Never."

"You're not legally married."

"Nae. I'm not."

A huge grin lit up his face, but she put a hand over his mouth and shook her head. "It willnae succeed," she said. The grief of her knowledge was deep in her eyes. "If I try to say the marriage doesnae exist, he will but point to the boy to say it was consummated and the courts will believe him. As much as he hates Ciaran, and hates me for refusing him, he needs the marriage to protect himself in case James one day rules. He's also written an early will, in which he's declared Ciaran illegitimate and the marriage null. If he dies, we will be not only destitute, but shamed."

"Your father would take you."

She shook her head. "He willnae. You *know* he willnae. Further, if you believed he would, I know for a certainty Connor would be dead by now. You would have seen to it. But I know you let him live because there is no other place for me as long as you're an outlaw. Iain Mór cannae have an illegitimate grandson."

Dylan sighed as hope died, and he kissed her palm. As much as he hated to admit it, she was right.

CHAPTER 9

The pale dawn barely outlined the windows to either side of the hearth when Dylan awakened with a start. *What am I doing?* It was too risky to sleep here. He should have left. But as he looked around at the still-deep shadows, listening to the house, sensing the floor under him, he felt the stillness and saw the color in the windows was only a false dawn. There was time left. He kissed Cait's forehead, and she stirred.

She seemed to recognize him before she was conscious, as if she were aware of his presence even in sleep. Without opening her eyes, she slipped her arms around him and snuggled to his body. He pressed her to him, and whispered, "Tell me, how come we slept on the floor?"

A smile curled her lips and she looked up at him, then she raised herself on one elbow to reach past him to the footboard of her bed. She gave it a shove, and the entire bed swayed with loose joints and the headboard tapped the opposite wall.

Dylan chuckled. "Oh. Are all the beds in this house like that?"

She giggled, and kissed him. As he lost himself in her again, unwelcome reality soured the moment. He kissed her cheek, then her forehead, and said with his lips against her skin, "I can't come back to this room."

There was a moment of silence, then she replied, "I know."

"I'll be downstairs, though. I won't let him hurt you again."

"I know."

His mouth returned to hers, and they made love again on the floor, before a fire that appeared cold but nevertheless held life deep inside its embers.

Before the servants were up, he stole to the guest room, seen off with kisses and repeated avowals of faith. The house was cold as he hurried down the stairs to the relatively warm guest room, in which Sinann had kept the fire from dying. Dylan sat on a footstool before it and stared into the coals. The faerie, perched on the headboard, awoke. "Yer back."

"Aye."

He stared at the red talisman on his wrist, glad the magic had been done, but also wondering. Just as he opened his mouth to thank her, she said, "Yer welcome."

A smile flashed across his mouth, then he was serious again. "Tink . . . how come—?"

"How come the magic caused her to refuse him but not yourself?" Dylan nodded. "I daresay you're a rare man to even think of that question, let alone ask. The truth of it is, the talisman wasn't that sort of enchantment. It was but an aid to strength so she could do the thing she already knew she must."

"You were in Glen Ciorram when you did this, but you knew she would refuse Ramsay?"

Sinann nodded. "Some things are just plain to the eye. If she'd accepted him, it would have been the end of her, for neither her soul nor her body could have survived it. She needed but little help, though she did need it."

Dylan picked absently at one of the knots. "Thanks, Tink."

"You might not be thanking me after the two of you are married and have your first spat, which she will assuredly win."

He closed his eyes and prayed he would live to see that day.

"Dylan . . ." It wasn't Sinann, though he looked up to be sure. The faerie stood on the headboard, a deep crease in her brow. The voice came again, "Oh, Dylan . . ."

Sinann waved him over to the bed. "Quickly, lad. Throw off that robe and lie down." He did as he was told, and lay atop the blanket in the predawn cold. "Now, accept the voice."

"Is it Cait?"

"Shhh . . .'Tis not. Accept the voice and hear what it says."

He squeezed his eyes shut and tried to relax, but his pulse surged and wouldn't respond to concentration techniques. The tension increased till his body quivered, and he gasped as the voice seemed to enter him. It vibrated his spine. It faded in and out, and as he listened, he realized some of the words were backward. Like a tape run in reverse. "Make it go straight," he pleaded with Sinann. "Make it go forward." The blanket bunched up in his fists and his heels dug into the mattress. Sinann hovered over him, gesturing over his face. His chest heaved.

Frustration colored her voice, "I cannae." She muttered something in the ancient language Dylan hadn't begun to master, and waved her hands back and forth over his face. "It's . . . it cannae find you."

He said through clenched teeth, "I'm here! I'm right here!" A vibration on frequency with his body took him, like a huge fist shaking him by the spine. The bed frame rattled under him. He could feel the voice in his bones.

Sinann emitted a long, furious growl that ended in a loud wail. "*No!*" She fluttered away from his face, settled on the floor, shaking a fist at the ceiling, and shouted, "Come back!"

Then the voice was gone. Dylan went limp on the bed and moaned. His head throbbed and his stomach heaved with the nausea of one too many rides on a roller coaster. He rolled to the edge of the bed to vomit, but though his gut lurched, he controlled it until it settled. Then he sagged onto the mattress with his face against the edge. "It was backward."

"How do you mean?" Sinann was panting, collapsed on the floor, which Dylan had never seen her do before.

"I mean, it sounded backward. Like a recording in reverse." He looked over at her, and at the utterly baffled look on her face, he said, "Where I come from, we can . . . well, sort of capture a person's voice in a machine, then play it back later. The machine makes the same, exact sounds the person made. We did it with music, too. When I was a little kid, there were people who claimed those who made music recordings did them in such a way that if you played them backward they would say nasty things. So when my friends and I found out about this, after school we sat around with a record player and pushed the turntable around backward with our fingers so we could hear the records play in reverse. Never found anything, but that's what this sounded like. It was like listening to a recording running backward."

"In reverse time ye say?" Sinann was thinking hard.

"Aye. Like someone moving backward through . . ."—his heart lurched—". . . time."

Dylan was able to grab the next couple of hours for sleep before he was awakened to dress for breakfast. Stepping into the Great Room on his way downstairs to eat with the servants, he was surprised to find a place had been set for him at the family table. Ramsay and Cait were already seated, Ramsay at the head and Cait to his right. The master of the house gave a graceful wave to the empty seat at his left. "Sit and eat. Don't dawdle."

It would have been better to have gone to the kitchen than to sit across from Cait and pretend she was nothing to him. He didn't dare even look at her, until he noticed she wasn't looking at him, either. She sat perfectly erect in her stays, her body almost thrust forward in her seat. The low bodice of her overdress was edged with lace, as were her sleeves, and the silk blouse underneath was a mass of ruffles down the front and at the sleeves which turned back at mid-forearm and dangled nearly a foot. She wore it all gracefully, but he hated to see her mashed into the costume. The soft wool she'd worn in Glen Ciorram had shown off her curves, which he much preferred, and he imagined must have been far more comfortable than being bound up in wooden stays.

He also noticed she'd learned to use a fork since coming to Edinburgh. Not much of a stretch for her, since she'd always been accustomed to spoons and knives. Dylan picked up his fork and used it exactly the way they did, leaving it in his left hand as he cut the beefsteak in front of him with his right.

Nobody spoke. Ramsay ate at a leisurely pace, each movement a flourish on its own. Dylan wasn't sure why he was allowed to eat with the family, but figured Cait had engineered it, the way she had put him in the guest room the night before.

A door opened on the balcony above, and a woman in a gray linen dress came from the nursery with Ciaran in her arms. Dylan watched their progress to the stairs, then waited to see them emerge at the first floor. The boy was dressed in a little blue suit with short pants and white ruffles at the neck and sleeves. In one hand he gripped Dylan's gift, the wooden toy jet plane.

A smile he couldn't banish crept to Dylan's mouth. He focused his attention on his plate as the nurse carried his son into the sitting room. Sinann appeared to Dylan's left, sitting cross-legged on the table top. He only glanced at her, then returned his attention to the boy, who was chewing hard on a wooden wing. Ciaran smiled at his nurse, a big, pink, wet grin with a single white dot at the middle. He kicked his little feet against the nurse's skirt.

Dylan found himself marveling. He'd seen lots of kids before and as a teacher had always liked them, but this one was a part of him. Pride swelled his heart until swallowing became difficult. It was all he could do to keep the corners of his mouth from curling, to keep from going over there to lift Ciaran to his shoulders, carry him into the street, and announce to all who would listen that this was his son; this miracle of perfection, this child who would grow to be a fine man, was his boy. He ached to do it, but instead returned his attention to his breakfast and finished eating, his gaze only on his plate.

Sinann's voice was soft. " 'Tis a hard thing, lad."

He glanced over at her, then back down. There was no answer for that, even if he could have talked to her then. He wondered why she was being so nice to him. It wasn't like her.

That day, activity at the office was business as usual for the morning, then a long lunch at the coffee shop on the High Street. Dylan ate his bread stuffed with cheese, washed it down with a tumbler of ale, and listened to the talk of prices and markets. He didn't care for the tone of the Englishman's voice, and he could sense Ramsay wasn't comfortable, either. Charles was hiding something. Or, maybe, he seemed disinterested in the conversation. There had been girlfriends in Dylan's past who had sounded just like that right before breaking up with him. Like Ginny, who had suddenly and arbitrarily broken it off with him just before he'd been brought to this century, this man seemed bored.

Dylan looked over at the door as someone came through it, and a cold sweat broke out. Three men in red dragoon coats and charcoal gray breeches were there, and one of them was Major Bedford. His hat was under his left arm, and he was removing his riding gloves as he looked around.

Sinann hissed, "Dinnae move."

Dylan wasn't about to. Anything he might do at that moment would only attract attention. There was but one public door in this place, a small and narrow one, and Bedford was standing in front of it. Dylan hissed under his breath, "Do something."

"Such as . . . ?"

"Anything."

"Your wish is my command, as they say." She giggled and leapt into the air, hovered by Dylan's shoulder, and waved her hand. Immediately, buttons began to pop from Bedford's uniform. Like corks from champagne, they went flying from the red wool coat and rattled across the floor and under the tables.

Bedford swore. Ramsay turned to look, and chuckled along with everyone else in the room at the sight of the stiff-necked English Army Major holding his coat together with his hands and sending his escort after the AWOL buttons. Sinann squealed with glee, then several more buttons rattled to the floor at Bedford's feet in a rain of little hardwood bits. The Major's eyes went wide as his other hand went to hold up his pants. When the gold bric-a-brac began peeling and unraveling, he gestured to his men to accompany him from the coffeehouse. Struggling to maintain his dignity, he hurried from the room, grabbing at pieces of fabric as they deserted him.

In a gale of hysterical laughter, Sinann collapsed onto the floor to roll in the straw scattered there. Dylan bit his lip to keep from laughing, and Ramsey snorted into his coffee as everyone else in the room went into an uproar over the ridiculous spectacle. Dylan leaned down and whispered, "You like doing that."

Tears fell onto her cheeks. "Aye, I do, a great deal."

"He must go through a lot of valets, then."

Sinann nodded, and was lost in a fresh peal of laughter.

Once Ramsay was finished with his meeting, he proceeded toward Canongate. It was time for another visit with the mistress there. Dylan waited outside, his coat and plaid pulled around him in the cold. He chatted with Sinann. "So how do I go about turning Bedford in to obtain my pardon? Who do I talk to?"

"Good question, and one for which I have nae answer. Alas, there's nae telling that anyone you might approach willnae simply haul you off to the Tolbooth and ignore your information in defense of one of their own. And even should they take ye seriously, they'll nevertheless have to arrest you and keep you until yer tale is confirmed. A great deal of mischief can happen to a body during that time when one is helpless behind bars."

No one needed to tell Dylan that. He sighed and wandered to a corner of the close in hopes of getting out of the wind. "Then what good is my information?"

She shrugged. "It could be useful eventually. If you bide your time, an opportunity might present itself."

"There's got to be . . ." He fell silent as two horses bearing Redcoats arrived at the close. One of them was Bedford, dressed in a fresh uniform. "Damn," muttered Dylan as he started to turn away, but was too late to avoid being seen. He pulled in his chin, tugged on his turned-up coat collar, and stuffed his hands into his armpits as if hiding from the cold.

Sinann said, "It must be Ramsay he's wanting to see today, and badly."

Bedford knocked for entry at the house, then, as he waited, checked out Dylan, who nodded a respectful greeting without looking him in the eye. Nothing in the Major's demeanor indicated recognition, and he passed quickly into the house of Ramsay's mistress.

Sinann raised her hand, "Shall I—"

Dylan hurried to whisper, "No. It's plain he's determined to see Ramsay. He doesn't seem to recognize me; maybe he won't make the connection."

Ramsay's visit with the mistress was much longer than previous ones, possibly because of the meeting with Bedford. Dylan huddled into his coat, mostly for warmth but also to avoid contact with Bedford's Lieutenant. The Redcoat stood by the horses, braving the cold in a solid display of discipline that impressed even Dylan. After a while, the Lieutenant commented in Gaelic, "Cold day."

Dylan's attention sharpened, and he realized this was the round-faced soldier he'd seen outside Ramsay's offices a while back. He replied, "You speak excellent Gaelic, for an Englishman."

The Lieutenant chuckled. "I'm from Skye. And I'll say you speak adequate Gaelic, for a colonial."

Alarm surged. "Not many recognize my accent." Usually he was queried about his origins rather than readily identified as American, for more Scots went to the Americas than colonials came to Scotland.

"I was there for three years and recently returned. Garrisoned in Virginia. Though I must say your speech is not quite the same as I heard over there."

"It's a big place." Dylan relaxed some. "Did you like it there?"

The soldier shrugged. "If one cares for cutthroat savages, deadly snakes, and blood-sucking insects the size of vultures, it's Paradise. For myself, I'm happy enough to be home."

It was Dylan's turn to chuckle. He asked, "Why would an Islander such as yourself want to join the English Army?"

"It's far more attractive than starvation."

Dylan couldn't argue with that, but wondered, "You're an officer. How does one from a starving family pay for a commission?"

"Luck. An Indian attack decimated my regiment. His Majesty promoted me gratis, out of necessity."

Ramsay and Bedford emerged together from the house, chatting. The Lieutenant, readying the Major's horse for mounting, reverted to English and said to Dylan, "You should consider enlisting. You might find yourself lucky as well, especially if those Jacobites continue stirring up trouble." It was a friendly invitation. Dylan bit back a wry comment that it would indeed be fortunate for him, were the Jacobites to decimate the English Army.

He only smiled and nodded, but nearly groaned when Bedford took an interest in the discussion. The Major turned to him and said, "Are you considering signing up, young fellow?"

Now Dylan was stuck. The Lieutenant knew he was an American, but if Bedford heard his voice and native accent . . .

Ramsay inserted himself just in time. "Now, now, now, Daniel. Dinnae be wooing my help away from me. A good man is hard enough to find without the Crown stealing him for cannon fodder."

A sly smile curled Bedford's mouth, and he approached Dylan. "Ah, Connor, all's fair, and so on. If your man can fight . . ."

Before the Major could get too close to Dylan, Ramsay held his arm, insistent. "Seriously. Do not go near him, or I'll have to hold it against you. He's mine, and you cannae have him." Ramsay's tone was still light, making a humorous undertone of romance, but it also took on an edge that meant he would make Bedford suffer for recruiting Dylan. He wouldn't let go, and the Major came no closer to Dylan.

Bedford shrugged. "Very well, then, if you feel that strongly about him, keep him. You two should be quite happy together." The good-humored rib reddened Dylan's cheeks, but Ramsay gave a leering chuckle that Dylan found even more creepy. The Major continued, "Bring him to the next Benison, then, if you're that fond of him."

That brought a great, rolling laugh from Ramsay. "Just for that, I believe I shall."

With a big, white grin, Bedford mounted. "I'll see you both, then." He chuckled. "As it were." His Lieutenant mounted, and they were off.

Dylan knew what the Beggar's Benison was, and just then wished he could leave Edinburgh that day, and never come back.

On the walk from the office to Ramsay's house that evening, Dylan's boss said, "Tell me, Mac a'Chlaidheimh, does Bedford know you?"

Dylan blinked, having been lost in anticipation of seeing Cait again, and forgetful of everything else. His mind flew to figure out what to answer. Stalling, he said, "Why do you ask?"

"Had there been a hole nearby when he saw you this afternoon, I'm certain you would have crawled into it. You're an outlaw, so it stands to reason you have had unhappy encounters with the authorities in the past. But the Lieutenant didn't seem to give you any trouble. It wasn't until the Major addressed you that I could see you wished to be elsewhere."

Dylan sighed. "Aye. The Major would recognize me if he ever had a good look, and would most certainly arrest me in a heartbeat."

"For what, may I ask?"

With a shrug, Dylan replied, "The usual. Treason and murder."

"Well, given that you were working for Rob Roy MacGregor, I don't imagine I need ask whether you are guilty. Not that it matters a whit."

Anger tinged Dylan's voice, "I did a lot of things while working for Rob, but not murder. I've never killed but in self-defense or in battle."

Ramsay considered that, then nodded and said, "As you say. Though it still makes not the least difference. I knew when I hired you, I wasn't hiring a man of impeccable reputation. My only concern is whether you are motivated to keep me alive. I . . ." A hand went to his coat pocket, then the other one. "Damn."

"Sir?"

"I've left a letter in my office." He looked back along the street with a sour expression on his face. "It's too far to return. Blast it."

"I'll go back, and bring it to the house."

That didn't seem the best idea to Ramsay, either, but he said, "Yes, I suppose there's nothing else for it. It's in the middle of my desk, and the seal is blue wax."

Dylan hurried away, back to the office. He ran up the spiral staircase, but paused at the top when he saw the trapdoor from the attic was open. He took a couple of steps toward it. "Felix?" No answer.

The clerks, including Felix, had all gone downstairs to their quarters, where they slept on cots and kept a sort of communal bachelorhood much the same as in the barracks at Glen Dochart. Dylan shut the attic door and cursed the lazy clerk who had left it open.

Ramsay's offices were dark and deserted. In the outer office the remnants of the day's fire were dying in the hearth. Dylan went through to the inner door, but stopped cold as he reached for the doorknob. The door, which Dylan himself had shut half an hour before, was ajar.

CHAPTER 10

"Shhhhit," Dylan said under his breath as he reached down for Brigid. He pointed to Sinann, then to his eyes, then toward the room, that she should reconnoiter, and she popped away. In an instant she popped back. "He's behind the desk, rifling a box of letters. Step to the left of the desk, but be quick about it, for he's facing the door."

Dylan took a deep breath, centered himself, then shoved the door open and charged. The intruder was small and quick. On seeing Dylan, he made a squeaking noise and tried to run, but Dylan cut to the right and headed him off as he came around the other end of the desk, and body-slammed him against a bookcase by the window. The case shook, and a ledger fell from the top shelf to the floor with a *whump*.

Then Dylan realized what he'd caught. "Whoa! You're just a boy!" It was the raggedy kid in the faded red military coat. The boy tried to run, but Dylan shoved him against the bookcase again. More ledgers teetered.

"Aye, I'm a lad." The boy snarled in a *What of it?* tone. He struggled to get away, and it was all Dylan could do to hold him still against the bookcase. When Dylan pressed a hip against the red-coated back to grapple with both arms, the boy said, "But I can pretend to be a lass if ye like." The wriggling turned suggestive, and Dylan took an instinctive step back.

The boy ducked out of Dylan's hold and ran. Sinann slammed the door shut in the kid's face and held it there while the boy yanked desperately on the knob. Dylan grabbed a skinny arm and twisted it, angry now. "Hold still, you little punk!" He slammed the boy against the door and pressed Brigid's point against his neck.

"I dinnae take nothing!"

"Ask me if I care. I want to know what you're doing here. There's nothing to steal in this office." Nobody with a brain kept cash around employees who were unsupervised at night. "Who are you working for? What did you want with those letters?"

"I work for nae man."

Dylan twisted harder. "I said, who are you working for?"

The kid gritted his teeth with the pain and affected a voice of infinite patience. "I said, *nobody*."

"We can stay here all night, if you like. You're not going anywhere until I find out what is going on." He twisted the arm until the boy squeaked.

"*Och!* It was a Redcoat! A Major! Big, fair-haired fellow! Talks like he's got a mouth full of marbles and walks like he's got a rod up his arse. Ow! Let me go!"

Dylan squeezed his eyes shut and fervently wished Bedford had died at Fort William. "What's he want?"

"For a certainty, he'll be after you if I go missing! He wanted some letters. That Ramsay is a traitor, ye ken!"

"You read?"

"Of course, I read." The boy shrugged. "A bit. I wouldnae be here now if I dinnae."

"And what has Ramsay done that is so traitorous? Tipped a glass to King James, I suppose?"

"He's sending reports of military strength to the rebels!"

"And you're so sure of this because . . . ?"

The boy reached into his shirt and produced a wad of letters. "Says so, right here." Dylan let go of the arm to take the letters, and just as he did so, the boy reached into Dylan's sark to grab his *sgian dubh*. In a flash he stabbed Dylan in the side.

Caught by surprise, Dylan erupted with one long bellow, and in enraged reflex thrust Brigid into the kid's neck. Blood sprayed, and Dylan stepped back, dismayed, with the *sgian dubh* lodged in his side. The boy collapsed onto the floor, blood running in a gush and choking him, and within seconds he went still.

Dylan pulled the dirk from his side and dropped it, held his wound, and cursed vehemently. The little blade had reopened his battle scar, where he no longer had spleen nor kidney. But when he looked, there wasn't much blood. In fact, much of the blade's length seemed to have been taken up by the thickness of sark, plaid and coat, and hadn't gone deeper than muscle.

The boy, however, hadn't fared so well. He lay in a puddle of blood, quite dead. Dylan's stomach turned and hitched, but he couldn't let himself wallow in sorrow for the boy. That would come later, in quiet moments when his conscience would catch up with him and he would go cold with the horror of things he'd done. But for now, he needed to get the hell out of there. He wiped Brigid clean on the boy's coat and scabbarded her. Then he retrieved his *sgian dubh* from the floor, wiped his own blood from it, and returned it to its scabbard under his arm.

Felix's alarmed voice from downstairs called up the spiral case, "Who's there?"

Great, now he's paying attention. Dylan cracked the door and called out, "It's just me. Mr. Ramsay sent me to retrieve a letter." When there was no further inquiry, Dylan turned to grab the blue-sealed letter from Ramsay's desk. But there wasn't one. There were no letters at all on the desk.

He went to the wad of letters that had fallen to the floor and paged through them, but none had been sealed with blue wax, broken or otherwise. He returned to the desk and looked around it, and in the box the boy had been rifling. No letter with a blue seal. Finally he searched the body of the dead boy. Still no letter.

"Sinann, I don't believe this is happening."

"Perhaps the letter was gone before the boy came?"

Dylan groaned. Ramsay was going to have a hissy fit.

Bloodied as he was, and not a sight to go unnoticed even in this city, he took a roundabout way to Ramsay's house, through alleys no wider than his shoulders and across darkened closes. He knocked at Ramsay's door, which was answered by the cook, then slipped inside unseen by neighbors. In the Great Room, Ramsay and Cait were at supper, Dylan's own place set but not served.

Cait gasped when she saw the blood on his sark and his hands, but though she jumped in her seat she stayed where she was. *Good Cait.* He leaned against the door frame, the heel of his hand pressed against his side, and said, "The item is missing." Then he looked at his wound and muttered, as if to himself, "*Tha gu slàn,*" so Cait would know he was all right, since Ramsay wasn't likely to ask.

"Bloody hell!" Ramsay rose from the table. "Get into your room," he ordered Dylan. "Cait, send Nellie to me." Ramsay hustled Dylan into the guest room as Cait left the table in search of Nellie. "What on God's earth happened?" Ramsay nearly shouted as they went.

Dylan waited until they were inside the bedroom and the door closed before he replied, "I walked in on someone ransacking your office. It was a street boy, but he got me a good one." He took off his coat to examine the hole in it, then set it on the bed and went to pour water from his ewer into the bowl.

"You dispatched him, I expect?"

Dylan pressed his mouth into a hard line and nodded as he cleaned blood from his hands. "He's dead. And he's lying on the floor of your office. You'll want . . ."

There was a knock, and Ramsay answered it. Opening the door just enough to speak through the crack, he said, "Nell, fetch me Williams. Have him report here with utmost haste." Nellie departed without a word.

Dylan opened his shirt to examine the wound. It had stopped bleeding, but was swelling and turning all shades of purple. It would be mighty sore for a while. "The boy was sent to steal letters. There will need to be an explanation of his disappearance." He dabbed around the wound with a wet towel, cleaning his skin but dribbling pink water onto his sark.

"Williams will handle that—put out a rumor of stolen money, or a press gang, or the like. Whatever . . ." Ramsay, turning back from closing the door, made a noise when he saw the wound, and stared hard at the seeping blood. "I'll have Cait come sew that up for you."

"Before the boy died . . ." Dylan raised his voice to get through the distraction. Ramsay paused, listening, and Dylan continued in a lower voice, "He told me he'd been hired to find letters implicating you as a spy for the Jacobites. It's Bedford who suspects you."

That gave Ramsay long pause. Then he shook his head as if to clear it. "What does he know?"

"Bedford? I'm not sure. The boy told me what he'd found in the letters, but of course never made it out of the office with them. The Major suspects something, though. Whether he was looking for something specific or was just fishing is anybody's guess."

"He already knows enough about me to have me arrested, were he inclined."

"But does he have anything on you in which he's not involved?"

Ramsay frowned. "*On* me?"

"Does he have proof you committed a crime, that would not also implicate himself?"

"Nae." Ramsay shook his head.

"So maybe he just sent the kid for a look-see? Nothing specific in mind, just browsing?"

"One should hope." Then Ramsay took a deep breath. His eyes narrowed and he said, "If none of the letters left the office, how is it the one letter is missing?"

"Someone in your office has it. There's no other possibility."

"Is it possible you are as good a reader as you are a listener?"

Dylan leveled his gaze. "Are you suggesting I would be so low as to betray my employer? For if you are, let me assure you I take slights to my integrity no more lightly than my Highland cousins, any of whom would cut your throat for saying such a thing. Whether I read or not is of no importance, for it was not I who stole that letter. It had to be one of your clerks."

He lowered his voice even more and continued, "Furthermore, you might give a thought to who it was that arranged for the shipment of casks out of Perth to be attacked, and who knew—and would care—that Bedford should not be crossed. Thirty guineas is an awful lot of money; it must have been someone who had a high stake in keeping you on Bedford's good side."

Ramsay was silent for a long moment, his mouth pursed in deep thought. Finally, he said, "Well. It's good to know I've hired a man with a sense of loyalty, who won't turn me over to save his own skin with the authorities."

Dylan said, "I did what I'm sworn to do. No more, no less."

Without missing a beat, Ramsay replied, "Of course." Then, with another uneasy glance at Dylan's bloody sark, he said, "Take steps to secure my offices from the depredations of my clerks."

"And Felix."

"Not—"

"*Especially* Felix.

There was another silence, then Ramsay said, "Very well. Do it." Then he left the room.

Sinann, perched on the headboard, said, "It would be the height of irony, would it not, for you to gain pardon by handing Ramsay over to Bedford?"

Dylan sat on the bed, pulled his sark from his kilt and over his head, and dried himself with it. "I didn't do it before, and I won't do it now. Turning Ramsay in would implicate Cait's father. If Iain Mór's lands were confiscated, it would destroy the entire Glen. And it would destroy Cait. It's not an option." He said it like a litany, having said it so often already.

"Bedford suspects. What if Ramsay is caught after all?"

"Then we're screwed."

It took so long for Cait to come with her needle that Dylan was almost ready to go looking for her. He went to open his door, but stopped when he heard low voices in the Great Room. It was apparent Ramsay was giving orders to the man named Williams, to the effect that the dead body in his office was to be weighted with chains and sunk in the harbor. Without a murmur Williams left to obey, and Dylan sat on his bed to continue waiting for Cait.

Several minutes later, she finally appeared at his door. In her hands was a tray containing a steaming copper pot, a pewter bowl, and a towel. She pointed with her chin to the low stool by the fire. "I cannae sit on the bed with you."

He moved to the stool, and she knelt on the floor next to him, leaving the door to the hallway open, for a closed door would cause the entire household to gossip. When Cait poured the water from the pot to the bowl, Dylan had to smile as she lifted the suture from it by its thread because the needle was too hot to handle. It touched him she remembered he wouldn't let her give him stitches with a needle and thread that hadn't been boiled. Gently, almost as a caress, she pressed a hand to his chest so he would lean back against the foot of the bed, to flatten the skin of his belly. "I won't need more than a coup—" She stuck him, and he grunted.

"Who did this?" Her voice was distant as she concentrated on her work, gently pulling the suture through Dylan's skin.

"Some kid hired by the Redcoats, rifling Ramsay's office, looking for evidence of him running information to the Jacobites."

That seemed to take her by surprise, and she frowned up at him. "Was there any to find?"

Dylan chuckled. "About a ton of it, I expect."

"Connor is a spy?"

He frowned. "You didn't know?"

She shook her head. "If the Crown suspects him, why do they not simply have the Army search the office themselves?"

Dylan shrugged. "Bedford must not want them to find anything to implicate himself."

"But he does want to find evidence of spying?"

Dylan nodded.

"To give to his higher-ups?"

Again, Dylan nodded and said, "Or to blackmail Ramsay."

Cait fell silent and returned to her work. The third and last suture went in, and Dylan blew air through his nose at the sting. Cait said nothing further. She tied the thread and leaned down to bite it off. Dylan laid his hand against her cheek, and for a moment she pressed her face to his belly. But then she rose, gathered her things on the tray, and stood. With a quick glance at the open door, she bent to kiss him lightly on the mouth before leaving.

He watched her go, and tried not to ache too much for what should have been.

CHAPTER 11

"Oh, Dylan . . ."

"Cody, what's the matter?" Ray's voice startled her, though he'd been sitting in the chair next to the sofa since dinner. She had a stack of photocopies in her lap she'd been reading, but at some point had stopped and was staring into space, thinking hard. Ray was watching TV, which she'd heard only as distant background noise.

Her mind hadn't been in the room. Nor even in the century. For one very strange moment she thought she'd seen Dylan, but the image had passed so quickly she couldn't tell what her imagination had conjured. Especially since, if it *was* him, he'd been naked. Her cheeks flushed to have those sorts of daydreams about her childhood buddy.

Ray's foot jiggled, perched on his opposite knee, and impatience tightened his voice. "I think you need to put those papers down for a while and quit talking to yourself."

Uh-oh. Talking? "What did I say?" She wished he would go back to watching television and leave her alone.

He shrugged. "You're just muttering. Keep that up, I'll book you a room at the laughing academy." He meant it as a joke, but often Ray's humor fell flat. Especially lately. Sometimes it seemed he was always irritated with her. Not like when they'd first been married. He'd been sweet back then. Sometimes a little boring, but still sweet.

She shook her head and mumbled an apology, then tried to focus on the page again. On her lap, and spread across the couch and coffee table, were huge stacks of papers, shipped to her from Scotland. Several months before, she'd written to the public library in Ciorram in hopes of finding some local information about Dylan—anything about Dylan. They'd forwarded the letter, and the town historian, an elderly gentleman named Ewan MacDonell, had kindly come to her rescue in her frustrated hope of finding records.

Though in his reply he'd said he hadn't the resources to track down a particular Matheson, he happily had sent photocopies of some old church records to which he had access. He also had sent her a small self-published booklet about his own family ties to the Battle of Culloden in 1746. She'd glanced at it, then set it aside, more interested in the photocopies, which were more likely to mention a name other than MacDonell.

Being acquainted with others in the area who were caretakers of records unwanted by the chroniclers of those more famous than the inhabitants of tiny Glen Ciorram, Mr. MacDonell had been able to send quite a lot of paper. Now she paged through it, stunned at how many Mathesons there had been in the area during the eighteenth century. The documentation wasn't nearly complete, but the baptismal records showed a good many Mathesons. Some of them in the 1720s and 1730s were named Dylan, Dilan, Dilean, or Dillon. It was horribly confusing.

It was slow going to decipher the scrawled writing riddled with creative spellings. Earlier in the day, she'd spent a bit of effort looking for Ciaran Matheson's baptism before she remembered with a flush of embarrassment that Dylan had told her the boy had been born in Edinburgh. So she sighed and went looking for other names. A thrill of triumph took her when she located a Caitrionagh Matheson who had been baptized in 1693. Apparently she had two younger brothers . . . no, wait, they were uncles, Coll and Artair, who had been baptized in 1694 and 1695, respectively. There were no marriage records in the stack, and she debated with herself whether she should impose and ask for them. Mr. MacDonell had already been so helpful, she hated to burden him further.

In any case, gazing at the lists of names, searching for familiar ones and thinking she might stumble across a reference to a name she recognized, she drifted off yet again. What was Dylan's life like? Had he found

Cait, as he'd said he would? Where had he been buried? *When* had he been buried? She took a deep breath and paged through to find the death records, starting with 1715. Now she hoped she wouldn't find him soon.

Dylan wasn't there, but what she did find broke her heart. Ciaran Robert Matheson had died in 1718. The poor little boy had been the victim of violence, the cause of death given as "beheading." Cody had to close her eyes and turn away from Ray as tears came. The boy had been only three years old. Poor Dylan.

Sleep wouldn't come that night. Cody lay in bed, staring into the darkness and listening to Ray's light snoring to her left. All her muscles and joints ached. Vivid images of Dylan buzzed in her brain. Dylan fighting English soldiers. Dylan herding sheep. Dylan holding his son's body, covered with blood. She sat up on the edge of the bed and groaned. There was an over-the-counter sleep aid in the bathroom medicine chest, but she didn't want to take it. She hated feeling drugged in the morning.

Instead, she pulled on her robe, stepped into her fuzzy slippers, and went to the living room to leaf through the material Mr. MacDonell had sent. She sat on the floor, going over the pages again, one by one, and still failed to find Dylan. When had he died? Had he even outlived his son? The pages covered fifty years, from 1690 to 1740, but though the village of Ciorram had been tiny, even for back then, the records weren't necessarily complete. School records gave lists of children, but no ages. There were some arrest records and tax ledgers kept by the local British authorities, but they were extremely disorganized and the early modern penchant for creative abbreviation made them almost gibberish. Birth records consisted strictly of church baptisms, and she had only the records for the Catholic church in the glen. The death records were from the same church. But, even assuming they were complete for the entire glen during those years, she still couldn't know whether Dylan had lived past 1740 or had simply died somewhere else. For instance, if that faerie had returned him to the Battle of Sheriffmuir . . .

She shook her head. No, he couldn't have died that soon after going back. He just couldn't have. She wouldn't allow herself to think that.

The page of death records with Ciaran's name on it caught her attention again, and it occurred to her that something had happened to bring the child to Glen Ciorram from Edinburgh. She wondered if the boy's mother had left that man she'd married and returned home. Had Dylan gone with her? Had he found her there after the uprising? If not, had she left her husband to go to Dylan in Ciorram? Then Cody began to wonder about the circumstances of Ciaran's death, for she couldn't imagine Dylan letting anyone hurt his son. Had he been there at all? Again, she was back to wondering whether he'd died at Sheriffmuir. Then she realized it might have been merciful for him to have died then, for he would then not have had to outlive his son. She couldn't imagine anything more horrible than the death of a . . .

Culloden. Ciaran Robert Matheson had been at Culloden. Okay, it might have been a different Ciaran Robert Matheson, but what if it was the same? What if they were both Dylan's son? Two conflicting records would mean that history could be changed. Excitement filled her, and she sorted through the pages some more. Perhaps, if there was another death record further on . . .

Among the scattered papers, a pamphlet slipped into view. She picked it up. Had she seen this before? She couldn't remember. It was an inexpensively printed tourism advertisement, extolling the attractions of Glen Ciorram. A smile curled her mouth. She bet Dylan had never thought of that place as a vacation spot.

Inside the tri-fold card were photographs of the local sights. The town boasted a whiskey distillery that gave tours, which sounded to her as exciting as watching paint dry. Another hot spot was a historical monument called the Queen Anne Garrison Museum, a two-story stone army garrison that had been converted to a museum which was open from April through October. Ciorram's third claim to fame did perk Cody's attention, though. *Broch Sidhe* rang several bells in her memory, for Dylan had told her quite a bit about the faerie who was responsible for his abduction to the eighteenth century. She had lived in an incredibly old tower. This pamphlet translated *Broch Sidhe* as "Faerie Tower." It was also the place where the Ciorram police had found Dylan's belongings when he'd disappeared.

Cody's heart beat faster. An idea was forming.

"I need to go to Scotland."

"Like hell, you do." It was breakfast, and Cody hadn't slept all night. Ray looked like he had, and seemed in a good mood, so she blurted her idea to him as soon as she put his oatmeal in front of him.

"I do. And I'm going." As far as she was concerned, the issue wasn't up for debate.

He peered at her as if she'd grown a third eye. "Are you nuts? By yourself?"

"You can come, too. I don't mind." She brought her own bowl to the table and sat down.

"Oh, like I can just take off from work—"

"Then I'll go by myself. I won't be long." As far as Ray was concerned, his job was the all-important, sacrosanct center of their lives. But Cody wasn't about to give in on this one. She couldn't give in. She gripped her spoon hard and found herself no longer hungry.

Ray snorted. "Oh, sure. *'Bye, honey, I'm off to Scotland. Won't be long. Dinner's in the microwave.*"

Irritation rose. "I need to do this, Raymond. I have to go there." If there was a chance of changing history, she had to find a way. She couldn't just let Dylan's son die a little boy.

Ray wasn't eating, either. His face began to darken. "Why? What's the big deal that you have to go five thousand miles to look at the place where Dylan died? I know that's why you want to go."

Why couldn't he just let her go? "I can't explain it. I just have to do it. It's not like we don't have the money." She started to sprinkle sugar into her bowl, but stopped as Ray scooted his chair back from the table, wide-eyed.

He was aghast. A complete overreaction. "Not for this, we don't. Not for your dead *boyfriend*, we don't!"

Her eyes went wide, then she blinked, stunned he could say such a thing. She dropped the spoon back into the sugar bowl and stared at it. "He was never my . . ." Fury choked her words, and no sound came though her throat worked and her mouth opened and closed. Tears rose. This was too much. She'd taken far too much of his snarky crap, and was quite finished with it. She forced her voice to come. "I'm going."

"Cody . . ."

She stood to lean across the table, and pointed a finger at his face. A quivering took her as the rage vented through clenched teeth. Tears stung her eyes. "I've never expected you to understand my friendship with Dylan." A sob choked her, but she coughed and went on. "I've only asked you to accept it and respect it as part of who I am. I've never given you cause to feel threatened by him—"

"You spend more time mooning over him, now that he's dead, than you ever did paying attention to me."

Her mouth gaped, once again, in astonishment. "That's not true! I looked forward to those classes because they were the only time I had for myself. I deserved that aspect of my life. I deserved . . ." Tears spilled onto her cheeks, and her heart clenched. "I deserved . . . I deserve to *grieve* for him. He was my friend as far back as I can remember, but I can't mention him around you. Do you know how that makes me feel, to not be able to talk to you about something that hurts me?"

Raymond's eyes were afire with rage, more emotion than she'd ever seen in him. "Excuse me, but from where I stand, you never talk about anything *but* him."

Now tears were streaming down her face. Her lips were swollen and her nose was starting to run. "I *don't!* I read! Talking doesn't happen! I *used* to talk about him, but every time I did, you said something disparaging, so I stopped talking." She went to the kitchen counter to pull a paper towel from the roll and blow her nose. Then she turned back. Her voice was dead flat. Nothing was going to move her. "Listen, Raymond, I'm going. Nothing you can say will change my mind." She retreated to the bedroom. That was the end of the discussion. She would go, and if he was still here when she came back, then fine. They would talk. If not, then *oh, well.*

G len Ciorram, Scotland, surely qualified as Cody's idea of "the sticks." Smack in the middle of the Western Highlands, it was a majestic valley with steep, barren mountains to the south and lower, wooded ones to the north. There was a bend at the near, narrow end, so as one drove the narrow road, which was the only convenient way in, there was a feeling of passing the gatehouse of a fortress. In fact, the Queen Anne Garrison Museum wasn't far from the road, set just at the entrance to the glen.

Her little blue rental car took her past a big, brown sign with white lettering: *Fàilte do Gleann Ciorram* and, below it, *Welcome to Glen Ciorram.* A thrill skittered up her spine. She'd arrived.

The drive up from Glasgow had been a white-knuckler, running with the traffic at seventy miles an hour, up winding roads barely wide enough for two small cars to pass but which semi tractors and trailers nevertheless negotiated at full speed. It was impossible to convince herself the oncoming traffic wasn't going to want her side of the road, so for three hours she had flinched every time she met another vehicle. For the final half-hour before reaching Glen Ciorram, the road was a single lane with the occasional wide spot where one was expected to pull over to let past oncoming cars. By the time she passed the *Welcome* sign, she was quite exhausted.

At a narrow spot in the glen where hills rose sharply on either side of the road, a small, stone church caught her eye on a rise to her right, and she had a glimpse of a dirty, painted sign. *Our Lady of the Lake Catholic Church.* It was an ancient building, looking like it had been built back in the Middle Ages. But she couldn't gaze long on it, lest the road get away from her. She blew around the curve, into the glen proper.

The valley opened up before her, an expanse of rolling, green pasture tucked between the slopes. In the distance lay a cluster of houses and businesses, dominated by a gray castle just beyond. West of that was a lake that seemed to go on forever, the mountains on the other side of the water appearing vague and grayish at this distance.

From here she could see the second largest structure in the village, the whiskey distillery. The cut stone structure sat near a low hill, where a stream issued from the north slope of the valley to make its way toward the lake. Scattered clouds overhead threw shadows across the green pastures dotted with white sheep. As Cody drove, she noticed some of the animals had numbers painted on their fleeces in bright pink. Easier to see than branding, she guessed.

Wildflowers touched everything with patches of purple, yellow, and white. Crumbling stone walls could be seen here and there, occasionally still doing duty as fencing between stretches of wire. The road meandered some, then widened to two lanes again and took her straight into the village. It took her a couple of seconds to remember which of the two lanes was supposed to be hers.

Most of the buildings in the village were whitewashed brick, though there was one red brick storefront with *MacGregor's* painted on the window, and a pseudo-Tudor office building just before the roundabout. The streets were barely two lanes, but people nevertheless parked at the curb, which forced traffic into a single lane, coming and going. Cody kept as close as she could to the left, away from oncoming traffic, but was terrified she might sideswipe one of the parked cars for being unable to gauge distance to the left. Fortunately, traffic was light and oncoming cars were few. Pedestrians were even fewer, consisting of only one young mother pushing a stroller.

Six roads converged on the roundabout at what appeared to be the center of the village, and as Cody circled it a few times to get her bearings, the signs told her which direction to take for the distillery, the castle, the high school, the Presbyterian church and *Broch Sidhe*. The direction suggested for the tower was back the way she had come. She sighed as she veered away from the roundabout and headed back up the valley.

She was almost to the Queen Anne Garrison Museum, nearly leaving the valley again, when she finally spotted the tiny white sign to the left, directing her to the tower. The parking lot was situated in a nook within the wooded hills, and a carved wooden sign bearing an arrow pointed the way up a narrow trail. Cody parked, locked the car, and began walking.

Giant pines and oaks grew all around, and the grass beneath was alive with clusters of toadstools in circles of brown and white. Faerie rings, Cody had read somewhere. The toadstools looked like tiny, dancing people, women's skirts flying up with the spinning.

The trail ended at the tower. Even in a country where the very air was thick with history, this tower struck her as immeasurably ancient. The gray stone seemed half-melted, covered with thick mosses of varying shades of green and gray. Inside the tower, the well-groomed grass was laced with black fungus. Crumbling steps ascended the wall in a circle, ending near the top where a monstrous oak tree thrust a huge branch through a straight-edged gap that must once have been a window.

The summer sun was high, but at this latitude and altitude the temperature was no higher than barely comfortable without a jacket. Half the tower interior was in shade below the spreading oak, cool and still as a grotto.

Now what? Cody stood at the center of the tower and turned. The place was empty except for herself. No tourists, and certainly no locals. No faeries, either, not that she'd expected to find the wee folk dancing around everywhere like toadstools. Now she wondered if she'd been a fool to come here. She had to remind herself that this was the last place Dylan had been traced.

"Hello?" How did one address a faerie? She'd read horrible stories of faeries luring people away to magical lands, exchanging human babies for their own, and flattening car tires. They had a long reputation for mischief, and Dylan's stories of Sinann supported it. Cody's heart beat faster for fear of what might be done to her for coming here if she did find the faerie. Which didn't seem likely. "Hello?"

There was a large stone nearby, lying in the middle of the tower floor as if it had fallen there and never been moved. She put her rental car key in her purse and set it on the ground, then sat on the stone and tried to calm herself. Stressing out wasn't helping anything.

Her eyes closed, she concentrated on her breathing until it slowed. Her limbs relaxed, and slowly her breathing came under control. It was a meditation technique she'd learned from Dylan during her classes with him. Sometimes he taught martial arts tricks in his fencing classes, saying that a good fighter always used whatever worked, regardless of style. The sun on her head was warming, comforting. The smell of damp moss and grasses was thick and earthy.

Her mind drifted to the times when she and Dylan had been children, playing in the forests near the neighborhood. She'd never had a brother, and he no siblings at all. There had never been a time when she and Dylan hadn't been inseparable. Even in adulthood, he'd been like a brother to her. He'd taught her to handle a sword, and she'd shared his interest in things Scottish. Especially now; but even before he'd left, she'd loved to dress up as a Scottish maid. And now she could sense him. Something about this place gave her such a strong *sense* of him; she thought she could almost smell him. Almost as if he were standing before her, sweat beading on his forehead and soaking his shirt, as he had been so many times . . .

"Cody?"

"Dylan . . ." She opened her eyes, but there was nothing there. No Dylan. It had been his voice, though. Surely his voice. Her heart thudded so hard, she could feel it in her ears. Then a niggling sensation crept up the back of her neck, and she slowly turned around.

Nothing there. *No, wait.* Cody jumped. A figure crouched on the steps, just beneath the oak branches. A tiny, white figure, hugging her knees and staring. The eyes were ice blue, and so piercing it was no wonder Cody could feel her gaze. "A more natural witch I've never before seen."

"Sinann?"

The tiny creature didn't reply at first, but raised her head. Finally, she said, "He told ye of me."

Cody nodded.

"And what did he tell that brought ye here?"

"That you sent him to the eighteenth century. And that you saved his life once or twice."

The faerie snorted. " 'Twas far more than once or twice. He was forever getting himself into trouble, that one."

"Sorry for the slight. But to be perfectly fair, you knew him until he died. When he spoke to me of you, he was only thirty. I mean, thirty-two."

The faerie had no reply to that. Her thoughts seemed to withdraw for a moment, then she returned. "What is it ye want? As if I didn't already know." She sounded as if she were sure Cody's motives for being there must be less than honorable. Cody wondered what the faerie did know.

"If you already know why I'm here, then you tell me."

Sinann stood and fluttered down a step, then another. "I could tell ye to bugger off, then where would ye be?"

"But you won't. And you know you won't, because you already know you're going to send me back in time."

The faerie made a hawking noise in her throat, then uttered some words in a foreign tongue that might have been Gaelic, in a tone that suggested she was better off not knowing what was said. Then Sinann switched back to English. "Two peas in a pod, that's what ye are! Himself said that very thing to me some months ago. And 'tis true. I would nae sooner not send you back than to thrust a dirk through his poor sore heart. What's done cannae be changed."

The triumphant smile that rose to Cody's lips died in an instant. "But, wait, that's why I want to go back. I have to change history."

"I assure ye, lassie, you will go back, but you'll change naught. Nae more than Himself did at Sheriffmuir, and nae more than I have all these centuries. Nevertheless, lass, I wish you to take this with ye." The faerie reached into the front of her dress and pulled out a small, folded packet of paper yellowed with age. "I dinnae ken when I wrote it, but I must have, for 'tis my own writing. I've kept it a good many years, read it and read it again, wishing it had come to me sooner. Now I need you to take it." She handed the paper to Cody, who held it between two fingers. "Take it. Put it in a pocket." Cody obeyed and slipped the packet into the front pocket of her blouse. Sinann continued, "Give it to me when you arrive, not that it will do any good."

"But if I can't change history, why will you send me back?"

Sinann put her hands on her hips and leaned forward. "Because, ye sumph, if you dinnae go back, it *will* change!"

"But—"

"*Och!*" The faerie waved away the pointless argument and hopped down a few more steps to be at eye level with Cody. She raised one hand and closed her eyes.

Cody had a sudden rush of alarm. "Wait a minute! Will I be coming back? Or will I be stuck there forever, like him?"

Sinann set her hands on her hips again. "Oh, now she isnae so sure she wants to go. Hear me, lassie. If ye stay, the laddie will die. If ye go and yet dawdle, the laddie will die. So, I hope ye're ready, because you're a-going." With that, she raised her hand.

Cody cried, "No! I need to know."

The faerie's impatience was palpable. "Whatever for? If I answer and give you a reply ye dinnae like, will it keep you from going?"

Cody thought about that, then shook her head. "No. I have to go."

"*Och*, aye, you got that right." Sinann's expression clouded over. "Further, the tragedy of it is you'll be a day late." Cody's heart clutched with alarm, and the faerie continued, her voice thickening and tears filling her eyes, suddenly talking as if to herself. "If only I hadnae tried to send him back. If only the magic hadnae been done on that day." She squeezed her eyes shut. "I would appeal to Yahweh, please let her be a day earlier. Please let me change just this for my poor Dylan. Dinnae punish him for my error."

Before Cody could ask what she was talking about, Sinann snapped her fingers, and for Cody the world went black.

CHAPTER 12

The explanation for the disappearance of the street boy was put out on the streets of Edinburgh: he'd been carried off by a press gang and was on his way to New York as a cabin boy on a merchant vessel. Dylan knew Bedford's suspicions of spying wouldn't end there, but at least Ramsay's hand wouldn't be tipped that he knew of Bedford's attempt at catching him. It gave Ramsay time to clean out the evidence from his office and destroy it at home.

The missing letter had been from Polonius Wingham, and had made reference to the Major; therefore it was of no use to Bedford as blackmail. Dylan was certain it would have been returned quietly to Ramsay's desk before morning, had the theft not been discovered. It was a dead certainty the thing had been taken by one of Ramsay's clerks.

The next couple of weeks, living in Ramsay's house, were among the most awkward Dylan had ever spent. Being around Cait without being able to touch her, or even speak to her casually, emphasized the distance between them and the impossibility of the situation. He hated to the point of red anger not being able to spend evenings with her and with Ciaran, but neither could he sequester himself in his room. Most nights he was expected to be visible to visitors, but not participating—still and silent like a watchdog. Cait was usually present downstairs, and Ciaran was hidden away in the nursery. Dylan ached to ask after the boy, but didn't dare even glance in the direction of the nursery door at the end of the balcony.

Each day he was expected to take breakfast and supper with Ramsay and Cait, but made conversation only with Ramsay, unless addressed by Cait first. It wasn't even safe to look at her too long, so he confined himself to quick glances while giving short, careful replies to polite, superficial queries.

Ramsay himself almost never spoke to Cait, except to criticize. Cait rarely spoke to either of them for fear of attracting unwanted attention. Dylan focused on Ramsay for fear of giving too much attention to Cait. Meals became monologues in which Ramsay expounded an opinion on whatever came to mind, and Dylan agreed just often enough to let Ramsay think he gave a damn.

That week Ramsay's temper became especially nasty, when it became clear that his English friend, Charles, was ending their business relationship. Like a lover who has found someone better and moved on, the Englishman began avoiding Ramsay. It was apparent Charles had found better prospects elsewhere, for it was soon learned he had departed for London and closed his offices in Edinburgh. Ramsay, Ltd. would weather the lost business, for there were other irons in Ramsay's English fire, but his sore pride made him difficult to live with.

Cait took the brunt of Ramsay's anger during this time. Though he never took another swing at her while Dylan was around, Ramsay was quite free with aimless abusive language. Both Cait and Dylan suffered under the tirades. Cait avoided her husband as always, and especially kept Ciaran out of his way. Dylan was grateful the baby was still too young to understand most of what was said by the adults around him.

On Friday night Dylan was made to attend a performance of chamber music, put on by Ramsay for the entertainment of some prominent Edinburgh businessmen. There for show, Dylan stood to Ramsay's left and to the rear, at attention like a sentry, mortally stultified for an hour and a half by a string quartet playing lilting music that damn near put him to sleep. Never mind that this was the latest sound from London, Dylan still longed for a Walkman and a couple of Springsteen tapes just to keep awake.

During these days Ciaran was rarely brought from the nursery, and never when Ramsay was in the house. Therefore, Dylan saw his son only if Ciaran and his mother were already in the sitting room when Ramsay arrived home from the office. Then Dylan couldn't *not* look at the boy, and tried to keep behind Ramsay so he could watch the baby freely. But those times were seldom, and Ciaran wasn't allowed to remain downstairs in the evenings once Ramsay was on the premises. Dylan dreaded what would happen to his son later on, when his world would need to expand beyond this house. Would Ciaran be locked up in the nursery all his life?

But there was nothing Dylan could do about it. His day was spent in Ramsay's office or following him around town. Controlling what happened at the house wasn't possible.

One evening when Ramsay and Dylan arrived from the offices, they walked in on Cait reading to her son in the sitting room. Ramsay's entrance was disruptive and curt as he ordered the servants this way and that, and Dylan heard only a word or two of Cait's voice before she hushed. Sitting in the far corner by the fire, she was inconspicuous, and whispered into Ciaran's ear for the sake of keeping him quiet. Dylan knew she would stay that way, like a rabbit waiting for the hawk to pass, until an opportunity would arise to sneak unseen up the stairs to the nursery. Afterward, she would return for supper with Ramsay and Dylan.

But tonight Ramsay dismissed Nellie with a wave and made directly for the stairs. "I'll eat in my rooms, Nell. See I'm not disturbed for the evening."

Dylan's heart lightened as he watched Ramsay go. He glanced at Cait, who seemed equally relieved. Ciaran was banging his heels against her shins and uttering something in babyspeak as he slapped the book in his mother's hand. Startled back to her reading, she blinked and said, "Oh, yes. Where was I?" Her eyes scanned the page, and she read, continuing where she'd left off, *"Thou art my life, my love, my heart, the very eyes of me."* At that, her eyes flickered in a glance at Dylan.

He stood in the Great Room, a smile curling the corners of his mouth, for he recognized the book in her hand. It had once belonged to him, and he'd read to her from it many times, and she to him. Cait continued, *"And hast command of every part, to live and die for thee."* Her voice trailed off, and Dylan knew she wanted to look over at him but didn't dare with Nellie in the room.

Dylan said to the maid, "I'll eat in here, Nell." She nodded, and went to serve her master before she would bring Dylan's supper. There were a few minutes before he would need to wash up. He turned the chair at the end of the dining table so it faced the sitting room, sat, and said, "Continue."

Cait smiled, sat back, and returned to reading aloud. For a while, at least, Dylan could imagine they were a family, reading to each other for entertainment before bed.

That week the Welshman Gilman arrived from Perth at Ramsay's invitation, which brought joy to the offices of Ramsay, Ltd. Over the course of two or three meetings, an arrangement was negotiated and agreements were made that enabled Ramsay to attempt participation in the Amsterdam Exchange, with Gilman as his associate. The entry would be slow, for the risk was too great and the repercussions of intrusion too dangerous for a full-on assault on the Exchange, but it was a toehold for which Ramsay had searched many years. He was so thrilled with the results of the negotiations, he even thanked Dylan for bringing Gilman to his attention. No finder's fee, though, which didn't surprise Dylan at all.

One night during that week, Dylan waited till the house was quiet, then slipped through the window of his bedroom to the alley back of the house. In utter darkness and bitter cold he wended his way through the Edinburgh labyrinth to the road that took him out of the city and north to the harbor. It was a long walk, so he would have to be quick about his business in order to make it back to his room by dawn. He went to one of Ramsay's warehouses, where he found Seumas alone and asleep on the floor next to the fire, snoring heavily. Dylan knew better than to approach. "Seumas . . ."

The guard opened his eyes and threw back his plaid to reveal the gun he had at the ready, pointed at Dylan. "*Och*, it's you." He let down the hammer of the pistol and set it aside, then hauled himself to a sitting position and adjusted his plaid over his shoulder. "What in creation brings ye here? I heard you've a comfortable bed; you should be asleep in it."

Dylan crouched by the fire to warm his numbed hands as he spoke. "I need some help, Seumas, and I can't have Ramsay listening in when I ask for it. I want to know about people leaving from that dock out there, in the middle of the night."

"Smuggling people, ye say? Jacobites fleeing the noose?"

Dylan shook his head. "Prisoners. Women and children. On New Year's Eve a wagonload of them were taken from here. I need to know where they're being held before transport."

"Ye think there will be more of them taken?"

"Well . . ."—Dylan shrugged—". . . not anytime soon. Near as I can figure, there's only one ship engaged in the activity. The last shipment was headed for Singapore, so it's not likely to return right away. Which means there has *got* to be a place where they hold the prisoners. Keep an eye open and an ear to the ground for anything that would point to such a place: food going in and not coming out, buildings with no apparent purpose, that sort of thing. Talk to the dockworkers. Ask about people disappearing. Or maybe even people *appearing* out of nowhere . . . bodies . . . whatever."

Seumas nodded. "Aye, man. I'll have a look about the place, and tell Alasdair and Keith as well." He reached for a peat to renew the fire. "Come, sit, Dylan. Warm yerself."

Dylan shook his head and adjusted his plaid around his shoulders in preparation for the walk back to Edinburgh. "I can't. I've got to be in that comfortable bed when Ramsay awakens, or all hell will break loose."

"*Och!* We wouldnae be wishing for that!"

A chuckle rose. "No, we wouldn't." He bade Seumas good night and went on his way.

R amsay continued to visit his mistress and to bang the woman living on the third floor, but toward the end of January he surprised Dylan with an invitation to a social engagement as a guest.

Ramsay was in a rare mood at supper that night, giggling and glancing at Dylan with a leering eye that was annoying. Dylan wasn't sure he wanted to know what was up, and tried to decline the invitation. "If you don't need me in my professional capacity, I'm sure I'd rather stay in my room tonight, if it's all the same to you."

Ramsay threw him an odd look. "Yes, I expect you would rather stay at home, and it is not all the same to me. The more, the merrier, and so you must come." A laugh snorted through his nose. "So to speak. Though it will still be inferior gratification, at least the vice, then, is not solitary." He then brayed with laughter at his own joke, and Dylan frowned, confused. But then it came to Dylan where they were going, and he swallowed a groan.

While reiving cattle with Rob Roy, he'd heard rumors of an elite club in Edinburgh called The Beggar's Benison. The word was, some very rich men got together twice a year to stare at naked women. Dylan understood it to be something on the level of a twentieth-century strip club, with drinking and rowdy behavior, dirty jokes and perhaps the chance to engage a prostitute afterward.

Cait threw him a look, and he threw one back, hoping she either knew nothing about this club or at least had enough faith she wouldn't think he was going whoring. He hoped she knew he wouldn't risk exposure to the "French pox." He had to admit to himself the Benison was intriguing, and probably harmless. In any case, he was cornered into going and had no say in the matter.

"As a rule," said Ramsay as they proceeded along the wyndes toward their destination, "the help arenae welcome at these meetings, so I must introduce you as a colleague from Skye, if you don't mind." Dylan shrugged and nodded. He didn't care if Ramsay called him Santa Claus to his friends. " 'Twill be best if you keep shut for most of it. I'm letting you accompany me because I've taken a liking to you. You'll not want to ruin it by talking overly much. If anyone addresses you, say something in that Gaelic of yours. Most will leave you alone then." Dylan nodded.

Dylan had his first inkling that this gathering was not so much like a strip club as he'd thought when they arrived at a private home and were escorted by a manservant to a room where a number of monks' robes lay across a bed. "The others are upstairs," said the manservant.

"Tell them we'll be along directly," said Ramsay. When the servant backed through the door and closed it, he said to Dylan, "Remove your clothes and take one of these."

Dylan chuckled. "You're not serious."

Ramsay began to undress. "I'm quite serious. Hurry, or we'll miss Nancy."

"Everything?" He put his hand on his sporran, which contained everything he owned except his weapons.

"Aye. Everything. Don't worry about your things." His voice took on an even more condescending tone than usual. "You've nothing worth taking by anyone in this house."

That was probably true. Many other sets of clothing were lying around the room, all of them worth far more than anything in his sporran. He sighed and unbuckled his belt. He would keep his *sgian dubh* strapped under his arm, at least. The robe was brown silk satin, its resemblance to a monk's habit extending only to color and cut. The arms were long, and the hood was so large and droopy, he had to pull it back a little in order to see out. The silk felt good to wear, and was a nice change from linen and wool. Having cinched the large, floppy robe around his waist, Dylan followed Ramsay from the room and up a flight of stone stairs.

A large bedroom upstairs was filled with milling figures in identical brown robes, chatting among themselves. The voices all had an excited quality, the sort of quaver people get when they are about to do something they know they shouldn't. One of the robed men was telling a dirty joke to the room, and the laughter was uproarious enough to make Dylan wish he'd heard the beginning of the joke. Wine was available on a nearby table, and he went to take a glass. Ramsay approached one of the robed men, greeted him with a few words and a hearty laugh, then pulled out his erect penis to touch it to the other man's equally erect member. Dylan's jaw dropped and he looked away, no longer sure where it might be safe to gaze. This evening was becoming weirder by the minute.

Then Dylan's stomach turned, because from somewhere in the room came Bedford's voice. "Whatever has happened to the cully? She's late." The lighthearted tone sounded strange coming from the Redcoat. "I wish a closer look this time." Dylan guessed him to be the seated figure who now put his long, bare feet up on the mattress of the bed.

Dylan pulled his hood completely over his face. *Damn!* Ramsay, now at his elbow, began laughing so hard Dylan thought his employer might choke. *Very funny!* It occurred to Dylan he should have known Bedford would be here, but somehow he'd assumed an Army officer would have better sense than to open himself to court-martial for something this frivolous.

Another voice said in reply to Bedford, "A closer look might get your nose stuck in her quim, Major. Or have you turned French on us? Is it your tongue you wish stuck?"

That brought uproarious laughter among the group. The ones standing looked around for seats, and one of them began reading from a book a ribald passage that referred to "rising hillocks," "grizzled bush," and "red truncheon." While the others listened, rapt, Dylan struggled not to laugh. He sipped his wine and faded toward the back of the room. He wanted to be as far from Bedford as possible. The reading went on, several men taking turns reading bawdy poetry and ribald stories. Some were interesting, bordering on truly erotic, but most were just silly. It appeared that cheap porn was cheap porn, no matter the century.

Someone in a hurry brushed past Dylan, and he looked to see a young girl, sloppy drunk and stinking of whiskey, make her way toward the bed. Approving murmurs rippled across the room, and the reader quit and shut his book. Dylan leaned against the door frame, sipping from his glass and observing the spectacle. The girl sat on the bed, facing the seated men with her knees bent and her heels at the edge of the mattress. She beamed at the assemblage, her grin wide and ragged with missing teeth, then reached down to the hems of her skirts, pulled them over her head, and lay there with her feet splayed as wide as they would go, exposing herself to the gawkers.

Dylan's eyes went wide. Not because he'd never seen such a thing before, but because he *had*. His first thought was *Big deal*. Was this what all the fuss was about? Where he came from, every magazine stand in the Western world had magazines containing photos of female genitalia, most of them a lot more artful and appealing than this. True, he was not unaffected by the sight—it was, after all, a mostly naked woman. He waited for her to do something. Dance, perhaps, or touch herself—anything—but she only lay there.

It was the *men* who were touching themselves. When Dylan realized most of the men in the room had hands disappeared inside their robes, the hair rose on the back of his neck. Some were masturbating vigorously, a couple of the fatter men with their hands disappeared up under their huge bellies. Dylan glanced around to be sure nobody was checking to see where his hands were, then took another long drink of wine. The reading resumed, but the reader's voice faltered now. There was an overall undulating movement in the room and Dylan watched, unable to look away, as if witnessing a chainsaw massacre: horrifying, yet fascinating.

After a few minutes of this, the manservant entered, carrying a large, ornate silver cup. One of the robed ones gestured to him, and the servant brought it close. The robed one stood, held the cup to his front, and in a flurry of motion ejaculated into it. Others stood, ready to take their turn at the cup.

That was it. Too much. Dylan set down his glass, ducked out of the room, and slipped back down the stairs. He found the room where he'd left his kilt and sark, dressed, and was out the front door without anyone noticing he'd gone. The night air washed over him, and he took deep gulps of it. Embarrassment warmed his cheeks as he realized his pulse was racing and his groin ached. He started to head back to Ramsay's house, but realized he had to return to the wynde in front of the Benison house.

Ramsay would not take kindly to being left behind. Dylan sat on a mounting block by the steps to wait.

Sinann appeared, hovering cross-legged above the muddy ground in front of him. "Lost yer nerve when it came down to it, did ye?"

He glanced around to be sure they were alone. "Communal masturbation just isn't my fascination, Tink."

She giggled. "Ye prefer yer onanism solitary, then?"

He blinked and made a disgusted noise. "Well, yeah, actually." She giggled again, and his eyes narrowed at her. "How long were *you* gawking?"

"I left about the time ye began to slaver."

"Tink!" He couldn't help wiping his mouth with the back of his hand, just to be sure she was kidding. She giggled some more.

He waited about an hour, wondering how the attraction could possibly last that long. Then, when the door of the house opened, he hid in some shadows behind a tree, watching for Ramsay.

Men wandered out in languid fashion. Dylan observed the tall, blond Major emerge, wearing civilian clothing in muted shades of brown, and watched him stride away at a march of sorts. Dylan wondered if that guy ever walked anywhere that he didn't look like he was marching. Ramsay strolled out soon after, looking around. Dylan came out of hiding and approached.

"Ah, there you are, Mac a'Chlaidheimh."

"I lost you among all those robes in there. I came outside, thinking you'd be here."

"Nonsense. You were hiding from Bedford." Ramsay led the way back toward his house, and Dylan followed.

"Uh, yeah. That was it, you figured me out. I didn't want Bedford to see me." Nor did he want anyone else to see him, but he didn't need to tell Ramsay that. All the way back to the house, he struggled not to wonder what the hell they did with that cup once it was full.

The next night, a knock came at the outer door of Ramsay's house during supper. Nellie went to answer it, and in a moment Felix appeared at the door to the Great Room. "A word with ye, sir?" he said, his hat in one hand and his other hand pressed to his chest as if he were protecting something inside his coat. With a sigh, Ramsay left his supper and the two retreated into the stairwell.

Dylan and Cait continued to eat in silence, guarded against conversation which might interest Nellie too much. The maid was in the habit of standing at attendance, and her stare was an unavoidable accompaniment to supper.

When Ramsay reappeared, excitement flushed his cheeks. "I've an errand for you tonight." He now held his palm against his coat the way Felix had, and Dylan wondered what had been brought which he would be asked to deliver somewhere else. Something flat: a letter, no doubt.

Dylan stifled a sigh and said, "Yes, sir?"

Cait's mouth was a straight, tight line, but she kept her gaze on her plate.

Ramsay said, "There is a ship coming into the firth. You are to meet it. Afterward, you are to report delivery of the cargo which I will send with you." He cut a glance toward Cait, but not a flicker of understanding passed over her face. A smile tried to curl Dylan's mouth, though, for he knew she understood far more than she let on.

Ramsay motioned for Dylan to join him, and Dylan rose from the table to follow down the back hallway to his office. Ramsay closed the door behind them and continued his instructions as he lit a candelabra on a table by the door. "Once you've accomplished delivery, present yourself at St. Giles and kneel for a prayer at the far right of the very last pew."

Dylan looked up with alarm. "St. Giles? Isn't that a little risky? The High Kirk being right next to the Tolbooth and all, and the place crawling with Redcoats."

"Aye, it is. Also, your rendezvous point will most likely be within sight of the castle." He shrugged. "I don't see the significance. I assure you the Landguard is well secured, with cash sufficient to sink a man-o'-war. Nothing could be more safe."

Dylan found those words suspect, just for their arrogance. "How will I know where to make the rendezvous?"

"You are to go where the Landguard are not."

Dylan's eyebrows raised. "Excuse me?"

"I am informed the excise officers are patrolling north of the river, and tonight may be as far north as Kirkaldy. You will go to the near side of the Forth, to the promontory near Queensferry, and signal the ship at sea. It is a light craft and will make good time through the firth. You will then hand over the cargo to Wingham, whom you know by sight, and he you. You will give him this." He drew the letter from his coat and handed it over.

Dylan transferred it directly to his own sark without glancing at it. The contents of the letter were none of his business, and it would be unseemly to evince too much curiosity about it. "This isn't an ordinary smuggling job."

A smile played around Ramsay's mouth, which set off alarms in Dylan. "It is not."

"But the Landguard doesn't know that."

"Of course not. Simple smuggling is merely an economic expedient, but this is something else entirely."

"Then, tell me, if the Landguard is so bought off and they think this is a simple exchange, why do I need to be careful of being seen?"

Ramsay chuckled. "Because it's so very less expensive to buy a few excise men than it is to pay the entire English Army."

"Even with Major Bedford in your pocket?"

Ramsay grunted. "Even so. And would that he were entirely *in my pocket*, as you say."

Ramsay put a hand to his belly and belched. "I'm off to bed. You have your orders. I'll see you tomorrow." With that, he left the office, then climbed the stairs. Dylan followed as far as the Great Room. At the second-floor balcony, however, Ramsay leaned over the banister and called down. "Be sharp tonight, Mac a'Chlaidheimh, for loss of this cargo will mean your life."

Cait looked up from her supper, and the blood drained from her countenance.

CHAPTER 13

Dylan and Cait continued eating in silence, under the watchful eye of Nellie. Cait's silver clattered against the plate and her eyes swam with unshed tears. Dylan hoped the maid didn't notice Mrs. Ramsay's sudden case of nerves. He longed to console Cait, but didn't dare. There was nothing he could do to calm her that wouldn't attract the attention of that cantankerous busybody. Finally Cait left the table, her supper unfinished, and went to the nursery.

Dylan then left the table to prepare for his ride, and in his room took the letter from his sark to examine it. The seal was huge, the most elaborate he'd ever seen, and accompanied by a purple ribbon besides. The crown in the imprint made his pulse surge. King James? Certainly not George. Was the King hiding in St. Giles? Dylan sifted his memory for James' whereabouts. Had he fled Scotland yet? He shook his head. No, the escape would be sometime in February, and it was still the last of January. But James probably wasn't at the High Kirk, either. Only the letter was in Edinburgh, and the message must be of paramount importance, relating to the escape. Ramsay had surely meant it when he'd said letting the thing be taken from him would get him killed.

Now a question niggled at him. Was he to be instrumental in aiding the escape of King James? He knew the King would survive to return in

1719. Had Dylan always been a part of that history? And if he was, could he *change* that history by failing to deliver the letter? James' son, Bonnie Prince Charlie, wouldn't be born until late 1720. If the King were taken by George's army, contrary to what Dylan knew to have happened, would the Prince never be born? Would the uprising of 1745, so disastrous for the Highland people, then be prevented?

But not to deliver the letter would mean his death, and no guarantees of preventing the uprisings. Cait and Ciaran would be left without him, at the mercy of a man who hated them both. There was but one choice to make.

Dylan slipped the letter back inside his sark, pulled on the coat and the gloves he'd recently bought, then hung his baldric across his chest. He addressed the faerie perched on his headboard, "I want you to stay and watch—"

"I'll be going with ye."

"Sinann—"

"I invite you to recall the times past when you left me behind. The one time, you were nearly dead by the time I caught up with ye. More recently, you came within a hair of being recognized by the *Sassunach* Major and then were nearly killed by men you have still to identify. Nae argument, I'll be accompanying you and that is that."

Dylan narrowed his eyes at her and considered the value of arguing.

Sinann continued, "And besides, we'll nae be gone longer than noon tomorrow."

That was true. "All right, come on."

Once again he took the horse from David's stable in Cowgate, and this time a signal lantern as well. With Sinann perched behind him, he rode northwest toward the narrow end of the Firth of Forth. The road was deserted, it being a cold, moonless night, and Dylan encountered nobody at all, let alone anyone in uniform. They took most of the trip at a light canter, which ate up the distance quickly.

The land near Queensferry jutted into the firth, and to the east the entire harbor was visible. Out to sea were anchored several vessels showing flickering yellow lights, but Dylan knew the ship he wanted to signal would be darkened. He unhooked the small lantern from the saddle, lit it with iron and flint, pointed it straight down the firth, and opened the lens. Two flaps shielded the light from being seen from either side. He held the thing, braced against his leg as he sat on the horse, and he waited.

Having been raised in a world where instantaneous worldwide communication was taken for granted, and the top speed of a horse was considered unbearably slow travel, Dylan quickly became antsy. Even his years in this century had not broken the lifelong habit of expecting things to happen immediately.

"They're not there," he muttered. The wind tossed his shaggy locks, and though he held back his hair from his forehead to see, the ends occasionally whipped into his eyes. In spite of his dislike for Lowland fashion, just then he wondered if tying his hair into a queue might be a good idea.

"And how would you know where they are?" Sinann perched on the horse's rump, hugging her knees and huddling against Dylan's coat for warmth.

"It's taking too long."

"You've not waited half long enough."

Dylan sighed and adjusted his seat.

It felt like forever, but eventually a shadow moved across one of the boats on the firth. "There it is." He couldn't keep the relief out of his voice. Being stuck out in the open like this was far too risky for comfort. He was sure he could smell Redcoats, and shook his head at himself for his paranoia. The Landguard was still undermanned, the Crown not yet having cracked down on free traders running goods. Ramsay's faith in the laxity of the gadgers was well founded in fact.

When the ship was close enough for him to hear the creaking of masts and rigging, he covered the lantern and dismounted to make his way to the shore. Soon the darkened ship was near enough to put out a dinghy. Two rowers and a third man came to the rocky shore.

The passenger was Polonius Wingham, all in black and wearing a black cape. He hopped from the boat and picked his way over rocks toward Dylan. When he saw who was there to meet him, he chuckled. "Ah, it's the famous Dilean Dubh. Good e'en, Mr. Dubh." He doffed his hat with a flourish, then restored it to his head. "You have something for me, then?" His smile was wide and utterly cheerful, as if he were there to pick up a gift for his girlfriend.

Dylan reached into his sark for the letter. Wingham went for his dirk. Dylan spread his palms. "Whoa. It's a letter."

Wingham stood down, surprised at this development. Dylan took the letter from his sark. "You can make a guess who it's from, and it's addressed to *The Ship's Captain*. I imagine that would be you."

Wingham inclined his head in acknowledgment as he noted the seal. "It would be whatever ship's captain might not mind running errands for the Pretender in exchange for a great deal of money." He reached for the letter.

Sinann, still near the horse, emitted a piercing scream and shouted, *"Run! a Dhilein! Redcoats!"* Dylan spun and ran, ignoring the shouts from Wingham behind him. At that same moment, muskets reported from the slope above. Wingham collapsed onto the rocks with an ugly, gurgling sound, and the two men in the dinghy scurried to push off, shouting to each other as they manhandled the boat back into the water. A large gun was discharged on the ship, followed by a loud, low whine, and some rocks flew into pieces nearby. Dylan ducked the flying stone fragments, then continued to scramble away from the musket shots.

But just when he thought he might be able to hide himself before the Redcoats could reload, more musket fire came from straight ahead, kicking up dirt and rocks all around him. Dylan wobbled to a stop, raised his arms, and shouted in English, "I surrender! Don't shoot! I surrender!" He kept his arms high and his head low for fear they would shoot again, and he repeated for good measure as loudly and clearly as possible, "I surrender!"

Sinann swooped down and hissed at him in Gaelic, "Coward!"

He muttered through his teeth, "It beats having a musket ball through the skull, you little shit!" When the soldiers came to surround him, he could see there were far too many for him to have escaped. Wingham was dead, and the oars of the men in the dinghy could still be heard as they struggled to escape. But out on the firth an excise ship blocked them, lit up like a twentieth-century Christmas tree. The Crown had succeeded in capturing a notorious smuggling ship, and in a moment the Redcoats would find they had a Jacobite spy as well.

The letter was snatched away by one of the soldiers, and Dylan was disarmed in a hurry, down to his hidden *sgian dubh*. His sporran was taken from him, its thongs cut from his belt. The Redcoat with the letter was struck silent at first glimpse of the seal, then without another word hustled Dylan at bayonet point to his horse for the ride back to Edinburgh. Wingham's body was slung across the back of the same mount, behind the saddle, his arms dangling and swaying with the rhythm of its gait.

Sinann flew beside him and said, "Shall I pop some buttons for ye, lad?"

Dylan shook his head. There were several muskets aimed at him.

Sinann's powers erratic as they were, she could confound only one soldier at a time, and was unable to kill anyone at all. Pissing off any of these men was not his idea of a brilliant strategy. Sinann flew with him all the way to the Edinburgh Tolbooth, where the soldiers hauled him from the horse and escorted him inside. Down a spiral staircase, the detention cells were just below street level. The bayonet poked Dylan in the back as he was urged into a small cell at the end of a corridor. Then one of the Redcoats shackled his leg to an iron pole anchored to the floor down the center.

Dylan was left there in the dark, and he lay down on the straw-covered floor to sleep.

"I dinnae see how ye can sleep." Sinann hovered and crossed her arms, angry.

He sighed. "I *dinnae* see how I could do otherwise. I figure I'm ahead of the game, seeing as how they haven't shot me yet. Not like last time. If I don't sleep at all, I'll be good and sick by morning and worthless to everyone, especially myself. I might as well rest. There's nothing I can do about any of this right now."

Sinann snapped her fingers, and the door to the cell popped open.

He grunted and pulled his collar up around his neck. "Close it, Tink."

"Ye're daft."

"I said, close it. I'm not going to run again. Even if I got away without being killed, I'd never be able to go near Cait or Ciaran again. Ever. Then what would be the point of escaping?"

"Ye'd be alive."

"Big deal." There was a long silence, then he looked over at the open cell door. "Close the door, Tinkerbell."

"Ye'll hang."

"Then I'll hang."

There was another long silence, then the door squealed as it slowly closed, and the lock clanked shut. Dylan curled up in the dirty straw to sleep.

The next morning, the ache in his bones at dawn told him how spoiled he'd become lately, sleeping in Ramsay's guest room. He sat up to stretch, and hoped he would be fed soon, though he knew whatever they gave him would certainly be less than edible. Gray sunlight made its way through one high, barred window directly above him. The whitewashed stone walls were irregular, as if this building had been nestled in living rock and the first three feet of wall were not man-made. The wall above the rock was stone blocks, neatly mortared.

It was a narrow cell, and down the middle of it ran the pole to which he was shackled. That pole was bolted to the floor at either end, but the iron to which Dylan was chained could slide the length of it. If he wanted, he could go to the door and look out the tiny, barred window in it. He didn't bother, but sat where he was at the far end and waited.

His stomach growled, and the cold continued to stiffen him. It was a nasty winter day outside, and there was no fire to warm himself. "Sinann?"

"Aye?" She was still there, but not showing herself.

"May I have some heat?"

"*Och*. Of course." The rock behind him began to warm, and he huddled to it. He gathered some of the straw from the floor to cover himself, and hugged himself inside his plaid and coat. He was fed once that day, a piece of bread and some dirty water. The bread was a pleasant surprise, for it was better fare than he'd had in the dungeon at Fort William.

Another day dawned, as cold as the last and far more rainy. The rock behind Dylan had cooled during the night, but when Sinann awoke, she heated it again. Dylan curled up against it and waited.

At midmorning, long before time to eat, keys rattled at the door, and Dylan looked up to see it open and admit a tall dragoon officer. The Redcoat ducked through the low door and stood to address Dylan in precise tones. "Good morning. I pray you slept well." It was Bedford.

Dylan peered at him from the corner of his eye, head down, hoping against hope the *Sassunach* wouldn't recognize him. But it was in vain. The Major's jaw dropped and his eyes went wide for a moment before he recovered himself. His voice was low, soft with wonder. "Matheson."

Dylan declined to reply.

The Major regained his poise and said, "Well, then, this is going to be far more enjoyable than I'd anticipated. When they told me an overzealous Landguard had stumbled onto a rebel spy, I had no idea they'd made such a find! This is truly my lucky day." His hand pressed absently to his chest, roughly the spot Dylan had stabbed him in 1714 while escaping the garrison at Fort William. "I take it you've gone over to the *cause* after all."

"Just letting the crime fit the punishment."

"You've come up in the world since leaving the influence of a third-rate laird in an unimportant dale. You were found in possession of an encoded message bearing the seal of the Pretender, James Stuart. We want to know what was said in that letter, and we want to know who sent it."

Dylan blinked as he realized Bedford still didn't recognize him as Ramsay's bodyguard, Mac a'Chlaidheimh. "If it's got James' seal, my money is on him for the sender."

Bedford said with strained patience, "Who gave it to you?"

"My old Aunt Fanny. She's been banging His Majesty since the Treaty of Union, don't you know."

A tiny, puzzled frown crossed Bedford's face, but then he seemed to get that Dylan was joking. His lip curled, and he said, "Perhaps you would remember, I have no compunctions about flogging a prisoner to death. Since you're still an outlaw, whose family has thought you dead for nearly two years, you may be assured I won't hesitate to take the whip to you until you've told me all I wish to know."

The memory of torture in the garrison made Dylan shiver. He thought quickly about turning in Ramsay, but Bedford's relationship with the rich merchant kept him from it. Turning in Ramsay to Bedford would do nothing for his own case. Besides, Dylan was the one with compunctions regarding loyalty to his employer. He'd sworn silence, and wouldn't talk unless there was something at stake more important than his honor. His life, as it stood, just wasn't worth turning in Ramsay, who surely wouldn't be arrested.

He forced a sigh and said, "It would be more time efficient for you if you just took me out to hang me. There's a gallows upstairs, right there handy. Take you five minutes. You wouldn't learn anything, but you already know you won't learn anything from me. We've been here. I'm no different than I was then, so let's move on."

"I don't intend to beg."

"Good. That's about at the top of my list of Things I Don't Care to Watch."

Another tiny frown crossed Bedford's face and Dylan knew he'd scored again. "Very well," said the Major, and he straightened as if the rod up his butt had just been shoved farther in. "I'll arrange for an interrogation room." With that he departed, and the door was locked behind him.

Dylan sighed and laid his face in his arms, crossed on his knees. He whispered to Sinann, "You might have to spring me after all, Tink." Living without Cait would still be preferable to death by flogging.

Later that day, Dylan perked to hear Ramsay's voice in the corridor outside. Hope blossomed, but then died as he grasped what was being said.

"I tell you, 'tis a lie!" The terror in Ramsay's voice was palpable. It seemed he was arguing himself out of a bad spot, and failing. "That cunt is a liar of the first order! She'd say anything to destroy me! I'm telling you, when all is made clear, you will suffer personally for this!" He went ignored, and the unmoved soldier to whom he was speaking opened the cell door and shoved him roughly through it. Then Ramsay was shackled by an ankle to the iron pole just as Dylan was.

The Redcoat left, and Ramsay shouted after him, "You will live to regret this! I'll see to it!" A string of expletives burbled from him, and he kicked the door for good measure.

Once Ramsay was finally silent, Dylan said calmly, "You're in luck. You haven't missed lunch."

Ramsay spun, agog, and his leg iron clanked. "Mac a'Chlaidheimh! You! You buggering sonofabitch! I trusted you, and this is—"

"Oh, shut up!" Dylan was quite finished toadying to this asshole. "Someone betrayed you, but it wasn't me. The Redcoats were waiting for us when Wingham landed. Your pet smuggler is dead, and the ship is captured. They weren't after the letter, I'm sure of it; they were too surprised when they found the thing. Whoever you paid off didn't stay paid, and they thought they were getting a shipment of salable goods. It was Redcoats who arrested me. Your betrayer was probably Bedford, though I know I'm pissing up a rope trying to convince you of that."

"Bedford wouldnae come after me. Also, if they found no salable contraband, and he hasn't connected you to me, and you didn't give him my name concerning the letter, then why was I arrested?"

"How should I know?"

"You lie! You betrayed me!"

"Bite me!" Dylan turned his back.

There was a long, ugly silence, then Ramsay said, "The letter. Do you have it still?"

Dylan turned and threw Ramsay a look as if to ask whether he were nuts. "They searched me as thoroughly as they could without rubber gloves. I don't know what was in that letter, but it's the property of the Crown now."

"You should have died before—"

"They would still have the letter. My dying wouldn't have helped that."

Ramsay threw himself down on the straw against a side wall, in a sulk. "It was instructions for Wingham's ship to rescue King James and the Earl of Mar at Montrose."

The escape of the two ringleaders of the failed rebellion concerned Dylan not at all, beyond that he'd nearly been killed yet again for their lack of planning. Heavy sarcasm crept into his voice and his drawl gained prominence. "Huh. I guess Our Heroes will have to catch another ride, then, 'cause that ol' smuggler ain't a-going noplace. And I think them boys better move with unaccustomed alacrity, else they're liable to be caught." His disgust for the Earl of Mar, stemming from the unnecessary failure at Sheriffmuir, rose in his gut until he could taste it in his mouth.

"I was under the impression you sided with the cause."

"I side with those I care about. The royal succession means nothing to me, and King James VIII can go to hell, Catholic or not. He's a kid, for crying out loud. Twenty-seven years old is not, in my book, old enough to run a country, let alone send men into battle. Men with families—with something more important to lose than just their lives. Let him get a family, then we'll talk about whether he should decide what's best for the country. Meanwhile, some peace would be nice for a change."

There was a silence, then Ramsay said in a low, careful voice, "Strange words, coming from the father of Iain Mór Matheson's only grandson."

A chill skittered up Dylan's spine, and he threw Ramsay a sharp glance.

Ramsay's voice took on a bitter edge that sharpened as he spoke. "I knew it the instant I first saw you and the boy in the same room. The resemblance is so striking, I was shocked I hadn't realized the relationship when I first laid eyes on you. I suppose you've been fucking her the entire time you've been in my house. Not at night, of course, for I've been watching since the first day." His voice took on a definite whining quality. "But I imagine you found ample opportunities during the day for sneaking the pillock into that sow." He hunched inside his dirty, green coat, sullen.

Dylan blinked at the language, but kept shut. Though guilt pried at him for the one night he'd spent with Cait, he brought to mind her bruised face looking horribly like his mother's often had. He sucked on the inside of his lower lip and refused to acknowledge he'd even heard what was said. Staring at the shackle around his leg, he noticed the skin under and around it was turning purple.

Ramsay continued, spit flying from his lips as he spoke, "Aye, ye've been creeping to her room at every opportunity, I imagine. Niggling the cunny behind my back, myself the perfect cuckold. And there you stand on your honor, taking my wages and doing your level best to foist another bastard on me."

A warmth crept into Dylan's cheeks and ears. His jaw clenched, and he pressed his lips together to keep from speaking.

But Ramsay was relentless. "I daresay, though, even you cannae be sure all your bastards are yours. After all, a woman who is a slut with one man will be a slut with all and sundry. I suppose if your friend Seumas were to so much as enter the house, she would surely throw her legs wide for him as quickly as for you. Further, were Alasdair and Keith to sniff the air and come a-running, she would no sooner finish with Seumas than rub her rump against the groin—"

Dylan's temper broke, and he rose to grab Ramsay's shirtfront with both fists and haul him to his feet. He slammed his former employer against the rock wall, then again, and when Ramsay wrestled loose from Dylan's grip, Dylan hauled off and belted him. Ramsay collapsed into the straw.

"*Prick!*" Dylan said through gritted teeth. "I should kill you right here for how you treated her." He grabbed the shirtfront once more, hauled Ramsay to his feet, and shoved him against the wall to hold him there. "You're not a husband. You're *not!*" Ramsay grunted as Dylan slammed him against the wall again. "You're a whoring, battering, coward!" He punctuated each word with a shove. "You don't deserve to look upon her. You don't deserve . . ." His throat tightened, and the words stopped. Mouth open, throat working, all he could do was renew his grip on Ramsay and slam him against the wall again.

But Ramsay, half-stunned, croaked, *"Doxie."*

The world went red. Dylan no longer wanted anything more than he wanted Ramsay dead, and his hands went around the skinny neck. Ramsay's eyes went wide, protruding, as Dylan's fingers closed hard around his throat. The tendons and Adam's apple worked, struggling to admit air, but Dylan's aim was to kill Ramsay, and he clamped down harder in hopes of breaking the larynx.

"Kill him!" yelled Sinann, fluttering about the cell. "Kill the whore-son!"

A gurgling sound let Dylan know he wasn't gripping hard enough, so he adjusted his hold for a better grip. Ramsay writhed and gasped one word at full voice, "Murder!" before Dylan regained hold and silenced him again.

But that was enough to attract the attention of the guard outside the door, who burst in and with the butt of his musket pounded Dylan's back and shoulders. Dylan felt nothing. His grip stayed firm, and his heart lightened to see Ramsay's eyelids begin to droop. Finally, the Redcoat slammed Dylan in the head, and the world went from red straight to black.

"Wake up, lad." Sinann's voice seemed far away. "Wake up! Hurry, for she's coming!"

She? Who? There was no "she," there was only darkness. Time had stretched to infinity, and existence had narrowed to nothing.

"Open yer eyes!"

The pain in his head finally registered in consciousness, and let him know he was still alive. Then he realized he hadn't killed Ramsay, and he groaned, disappointed. He opened his eyes, raised his head, and peered around the dim cell. Ramsay was still there, crouched against the wall and staring at him. Dylan's voice was low and ominous. "Why are you still here? How come they didn't move you to another cell where you would be safe?"

Ramsay said nothing, but shrugged. His wall-eyed gaze followed Dylan as he sat up. Dylan looked away from Ramsay, for the sight turned his stomach. He'd calmed enough to refrain from killing, but not enough to be sanguine about the man's presence. There was a sore lump at the back of Dylan's head, which he probed with the tips of his fingers. He idly wondered when one of these concussions would put him in an irreversible coma, and just then wished this one had.

"Dylan?" It was Cait. He leapt to his feet, swayed a bit, then went toward the door. The chain on his leg stopped him halfway as it came against Ramsay's shackle, which was nearer the door along the iron pole. Dylan turned to grab Ramsay and haul him along, but his cellmate scurried like a crab along the wall toward the door lest Dylan lay hands on him. Dylan shoved Ramsay's shackle along the pole with his foot, and went to the door.

"Cait." The window in the door was only a foot square, and barred with three iron rods half an inch thick. Cait put her face near the bars, and Dylan touched her cheek. Then he leaned down to kiss her, and without a thought she pressed her mouth to his. Ramsay coughed, startling her. She pulled away and looked in at her husband. Dylan whispered, "He knows."

She considered that for only a moment, then reached in to press the back of Dylan's neck and bring him close for another kiss. She opened her mouth to him. He accepted the invitation and groaned for wishing to be on the same side of the bars as she, at the same time heartsick this might be the last time he would touch her.

Then she turned her lips toward his ear and whispered, "We can be married."

He pulled back to look into her face. Was she nuts? "Cait, they're sure to hang me. And even if they don't, nothing has changed."

"Nae." Her voice revealed a reluctance to talk near eavesdroppers, and he was also unwilling to tell her in earshot of Ramsay the details of his chat with Bedford. But she shook her head and insisted, "Nae, it's Connor they will hang." She smiled. "We'll be married."

He kissed her again, and wished it were so.

The visit was short, and Dylan ached for a long time after she'd gone. His heart clenched, and he feared for Cait as the wife of a man who would most certainly hang for treason. He was terrified of what would happen to her and Ciaran after both he and Ramsay were dead.

CHAPTER 14

Ramsay was removed from the cell in the early evening, leaving Dylan alone with Sinann and his own thoughts. Escape looked better and better. He told the faerie he wanted her to open his cell again that night, late, when the streets would be quiet and the guard sleepy.

But when the night was at its darkest and coldest, and Dylan was about to signal Sinann to let him out, the silence was split by loud shouting and gunfire. A clopping of horses erupted outside the window, then with a burst of speed went racing past his cell. Though he hauled himself up on the bulging rock under his window, his shackle prevented him from getting near enough to the bars to look out. The racket outside died, and then there was silence. "What was that?" he muttered.

Sinann, at the window, said, "Someone escaping, it would seem. I dinnae imagine now would be the time for you to bolt."

Dylan slid down the wall to sit in the straw, dejected. "I expect not." The guards would be alert, and angry besides. At this point, an escape attempt would be suicide. Hanging, on the other hand, wasn't any more attractive a death. He curled up beside the rock, which was cooling, and figured he'd make a run for it as soon as the guards were relaxed again.

The next morning, Dylan found the guard on his cell tripled. One

Redcoat stood on either side of the door, and one stood across the way, facing his door. Sinann groaned. "You should have let me take ye from here when there was a chance. Three are far too many for me to confound at once."

Dylan was very quiet. He scratched his itchy new beard. "We'll have to wait, and choose our time. This ain't it."

The waiting was interminable. Day after day, Dylan sat by his warm rock, his muscles stiffening with inactivity and his imagination torturing him with fears for Cait and Ciaran. Weeks passed. The weather warmed some, and his unwashed body developed sores under his belt and at his neck. The food was adequate to keep his stomach from rumbling, but cravings for meat made him ask Sinann for some.

"I cannae give you meat fit for eating, but I can provide a creature. A rabbit, perhaps, or a fowl. Ye'll have to kill it on your own."

He looked around the cell, which contained only dirty straw and a slop bucket. "I could tear it apart with my bare hands and eat it raw, I suppose," he said, then made a hawking noise in his throat. "Or not."

"Here, then." She waved her hand and a small cheese appeared in his lap.

He broke it apart and took a bite. "Thanks, Tink." After so many weeks of bread and dirty water, the cheese tasted wonderful.

Time lost much meaning beyond changes in the weather. As winter relinquished its hold and the sun appeared more often, the stench of Edinburgh sewage was renewed. Though the nights were still cold, Dylan's little cell became stuffy if the sun was out all day. Finally, one morning a Redcoat entered the cell. Dylan stood because he knew it wasn't time to eat. Something was up.

The soldier unlocked the shackle around the iron pole, then attached it to Dylan's free foot. Another, smaller set of irons secured his wrists in front of him, then he was shoved through the door into the corridor, clanking like Jacob Marley.

He figured he was being taken to trial, but instead the guards escorted him up the spiral stairs all the way to the top. There was a large, open room beneath the sloping rafters, equipped at each end with a hearth burning high and bright with fresh pine. In addition to the fires, a generous number of candles stood in candlesticks everywhere. The room was almost unbearably warm. A large oak table occupied the center of the room, surrounded by high-backed chairs, and several side tables stood against walls. It was an impersonal meeting room, public for certain people but far from the higher traffic areas of the courtroom and offices below.

Perched on the edge of the center table was Major Bedford. Near him on the table, Dylan recognized his weapons and his sporran. Next to them were some folded papers.

Dylan stopped just inside the door, and stared as a horrible sense of déjà vu swept over him at sight of the tableau. Memories of Fort William rushed back on him with staggering power. On reflex, he glanced around the room to see where he would be hung for flogging, and was relieved to find no loops or rings anywhere. On reflection, it made sense he wouldn't have been brought here for torture, where the sounds of screaming would drift out over the entire city. Now he wondered why he *had* been brought here.

Bedford said to the guard, "Remove the chains, then leave us. Take a post in the stairwell." The guard obeyed, and closed the door silently behind him.

There was a long silence as the two men stared at each other. Dylan wished to attend to his sore ankle, which itched where the shackle had been tight, but he refused to move. Finally, Bedford said, "You've been a naughty fellow, Matheson."

Dylan declined to reply. Sinann, also, was uncharacteristically quiet. She stood to Dylan's left, staring at Bedford. Something strange was in the air.

Bedford gestured behind Dylan, who turned to find a table in the corner; on it were a ewer, a washbowl, a towel and some clothing. "You may wash, if you like." His nose wrinkled. "I would consider it a blessing."

Still Dylan stood, staring hard at Bedford. "What do you want from me now, you limey bastard? You had Ramsay; if you let him go, it's your own damn fault."

Bedford took a slow, deep breath. "Ramsay is dead."

That shook Dylan to his soles.

Bedford continued, "He was killed trying to escape, on the first of February. There's one less traitor in our midst."

Dylan's mind buzzed with questions, none of which he dared ask. Where was Cait? Were she and Ciaran all right? Were they even still in Edinburgh? He hoped not. With Ramsay dead and his last will and testament read, the only place she could have been safe these past months was with her father. But her father might not have taken her back, with

Ciaran declared illegitimate. He swallowed hard, and his cheeks warmed at the high amusement in Bedford's eyes.

"Your draggletail and her brat have fled to that dreary dale in the north. I venture a guess she is terrified of repercussions on the reading of her husband's will. Far too amusing, since the will is not to be read." He reached for the top document in the pile of papers, and Sinann leapt into the air, swooped in, and landed on the table behind him to see what he had. Bedford glanced inside the folded paper to be sure of what it was, then pushed off the table and took the document to the near hearth.

Sinann's eyes were wide. "It's the will, lad. He's telling the truth." She turned her head and lifted the top fold of the next paper on the stack. "And that isnae all of it."

Bedford said as he strolled, "Having been found guilty of treason, he leaves no property for her to inherit. Also, it seems he's filled his last testament with a great deal of drivel—accusations and such." As Bedford dropped the document on the fire and watched it flame, Dylan figured some of those accusations had been about Bedford himself. "Invective which does no one living any good at all."

Sinann confirmed Dylan's thought. "Aye, ye *Sassunach*, especially yourself." A sense of relief stole over Dylan, as he watched the burning, that the truth of Ciaran's illegitimacy was no longer in writing. Nothing official would be done about it now.

Bedford returned to the table and continued, "You'll be interested to know that before she left, your whore was quite energetic on behalf of her fuck-beggar." Dylan bit the inside of his lip hard as his vision turned red, and he held his fists at his sides. A leer rose to Bedford's face, but Dylan continued to stay his temper. Something strange was about to happen, and letting Bedford bait him would be pointless and stupid. He let the Major continue in contemptuous tones. "In fact, she is the very heroine who surrendered her traitorous husband to the authorities, on the understanding His Majesty would look benignly on your case."

Dylan's pulse picked up. A pinpoint of light appeared at the end of the long, dark tunnel he'd lived in for two years, and he held his breath lest it turn out to be an oncoming train.

Bedford reached for the next page on the stack of papers, and handed it to Dylan, who opened the triple fold. Dylan's jaw dropped at sight of the heavy royal seal at the bottom of the page, decorated with purple ribbon and gold foil. His fingers trembled as he read:

By order of His Majestie, King George

These are to pardon and release from all culpabilitie Dylan Robert Matheson of Glen Ciorram, Scotland, alias Dylan Du MacAclay, for various actis relating to ye late and infamous rebellion and mutinie against His Most Sov'reign Majestie. Insofar as Dylan Robert Matheson hath in all diligence and sinceritie repented before God and ye Crown for his crimes, come to account for his deeds by turning evidence to ye Crown, and further hath removed himself from the wicked influence of all Guard or Company in defiance of ye law, His Majestie is well satisfied of ye prisoner's redemption, on condition Dylan Matheson remain faithful to ye Crown from hence forward.

Given at London ye twenty-sixth day of March, 1716, under the Great Seale of England, Scotland, Wales, and Ireland.

His Majestie, George, King of Great Britain and Ireland, Elector of Hanover

To all whom this may concern.

Dylan read it over twice, then began again. When he came to the end again, he finally spoke. "I'm free?"

"Utterly."

"Why?"

Bedford blinked. "Because His Majesty wishes it."

"How come I'm not dead like Ramsay? That escape attempt stinks of setup. Why not kill me as well?"

Sinann hissed from atop the table, "Be still, ye sumph! He's letting you go!"

The Major's lips pursed in a stifled smile. "Am I to understand you wish to decline the pardon?" Amusement lit Bedford's eyes again as Dylan folded the precious document and pressed it to his side. Bedford said, "You'll want to wash now, for there is one other item I, myself, arranged to be added to your redemption for good measure." Now he handed over the last paper.

It was a land deed with Dylan's name on it. As he read, he realized it referred to the very piece of property confiscated from Alasdair Matheson, Iain Mór's cousin, the day Dylan had arrived in Glen Ciorram in October 1713. Sinann made a high noise that sounded like *eep*, then pressed both hands over her mouth. Before Dylan could ask "why" again, Bedford said, "I want to know where to find you."

There it was. Dylan was free, but not free of Bedford. Though the Major couldn't do anything about the pardon, and two deaths by escape would beget too many questions, he had no intention of letting go of a man who had once nearly killed him.

Dylan raised his chin. *All right, fine.* He looked at the door and considered making a hasty retreat, but then turned to look at the ewer and basin. It wouldn't do to appear afraid.

He turned back to address Bedford. "I think I'll have that wash now." He turned to the basin and carefully set his papers to the side. Then he removed his coat and set it on top of them to keep them safe.

Sinann fluttered wildly about. "Go! Get away! Have ye gone completely mad? Get away from this place, before he changes his mind and has ye done away with! *Run!*"

Calmly, as if Bedford weren't there and Sinann weren't going nuts overhead, Dylan unbuckled his belt and unwound his kilt from his body. The filthy wool plaid was also set on the table. Then he unbuttoned his sark, his back to the Major. As casually as he could, he removed the sark, the scars in full view of the Redcoat. He laid the sark on top of the kilt, and began to wash. Methodically, thoroughly, even slowly, with a calm, unhurried motion, he cleaned himself, soothing the reddish spots where his dirty clothing had bound and irritated over the months. Allowing Bedford a leisurely view of his mutilated back, he gave a reminder he, too, had a score to settle.

Dylan wet the towel for a washcloth to clean his privates. Bedford said, "There are proper breeches for you on that table, but you'll find them more binding than what you're accustomed to. Attend to your fartleberries, or you will regret it."

Dylan turned to peer at him. "What-berries?"

Sinann said quickly, "Leavings in your arse." Dylan blinked, amused now.

Bedford said, "As dirty as you people are, I expect they're common where you come from."

A laugh snorted through Dylan's nose. "Where I come from, we don't even have a *word* for them, that's how common they are."

That silenced the Major, and made Sinann renew her urgings that they leave at once. Dylan finished washing. No "fartleberries," since there had been plenty of straw in his cell.

Dripping and covered with goose bumps now, he looked down at the folded breeches and ruffled shirt on the table. No way. He left them there and dressed in his sark and kilt. Though they were dirty, they were his. Then he picked up his pardon and land deed, and turned to face Bedford.

The Major stepped back and away from the table, and Dylan approached it. There he found his sporran, *sgian dubh*, and Brigid. No sword. That didn't surprise him at all, for disarmament of the clans was an ongoing struggle for the government during most of the century. It was a surprise to see even his dirk again. He scabbarded Brigid, put the smaller dirk into his sporran, then folded the documents together once and slipped them in as well. His fingers touched the silk drawstring purse inside, and he was not the least surprised to find it empty. All the cash he'd saved while employed by Ramsay was gone.

The thongs from which his sporran hung having been cut, he drew Brigid and reached under his kilt for the hem of his sark. He cut and tore a thin strip of the linen, then halved it. With Brigid returned to her scabbard, he then tied his sporran to his belt with the two strips.

Then he straightened and looked at the door, and his heart lifted to know he was about to walk out, a free, propertied man. A smile lit his face.

But Bedford said, "Enjoy your freedom while you can, Matheson. Be assured you rebellious Scots will be crushed. You will remain a part of Britain."

Dylan's smile died. "Danny, boy, there is not a living soul on this earth who knows that better than I." That brought a baffled look, and Dylan continued, "However, I also know that, in the final analysis, Scotland will win."

Bedford's mouth became a hard line, and his eyes went cold. "I will die first."

Since Bedford certainly wouldn't live long enough to see the end of the Clearances, when Scotland would finally begin to benefit from peace with England, Dylan gave a hearty, rolling laugh. "Of course, you will." Then he raised a hand in farewell. "Later, dude," he said to his former captor as he waggled his hand with thumb and little finger extended, "It's been real." And he walked out.

In the square at the front of St. Giles, the air of Edinburgh had never smelled fresher, nor the sky seemed brighter, nor colors more vivid. Dylan was barely able to contain a whoop of joy. *Cait!* She would be waiting for him in Ciorram. It was noon and he was hungry, but he hurried up the High Street to get out of Edinburgh as quickly as possible.

"Dinnae turn around," said Sinann, fear in her voice.

Dylan returned to reality and muttered, "What is it?"

"Two men following. It's pistols they're carrying."

"All right." He should have known better than to think Bedford would let him get away easy. "What do they look like?"

"One is wearing an unkempt brown wig and a coat too small for him, and the other is bareheaded."

Dylan ducked down a wynde, then took another turn quickly, and stopped immediately behind the second turn. He drew Brigid. Sinann posted herself to watch, and said, "They're nae stupid. They know where you've gone and have their guns out, and dirks as well. Keep back."

Dylan pressed his back to the building giving him cover, and waited. There was no sound, but he could sense their approach. Then Sinann said, "*Och!*"

A roar of angry men went up from the street, like the cry of Berserkers on the attack. Dylan looked around the corner and saw Seumas, Alasdair, and Keith rushing down on the two would-be attackers, who nearly dropped their guns from surprise. The wigged one tried to swing around and take aim, but was far too slow. Seumas launched a flying tackle, and they went rolling down the slope. Dylan had to step back or be bowled over himself. The bareheaded assailant got off a shot, but it missed entirely as Alasdair and Keith grabbed him, threw him against the building, and pummeled him. Gun and dirk clattered to the ground. In short order, the strangers were beaten unconscious and lay, bloody, in the street. Dylan returned Brigid to her scabbard, unused, and gawked, speechless.

Once Dylan's friends were sure the men in breeches were no longer a threat, Seumas wiped blood from his lower lip and wiped his bloodied knuckles on his kilt, then poked at a cut on one of them.

Then he looked at Dylan and a huge, white smile lit his face. "*A Dhilein!* We were hearing an ugly rumor of a pardon, so the three of us kept a lookout to see whether this outrageous thing might be true. For a certainty, the streets arenae safe to walk, with His Majesty forgiving every felon in Edinburgh for the asking."

Dylan laughed. "Yeah, there oughtta be a law."

With a warm laugh, Seumas threw his arms around Dylan and slapped him hard on the back. Alasdair and Keith threw in their two cents and clapped his shoulders until he staggered. Dylan found himself laughing so hard he could barely stand. It was good to see his friends again.

Then he looked at the two unconscious men who were bleeding onto the street, and said as he sobered, "Let's move along before they wake up." He, Seumas, and Alasdair took off at a brisk walk, but slowed to wait as Keith picked up the dropped pistols, slipped them into his belt, and relieved both men of their leather bags of shot and powder cartridges. Then he followed at a run.

Safely away from the scene, Dylan asked, "Seumas, what do you hear of Cait and Ciaran? Did they make it safely away?"

Seumas nodded. "When we heard of Ramsay's arrest and his death after, I went to the house near Lawnmarket. She'd already gone, and the house was sealed for the inventory of confiscated goods. Ye'll be interested to know that our good friend Felix has disappeared and cannae be found."

Dylan frowned. "You didn't kill him?"

"*Och*, nae. Naught has happened to the lad, to the best of my knowledge. He's but departed from the focus of the attention of the authorities."

Dylan grunted. "That slimy little shit. He's probably off, now, in search of another employer to steal from." The other three Highlanders grunted in agreement and disgust.

Seumas said, "That place you wished me to find remains a secret, I'm sad to tell. Though we scoured Edinburgh, we couldnae find, nor even hear tell of, a place where people might be kept hidden for transport. Could be it's elsewhere. Out in the countryside, somewhere."

"Maybe." Though the stolen people were a concern, they weren't Dylan's immediate worry. He looked toward heading for Glen Ciorram. He turned to address all three men. "Where are you all off to?" The Grassmarket was dense with people, and the four Highlanders went ignored in the noon bustle.

"We go where you go." Seumas was matter-of-fact, as if Dylan should have figured this.

Dylan laughed, but realized Seumas was serious. He said, "I'm going . . . home." Glen Ciorram was home now. He said to the three, who looked to him with expectation he wasn't sure he could fulfill, "There will be trouble when I get there. The Laird won't be pleased I came to Edinburgh.

He'll blame me for Cait turning Ramsay over to the authorities." Dylan shrugged. "And he would be right. It might be a struggle to take Cait from her father."

The men all smiled, and Seumas laughed. He said, "Then let us go free your Cait. A man shouldnae be kept from his son, in any case. 'Tis a just cause." The other two declared their agreement.

"In addition," Seumas continued, "we've naught else to do with ourselves, and may as well go with you as to remain about this filthy and evil place. Then, at least, we'll be out of the Lowlands." He turned to the others and said, "Will we not, lads?"

Alasdair and Keith agreed, and Seumas nodded at Dylan.

Sinann said again, "They're your men, laddie. They trust ye and wish to follow ye. Accept it, for you need them as they need you."

Dylan bit the inside corner of his mouth, then said, "Come. If we make a steady pace, we'll be in the hills before sunset." He headed west out of the city, and the three went with him.

CHAPTER 15

The four spent the night in the Ochil Hills, and fed on oatmeal Alasdair bought in Edinburgh plus a rabbit that Keith shot. By the second day they were in Glen Dochart and spent the night in the hospitality of Keith's parents. The following day the travelers met two more of Rob's former group by the Dochart River, and they joined up for the sake of adventure. Rescuing Dylan's son and the boy's mother from the tyrannical Laird of Glen Ciorram had an appeal that was irresistible to men who otherwise had nothing to do.

On the third day the group didn't make much distance, for the weather was sunny and springlike. That afternoon Dylan called a halt to bathe in Loch Lyon and scrub their clothing.

The others stared at him as if he'd just suggested they all dance a hula, but there were no objections. They all stripped to the skin on the grassy shore and waded ankle-deep into the icy water to scrub their kilts and sarks. Dylan had an urge to swim. It had been years since he'd been swimming, not having been inclined to recreation while an outlaw, and the lochs being very cold even in summer. Now he waded farther out, took some deep breaths, and plunged in. When he broke surface, for a moment he could take only short, gasping breaths. But he soon grew accustomed to the temperature and swam around some, floating on his back, on the surface where the water was a mite less cold. It felt wonderful to float, then dive, moving through the water with a relaxed sense of joy.

The men watched from the shore, agog. Seumas grinned and shouted to him, "Ye'll find yer balls lodged behind yer eyes when ye come out of there, laddie!"

Dylan laughed and continued with his swim. It wasn't long, though, before the chill crept in to make him shiver. He swam to shallow water and took a moment to scrub his skin and scalp with his fingernails, then climbed, dripping, to the shore. Quickly, he rinsed his sark and kilt and laid them out on a rock to dry with the others, then stretched out on the grass to sleep in the sun.

The Highlanders chatted among themselves while lounging in the lazy afternoon. One of the Glen Dochart men had a deck of cards he carried in his sporran, wrapped in an oilcloth, so the few coins between the five of them changed hands, back and forth, all afternoon. A line of wet woolen stockings graced a nearby tree limb, and a boulder rising from the ground was covered with a patchwork of woolen kilts and linen sarks. The grass nearby was littered with leggings, shoes, sporrans, and weapons.

Listening to the idle conversation and occasionally adding to it, Dylan dozed some, feeling entirely clean for the first time since his arrival in Edinburgh. The fresh air and pale, new grass all around him, the light scent of spring flowers in the air, all perked his senses and brought memories of spring and Cait.

Then Sinann settled onto the grass near his head and said, "Do ye recall the tapestry hung in Iain Mór's private chamber?" Dylan grunted softly to acknowledge her. Of course he remembered. A number of years before, when Iain's father had been Laird, she'd placed an enchanted tapestry in that room containing an image of herself, in order to be able to see and hear the goings-on there whenever she wished. Now she said, "The Laird is nae pleased with the turn of events concerning his daughter and Ramsay, and moments ago had a meeting with his brother, Artair." Dylan grunted again. This was no surprise.

Sinann continued, "Also, he knows nothing of yer coming." That made Dylan open his eyes to search the faerie's face. She said, " 'Tis true. Yer Cait has kept to herself the knowledge you dinnae die at the garrison, and so has Robin Innis."

Now Dylan burned with questions, but couldn't ask with the others so near. Thankfully, Sinann couldn't keep anything to herself, and went on. "Robin last knew of your whereabouts before the uprising, and thinks ye must have died fighting for King James. As for Cait, her aim is to protect you. She wishes to keep her father off his guard, lest he send men out to find you and fight ye in an ambush. Iain couldnae kill you in sight of the clan, for there would be trouble after. She knows if you make it to the castle alive, the clan will support you."

Dylan cut her a questioning glance, and she said, "Aye. They will. I must say, because of your influence in the glen, Artair could hardly contain his joy at news of your demise at Fort William. Were he to learn of your approach, he would be ever so eager to lead a band of men against ye. Yer Cait is saving your life again, lad, perhaps at the cost of her father's."

Dylan closed his eyes and sighed, worried for Cait. But at the same time a warmth of pride filled him as he realized how strong a woman she was, and how deeply that strong woman cared for him. More than ever, he wanted her for his wife.

As the day waned, the men dressed, then spent the night by a fire Seumas built for making bannocks. A sense of well-being swelled in Dylan, and he felt he was truly going home.

On the fourth day, as the sun dropped behind mountains touched with spring green, they pushed on past Fort William, not stopping for the night until they were beyond Banavie. Dylan had no love for the area near the garrison, and none of the others could afford an encounter with the Redcoats, all of them being known cohorts of Rob Roy. Well after dark, they accepted hospitality in Glen Affric, at the home of an old couple with five sons and three daughters. They were fed bannocks and honey, a treat that spoke to the generosity of the household. By the fireside, men lounging on the floor, women in chairs, and smaller folk alert in bunks along the peat walls, stories were told throughout the evening.

"So the lot of ye are making your way toward the *Tigh a' Mhadaidh Bhàin?*" On a stool sat the old wife, the pudgiest soul Dylan had seen in Scotland. She gathered her skirts into her lap and held them between her knees, leaning forward excitedly. The wide smile and lilting, easy laugh suggested the source of the old stereotype of the jolly fat person. In this place and time, anyone who was eating well enough to be fat had reason to be jolly.

Dylan nodded as he sucked a last bit of honey from his thumb. He wasn't inclined to elaborate further.

One of the sons, a light-haired teenager, said, "Tell of the white dog, Mother."

She threw him an ever wider smile and said, "There is a story regarding the naming of that place." Dylan sat back against the peat wall behind him, silent, for it would be impolite to let on he'd heard the story before. Most stories told had been heard by most listeners, and the enjoyment came from hearing an old story told in a new way.

This one had certainly changed since he'd heard it last. The woman said, "When I was but a lass, there was a Laird of that castle called Cormac Matheson. . . ." Dylan had originally heard the story as having happened centuries before, and he knew the Laird in the previous generation was named Donnchadh, and the one before called Fearghas. But he kept his mouth shut and listened. ". . . who had an enormous white dog. That dog was so devoted to Cormac, nowhere was there a man who would harm the Laird when the dog was about. The Laird was a good man, who was heartstruck by a faerie to fall in love with a neighbor lass of the MacDonell clan." Dylan threw Sinann a glance, but the faerie shook her head. *Not I.* He attended to the storyteller. "But her father wouldnae let her go to the Mathesons, for the MacDonells have long hated the Mathesons of Ciorram. Cormac was so lost in enchantment, he kidnapped his bride, and forced her to marry him."

Dylan raised his eyebrows at Sinann, who nodded and said, "It's done, but 'tis thought little better than defilement and can get a man hung by the authorities if her father and brothers dinnae kill him first." Dylan nodded his understanding and turned his eyes to the old wife again.

"When the MacDonells came to reclaim their kinswoman, Cormac and his men met them before the castle. Cormac pleaded with the girl's father to keep his young bride, but MacDonell rose up in rage, his face burning red as metal heated in a forge. He shouted to his men to destroy the Mathesons. So they attacked, with swords and pikes and all manner of destruction. The MacDonells laid waste to Ciorram. Every man in the glen of fighting age fell.

"The white hound fought like a hellion, taking many a man with its gigantic maw. But when the battle was over and the Mathesons defeated, Cormac was dead and his white dog lay at his side, its throat cut with a dirk. The MacDonells were victorious and carried off the bride as well as a number of cattle. However, MacDonell never made it home. Nobody knows exactly what happened, but sometime during that night the

MacDonells were attacked by an animal. Every last soul in the camp had his throat torn from him, including Cormac's bride. It was the dog killed the MacDonells. And to this day, you can sometimes see the white hound guarding the gate to the castle, with blood dripping from its mouth. And so the castle has been known since as House of the White Hound."

Dylan had an urge to tell of the time he'd seen the ghost himself, but resisted, for it wasn't a pleasant memory.

Another story request was made, this time by one of the daughters. The old wife sipped her quaiche of ale, took a deep breath, then began a story about a stranger who had come from the sea. "Once there was a young man from Glen Ciorram who had been carried away by selkies." *Seals.* Dylan had heard stories about seals who became people and vice versa, but didn't know much about them. It seemed to him that everyone who went to sea and didn't come back was said to have become a selkie. The woman continued, "That young man was never heard from again, but one day his son came to Ciorram from over the ocean. Braw and bonnie, he was. So tall, every man in the glen was required to look up at him. And his hair so dark and shiny, and his eyes such deep blue, everyone knew for a certainty he was the son of the man who had gone to live with the seals, for, as he said so himself, his hair was the color of his mother's but his eyes were the color of his father's."

A dim bell rang in Dylan's memory, and a creepy feeling stole over him as the storyteller continued. "He had an odd way about him, that one. Any man who tried to fight him, he defeated with uncommon cunning, for he was never where ye expected him to be. His skill with a sword was beyond imagination. He once killed a man by cutting his head off with naught but his finger."

"It was a *sgian dubh*," said Dylan.

The old wife blinked and threw him a haughty look, "Was it indeed? And how would you know?"

Dylan reached into his sark and pulled out his little dirk. "It was this very knife. And I didn't cut off his head, I only cut his throat so he bled to death."

Everyone in the room began to talk, shocked. The woman's eyes narrowed. "Nae, it isnae you. It couldnae be. For, ye see, the English tried to arrest him, shot him in the left leg, they did. But he escaped by turning himself back into a seal, and went to live with his selkie family. A fisherman from Inverness once reported the sighting of him. A long, dark seal, he was, with a mark on his tail where the English musket ball had wounded him."

Dylan shook his head and began to untie the straps of his left legging. "He was shot in the leg, arrested by the English, taken to Fort William, and escaped from there. Then he went to work for Rob Roy MacGregor until the recent uprising. Now he's returned, on his way to marry the bride promised to him by Iain Mór of *Tigh a' Mhadaidh Bhàin*. His name is Dylan Matheson, and I am himself." Dylan removed the legging, shoved down the wool stocking covering his calf, and turned his leg out to show the white scar from the musket ball. The entire family and all his men gathered for a look.

Seumas nodded. "Aye. I've fought him, and it's true he is never where ye expect him to be." Alasdair and Keith laughed and nodded.

The family fell silent, in awe; the woman said only, "*Och.*" Dylan was certain he'd made a mistake in speaking out, but the chatter started up again and he was urged to tell a story about working for Rob Roy. So, relieved, he restored his stocking and legging, and told of how he'd escaped the dungeon in Fort William, leaving out the part about Sinann helping him get over the wall by flying. He figured some later storyteller, the old wife herself, perhaps, would invent that part anyway. He told of how Rob had found him, half dead, by the River Nevis, of kidnapping Connor Ramsay, and of the time Rob had provided a widow her rent money then promptly stolen it back from the rent collectors.

The stories lasted well into the night, and it was an exhausted group that finally curled up on bunks and in clusters on the floor by the fire.

Next morning, Dylan wasn't surprised when the fair-haired teenage son announced his decision to accompany Dylan's group to Ciorram. As the boy had the blessing of his parents, Dylan allowed him to come. It was a lad flushed with pride who donned his sword and dirk to become one of Dylan Dubh's men.

Hence there were seven men who climbed the rocky hill behind the new stone garrison at the mouth of Glen Ciorram in mid-April of 1716, ducking low and circling behind the peak to avoid the gaze of a red-coated sentry. Clusters of bracken hid their descent to the glen, where, below the church, they emerged onto the track that would take them to the castle.

As small and rural as Ciorram was, naturally the travelers hadn't made it very far into the glen before folks noticed the group of heavily armed men, all strangers, walking out in the open all brazen-like. Dylan led the way, intent on the castle, and was not surprised to notice people running from house to house along the glen. Most of them looked familiar, and he struggled to pull names from repressed memory. Many names simply escaped him, it had been so long since he'd allowed himself to think of these people he'd missed. The seamstress Nana Pettigrew, he noticed, was still around, standing and talking to the wife of the house nearest the church. That house must have been recently built, not having been there before, as far as Dylan could remember. He waved to Nana, who only stared.

Farther on along the track, which wended its way between the Matheson tenancies, was a young woman he thought might be Marsaili Matheson's oldest daughter, but it was hard to tell, for this woman was wearing a kerchief and hugging a huge pregnancy. The last time he'd seen the daughter, she'd been too young to marry even in this place where most girls married by eighteen. Marsaili herself had been ill before he left, and Robin Innis had brought him the news of her death at the same time he'd told Dylan of Ciaran's birth. Dylan smiled to remember Robin as he and his men continued on their way toward the castle. Innis was a good man and a good friend. It would be a fine thing to see him again.

People began to cluster and stare. A little boy ran straight toward them, and by the time any of the villagers saw what he was doing, it was too late to head him off before he reached Dylan and his men. The boy skidded to a stop on the grass a few yards from Dylan. He was about eight years old and only vaguely familiar. Dylan stopped and lowered his head to peer at him. "Eóin?"

The boy grinned. "Dylan!" Eóin Matheson, son of Alasdair Matheson, turned to shout across the glen, his voice cracking from excitement. "It's Dylan! Everyone, he's returned! It's Dylan!" Young Eóin was growing tall and healthy. He ran to hug Dylan around the waist; Dylan returned the hug and patted him on the back.

Those who had hung back now lost their shyness and hurried to see. "Dylan?" Everyone within hearing came, and called to those farther on. Faces lit up with joy to see him. Men clapped him on the back. Tormod Matheson, the blacksmith, was there, and as the crowd moved with Dylan toward the castle, even more clansmen came to see. Names came back to Dylan in a flood: Coinneach Matheson, Dùghlas Matheson, Marc Hewitt, Colin Matheson, and the old widow of Myles Wilkie. Myles had been hanged in 1714 for the murder of Seóras Roy Matheson, who had been Marsaili's husband. Nana ran up, her enormous breasts bouncing, and began talking so fast he could hardly understand her.

Eóin's mother ran up, out of breath. "Dylan?" He looked up, and his heart sank a little to see the same heartstruck look in her eyes she'd had before, as she tucked stray ends of chestnut-colored hair into her kerchief. Poor Sarah Matheson suffered from a love spell Sinann had evoked shortly after Dylan's arrival from the future, and he could see she still had an affection for him he couldn't reciprocate.

Politely, he nodded to her. "Sarah."

"You look well." It was plain she'd calmed some during his absence. There had been a time she would have thrown her arms around his neck and wept, but now she refrained though the struggle within her was apparent.

"I am well, thank you." Then Dylan winced and grinned as Ranald shrieked at sight of him and started babbling about seals, leaping up and down, waving his arms. Dylan accepted a hug from the retarded teenager before pressing onward. It was good to be home.

But as he stepped onto the drawbridge to the island on which stood *Tigh a' Mhadaidh Bhàin*, the crowd hung back. The castle of the Ciorram Laird was a crumbling gray relic of a much earlier century, no longer a true military stronghold but still the residence of the local Laird. Dylan took a deep breath as he and his men crossed the drawbridge and approached the gatehouse along the dirt track.

Inside the castle bailey several men, bristling with swords, dirks, and flintlocks, could be seen approaching from the other side. It seemed someone had run to warn Iain, and Dylan gathered that Cait's father was not as thrilled to see him as was the rest of the clan. He halted his men just outside the raised gate.

"Iain Mór!" he shouted.

Nobody spoke. Dylan opened his mouth to repeat the summons, but Robin Innis stepped forward. "He's coming." Dylan nodded to his old friend, wishing they could greet each other, then simply relax, share some ale, and catch up on things. Robin said, low enough not to be heard by the others, "Are ye well?"

Dylan nodded, and resumed waiting.

Soon a large figure pushed through the crowd, which parted in a hurry so as not to be bowled over. Iain Mór wore the silver-hilted sword that had been handed down from his and Dylan's common ancestor, who had received it in the service of King James I of England. Hung in a steel scabbard from a black leather baldric, it glinted in the evening light.

The Laird bellowed, "What is it you want?" His blond hair was wild, and his beard was longer than Dylan remembered, which mitigated the original impression of him as a redneck. Even through the hair Dylan could see the habitual anger in the Laird's blue eyes.

Dylan took Brigid from her scabbard and handed her off to Seumas, then did likewise with his *sgian dubh*. Fully disarmed, he stepped forward. "I have matters of importance to discuss."

"Such as?"

"I've come to marry your daughter."

"I willnae allow it, for she's been hurt enough by you." Iain drew the King's sword. "I willnae allow her to marry the man who betrayed her husband to the *Sassunaich*. It's enough she's been made a widow."

Dylan's jaw clenched. Fed to the teeth, he was through taking this crap. He'd come through hell for Cait, he was the father of her son, and nobody—not Iain Mór, not Major Bedford, not King George himself— was going to give him an argument about marrying her.

He reached out for Brigid, and Seumas set the hilt in his hand. Dylan said to Iain, but at full voice for all to hear, "I will marry Cait. Either you will stand down and talk like a civilized man, or I will order my men to take her by force." In a flurry of singing metal, each of the six men in his company drew a sword, and Keith added a loaded flintlock to the threat. In his belt were two more loaded and primed pistols.

The castle guard drew in reply. Dylan's voice was hard. "I'm done playing games, Iain. Let me in, or I will kill you."

Anger flushed Iain's cheeks. Great, heaving breaths filled his chest, and his knuckles were white around the gleaming hilt of the King's sword. He looked past Dylan at the men, then beyond them to the clansmen beginning to creep forward onto the drawbridge.

Sinann said into Dylan's ear, "Remember they support ye, lad." Dylan was counting on Iain remembering that, for a battle, however small, would only hurt and divide the clan. The land awarded by the Crown was not far from the castle, and to live there in animosity with Iain Mór's successor would be a difficult existence.

Apparently, the Laird did remember how the clan felt about Dylan. His eyes lost their flame and his shoulders their bravado. The tip of his sword lowered, and he returned it to his scabbard. Then he lifted his baldric over his head and let Robin take the weapon.

Dylan handed Brigid back to Seumas and stepped forward to meet Iain, who came halfway, at the very spot where Dylan and Cait had seen the ghost of Cormac Matheson's white dog. Iain said in a voice for only Dylan to hear, "Ye've got balls, lad."

"I won't let you keep her from me any longer. I've come too far." He closed his eyes for a moment at the centuries he'd crossed for her, then opened them. "And I can't let you take my wife and my son from me."

"She's nae your wife."

"She wasn't Ramsay's, either. Not that I give a damn what you think anymore, but this is the deal: I have a pardon from the King and have been awarded Alasdair's confiscated lands. I'm going to marry Cait, and be a father to her son. I'll abide peaceably on my land, swear my allegiance to you, and Cait and I will give you grandsons to make up for the sons you lost as children. If that doesn't suit you, and you think there's anything you can do to stand in my way, I'll be quite happy to take you out by whatever means is at hand."

Anger rose in Iain's eyes. It appeared there would be a fight, and this time Dylan wouldn't let the old man win. He prepared to order his men to attack.

But slowly the flush left the Laird's cheeks, and he took a long, deep breath. Finally, a big grin struggled to his face, and he slapped Dylan's shoulder. Then he shouted, for the benefit of everyone watching, "*Och,* lad, why did ye nae tell me this before? Come in! Come in and take a seat by my fire!"

A collective sigh of relief riffled through the crowd. Dylan's men and the castle guard scabbarded their weapons. Iain threw his arm around Dylan's shoulders, and escorted him through the assemblage of castle residents into the bailey. The crowd parted to let him by, talking excitedly among themselves.

Then, there she was, standing by the giant doors to the Great Hall, the vision he'd conjured so many times, dressed in a simple, pale overdress threaded in blue, no stays to distort her curves or bring pain to the corners of her mouth. Even in the harsh, orange light of sunset, her eyes shone with a joy that lifted his heart. She picked up her skirts and ran to him, and when she threw her arms around his neck, he gathered her to him and lifted her off her feet. They kissed as he set her down, long, hungry, and joyful, and he hugged her so tightly, she squeaked. Then she hugged him in return.

"I knew you would come," she whispered in his ear. "I knew you would come, I knew it." There were tears on her cheek, wetting his face, and he struggled to keep his own tears down. His throat closed, and speech was no more thinkable than letting her loose from his arms. He wanted to hold her forever.

But then Iain's brother Artair came to take her arm. "Come, Caitrionagh. Your father will send Marc for Father Buchanan, and he'll be here tomorrow. For tonight, you must stay in your chamber."

She twisted her arm away from him. "I'll go where I like, Uncle." Dylan held her other hand, but Artair took hold of her arm again.

"Let go, boy," said Dylan.

A hearty slap landed in the middle of Dylan's back, and Iain's voice boomed with forced cheer. "Such an impatient lad! I hope you arenae expecting to sleep with my daughter under my roof with yourselves still unwed. I surely willnae countenance such a thing, even were you to insist." That brought a laugh, for he said it in a pointed tone that made light of Dylan's earlier insistence.

Dylan realized he had to give in on this, just for the night. He sighed, and nodded, then patted Cait's hand and kissed it. "Your father is right. You must go." A smile curled the corners of his mouth, and he leaned in to whisper just to her, in English, for it was Shakespeare, "*Sleep dwell upon thine eyes, peace in thy breast. Would I were sleep and peace, so sweet to rest.*"

She smiled and kissed him, then allowed herself to be led away by Artair to her room in the West Tower, and he with his men to the Great Hall, there to accept the hospitality of the Laird.

It seemed the entire glen gathered at the castle that night. Dylan and his men were urged through the high doors, past and around the high wooden rack where weapons were hung, and into the Great Hall. Memories flooded Dylan's mind, and there was an odd sense of *home* in this place where he'd spent only a few months.

Many torches had been lit, he assumed in response to the news of his approach accompanied by armed men. Tonight even the high rafters could be seen in the flickering orange light. Tables and benches stood all across the stone floor, which was scattered with straw and reeds. The gigantic stone hearth at the east end of the hall boasted a high fire, and women entered from the kitchen, bearing plates of bannocks and cheese, for it was too early in the season for fresh meat and too late for salted. But there was an abundance of ale, and soon several quaiches were making the rounds of the men. Dylan's men sprawled on the benches, hungrily accepting the food. Out in the bailey a piper started up while names and peaceful greetings were exchanged between Dylan's men and Iain's castle guard.

"Where's Malcolm?" Dylan asked Iain. Malcolm Taggart was Iain's cousin and closest advisor—fear-còmhnaidh—and one of the few men in the castle Dylan was able to trust with his life.

A shadow crossed Iain's face, which Dylan found impossible to interpret. "He's alive and in the castle somewhere. Sleeping, more than likely. He's an old man, and no longer as vigorous as he once was."

Dylan hoped Malcolm wasn't ill, but it seemed he must be declining quickly. Two years before, Malcolm had been as hearty and hale as anyone in the glen.

As more people joined the party, Iain's three dogs bounded in from the pastures, shaking off the cold and looking eagerly for supper. Dylan grinned and called out, "Sigurd! Siggy!" One of the collies, the black one with the white underside, looked up and began to tremble. The dog searched the room, but couldn't see Dylan right away, though his nose twitched in its struggle to discern the scent among so many people. He took a step forward, but still couldn't find Dylan in the crowd.

"Yo! Siggy!"

That gave Sigurd the direction he needed to spot Dylan, and he took off toward him at a dead run. Skidding on the stone floor covered with straw, he nearly slammed into Dylan's bench but at the last second leapt up to brace his front feet on Dylan's lap. The dog's tail flailed, whapping everything in its path. He quivered with joy, but when Dylan commanded "*Suidh*," the dog's behind hit the floor with a thud. As much as he wanted to leap onto Dylan's lap and lick his face, Siggy did what he was told.

Dylan laughed out loud, and knelt to scratch behind the dog's ears and let him play kissy-face. Sigurd eagerly slobbered on him, and still wagged his tail furiously, though he kept his seat on the floor as he'd been taught.

Iain said, "I expect ye'll be wanting to take the dog from me as well as my daughter." There was only a slight edge to his voice now.

Artair's voice dripped with sarcasm. "Fitting, as the dog was once Alasdair's, same as the stolen land."

Dylan squeezed his eyes shut for a moment and took a deep breath. It was starting again. Artair saw Dylan as his competition for Iain's successor, and for good reason. Though Artair was Iain's half brother, and by the rules of succession his heir in the absence of a living son or grandson through the male line, Iain had once said he would prefer a grandson of his to one day be Laird. When Dylan had first been betrothed to Cait, Iain had encouraged the clan to regard Dylan as his heir, since Dylan was ostensibly Iain's first cousin and next in succession after Artair. Only Dylan and Sinann knew he was not the son of Iain's uncle Roderick. A direct descendant, yes, but fifteen or twenty generations removed.

Iain said to Artair, "I call it a good thing, lad, that the land is back in the clan. Nobody can bring back Alasdair, but Dylan has returned the land to us."

Dylan stopped playing with Sigurd to read Iain's face, but it was impassive. Might Iain make Dylan his heir after all? Dylan wouldn't have thought so from the reception earlier. But he looked at Artair and saw a young man verging on a tantrum. Artair was prone to bad temper, and had once tried to shoot Dylan through the head. Dylan now touched his finger to the nick that ball had taken from the top of his right ear, and knew he still needed to watch his back.

Dylan took a seat at a table with his men, and ate as he listened to his kinsmen tell of the events of the past two years. After Dylan's arrest, the English had sat hard on the glen, allowing nobody in or out for months. The priest was denied entrance to Glen Ciorram, and attempts to hold gatherings for prayer were dispersed by soldiers. All meetings of any kind were forbidden, and if more than two men were caught talking together at a time, they were questioned, often with beatings.

During the uprising, a number of men were sent to fight. Iain's participation was still more or less covert, and the men available in Ciorram were very few, so those men had fought under authority of MacDonald. Their absence during the rising was questioned by the English soldiers, and the unprotected women had the burden of maintaining the fields as well as their homes under the watchful eyes of soldiers eager to prove mastery of the Scots. Crops were commandeered, as well as horses and cattle. All the mounts from the castle were now property of His Majesty, and only a raid on the MacDonell cattle in the dead of winter had saved the clan from losing several children as well from disease caused by poor nourishment.

Dylan noted the stew he was eating was mostly young greens and onions, food that had grown only within the past few weeks. Usually at this time of year salmon could be brought in, but not if there was nothing to trade. A chunk of something dredged up from the bottom of his bowl told him the clan was eating eels from the loch. He rather enjoyed eel, and savored a bit from his wooden spoon, but knew the rest of the Mathesons considered them inedible. It had certainly been a hard winter in Glen Ciorram.

Aside from the struggle to feed the clan, as Dylan listened to these stories he had an odd sense that something wasn't being said. Something even more horrible had happened during his absence, which nobody would mention. They all talked around it.

Most of the men who had gone to fight hadn't returned. Now Ciorram was filled with widows struggling on their own. Young sons were learning in a hurry to be men. And though many restrictions had been lifted, the English soldiers still walked the glen, on the lookout for slights against King George.

"And ye should all know," Robin advised Dylan and his men, "the dragoons have been at Nana Pettigrew. Ye willnae be wanting to partake yourselves."

Dylan frowned. "Huh? She's sewing for the English?"

That brought a laugh that puzzled him even more. Robin said, "*Och, he's never had anyone but Cait on his mind!*" More laughter, and when it quieted, Robin said, "Surely ye knew Nana was the comfort of the single men in the glen."

Understanding struck. Dylan's eyebrows went up, and he felt like an idiot for not having known that before. Robin went on to explain that nobody was patronizing her as a seamstress anymore, either. Since she was without land, she was now left with no support other than the soldiers. Dylan gathered the consensus was that "comforting" clansmen was a community service, but whoring to the English was traitorous. The men of Glen Ciorram figured if she was so enamored of *na fir-striópachais Sassunach*, then the soldiers were obliged to support her.

Dylan wondered what would have happened to Nana if she'd refused the dragoons, but only said, "I don't expect Cait would want me to go too near Nana's in any case."

Robin joked, "Are ye certain, then, Dylan? With all the available women in Ciorram, are ye dead certain it's Cait ye want? I sensed a bit of hesitance in your greeting earlier."

That brought a laugh, and even Dylan had to chuckle.

Artair said, "I'd say it's nae healthy for a man to be so taken by a woman."

Dylan's eyes narrowed at Artair. He wasn't going to let anyone back him against that particular wall. He sat up and raised his voice for all to hear, "Cait is not just a woman. She's God's gift, made from my side. She's the other half of me, and any man who calls her *just a woman* is slighting her and myself as well, and will answer for it."

Artair snorted. "You think she was made for you only?"

Dylan shook his head, allowing no room for question. "I *know* it. I'm as certain of it as I am certain there's a faerie hovering over your head right now." Sinann giggled. "When God put Cait on this earth, he said to himself, *It'll be not just any woman for Dylan Matheson. She must be the fairest of skin, purest of heart, she must have the voice of an angel and a stubborn streak a mile wide.*" He looked over at Iain and said, "Aye?"

Cait's father nodded and smiled. "Aye, that's my Cait."

Robin said, "But what of Ramsay?"

This was not the time to explain the ugly truth of that nonunion, though Robin was his friend and would most likely be told eventually. Instead Dylan shrugged and said, "Ramsay and Cait weren't married in the Catholic Church. Doesn't count."

All looked toward Iain, whose face was turning red. This was a revelation to the clan. Iain said, "The lad is speaking the truth. Ramsay wouldnae consent to a proper wedding. They were married in the Kirk."

Artair said, "So all this time . . ."

"Further"—Dylan leaned toward Artair and said blandly—"I don't think it healthy for an uncle to be so deeply concerned with his niece's womanhood. Who she marries, and how, and whether she is God's gift or just a woman, is the concern of none but her father and her future husband." He sat back and hoped that would end it.

Artair cut a glance at Iain, crossed his arms, and shut up.

As the evening drew to a close, one by one Dylan's men wrapped themselves in their plaids and curled up before the hearth. It wasn't until the last clansman went home that Dylan was allowed to do the same, and by then the fire was almost out. It was less a sleep and more a passing out when he finally lay down.

Nevertheless, he awoke before dawn. One thing had to be done immediately, and it had to be done while he was completely alone. He looked over at Sinann. *Completely* alone. He didn't awaken the faerie, who had perched on a stool to sleep. Carefully, in utter silence, he made his way out of the Great Hall. Sigurd rose and silently followed.

CHAPTER 16

The old tower wasn't far, by the shortcut through the hills. Dylan had once thought it a long walk to get there, but any more it was nothing to him and the route along the burn that cut through the wooded north hills was a short climb. In the gray dawn the tower was a black shadow in a tiny gap between some hills across from the garrison. Dylan shivered, partly from the cold but also with the intense memories this place held. Sinann had first taught him about faerie craft and the Gaelic language here. Later, he and Cait had conceived Ciaran under the gnarled oak branches that reached inside over the crumbling stone.

He rubbed goose bumps from his arms, and went inside. Sigurd posted himself at the tower entrance and lay down. Dylan approached the stone block situated in the middle, and with all the strength he could muster after a long night of drinking, lifted the edge of that block until it turned up on its side. He looked at the muddy ground beneath in the scant light.

For one heart-stopping moment he thought the coins were gone. Alarmed, he thrust his fingers into the muck. Relief flooded him to find one of the gold guineas he'd left here when he'd known the *Sassunaich* were after him. He dug further, and found all of the five coins, wiped them on the grass to remove the worst of the mud, and put them in his drawstring purse.

Then he reached into his sporran for his last remaining cinnamon jawbreaker and squeezed it from its cellophane wrapper into his mouth. He'd been saving this one, for he knew he would find the wrapper there in November 2000. Gently, with a weird sort of reverence for his dwindling connection to his own past and the world's future, he set the wrapper on the ground before him. Then he went to the other side of the stone and shoved it back into place. The jawbreaker rattled against his teeth and stung his tongue, and as he shoved it around his mouth, he savored it as, possibly, the last refined sugar he would taste in his life. He tied his purse into a tight wad, to keep it from jingling, and put it into his sporran.

On his return to the castle, he found his kinsmen stirring as the day began. The castle kitchen was busy, he could see by the row of dead eels, accompanied by a few chickens hanging from the thatching frame over the animal pens. The chickens' heads had been cut off, and they bled into containers set along the top fencing rail. The blood would be used for pudding. Inside the Great Hall, tables had been stacked with bags of flour, cheeses, jars of God-knew-what, and bowls filled with goopy, white butter.

Screaming giggles approached from outside, and a gaggle of young women burst through the door, chattering and laughing, carrying baskets filled to overflowing with flowers. The women sobered a bit at sight of Dylan, but not much, and continued to gossip to each other about a romance in the glen between two people whose names rang dim bells in Dylan's memory. Marsaili's pregnant daughter was among the gossipers, and he then remembered the girl's name. Ailis. Ailis Matheson. She'd blossomed into a sturdy girl with bright Matheson eyes, but her extreme youth was still evident. After two years, she still couldn't be more than sixteen years old. Possibly as young as fifteen. As she passed, holding a basket filled with tiny, white rosebuds, Dylan indicated her condition and said, "Congratulations."

"Thank you." She blushed and smiled, fiddling with one of the flowers in her basket.

Though he knew who she was, he'd had little occasion to speak to her before, when he'd been a newcomer to the glen and she a child. He didn't know her very well. "Last time I saw you, it would have been hard to imagine you old enough to marry."

She giggled and glanced at her friends, who were listening closely. With a toss of her head, she said, "For a certainty, there wasnae a lass in the glen who dinnae imagine *you* married."

That brought a crescendo of hilarity from the girls and a flush to Dylan's face. Ailis took pity on him and calmed her laughter. Seriously, she said, "Marc and I married nearly a year ago, before he went off to fight."

Dylan blinked. "Marc? Marc . . . Hewitt?" Two years ago, the castle guardsman had been sleeping with a kitchen girl named Seonag. Dylan looked around the Great Hall. "Is . . ." How could he ask about Marc and Seonag without offending Ailis?

Ailis let him off the hook. "Seonag was taken from us the year after you left. It was . . . a sudden illness, in the summer."

That saddened Dylan. "I'm sorry to hear that. She was a sweet girl."

Something flashed behind Ailis's eyes, but it vanished quickly and she only said, "Aye, she was." There it was again, that awkwardness of tiptoeing around an ugly subject. He wanted to ask further questions about Seonag, but Ailis nodded farewell and went on her way with her friends and their flowers.

Breakfast for the castle residents was served amid the wedding preparations, and the parritch was the best Dylan had eaten since leaving this place. He'd become far too accustomed to the *drammach* he'd eaten from his hand while an outlaw living in the countryside. While eating, he glanced around in hopes of spotting Cait, but figured she was sequestered until the ceremony. Searching the clusters of playing children for Ciaran was also fruitless. The boy must be with his mother.

Malcolm appeared in the Great Hall at midmorning, which cheered Dylan. There had been a time when Malcolm was the only soul in Glen Ciorram he trusted. The old man now used a staff for walking, but still moved with a stately dignity, his head up and his back straight, not a tremor to him. He took a seat on the bench next to Dylan and congratulated him on the approaching wedding, then leaned his long, angular frame against the table behind him and propped himself on one elbow, his staff held upright in the other hand. Malcolm said, "Not to darken your day, lad, but I must perform my function as the Laird's *fear-còmhaidh*. There is the matter of the church fee. A dowry will be given, though Cait is a widow, but the fee . . ."

Dylan held up a hand to stop Malcolm, and reached for his sporran. From the silk purse he pulled one of the guineas and wiped a residue of mud from it. "This should cover it."

Malcolm's eyes went wide. "Twice over, I'd say! So you've come with cash as well as land and a love note from the King?"

"*Och*, no.". A sour look crossed Dylan's face as he recalled the dozen or so shillings he'd lost while imprisoned in the Tolbooth. "I had this hidden." He leaned close as if to speak confidentially. "Word of advice, cousin, and I tell you this because you're a trusted friend: never carry cash when you're about to be arrested. Just thought you should know that."

A chuckle burbled up from Malcolm, and he said, "Here, let me do this for ye." He reached into his sporran for his own purse, which had a respectable heft. Dylan's experience with other men's purses told him by bulk and sound there must be a couple of pounds in shillings there. Malcolm counted into Dylan's hand twenty-one silver coins bearing the image of Queen Anne, then slipped Dylan's muddy gold piece into the purse. "Give nine or ten of those to the priest during the ceremony, but nae more, or ye'll be taken for a fool. Half an English pound is exceeding generous at that."

Dylan then realized he had no idea of what he was supposed to do in the ceremony. "During?"

Sinann's voice came from behind him, sleepy and yawning. "No worries, lad. I'll tell you what to do." He threw her a look of gratitude, to which she responded, "*Och*, if I saw so much thankfulness when I saved yer life!" She sat cross-legged on the table behind Malcolm.

Una, Cait's mother, approached with a bundle of white linen in her hands. Dylan and Malcolm stood to greet her. Lady Matheson was one of the most beautiful women in the glen, and though she was getting on in years, she still bore herself with the regal grace she'd passed to her daughter. Now she smiled as she offered the bundle in her hands, which turned out to be a sark. "Dylan, Caitrionagh saved this and has asked me to give it to you."

Dylan reached for the sark, and his mouth fell open before he could catch himself and close it. This was the garment Cait had sewn and embroidered for him the month after they'd met. He'd worn it only on Sundays, and had intended to wear it on their wedding day. "She saved this? All this time?"

Una nodded. "She took it to Edinburgh with her. I told her at the time not to take it, for Connor would never have worn such a sark. She replied that it wasnae for him, but for her true husband. I thought she was being only silly and stubborn, but I've since learned that it was a matter of having more faith than I did. She knew even then that you both would return here and that you would wear it again as her true husband."

Dylan could only thank Una, and stood for a moment, fingering the white-on-white embroidery at the cuffs. When Una took her leave, Dylan said to Malcolm, "She kept this even after she'd been told I was dead."

Malcolm shrugged and smiled. "It takes a great deal of faith to rely that heavily on miracles." He clapped Dylan on the shoulder.

The wedding preparations came together with practiced efficiency, many hands making light work. When Father Buchanan arrived, the ceremony was set for just after noon. Dylan, dressed in the embroidered sark and still without a glimpse of Cait since the day before, was escorted to the church by his six loyal men plus Robin Innis and Marc Hewitt. It was a fine day and the men were in good spirits, joking and laughing aloud as they made their way down the glen toward the church. Exuberance rose in Dylan so that he threw back his head and let go a blood-curdling rebel yell.

His eight companions stopped in their tracks to gawk. He laughed and said, "I guess you all have never heard a rebel yell."

Robin said, "I've never heard a demon scream, either, though I expect that's close to it."

Dylan shrugged. "We picked it up from the Indians in America." He resumed the walk to the church, and the men followed. "It's a war whoop, and works a lot like a Berserker yell. Scares the snot out of the enemy. Then when the Confeder . . . when some men from my part of America went to war, they made the yell their own. Made them Yankees pee in their pa . . . uh, breeches."

Seumas threw back his head in imitation of Dylan, but his yell was more of a hoarse shout.

Dylan shook his head. "No, no. Keep that up, you won't talk for a week. Try it this way first: try singing a note in falsetto." When the men only blinked at him, he said, "Sing like a woman."

The eight all frowned, but Keith tried it. He uttered a clear falsetto note. Dylan said, "Now, take that same sound and make it louder." Keith tried it, and sounded like he was strangling. Dylan corrected, "No, from your gut. Make it come from your gut." He slapped his own belly with both hands.

Keith threw back his head and let go a respectable whoop.

"Now make it longer." Dylan demonstrated by filling his lungs to capacity and throwing back his head for a very long yell that ended in a yip.

Now the other men were doing it. The yells improved, until the group making their way to the church sounded like a band of Indians on the warpath. They whooped like that between bouts of laughter, the rest of the way down the glen.

But as the nine of them crested the rise to the churchyard, the group went silent at sight of a line of mounted dragoons arranged across the track leading from the glen. The men of the wedding party stared, and Dylan wondered what, exactly, had the English Army so interested.

Sinann said, "They're out to arrest the priest."

Dylan narrowed his eyes at the dragoons. He knew Catholicism was illegal, but there had never been much trouble from the garrison before. He threw a questioning glance at the faerie.

She replied, "They willnae disrupt such an important ceremony, but will try to single out Father Buchanan afterward."

He grunted. *They'd better not.*

Though Keith had left his pistols back in the castle and their swords had been left behind, everyone was armed with dirks small and large. Brigid was strapped in place on Dylan's leg. Dylan knew if the soldiers made trouble on this day, there would be a minor uprising, and he would be happy to lead it.

Seumas muttered, staring at the dragoons, whose muskets hung at their sides in holsters attached to leather baldrics, "Wouldnae wish for the rebels to forget for a moment who sits on the throne, would we? God forbid there should be a happy celebration without interference from the English Army."

There was a sullen murmur of agreement.

But the dragoons held their position, so far doing nothing more than glaring at the Scots, and the wedding party returned their attention to the business of marrying off one of their fellows.

Just outside the door to the church vestibule, Dylan was grabbed by the collar by the invisible faerie so he wouldn't go in. He turned and gave Sinann a questioning look, so she provided the answer to his unasked question.

"The entrance to the church is where secular and sacred come together. Marriage is a joining of both the spirits and bodies of a couple." Dylan nodded to indicate he understood and accepted.

The entrance was to the side of the building, because the vestibule was attached to the center rather than the front. Dylan had been inside the church many times before, and thought the unusual layout had something to do with the altar and the entrance both facing east, since the rear of the church was almost flush against the hillside behind it. Inside the sanctuary, over the altar, was a huge, round window of stained glass that during morning Mass filtered the rising sun in rich shades of red, blue, purple, and green.

Father Buchanan stepped from the vestibule to welcome the grooms-men, decked out in white raiment and looking somewhat the worse for wear for his hard ride the night before. His eyes shifted uncomfortably toward the dragoons. Nevertheless, he seemed glad to see Dylan. Though he was now more gray at the temples than when Dylan had last seen him, he was as hale as ever and his voice was filled with the joy of the day. The priest had always struck Dylan as the sort of clergyman with little pretense and strong faith in both God and man—a rarity in the world as Dylan had seen it lately.

Eóin Matheson joined the priest, in the robes of an altar boy and holding a tray bearing a small dish and a vial. He grinned up at Dylan, looking so proud of himself Dylan thought the boy might burst.

It wasn't long before the sound of pipers could be heard approaching from the glen. Dylan looked around the corner of the vestibule, toward the track that led from the glen below, and saw what must have been every member of the clan making their way toward the church. To be sure, nobody within miles would want to miss the wedding of the Laird's only daughter. Three sets of pipes raised lively, throaty music to the sky, but the many chattering voices could still be heard above them. The crowd moved slowly, to allow the oldest and youngest of the clan to keep up. In the midst of a cluster of women, Dylan saw Cait, chattering happily, sometimes laughing, and walking as if she were out for a stroll. Some of the women carried children, and Dylan thought one of them must be Ciaran. The one with the darkest hair, surely. Finally the party reached the bottom of the path leading to the church. At the front of the procession were Cait's parents, Iain and Una.

As Cait crested the slope on the path to the church, he saw she wore a pale blue dress over a white blouse. Her hair was in a kerchief, of course, but the kerchief was adorned with small wildflowers of purple, yellow, and white, among them the tiny white roses Dylan had seen earlier in Ailis's basket. Entwined in the flowers were green sprigs, and Sinann said to Dylan, "Rosemary, it is, for remembrance and loyalty. The roses are for love, eternal and pure." Dylan gave her a look of intense interest, that she should continue, but she shrugged and blustered. "*Och*, the primrose and dog violet are for pleasing color."

Dylan chuckled to himself and gazed on his bride as the clan gathered and arranged themselves around the vestibule, crowding behind Cait and Dylan. When that area was filled, the stragglers had to stand along the sloping trail and among the graves to the side of the church. Iain and Una stood directly behind Dylan and his groomsmen. The bagpipes stilled and the crowd hushed as Cait moved into place to Dylan's left.

The light in Cait's face filled Dylan so his heart swelled and he could hardly breathe. For a moment there were no others, and he and Cait were all that existed. The rosemary threw a rich scent, and to him the entire world smelled fresh and green.

Father Buchanan's voice startled him, bellowing out over the crowd. "We are here to consecrate union between Dylan Robert Matheson and Caitrionagh Sìleas Matheson. Is there any impediment?"

Silence. Dylan smiled.

The priest repeated, "We are here to consecrate union between Dylan Robert Matheson and Caitrionagh Sìleas Matheson. Is there any impediment?"

Dylan's smile faded, and he looked at the priest. Father Buchanan's attention was on the crowd. Still there was silence.

A third time Father Buchanan called, "We are here to consecrate union between Dylan Robert Matheson and Caitrionagh Sìleas Matheson. Is there any impediment?"

How many times was he going to ask this? Dylan opened his mouth to wonder aloud, but Sinann stopped him. "It's customary to say the banns three times. Be glad they dinnae make you do it at three different Masses. As often as this glen sees its priest, it would be June before you could wed her."

Dylan shut his mouth.

Satisfied there was no one living with a prior claim on bride or groom, the priest smiled wide and settled down to business. "Will anyone give dowry for this woman?"

Iain Mór stepped forward and announced for all to hear, "I offer five kine, four sheep, a goat, and my dog Sigurd for the future well-being of my daughter." He turned to receive a small bag of oats from a guardsman behind him. "In addition, enough seed to plant the land of my son-in-law." To symbolize the dowry, he held up the bag for all to see, then passed it to Dylan, who patted it to show he was pleased with it, then passed it to Seumas. Seumas broke out in a wide grin and held it up to the crowd like a trophy.

As Iain stepped back to his wife's side, Cait whispered to Dylan, "For Connor it was cash and political influence. It seems to me you've received the more worthwhile dower."

Dylan smiled and replied in a low voice, "I've more appreciation for the bride. I deserve the better dowry."

That brought a giggle and a blush, but she straightened up when Father Buchanan threw her a look. The priest then said, "Are you both willing to proceed?"

Cait and Dylan each said, "I am."

The next question was "Who gives this woman?"

Iain bellowed, "I do." The priest then directed Dylan to take the hand of his bride.

Dylan reached for Cait's hand, but Sinann said, "Your right. Take her right in your right." He switched hands. Cait's hand was covered with a soft, new glove. It was pale gray in color, and the leather was so thin, each bone of her knuckles was outlined and he could see the tendons on the back of her hand. Joining hands like this, he felt the connection begin. Before, he had merely loved her. Now a bond was beginning to forge that would tie them forever. He couldn't take his eyes from her hand in his.

Father Buchanan prompted, and Dylan repeated, "I, Dylan, take thee, Caitrionagh, to my wedded wife, to have and to hold from this day forth—for better, for worse; for richer, for poorer; in sickness and in health—till death us depart, if Holy Church will it ordain, and thereto I plight thee my troth."

Sinann said, "Now, let go." Dylan didn't want to, but released Cait's hand.

Cait then took his right hand in her right and repeated after the priest, her voice thick with emotion, "I, Caitrionagh, take thee, Dylan, to my wedded husband, to have and to hold from this day forth, for richer, for poorer, in sickness and in health, to be courteous and kind, in bed and at board—till death us depart, if Holy Church will it ordain, and thereto I plight thee my troth." Hearing those words on her lips made his heart soar. In that moment there was only Cait in the world. Nothing else mattered.

Then the priest presented the small silver dish from Eóin's tray, and Dylan was startled back to reality as Sinann prompted, "The ring. Where'd ye put the ring? And the fee. He wants the fee now."

Dylan reached under his sark for his crucifix and lifted it over his head to remove the gold ring he'd been carrying around, hiding it from his various enemies, for nearly two years. He returned the crucifix to his sark and set the ring on the dish, then dug into his sporran for his purse. Ten silver shillings went onto the silver dish, and Father Buchanan nodded, quite pleased. From Eóin the priest took the vial, and sprinkled holy water onto the ring as he said, "Bless this ring in the name of the Father, and of the Son, and of the Holy Ghost, that she who shall wear it may be armed with the strength of heavenly defense, and that it may be profitable unto her eternal salvation." He handed the ring to Dylan.

Sinann said, "Now, listen carefully. Hold it with your thumb and first two fingers only." Dylan obeyed. "Take her left hand in your left. . . ."

Father Buchanan interrupted, unaware of the faerie's presence. "Repeat after me."

Dylan listened, and said after the priest, "With this ring I thee wed and this gold I thee give; and with my body I thee worship; and with all my worldly cattle I thee honor." He cut his glance at Iain as it crossed his mind how meaningless that last vow would have been five minutes before.

Sinann's voice was urgent, and Dylan realized he was too slow. "Place the ring on her thumb and say, *In the name of the Father.*" Dylan obeyed, and she continued, "Now on her first finger, saying . . ."

Dylan got it and said with her, "And of the Son." Without further prompting, he moved the ring to Cait's middle finger and said, "And of the Holy Ghost," and lastly on the third finger, saying, "Amen." There he left it. Then he took a deep breath and smiled at her. Almost over, he figured.

He was wrong. The door to the church was then opened, and he and Cait were swept inside for the nuptial Mass. The two occupied chairs in the front row, amid the dark, close smells of beeswax and incense, damp stone and ancient wood while prayers were said over them. Dylan held Cait's hand as they listened to the priest, and knew all his prayers were being answered that day.

Finally the benediction was done, and Dylan received the passing of
the peace from Father Buchanan, a light kiss on the cheek. Sinann said,
"Now kiss yer wife, lad." For that, Dylan needed no prompting. The kiss
was gentle, but he had to let go when he found himself thinking things
that were inappropriate in church, even for married people.

The congregation began to disperse with a low buzz of chatter. Father
Buchanan hurried from his robes and stole, which were whisked away and
replaced with sark and kilt. Buckled into the secular clothing and surrounded by celebrating clansmen, he then made his way from the church
under the noses of the soldiers across the way. The bagpipes wheezed to
life outside, and the celebration moved from the church and back down
the glen to the castle. In spite of the mounted and heavily armed English
soldiers still positioned outside the church, the celebrants were joyful and
carefree, like children released from school. Father Buchanan wore a wide
smile as he moved among them.

The Great Hall of the castle was decked out in what must have been
every wildflower north of the Highland line. Garlands hung from the rafters, and bouquets graced every table. Amid the spicy, meadowy fragrance,
the thick aroma of meat and bread made Dylan realize how hungry he
was, and now his stomach growled from physical neglect and emotional
abuse. Gracie, the old woman who maintained the family living quarters
in the castle, led castle kitchen workers who brought wooden plates piled
high with chicken and bannocks.

The room was alive with noise and conversation, and the joyful em-
braces of everyone who came near made it difficult for Dylan and Cait to
eat. She didn't seem to mind, and laughed and chattered gaily until Sarah,
Eóin's mother, came to the table with Ciaran on her hip.

Cait cooed as she took the baby on her lap and fed him a piece of
bread from her plate. The boy was wide-eyed at all the excitement, kicking
his feet and laughing at everything he saw. Dylan stared at his son, joyful
that he was now allowed to stare, and had to laugh at the faces Ciaran
made at the new food.

Then, so she could eat, Cait handed the boy off to sit on his father's
lap. Dylan gave Ciaran a piece of chicken to gnaw, but that brought on
a grimace and it was spat out, dribbling onto the baby's chin. Dylan wiped
it away, then tried a bit of honey on the tip of his finger. His son's eyes
went wide. Dylan laughed, and dipped his finger again for Ciaran.

Ailis, passing on the other side of the table, giggled and commented,

"*Och*, Dylan, the wean couldnae look more like ye, were you his own father!"

Dylan's smile faded. As Ailis went on her way, never realizing what she'd said, the pain in Cait's eyes tore him in half. Quickly, he kissed her. "It's all right." A fresh smile struggled to his face. "It's going to be all right. You and I know who his father is. We're together. Nobody can keep us apart anymore. That's what matters. Everything else is . . ." He didn't know the Gaelic for what he wanted to say, and wasn't sure Cait would understand "technical" in English, so he said, ". . . everything else is just papers."

That brought a smile, and she kissed him.

The festivities moved from eating and drinking to dancing, singing, and drinking. Tables and benches were moved aside to make room for dancers. All through the afternoon bawdy songs were sung and naughty toasts made to the newlywed couple and their approaching wedding night. Ciaran was spirited away by Sarah early on, to sleep, and the other children fell out as they tired and became cranky enough to be tucked away in the servants' quarters or in the kitchen. The party continued without the wee ones, the suggestive songs now accompanied by suggestive behavior. Some couples chose dark corners to neck and tickle, and others chose secluded ones for more intense activity.

Dylan was quite shocked to see old Gracie coming from the tower corridor and appearing well-laid, pushing stray locks into her kerchief and smiling as if she'd just swallowed a canary.

Malcolm? Dylan looked around and found Malcolm among the men singing along with the bagpipes. But Tormod then came from the tower corridor, with such an air of forced nonchalance it was clear what had happened. Dylan had to smile. Gracie and Tormod. Good for them. He grinned and took Gracie to spin her across the floor a couple of times to the music, and when he let her go, she staggered from laughing too hard. He dove to steady her when he thought she might fall.

There was no telling how late it was when Robin and some others gathered the newlyweds to take them upstairs. Into the West Tower they went, a relatively small party, given the narrow corridors of the castle and the numbers of clansmen having passed out drunk. Outside Cait's chamber was the sentry's bunk Dylan had once slept on as Cait's bodyguard, and he smiled at the surge of memories. Many nights he'd lain on that narrow bunk, wishing for this day. Even after Cait declared herself to him, there was no going through this door, and evenings were spent in the alcove, reading to each other from his book of poetry. Now he made the party come to a halt before the door.

"Whoa! Whoa! Wait!" He held out his arms and resisted the push forward, then made a T with his hands in a "time-out" gesture nobody but himself could have understood. "Wait. It's my turn for a tradition. This is the way we do it where I come from." He then picked up Cait and carried her through the open door to the accompaniment of approving chatter. Then they followed him inside.

Dylan set Cait on the large bed inside and turned to shoo out the partyers. "Go! What, you want to watch?" That brought a roar of laughter, but the crowd parted as Gracie came through the door with a large quaiche in her hands and held it out to Cait, who took it and drank deeply. Then Cait gave it to Dylan, who peered at it and sniffed it. It was a milky sort of stuff, pink and loaded with little brown specks, and smelled like spiced wine, with cinnamon and nutmeg. He drank, and found it hearty. Not bad.

Finally the wedding guests seemed willing to go, and Dylan was able to herd them out and bolt the door. Some residual laughter burbled up through him like a surprise belch, but it settled as he turned to gaze at Cait in the candlelight.

His *wife*. The word, the fact of it, and the responsibility it carried, as well as the privilege, astonished him as it all sank in.

Her smile faded, and she said, "Are ye too tired?"

He shook his head slowly, and unbuckled his belt as he crossed to the bed. "Never." The belt and kilt fell to the floor, and he knelt to loosen the straps of his leggings and let them drop likewise, then removed his shoes and stockings as well. She untied the laces on her dress and stood to let it drop, then pulled her linen underdress over her head to stand naked before him, her kerchief having been lost much earlier in the evening. Her golden hair draped over her shoulders, and shone so he couldn't resist touching it.

"*Och,*" she said, and reached down to grasp the tail of his sark and pull it over his head so he would be naked as well. Then she slipped into his arms. Her entire length against his, her skin on his, he felt the wholeness of union symbolized by the ceremony that morning. They kissed. There was no fear someone might burst in to declare them adulterers.

Nobody would object, or even *could* object. He bent to pick her up and lay her down on top of the bed strewn with flower petals of yellow, purple, and white.

He kissed her as he settled onto the bed and into her. Joined with her, he saw the rest of his life lie before him, filled with moments just like this, making love in a real bed with a woman he knew would always be there. He showed her he wasn't nearly too tired for this.

Afterward they lay among the crushed flower petals, drowsy amid the earthy scents and textures of the bed and each other. Dylan moved a stray bit of Cait's hair where it stuck to her lip, and lost himself in the way it glittered in the candlelight.

Cait murmured, drowsy, *"Thou art my life, my love, my heart, the very eyes of me."*

Dylan made a low, pleased sound and smoothed more of the hair around her face. "I know what you did for me. And I know what you risked."

There was a moment of silence, then she said, "You mean, my father?"

He nodded. "When you turned Crown's evidence, you knew there was a chance your father would be implicated in Ramsay's spying."

She nodded.

"He might still be. If Ramsay told Bedford anything before he died . . ."

Cait raised up on one elbow. "He did not. I cannae stand the thought. But even if he did—even were the English to burst into the castle this very night and carry him away for hanging, there would be not one regret for what I did. For they were sure to hang you if I did not use what I had that would save you. My course was clear, for there was but one choice. I couldnae let you die any more than I could kill ye myself with these hands." She held up the palm of one graceful, well-made hand.

He took that hand in his and kissed it. She continued, "Dylan, you are my husband and Ciaran's father. Never will anything be worth your life to me."

His heart swelled. "Neither will anything be worth as much as your life to me." He ran his fingers into her hair, and kissed her.

Just barely had they caught their breath and were brushing the flowers from the bed when wedding guests returned to the door to pound on it. "Go away!" Dylan shouted. That only brought laughter, and the visitors began to sing, loudly and sloppily, about a man on his wedding night giving his bride fair warning that his member might be too big. "But I must do my duty!" cried one of the singers in falsetto as the wife, and another, singing the part of her husband, demurred with, "I'm sure to prove too manly for ye!" On the song went, the reluctant husband ever so concerned about hurting his poor, fragile wife with his *ball mór*, until the last verse, when the man finally did his conjugal duty and was swallowed up, whole, by the wife's *bolg*, never to be seen again.

Dylan dissolved in laughter, and Cait, also giggling, shushed him and put her hand over his mouth lest the revelers be encouraged and never give them peace.

When the partyers went away, the newlyweds slipped under the blankets and between the sheets, for the fire was dying and the candles guttering, and settled into each other's arms. It was time to sleep, and the long day had been exhausting, but as Dylan kissed his wife goodnight, he couldn't bring himself to stop. His own *ball mór* stirred again, and by the time Cait shoved him onto his back to straddle him, he knew it would not be time to sleep for a while yet.

CHAPTER 17

The land Dylan had been awarded lay just behind the peaks to the south of Glen Ciorram. A path rose to it between two steep hills, then behind one of those hills, to a high, narrow glen. Any higher and he'd be in the shielings, land worthless for farming. But the floor of this tiny glen had some good farming which had lain fallow for two years, used during that time only as temporary cattle grazing for *spréidh* reived from the MacDonells. In addition to the glen itself, the property encompassed the entirety of the hills along the south side of it. Though the peaks of those hills were bare rock, the lower slopes on either side of the glen were adequate grazing for sheep, and the south faces were thickly wooded. There would be raw materials for building, and game for Cait's pot.

Also, there was a spring near the top of one of the nearest hills just to the south of the entrance to the glen. It sent a thin but dependable trickle of water that fell over stones and through clusters of bracken to the glen floor, then wandered along to the west before tumbling off down the crevice and away from Glen Ciorram. Just as important as the presence of the water was that Dylan controlled it. He knew from his long talks with Malcolm, in preparation for becoming a farmer two years before, that control of one's water source determined the survival of the livestock, and could sometimes mean the survival of the family.

Dylan walked the length of his little glen, past the dogleg where it jogged southward, to where it narrowed to nothing and disappeared between two hills. Then he strolled back. It wasn't a terribly long walk. After seeing his property, cattle on the flat and the four sheep along the hillside with Sigurd in attendance, Dylan decided to increase his sheep stock as soon as he could, even if it meant selling some cattle. Though it would take another fifty years or so for sheep to become the backbone of the local economy, he was certain he could take advantage of the few things he knew of the future. It sure wouldn't hurt his children and grandchildren to already be herding sheep in fifty years.

"Ye know, this is where Sarah's husband died at the hands of the *Sassunaich.*" Sinann had been quiet and invisible during the walk, but now she spoke up and appeared to him.

"I know." He'd heard the story many times, of how Major Bedford, a Captain in the Dragoons at the time, had evicted Alasdair, Sarah, and their sons for taxes, and killed Alasdair in a pointless struggle over a Bible. He also knew it had been Alasdair's claymore sword Sinann had enchanted to bring Dylan from the future.

God knew where that claymore was now, somewhere on its journey of nearly three centuries and five thousand miles to finally be touched again by a Matheson—himself. This glen had been Dylan's first sight of eighteenth-century Scotland, for the sword had brought him to the dooryard of Alasdair's smoldering house. That house had stood, more or less, where Dylan's would soon be built. "The land is back in the clan, and it's mine now. Alasdair is dead, Sarah is well cared for at the castle, and we're all going to live happily ever after."

"Nae so long as the English rule."

Dylan closed his eyes and sighed. "There's no choice. History can't be changed. You saw that at Sheriffmuir."

Sinann made a disgusted noise and disappeared.

Now that the big wedding was over, the six men Dylan had brought to Ciorram quickly decided their own futures. Seumas, Alasdair, and Keith, along with one of the two other Campbells from Glen Dochart, were hired by the Laird for his castle guard, and to work as drovers when there was need for them. The remaining Campbell made a deal with someone who owned a boat, and began fishing Loch Sgàthan. The sixth fellow, the teenager from Glen Affric, returned home to his family, happy to brag about having helped celebrate the wedding of Dylan Robert Matheson, the mighty legend of Glen Ciorram, to Caitrionagh Matheson, the beautiful daughter of the Laird, Iain Mór.

With the help of several men from the castle and village, Dylan rounded up four white garrons from the half-wild herd that roamed the nearby hills, and began building his house. He cut peats from the bog just south of the loch, loaded them into baskets strapped to the tiny horses, and brought them to the entrance of his glen for drying.

Though material had been contributed by the clan for the interior partitions of Dylan's house, there had been no roof tree given, so on his property Dylan found a tree suitable to support his roof, and chopped it down with a borrowed ax.

"Allow me to stack the walls for ye, lad." Sinann was hovering over Dylan's shoulder, far too close to the arc of the ax for comfort. "As a wedding gift from me."

"No."

"*Och*, it'll take but a moment." She raised her hand and turned to face the drying peats, but Dylan reached up to grab her hand.

"No! If you do that, everyone will wonder how my house got built so fast. And you know the first thing they'll say is, '*Twas the wee folk did it.*"

"And they would be correct." She yanked her hand from his and raised it again.

He grabbed it again. "*No!* I mean that! Leave it alone." She sighed, and he continued, "Now, get back, because I don't want to catch you on the backswing here." She sighed again, and hovered farther away.

Younger, smaller trees were cut and stripped for the roofing, but straw for the thatching had to be obtained from the village. Dylan, though he had cash, was required to sign a promissory note against part of his harvest that year, for cash couldn't be eaten and nobody wanted to be stuck next winter with a piece of silver and no fodder for the cattle. Even at that, there wasn't enough straw to be had, so Dylan cut some bracken from the hillside behind his future house and it, too, was laid out to dry.

On the day they were to do the building of walls and roof, Robin, Seumas, Alasdair, Keith, and Cait came with Dylan from the castle. Cait had Ciaran on her hip, and the boy had grown large enough to be a burden. Dylan took him for the last half of the walk, sitting the boy on his shoulders astride his neck. Ciaran kicked his heels against his father's chest, and gurgled at everything around him. There was a risk of being peed on, but Dylan had been treated worse in his life, his neck was washable, and this was just something that went with having kids.

It was a bright, late April morning and all of them were in a good mood, joking and anticipating a good day's work. Sigurd expertly handled the four sheep, and Cait led the goat, which Dylan had named Ginny.

"An odd name for a goat," Cait commented as they passed the peat bog.

He simply shrugged and replied, "Well, she eats anything. Reminds me of someone I used to know."

When they rounded the last curve in the trail as they entered the glen, Dylan muttered an Anglo-Saxon vulgarism when he saw the house, completely built. They all went around to the front of it, stunned into silence.

The rising sun threw a pink and gold glow across the front. Dylan looked around for Sinann, but couldn't find her, and handed his son off to Cait to examine the construction. He said under his breath, "It better be solid, Tink. This thing comes down on us, you're dead meat."

Sinann's bodiless voice came to him, "Be assured, laddie, it's the sturdiest house in the Highlands." She giggled.

She'd put two windows in the walls, one to the front and one to the rear, simple wooden frames with crossbars, which in bad weather would be covered by wooden shutters stuffed into the gaps in the peat. He approached the door.

Cait said, "I thought we were to build it today."

"I . . ." Oh, boy, he needed a lie real quick. "Um, I did it yesterday. I . . . wanted to surprise you."

"All of it yourself?" She laughed and kissed him, so he thought it might be all right. "It's the hardest-working man in Ciorram I have for a husband."

She hurried to the front door, and he hoped the place was at least empty. "No wedding presents, please, Tink."

"*Och*, as if I would," she answered.

Dylan ducked through the tiny, narrow entrance. Doors in the Highlands were low, so any intruder would be at a disadvantage with his head presented for attack by a defending sword, something he'd been glad for many times during his months with Rob Roy. The house was empty and smelled of earth, like a cave. The ground underfoot was still grassy, so Dylan brought Ginny the goat in to let her graze. As he ran his foot over the green tufts, he had to grin at childhood memories of shag carpet. It wouldn't be long before the floor would be bare dirt like the rest of the houses he'd seen, and they would need to throw down reeds and rushes for covering, but for a while the dead roots would hold the dirt and keep the dust down.

Atop the peaks at either end of the house was placed the roof tree, and saplings had been laid over it and secured to the tops of the low walls, no higher than Dylan's shoulders, with wooden dowels cut from the stripped branches of those trees. Over those supports had been laid peats, like shingles, lashed to the saplings and also secured by dowels. Finally, over that, was the thatching, tied in close bunches and tightly secured in overlapping rows. Dylan gazed at the finished roof of straw and brown ferns, knowing it wasn't strictly waterproof, but also knowing it would keep out the bulk of the weather and hold the heat in. And knowing from experience, even thatching beat having no roof at all.

The house was rectangular, divided into four areas. One quarter of it was byre, sectioned off by a high wall of boards. The animals would enter and leave through the living quarters, so the opening of the byre was at the corner nearest to the front door, making the route to it a straight, quick shot across open floor. The byre door was tied closed with a rope.

The other quarter of the house at the byre end was the bedroom. Its partition was made of straw ropes woven tightly around wooden stakes, like wicker. Windowless, the room was very dark even in the daytime.

The public half of the house, which had the door, windows, and chimney hole, was not divided physically but still would have its functional divisions when furnished. The fire was more or less at the middle of the end wall. To the rear of the room would be Cait's work area, and the area near the door would be what Dylan thought of as the living room, a place for visitors to sit and children to play during bad weather.

Though thatching was too dear to be bought with silver, household goods could be had for cash. Dylan was able to buy from Tormod a small three-legged pot and a larger kettle, and, boldly ignoring the boycott, a mattress from Nana, who stuffed it with straw, bracken, and scraps of wool and flax. Dylan also bought a table, two chairs, a cabinet, and a plow from Owen Brodie, a craftsman who had recently come from Inverness. Some smaller items had been given as wedding presents, including candles, pitch-soaked rush lights and a couple of three-legged iron holders for them, a wooden hook to dangle the kettle, wooden dishes, bowls, and spoons, a kitchen knife, a ceramic jug, horn tumblers, and a few linen sheets.

There was a chimney hole in the ceiling over the shallow fire pit. The kettle hook was hung over the fire, from the roof tree, on a sturdy rope. In other countries and other centuries the hook would be iron and the rope a chain, but here iron was expensive so things were made of metal only when they had to be. Even his plow blade was wooden.

Cait's bed, though just a mite fancy for a peat house, was brought from the castle and placed against the far wall of the bedroom. Dylan and Cait were both happy to have it, for the mattress was stuffed with feathers, far more comfortable than straw, and the solid oak would hold up well enough even under a leaky roof. Ciaran needed a bed of his own, and when the family moved into the new house he slept atop the straw mattress on the floor of the bedroom. Bunks were needed, to have enough room for Ciaran and his future brothers and sisters.

Dylan could have had the bunks made, but decided to save his money and cut down another tree from his own property to saw into boards. Once the tree was found and felled, he hitched up the garrons to haul it to the dooryard of his house and left it there to season.

Meanwhile, his four sheep needed shearing before the weather warmed up too much and ruined their coats. It was simple enough to borrow a pair of shears from Iain Mór, but the operation itself was not the most fun he'd ever had.

"What is this gunk all over them?" Every winter Dylan had seen sheep with this black, goopy stuff all over them, but had no idea what it was for. It stank, too, of tar.

"Tar and butter." Sinann was lounging on the grass nearby as Dylan wrestled with the first sheep. Bright-eyed Siggy stood by with the rest of the herd, watching and panting, looking exactly as if he were laughing. Dylan reached under the ewe to grab the far legs, and flipped her on her side. Then he took the forelegs and hauled her to a sitting position, leaning against him. The animal kicked a little but had been sheared before, so she settled down quickly.

"What on God's earth is it for?" It was nasty stuff, greasy and black, and made a mess of his kilt.

"It's to keep off the nits and bugs, and to protect against the cold."

Dylan peered at her. "Parasites in winter? Only if you keep them inside where it's warm."

"Ye must, or the cold will kill them."

"No, it won't. That's what God gave them wool coats for. Which, incidentally, are less heavy if you keep the sheep warm. Kind of a waste, if you ask me."

"Nobody lets the livestock outside during winter. It's a good way to lose every head."

Dylan regarded the sheep between his knees. "Nah," he said, deep in thought about what he knew of Scotland in the future. "There's a better way, I think."

Sinann laughed. "Listen to the man who is about to shear his first sheep. There is nae better way. A piece of advice, lad; follow tradition if ye dinnae wish to kill yer stock."

The ewe kicked, and Dylan held her still until she settled again. "Tinkerbell, I lived through the final thirty years of the twentieth century. If there is one thing mankind learned during that time, it's that there's *always* a better way." Dylan squeezed the spring-loaded shears a couple of times, grunted, and set to work relieving this ewe of her winter coat.

Of course the greasy, tarry wool had to be cleaned before it could be used, which Cait accomplished by herself for the small amount of wool Dylan cut from only four sheep.

He came in from the pasture one evening, and a stench of ammonia overwhelmed him and made his eyes water. "What on earth is that?" He waved the door back and forth a few times to move some of the air out, then left it open and went to investigate the small, three-legged pot on the fire that seemed to be the source of the smell.

"It's for the cleaning."

His eyes narrowed, and an uneasy feeling crept over him. "Ammonia. Where did you get ammonia?"

"I know naught of *ammonia*, but this here is piss." She stirred the pot.

Dylan groaned. "I didn't need to know that."

"Then why did ye ask?"

He ignored her question as an even more ugly thought struck and he said, "*Whose* piss?"

"The kine. It's easy enough to put the pot beneath when one lets go, and they give more of this than they do milk."

He grunted. That was a little better than the thought of her waiting for him to use the pot so she could collect his urine. "You're boiling it, right?" She nodded. "Good. Boil it good and hard."

She laughed. "I dinnae ken why you've such an insistence on things being boiled."

"Humor me. Give it a hard, rolling boil." He flicked his fingers at it as if to ward off the stench. "And don't use that pot for anything else, or that spoon, either. Keep it aside for just this."

She peered at him as if he were nuts.

"Humor me." He blinked watery eyes. "Please. I'll buy you another pot, and I'll whittle you a spoon. Just don't use that pot for food anymore."

"Aye, I'll humor ye. I dinnae see the harm in it." She went on stirring the pot, and Dylan went back outside so he could breathe without choking.

Once the wool was clean and dried, in the evening Cait set about carding it and Dylan reached over to help her as they sat by the fire. A slap to the hand let him know she didn't want his help.

"What? Let me try."

"You would do women's work? I willnae let you. No husband of mine will be carding wool, nor even let on he knows how." He grunted and sat back in his chair, and she pointed to the door. "Go outside and find one of those tree branches you stacked for the fire. Whittle me a new spoon, like ye promised."

He obliged, and returned to the fire with a well-seasoned piece of pine. He took out his *sgian dubh* and began by cutting the twigs from it and rounding out the wide end. His dirk was still kept sharp, though he'd never gone back to shaving after his last arrest, and he took careful, precise pieces from the wood. As he worked, he thought he might be in a mood to visit the castle to see who was there for gossip and music, but Ciaran was asleep in the other room and waking him probably wouldn't be a good idea. There would be longer days during the summer in which to *céilidh*.

As he whittled, his mind wandered in the comfortable silence. He thought about starting the plowing, a little apprehensive about knowing exactly when to do it. Too early, and a late frost might kill the seed. Too late, and the growing season would be too short. June was approaching fast and . . .

He sat up in his chair. June was approaching in exactly ten days. Today was May 22, his birthday. He sat back and drawled to Cait as he worked, "You should know today is my birthday. I'm thirty-three." Actually, he was older. One of his time hops had taken him six weeks backward in the calendar year, while the first and last had been date-to-date. In real time, he'd been thirty-three for six weeks.

She smiled, but didn't look up from her work. "I cannae believe you're that old. I think ye lie. There are far too many teeth in your head for you to be as old as that."

He chuckled and ran his tongue over his teeth, checking for rough spots. Most of his molars had fillings put in by twentieth-century dentists, and he knew he would never have the luxury of another, so he kept his teeth fanatically clean. He said, "I can't believe I don't know how old you are. Judging by *your* teeth, you should be about twelve." Cait, her father, and her uncle had the sturdiest teeth in the glen. Only Iain was missing any, and he just the one lower incisor, as far as Dylan could tell. That had probably been knocked out in a fight.

Cait giggled. "You're nae likely to learn my age, neither."

Oh, boy, a challenge on this otherwise dull evening. He leaned forward. "Tell me." She shook her head, and he insisted. "Tell me. You can tell me, I'm your husband." He reached out with his foot and nudged her chair.

"Nae. Ye'll blather it all up and down the glen." A huge grin tried to come, all the way back to her ears, but she pursed her lips to hide it. Her hands became very busy, carding wool like a machine.

"*Och!* Like they don't already know! I bet all the old folks down there remember when you were born. Knowing Iain, he probably had a parade that day. More than likely, people were talking about it for years afterward. They said, *Remember the wonderful celebration the Laird had for the birth of his daughter? Why, I can remember it like it was just yesterday, but I know it was . . .*" He spread his hands, gesturing that she should finish the sentence.

She only giggled and worked faster.

"How long ago was it? I bet I could ask around. I bet Gracie would tell me."

"I think Gracie knows to keep shut."

He grunted and returned to his whittling. It annoyed him she wouldn't tell him how old she was. Ailis was only sixteen, but looked and acted as if in her twenties. Deep down where he kept things hard to admit, even to himself, he was concerned Cait might have been that young when they'd met, and his twentieth-century taboo against sex with minors was one he would never overcome. Ailis's condition still troubled him whenever he saw her, though the rest of the clan thought it a blessing.

In fact, there were several things about this place he still wasn't used

to. Looking around his home, he realized he might never be entirely rec-
onciled to living in a thatched house with a dirt floor. Back home, his
apartment had been free of bugs, except for an occasional ant and those
brown beetles that sometimes flew in through an open door. Here, the wee
creatures had easement rights over everything except his bed, his food,
and his person. Winter was the only time there wasn't a daily battle to
hold those small territories.

Back home, a flick of a switch had made his apartment as bright as
day. Here, not even day could do that. The peat house was in constant
dimness in daytime, even with the windows open, and in flickering shadows
at night no matter how many candles stood on plates or how many rush
lights were gripped by holders that looked like alligator clips on tripods.
Using many would be wasteful, so they didn't. The bedroom was the
darkest corner of the house. In a way that was a good thing, because
Ciaran slept in the same room and darkness was the only privacy to be
had. But not being able to see Cait's face while he made love to her took
something from the experience.

These things turned in Dylan's mind as he whittled and brushed shavings into the fire at his feet. When he was younger, he'd never thought
he would grow up to become a farmer living in a house of moss, dirt, and
straw, and if someone had told him so, he would have been horrified at
the prospect. Swordsmanship and martial arts had been his life, his con-
suming interest, and there had never been any question but that he would
own a dojo and teach in it. But now he watched his wife carding wool
he'd shorn himself, and thought of the little boy sleeping in the next room.
He knew he was meant for this. There was nowhere else in the universe
for him to be.

As the rush lights died in their holders and the fire in the hearth fell
to ashes, the room dimmed and cooled. Dylan's whittling had taken on a
crude shape which he could refine tomorrow. He stood to brush stray
shavings from his kilt, and returned his *sgian dubh* to its scabbard. Cait set
aside her wool and rose to straighten up in preparation for bed. Dylan
picked up a candle, took the bucket of water that had sat, warming, by
the fire all evening, and went on into the bedroom while Cait extinguished
guttering candles.

In the bedroom, Dylan set the candle and bucket on a small table, and
unbuckled his kilt. It and his sark he hung on a peg stuck into the peat

wall. He removed his leggings, stockings, and shoes, and set them under the stool. With a piece of linen for a washcloth, he bathed himself from the bucket.

Cait came, hung her clothes on a peg next to Dylan's, and followed suit with the washcloth. She'd always been one to wash daily, so she had been quick to adjust to his habit of washing at night. Dylan watched as he ran wet fingers through his hair, and a shiver took him as Cait's hand ran under her breasts and they rose and fell as she washed. Her skin was dusky in the orange candlelight, and he couldn't resist reaching out to touch her nipple. She smiled and placed her hand in the center of his chest, caressing him down his front, finally to fluff the hairs just below his navel. They'd been married only a month, and he couldn't imagine ever seeing her like this without wanting to make love to her at once.

But, though the cold water and chilly spring air did little more to him than raise goose bumps, it made Cait shiver and her teeth chatter. She reached for her nightdress, shook it out in case something might have crawled into it during the day, pulled it on and set to fastening the hundred or so buttons on it. Dylan murmured, "Don't button all of those just yet." He reached for his nightshirt, shook it out also, and pulled it over his head.

Cait brushed off her feet and climbed into the bed first, for she slept next to the wall, and Dylan blew out the candle before he followed. Under the blankets she burrowed into his arms, and he rubbed her back to warm her. His voice went low and he murmured into her ear, "Tell me what I want to know."

She giggled and nuzzled him. "And if I tell ye?"

"You won't regret it." His voice grew husky, and he reached for the few buttons of her nightdress she'd fastened. His mouth on hers, teasing with his tongue, he opened the linen and drew it back to expose her breasts. Her breathing was heavy now. He held her breast in his hand for a moment, then he scooted down to take it into his mouth.

She ran her fingers into his hair and pressed her lips to his head. He sucked hard, and she moaned, so he lifted his head and took the nipple between his fingers. He wished he could see her, to watch her face and know what this was doing to her. So he could hear her again, he took the nipple between his teeth and teased it with his tongue. He listened as she descended into delirium. He knew she could go on like this all night, but he couldn't take the ache much longer, so he opened her nightgown all the way down, pulled his nightshirt over his head to set it aside in a wad, and rolled onto her, settling his hips between her thighs.

She immediately gave him a shove back over and rolled on top of him. He had to chuckle at that. It seemed she was peculiarly fond of this position, for in over a month that was all she'd allowed. As she settled herself over him, he wrapped his arms tightly around her waist. Her body moving against his was delicious. The excitement in her breaths, her tongue in his mouth, made him know he was the most happily married man on earth. His hips began to move of their own accord, and he let her enjoy him until he couldn't help but surrender. One arm tight around her waist, his heels dug into the mattress, he shoved hard, shuddering, and emptied himself into her until it seemed there was nothing left inside his skin.

Afterward, she lay on his chest, soft and molded to him. He held her to himself, equally spent, a well-satisfied smile at the corners of his mouth. He smoothed her hair and closed his eyes to feel her breaths against his chest.

"I was twenty-two in September." Her voice was thin and wobbly.

Twenty-two. She'd been twenty when they met. He sighed, "Good."

P eats were needed on a continuing basis as fuel for the household fire, so cutting them from the bog was a weekly task. One day, during the last week of May, Dylan was at this job when along came Robin Innis to do the same for the castle. Robin tied his pack garron to a tree, stepped onto a section of bog that would support his weight, and thrust his peat spade into the thick, muddy moss. He threw the slices to the side, where they plopped one on top of another like dead fish. Dylan continued to do the same. The day was cold, but the work warmed him. He dug peats and chatted idly with Robin about being a father and a husband, and how Robin should find a wife. Robin shrugged off the idea, but the flush in his cheeks suggested he might already have a girl in mind. Dylan hoped for Robin's sake it was someone who was available to him, but the reluctance to talk suggested otherwise.

Once the pile of peats was high enough, Dylan began loading them into the baskets strapped to the back of his garron. Muddy water dripped from the baskets and down the white flanks of the shaggy little horse.

Hoofbeats came from down the trail, and Robin and Dylan both turned. The squeak of saddles and the jingle of bits caught their attention, for only the English soldiers had riding horses any more. Dylan stepped from the bog and drew his garron from the trail. Robin did the same.

Five dragoons came single file up the trail, led by Major Bedford on a leggy, black Thoroughbred. This was a new horse for him—young, and obviously very expensive. Dylan's pulse surged at sight of the Redcoat. He gripped his peat spade with white knuckles and looked at the ground in hopes of going unnoticed, but there was no luck.

"Ah, there you are, Matheson!"

Damn. Dylan looked up. Bedford reined in, as did the four men behind him. Dylan said, "You're looking for me?" Robin frowned, for he spoke almost no English and had no idea what was being said.

"I told you I wish to know where I can find you." His horse fidgeted, and he reined the animal in with a slight tug and a squeak of saddle. "I was just on my way to visit you and your fine family. To let you know I have returned."

"Why?"

"Why do I care that you know I'm here?"

"No, why are you stuck in Glen Ciorram again? I'd thought you'd been promoted out of here. What did you screw up to get sent back?"

A sour look crossed Bedford's face, but it was fleeting. Quickly a tight smile replaced it and he said, "His Majesty, in his infinite wisdom, is increasing his military strength north of the Highland line. You clansmen must be made to realize the futility of your cause, and that further unrest will be dealt with harshly."

"So you're on a saber-rattling mission." Dylan knew he should keep his mouth shut, but his mouth wasn't cooperating. It was all he could do not to haul off and take Bedford's head with the peat spade.

"I have reasons to be here. Be certain I have my eye on you, Matheson. You would do well to not give me an excuse to put you in chains again."

There was a long silence while Dylan refrained from saying the things that came to mind. Finally, he said, "Aye. I would, to be sure."

Bedford raised his chin. "Well, then. I'll leave you two to your work." His lip then curled, and he turned his gaze up the trail. "Or perhaps I should drop by for a visit with your lovely wife. I haven't seen that charming woman since she betrayed her last husband." He turned a concerned gaze on Dylan. "You haven't had any trouble with that, have you?" Then he shook his head and sat erect in his saddle. "No, I suppose not.

You certainly know better than to give her any damning information about yourself. A leopard and its spots, you know."

"I'll relay your regards."

"Do that, won't you?" With that, Bedford wheeled his horse to return along the trail. Each dragoon followed suit in turn. Dylan and Robin watched them ride off down the trail.

When the *Sassunaich* were gone, Robin asked what was said, and Dylan gave him the gist of the conversation, leaving out the comments about Cait. Then Dylan said, "The next couple of years are going to be very interesting times."

"Iain Mór willnae like this."

Dylan snorted and went back to work, muttering under his breath in English, "Iain Mór is going to have a hemorrhage."

CHAPTER 18

The weather warmed enough for plowing, and Dylan hitched the four garrons to his plow. The family worked long, exhausting days to accomplish that job, with Cait guiding the garrons, himself guiding the plow, and Ciaran perched atop one of the little horses, pretending to drive them. Then there were more long days to sow the oats and a little barley. The entire glen floor was planted, past the bend and on down to the very tip, leaving only a dooryard the size of a twentieth-century suburban lot for the purpose of keeping his garrons and goat.

At the far corner of the yard, nearest the oat field, he'd begun a small pile of leavings from the livestock, meat bones and other inedible garbage even Ginny wouldn't consume, and slop from the chamber pot. Every few days Dylan brought a cartload of dead leaves from the woods, to throw over the raw excrement. It tended to take the edge off the smell, and was good compost besides. He would have that much more fertilizer at the beginning of next season.

Sinann pleaded with him to let her help with the plowing, but he declined. Bad enough to have whisperings about the house being built so fast, he didn't need more talk. But he realized her ire when he walked out one morning to find the garrons' manes braided together in corn-row-thin plaits. The little horses seemed unhappy about it, stamping and shifting to get away from each other though they were quite stuck together. Dylan pulled out his *sgian dubh* to cut the manes, making a short, neat job of it lest Sinann try this stunt again. Cait could probably use the hair to weave rope or stuff pillows, or something, so he set it in a neat pile on the ground.

"I hate you, Sinann!" he said to the air. There was no reply, and he didn't expect one.

Then it started to rain, a soft day. Rainy days couldn't keep him from work, as neither did they stop anyone else in Scotland. Only a deluge could do that, and every farmer in Ciorram prayed there would be no such storm, for too much rain would wash away the seed. Father Buchanan prayed right along with them, and the subject of weather was central to church services at that time of year. Dylan surprised himself, suddenly caring fervently about things he had found boring back when his involvement in the glen extended only to his paying job, protecting Cait from immediate physical harm. Now it was his responsibility to make sure she and their son were fed, clothed, and sheltered, so the weather, over which he had no control, loomed large in his existence. He prayed sincerely every day.

Once the sowing was done, the tree Dylan had cut for boards was ready for sawing. Not owning a saw, and the tree being large, he made a bargain with Tormod to provide equipment and some labor in sawing, in exchange for half the resulting lumber. Tormod brought three sawhorses, a two-man saw, and a couple of one-handed saws to where the tree lay in Dylan's dooryard.

Dylan stood on the log, which they'd stripped of its branches and set on the sawhorses. Tormod crouched beneath, pushing and pulling at the other end of the large saw, and Dylan did the same from his side. It was hard work to rip wood by hand, and keeping the cut straight required intense concentration while hauling the flat steel through a log over two feet thick. The sun was high, the solstice nearly upon them, and both men sweated rivulets into their sarks. Dylan's leggings were left in the house, and both he and Tormod had removed their shoes and stockings not long into the job. They were still only halfway through the first cut when Tormod called for a breather.

Dylan nodded, and left the saw where it was. He sat on the log and Tormod crawled from under, then shook sweat from his face so that it flew in droplets. He began braiding the hair at the side of his face, to keep it out of his eyes. By way of conversation, Dylan said, "How come you're not married?" He knew Tormod could support a family. Everyone in the glen had regular need of the services of the blacksmith.

Tormod shrugged. "I've my eye on a woman, but she seems exceptionally uninterested in the likes of me."

Woman? It would be a widow then. "Do you care to tell who she is?"

Tormod glanced at Dylan, looking almost like a shy teenager though he was a few years older than Dylan. "Sarah, Alasdair's widow."

Dylan nearly groaned, for he knew why Tormod wasn't getting the time of day from Sarah. He said, "She's a handsome woman."

Tormod took a deep breath and said, "Aye." He wiped sweat from his face, then unbuckled his kilt and let it fall to the ground. Dylan stood on the log again, then took hold of the saw to continue the job.

A toothache began to blossom in Dylan's lower right jaw. He poked at it with his tongue and found a cavity he'd not noticed before. Damn. If it kept up, he'd have to use some of his aspirins for the pain or it would creep up his jaw and turn into a nightmare headache. He realized, with a cavity like this, he would eventually have to have the tooth extracted, and that would be an adventure in pain. Nowhere near the agony of flogging or battle wounds, but there was something about the idea of asking someone to mutilate him on purpose that made him cringe. He worried the tooth with his tongue as he worked the saw, and tried not to think about allowing someone inside his mouth with a pair of pliers.

Siggy barked from the hillside, and Dylan looked up to see the dog's attention was on the trail from Ciorram. There came a figure in black, a priest. Tall and thin, almost scarecrow-like, he was obviously not Father Buchanan. With a sort of lurching gait, he approached Dylan and Tormod, who paused in their sawing to watch the priest come, and to wipe sweat from their faces with their sleeves. Dylan was about ready to drop his kilt and finish the work in just his sark, for the linen would be much cooler without the enormous piece of wool over it. "Good day," said the priest in English, and smiled up at Dylan.

Tormod said, an edge to his voice because his English was weak and he tended to miss bits of conversations in that language, "Have ye nae Gaelic, Father?"

The smile never faltered as the priest leaned down to address Tormod under the log, "I apologize for having to speak English. I come from Lammermuir and understand not a word of Gaelic. I realize what a disadvantage that is up here, but I hope you will bear with me, and perhaps we might understand each other. I was educated in London, so I should be able to . . ."

Tormod muttered to Dylan in Gaelic, "He can understand any language, so long as it's English."

Dylan snorted so as to not break out in laughter. The priest straightened and said, "I intend to do my best to learn your language." He seemed quite annoyed, whether at Tormod or at Gaelic in general was hard to tell.

Dylan said to him in English, "I speak fluent American, Father, which I believe might be close enough to English as to be serviceable."

A look of relief passed over the priest's face and the crinkle-eyed smile returned. "Ah, yes. You would be Mr. Dylan Matheson, then. The fellow from Virginia."

Dylan nodded, surprised the priest already knew his name. He had a sudden uncomfortable sense that he needed a lawyer present. "And you are . . . ?"

"Father Turnbull. I've come to fill the vacancy left by Father Buchanan."

"Huh?!" Dylan leapt from the log, and at Tormod's request translated into Gaelic what Turnbull had said.

The priest's expression went straight from hail-fellow-well-met to patriarchal concern, as if someone had flipped a switch. "Yes, I'm afraid Father Buchanan has expired. The poor man was ill for a fortnight, and has now gone to God. I've been dispatched to preside over the parish."

"For how long?" It was rude, but it came out anyway. This was bad news all around.

Turnbull's mouth became a straight, lipless line, and he lifted his chin. "Indefinitely."

Dylan clarified for Tormod in Gaelic what Turnbull had said, then took a deep breath. Regardless of his initial impression of Turnbull, the priest was going to be around for a while. Dylan held out his hand and said as sincerely as he could at that moment, "Welcome to Glen Ciorram, Father."

The priest took his hand and appeared relieved. The corners of his eyes crinkled as the corners of his mouth turned up once more. "Thank you, Dylan."

Dylan climbed back onto the log to resume sawing, but hesitated when Father Turnbull continued, "I've heard many stories about you."

"Don't believe all you hear, Father."

A companionable grin crossed the priest's face. "It's not true, then, that you are a seal?"

Dylan laughed. "No. I'm not now, nor have I ever been, a member of the selkie persuasion. I merely carry a sporran of sealskin and my hair happens to be dark."

"Then I suppose the stories about knowing the future are also false."

Dylan's gut clenched, and his mind raced to think of how he might have slipped. "Knowing and guessing are two different things."

The priest nodded. "Yes. You guessed extremely well when you said George of Hanover would be Anne's successor."

Oh, *that*. Dylan breathed easier and said, "It was obvious, and had been obvious since the Act of Settlement. The only way Parliament will allow a Catholic king is for him to take the throne by force, and that's been true since James II was deposed. It didn't take a rocket scient . . . it didn't take great intelligence to figure out that by succession, the next Protestant choice was George."

Turnbull was smiling and nodding through all this, as if he'd known Dylan would say these things. But then, still smiling, he said in a disarming tone that suggested he was merely shooting the breeze, "I spoke with your friend, Seumas Glas, earlier today. He likes you extremely well." Dylan's heart sank, for he knew what was coming. "He boasts of your divining prowess. It seems you knew how the recent uprising would play out, even to which clans would side with James Stuart and when the struggle would end. You also seemed to know when James would arrive in and leave Scotland."

"I had access to privileged information." It was the truth. Never mind that he'd read the information in a history book; at one time it had been privileged.

But Turnbull shrugged off the explanation and his smile died. "Also, you've been known to talk to unseen beings." He raised his chin as if the subject disgusted him. "It can only be imagined what sorts of demons one might find to converse with in thin air." The priest took a deep breath and straightened as if steeling himself. "I think you should know, Dylan, the Church is less and less tolerant of the divining arts these days. Though the Catholic Church is more forgiving of it than the Scottish Kirk, some of us have been shown, by example from the Continent, the error of our ways. While Father Buchanan may have been lax in his vigilance against evil, I truly hope not to find pagan activity in my parish."

Oh, brother. "And, Father, if a faerie were to suddenly reach up and bite you on the ass?" A distinct possibility in Dylan's glen.

That brought a blink. "I . . . there are no faeries."

"If you say so." Dylan nodded to Tormod, and they resumed sawing. Over the noise, he said, "I'll see you in church, Father."

"Indeed you will, my son." With that, Father Turnbull departed.

Dylan muttered in English as the priest left, "Some people would drink sulfuric acid if it came in gin bottles." Tormod stopped sawing and looked from under the log with a puzzled frown, so Dylan explained in Gaelic, "It would seem Father Turnbull is more interested in appearances than in truth."

Tormod said, "*Och,* aye."

With the plowing and sowing accomplished, and the lumber cut for bunk beds, the daily workload became less intense. Dylan and Cait awoke at dawn, and while he stoked the fire and blew gently on its embers to return it to life, she prepared the parritch for breakfast. Once the fire was renewed, he went to the chamber pot in the corner, behind the curtain, to relieve himself.

One thing about this century Dylan had refused to accept was the concept of using the chamber pot with other people watching. In all his time with Rob Roy's outlaws, he'd never been able to bring himself to it, and had always waited for the barracks to empty before using the pot in the corner. Seumas had teased him horribly about never moving his bowels, and joked he soon expected Dylan's eyes to turn brown, but Dylan took the teasing rather than overcome the inhibition.

The castle had private garderobes, but there was no place for a construction like that in a peat house. For a while Dylan had thought about building an outhouse, but realized there was a reason why people here used chamber pots rather than walk outside in the relentless cold and rain. Also, since waste was kept in a pile near the house and used for fertilizer, digging a hole to bury it just wasn't done. Dylan could have rigged an outhouse over a bucket rather than a hole, but the extra work to carry it to the compost heap didn't seem worth the trouble, since there was a much simpler solution.

Dylan hung one of Cait's sheets across the far corner of the living room next to the wooden byre wall, and placed the pot on top of a stool there. Cait chided him about it, but didn't appear seriously upset. Neither did she seem to mind pulling the curtain when she used the pot herself.

While breakfast was on the fire and Cait tended to Ciaran, Dylan went outside to the dooryard to perform his usual workout. These days he was happy to do his form away from curious and ridiculing eyes.

Still without a sword since his last arrest, for a while he had used Brigid or a long stick that stood in for a quarterstaff. In June he finally made himself a real staff, whittled of yew, which Sinann said symbolized longevity. It was mostly straight and of quarterstaff weight, like the machined ones he'd used at the dojo. But it had a thick end which he carved in the shape of a bear's head, a totem associated with the dimly remembered origins of Clan Matheson, symbolizing courage and strength.

Of a morning he would begin his form facing the rising sun. He took deep breaths of cool air as mist drifted across his fields and hovered about the hills. Fresh smells of wet grass and nearby pine and oak forests mingled with musty burning peat from his own hearth, sharpened by a slight whiff of the compost heap out by the edge of the oat field. There was a musky scent of sheep from the new kilt he wore, which his wife had spun and woven for him from the shearing. The two-year-old rag it had replaced now served as Ciaran's bed blanket.

In dyeing the wool, Cait had used the colors of the kilt he'd worn when they'd first met, the *feileadh mór* in the Matheson clan tartan he'd brought from the future. Since the Matheson sett, like all setts, wouldn't be fully established until the next century, Dylan now wondered if he would have an influence on that. All his other kilts had been rust-red or shades of green, but his new one had black, green, and blue threads on a field of blood red, exactly as the Mathesons would wear in the coming centuries.

During these weeks he honed his body, trying to regain the physical tone and reflexes he'd had before his many injuries. He stretched the knotted scars on his back, and the muscles the *Sassunach* whip had cut, and toned the flesh outraged by surgery. Some mornings the pain of exceeding his limits made him pale enough to cause Cait to ask after him with concern. But he assured her he was all right, then the next morning he would stretch even further, moving through the prescribed exercises with all the strength and intensity he could muster, insisting his body do what it hadn't done in years. Gradually, he felt some improvement in his range of motion, and the pain lessened.

After his workout he washed up and ate quickly, for even while the crop was growing, there was plenty of work to be done. Peats had to be cut from the nearby bog, then laid out to dry for fuel. The kine, garrons, sheep, and goat needed tending. Calves were born that summer, one of them breech, and Dylan found out what it was like to shove his entire arm inside a cow, up to his shoulder, to pull it out.

Ciaran's bed was built with the new lumber, assembled with wooden pegs Dylan whittled from scrap and pounded into holes he drilled with yet another borrowed tool. He also built a trunk, using nails, hinges, and hasp from a crumbling, old trunk Cait had finagled from the castle.

During the second week in June, a healthy son was born to Ailis and Marc Hewitt. Dylan heard the new mother was very weak afterward, but the entire clan prayed for her health and she was expected to recover. They named the boy Aodán.

At the solstice, when the lower pastures were nearly grazed out, the Matheson stock was herded to the shielings, sparse pastureland high in the mountains at the south shore of Loch Sgàthan. Dylan went with the clan to help organize those who would mind the cattle and sheep during the summer, and to help repair the huts where they would stay. After a few days he returned to the glen with the bulk of the men, to take his turns guarding crops from deer and birds so that his land would be included in the rotation. He hurried, pressing on ahead of the other men. Being only two months married, he was eager to be home with Cait.

He climbed the trail to his land, Sinann fluttering behind him, and when he rounded the corner of his house, found the door ajar. A niggle of alarm fluttered in his belly, and he hurried inside. Neither Cait nor Ciaran was there. A pot was on the fire, filled with boiling cabbage, so he knew he was expected, for Cait hated vegetables and would never cook them except for him. He stepped outside, where his ears perked to hear Cait, and he saw her waving at him from a slope down the glen. Ciaran was on her hip, and she was returning to the house. A smile lit his face as he watched her come.

Sinann popped in and said, "Ye care for her a great deal, lad, I ken."

"Aye." The word was almost a sigh. "You know, Tink, I knew a lot of girls before I came here."

"*Knew* as in your Bible?"

A chuckle rose, and he shrugged one shoulder as he cut a glance sideways. Cait was walking along the foot of the nearest hill now, hefting Ciaran to her other hip. "Well, yeah," Dylan said to Sinann. "And I cared for most of them. But I'd never imagined what it might be like to be with any of them every night. They came, they stayed, then they went home to their own apartments. Each one, I knew, would move on. Or I would move on. It was the way things were. It was expected.

"But Cait's going to be here for the rest of my life, and I can't imagine it otherwise. It's like she's a part of me. When we're asleep, she moves and I adjust, and it's like I'd wanted to roll over, too. When we're apart, it's as if something is missing, like the arm of a chair you expect to be there, but when you try to lean on it, you fall. That night when she made me show her my back . . ." His voice failed for a moment, and when it returned, it was soft. "She's the world, Tink. She's just . . . the world. And I sometimes can't believe my luck she loves me in return."

When she reached him, he saw lines of fatigue at the corners of her mouth. He took Ciaran and kissed them both. "Is something wrong?"

She shook her head. "Naught but missing you."

That made him smile.

In July, there was business to be done with cattle buyers from the south. Dylan surprised the folks of Ciorram by selling two of his kine to the Lowland buyers gathering a herd, then keeping the note of exchange instead of sending it with Seumas to Glasgow. Seumas was to go with the herd to Glasgow along with a cartload of cloth and other surplus goods to barter for goods neither produced in Ciorram nor brought there by itinerant peddlers.

Dylan intended to make a trip himself, to Inverness, and had plans for the money he didn't wish to announce yet to his neighbors. To improve his sheep herd, he wanted to buy some sheep of the type from the Cheviot Hills in the Borderlands far to the south. Also, if he could find one for sale at a good price, he wanted a still for making whiskey. If the oat harvest was adequate, there were plans for the barley Dylan had sown. So Seumas left with the herd and most of the available cash in Ciorram, with the exception of Dylan's note.

In the Great Hall of the castle one Sunday night, Dylan was contemplating his next move in a chess game against Robin Innis when he mentioned to his friend his intention to buy the sheep. Robin replied, "They cannae survive a hard winter, those southern sheep."

Dylan grunted, his eyes on the board. "I don't see why they shouldn't, the way sheep are coddled around here." He moved his knight to threaten Robin's queen, then finally looked up.

"Coddled, ye say?"

"Aye. Many a time over the past couple of years I've wished for a byre to sleep in, rather than snow-covered heather. You'll notice I'm still breathing."

"A man is not a sheep." Robin moved in haste, as Dylan saw it.

"No, he's not. A sheep has a thick wool coat, given to him by God, that would be even thicker if left in the cold, and a man is naked except for borrowed wool." He then saw his endgame, but waited while Robin became more agitated over the sheep discussion. When his knight wobbled and began to move, he grabbed it in a flash and held it until Sinann let go. Then he carefully removed his hand to consider the board some more.

He said—lightly, to keep from his voice his irritation with the invisible faerie—"My aim is to cross the Cheviots with my own sheep, and leave them outdoors during winter besides. I figure eventually my entire herd will be bigger animals and give more wool. And I daresay my house will smell better for it."

Robin made a disgusted noise and shook his head. "Your sheep will be dead."

Dylan ignored that. "Oh, and that tarry stuff . . . I'm not going to use it on my sheep. All it does is make a mess." Dylan made his move that would lead to checkmate.

Robin's face was turning red by now, and attacked Dylan's queen without seeing the danger to his king. "It's nae good. Ye'll lose yer sheep and yer two kine will be wasted as well."

Dylan moved. "No, I won't. Checkmate."

Robin gaped at the chessboard and swore.

Glancing around, Dylan saw Cait was in the midst of a cluster of women by the fire, several of them spinning yarn with spindles and bobbins, flicking them then feeding out the wool with their fingers almost absently as they talked. Children were playing under tables, chasing each other back and forth, and Dylan recognized the squeals of his own son who toddled with them. He leaned down to see, and found Ciaran clutching a bench to steady himself, slapping it with delight every time an older child ran past.

Artair, lounging against a table nearby, remarked, "Young Ramsay is growing like a weed."

Dylan's face warmed, and he sat up to reset the chessboard. "Another game, Robin?"

Before Robin could reply, Artair said, "Aye, Cait's first husband gave her a braw son, he did. You should hope your own sons will be so fine." Dylan hoped the little punk would leave it at that, but no such luck. " 'Tis unlikely, though, I think, for Connor Ramsay was neither traitor nor thief. He wouldnae claim as his own any land which rightfully belonged to a kinswoman, and wouldnae throw his honor away for the sake of a woman who was the wife of another man, nae matter how pretty and influential."

A disgusted sound gurgled from Dylan's throat, though he tried to keep shut. If he responded to Artair's baiting, it would only lead to a fight, which could escalate and force each Matheson in the glen to choose sides. Dylan refused to let this bratty kid cause a rift in the clan. He said to Robin, who was now glaring, red-faced, at Artair, "Want white this time?" Robin nodded, and Dylan turned the oaken board inlaid with ebony. A black rook toppled, and Dylan righted it. "Not that it matters which side you take. I'm still going to win."

Robin chuckled as he considered his first move.

Artair tired of being ignored, and moved to a group of men who were telling hunting stories. Robin made his move, and Dylan muttered, as if musing to himself, "When I go to Inverness, I'm going to adopt Ciaran. Legally."

Robin looked up, startled. "Why?"

Dylan's voice went low. "You and I both know he's no more a Ramsay than he is Robin Hood. I want to change his name to Matheson before he's old enough to know it was ever anything else."

"It still won't . . ."

"I know. Some will still think he's Ramsay's son, and others will know he's mine but not say it. But at least he'll have my name and my property when I die."

"Lawyers are expensive creatures."

Dylan nodded. "I have enough."

"Ye think Artair will shut his mouth then?"

The disgusted noise came again, and Dylan glanced over at Cait's strawberry-blond uncle. "No. I think he's going to keep it up until I have to kill him."

Robin grinned and snorted. "Let me know when you will do it. I wish to see it."

A chuckle rose in Dylan, and he made his first move of the game.

CHAPTER 19

In order to put meat in Cait's pot while waiting for the kine to fatten, Dylan whittled himself a yew bow and some arrows for hunting. He tipped them with metal arrowheads he bought from Tormod with the promise of a rabbit. His skills with a bow were still not the best, but the woods on the south side of his property were thick with game that had gone ignored, save the occasional poacher brave enough to trespass on Crown lands, for nearly three years. Soon he was able to pay his debt to Tormod, and thereafter when he ventured into the woods, he brought home a small animal or bird more often than not.

In the beginning of August he was returning from such a hunt, carrying a dead rabbit by its ears. The body swung and twisted loosely below the neck, which Dylan had snapped neatly after his arrow had not quite killed the animal. He'd hurried to break the neck, for he'd seen people bleed to death and couldn't stomach watching any creature die slowly.

Thirsty, he headed around the hill to where the burn from his spring trickled over a short cliff to pool at the foot of the hill among trees, bracken and reeds. It was a warm, dry day, and a drink would taste good before climbing the slope to his house. At the burn he knelt to drink deeply of the cold water, then picked some watercress from a patch floating near the bank and stuffed his cheek with it to munch.

Sometimes, when Cait would send a bannock stuffed with cheese with him for his lunch, he would come here for some cress to add to the cheese. The prevailing diet of meat and starch wore on him, and it was difficult to talk Cait into cooking green vegetables. She could trade with the castle for them, for the kitchen garden was well planted with cabbages, onions, and greens for the castle workers. But she disdained them as food for poor folks. Trying to convince her they were good for keeping healthy was futile. So during summer he ate a lot of cress and the occasional boiled cabbage when he could talk Cait into it.

He swallowed the mouthful of greens and leaned down to the water for another drink, then picked up the rabbit and headed home up the burn.

Soon he was close enough to his dooryard to hear children's voices. They were just beyond the hill, barely audible over the noise of the waterfall ahead. Probably Eóin and his younger brother, Gregor, who came often to play with Ciaran. But a noise among the bracken at the burn up ahead made him stop cold, alert to what else was at the pool below the fall. Silent, pulse quickening, he moved closer with all the stealth he'd practiced as an outlaw.

But what he saw as he peeked between ferns and trees made him smile. It was Cait, undressing for a bath. He stood as still as the trees around him, and watched her loosen the laces of her dress and step out of it. Then she released her kerchief cap to let her hair tumble over her shoulders, gleaming nearly silver in the sun. When she dropped her linen underdress, he had to take deep, silent breaths. His gaze feasted on her breasts, still round and full though she was no longer nursing. The curve of her behind was softer and sweeter now that she'd gained some weight since leaving Edinburgh, and two dimples perched over her buttocks. Her skin glowed golden in the afternoon sun, and as she bent over to brace herself on a rock while she stepped into the water, he nearly moaned for wanting her.

He set the rabbit, his bow, and his quiver on the ground, and knelt to loosen the straps of his leggings and unbuckle his belt. In a few moments he was as naked as she, and he crept silently toward her. Goose bumps rose at the fresh air on his skin and the thrill of this predatory game. The bank on this side of the pool was mossy, dotted with toadstools and patches of heather, and the slight sounds he made as he closed in were covered by the noise of falling water. The fall threw a mist over the pool, and little droplets, like a halo of tiny diamonds, formed in Cait's hair. He thought she looked like a faerie princess.

She sat in the water at the near edge of the pool, her back to him, humming a tune as she splashed water on herself. Dylan knelt behind her, struggling to keep from laughing out loud. He wondered how long he could stay here like this without her realizing it, but his body was impatient and the ache for her sharpened each moment. With an impish grin on his face, he reached around and tweaked her nipple.

She screamed and spun, and her fist nearly caught him in the mouth. But he grabbed it in one hand and took her around the waist with the other arm to haul her out of the water and onto the bank, into a patch of short, spongy heather, where he lay on top of her and pressed himself to her. She screamed again, but this time it was more of a squeal that turned into a giggle. "*Och!* You frightened the wits out of me!" She slapped his shoulder, but when he kissed her, she opened her mouth wide to him and writhed suggestively beneath him. Then she murmured into his ear, "But I would come here every day to sport with such a handsome wood sprite as yourself."

He chuckled and settled into her. When she tried to roll over on him this time, he resisted and wouldn't let her. He kissed her and muttered, "Uh-uh."

"Please. We must." Her breaths were heavy, and it seemed she could barely talk.

Moving slowly, but not stopping, he said, "Why?"

"I want a daughter."

That made him stop, but only for a moment. Then he continued, very slowly, and said, "Okay." He pressed himself harder, liking very much the thought of another child. Her hips came to meet his.

"But we must change positions, or it will be another son." She spread her knees and could hardly talk for panting, but explained, "Ciaran is a lad because when we made him you were on top. So . . ." She lost her train of thought for a moment and moaned, which made Dylan smile and press harder, but then she continued, "So . . . for a daughter . . . I must be on top."

That made him laugh. When he tried to speak again, he couldn't, and only chuckled some more. Finally, he was able to say, "It doesn't work that way."

"It does."

"Does not." Still moving, he couldn't explain. Even if he were in a mood to talk just then, his brain was too scrambled to recall facts learned in seventh-grade health class. But he made himself speak. "If we're meant to have a daughter, then we will."

"Dylan . . ."

"Shhh." He kissed her lightly on the mouth, then put his mouth near her ear as he held her thigh and pressed into her. He whispered as the last of his mind dissolved, "Let's make a daughter."

She took his earlobe between her teeth and wrapped both legs around his waist.

All summer long, Sunday evenings were spent at the castle more often than not. Dylan found visiting his in-laws more enjoyable than he had suppers with his own parents, so taking his family to visit with Iain, Una, and the rest of the clan turned out to be a pleasant break from daily chores. On discovery that family visits didn't have to be a pain in the ass, Dylan began to rethink his ideas of family. A knot loosened in his gut he hadn't even known was there, and a quiet joy suffused his life that even Artair and Bedford couldn't ruin.

Sundays in the glen were for playing games, listening to music, and talking into the night about cattle prices, the weather, projected crop yield, and the latest political news brought in by peddlers from Inverness.

During the long summer afternoons, boys and men played soccer in the pasture outside the castle gatehouse. Though the leather ball was heavier than the rubber ones Dylan had kicked around in his youth, and the players far rougher than the suburban American kids he'd played with, the games were almost a taste of his past. He distinguished himself enough as a player that the good-humored ribbing about his colonial origins eventually stopped.

Sometimes Dylan and Seumas squared off in the bailey to spar, with staffs or practice swords. Robin and some of the other men joined in, and the boys of the clan watched. Soon Eóin was begging to learn Dylan's Asian moves. The boy had been part of the class Dylan had taught for a few weeks before his first arrest, and already had a toehold on the basics. On Sundays Dylan began teaching Eóin the way he had his classes in Tennessee. Eóin's enthusiasm made Dylan forget he wasn't being paid for this.

It took only a couple of weeks for the men of the clan to join as well. Seumas threw himself into the sessions with as much energy as Eóin, for he began to realize that he, too, could master the art of never being where one's opponent expects. Robin joined in, and Marc was there when his family responsibilities allowed it. Even Tormod and Owen participated some weeks, though they were older and in general less inclined to fight.

Inevitably, Artair began showing up. Hot to prove himself a better fighter than Dylan, he challenged every concept presented to him. If Dylan taught a technique for disarming an opponent, Artair argued until the move was demonstrated on him. Before long, Artair was the student Dylan always called on for demonstration, for he knew he would eventually be forced to do it anyway. Nobody in the glen understood when Dylan began calling Artair "Crash Test," though Artair would surely have brought out his dirk if Dylan had added "Dummy."

As it was, Artair took every opportunity to do his teacher damage. If an elbow found itself in the vicinity of Dylan's face, he was sure to go home with a black eye that night. More than once Dylan limped for a couple of days because of a knee Artair had clobbered accidentally on purpose. Telling the little punk off about it was out of the question, as was banning him from the classes. Dylan wouldn't have it known he couldn't take a little pain, so he let Artair take his shots.

In early September the dirks came out in earnest. Eóin, Robin, Seumas, and Artair were the students that day, and the subject at hand was the roundhouse kick, which, as the name implied, was an attack from the side. Kicks were often tricky in a kilt, but Dylan found they could sometimes be useful just for the surprise factor.

Today he had the students strip to their sarks, which was a more common dress than the *feileadh mór* for battle among Highlanders. The tails of the sarks were about knee-length, except in the case of Eóin, whose sark was a mite long on him. Dylan took the four through the basic steps of the kick, and soon he had a short line of Scots throwing kicks in unison. Then Dylan said, "So how do you defend against this kick?"

Artair spoke up. "Dinnae need to. Nobody in the Kingdom would be fool enough to try it."

Dylan's tongue probed the bad tooth that was aching again. "Okay, let's pretend, then. Just say, for instance, you came upon a fool who tried to assault you with a roundhouse kick. What would you do?"

Eóin opened his mouth to answer, but Artair said, "I'd catch the fool's foot and hold it."

Dylan stifled a grin and said, "You would?"

"Of course, I would. Any idiot . . ."

"All right, Crash, show us."

Artair was only too happy to saunter to the middle of the bailey and bounce on his toes in readiness. "Try it."

Dylan, already in a casual fighting stance, threw a slow right roundhouse kick at Artair, who caught Dylan's foot as he'd said. In that instant, Dylan shifted the angle of his left foot to put Artair at his right, and transformed the roundhouse to a side thrust. Dylan's boot caught Artair in the chest and sent him reeling.

A string of vulgarisms erupted from the young man, and he regained his balance without falling. "That wasnae fair!"

"Tell it to the English." That brought a snicker from the other students, and Artair's face reddened.

"Let me try it again! I'll show ye what I meant!"

Dylan nodded and regained his casual stance. Another slow roundhouse, and this time when Artair grabbed Dylan's foot he twisted it to the right. Surrendering to Artair's energy and diverting it to his own end, Dylan transferred his weight to the foot in Artair's hands, leapt with the left, and clocked him in the jaw in a crescent kick, landing with his left having made a full spin in midair.

"*Och!*" said Artair, holding his jaw as he staggered. The other students laughed, and Dylan grinned. Artair reached into his sark, pulled the *sgian dubh* from under his arm, and came at Dylan with it.

"Whoa!" Dylan reached for Brigid and parried just in time. "Are you crazy? Put that away!" He backed off.

Robin and Seumas shouted at Artair to stop, but Artair wasn't listening. He came at Dylan again and slashed at his face before attacking low. Dylan kept backing, making Artair chase him, for he had no intention of drawing blood. He found himself backing toward the door of the Great Hall.

When Artair saw where Dylan was going, he stood down and walked away. Dylan guessed Artair didn't want Iain to see the fight. He scabbarded Brigid and watched Artair pick up his kilt and head for the West Tower and his sleeping chamber. The other students were silent as they all watched him go.

"Putz," Dylan muttered, and though nobody present knew Yiddish, they all had a pretty good idea of what he meant.

When Father Turnbull next arrived in Ciorram, he came to see Dylan about the fight classes while Dylan was chasing deer from the crops at the north side of Glen Ciorram.

"That sort of thing is against the Third Commandment of the Decalogue."

"In what way?" Dylan threw another rock in the direction a doe had taken, though she was no longer to be seen and probably well on her way to more likely pastures by now. The crop was approaching maturity, tall but still green, and whispering to itself in the summer breeze. He walked along the divisions between tenancies, in search of furry trespassers.

"The Sabbath is a day of rest."

Dylan nodded. "It's a day of prayer and introspection. A time to spend with family and friends." He took an arrow from his quiver and nocked it, against the possibility of finding a rabbit at the young oats, and for one fleeting moment wished to put it through the throat of the harridan behind him. Then he shook his head to clear it and mourned once again the passing of Father Buchanan.

Turnbull persisted. "Your teachings are practice for battle."

Dylan had an opinion of the priest's own teachings, having heard a number of sermons focusing more on obeisance to authority and the letter of the law than on anything truly spiritual. But kept that thought to himself. Instead he said, "It's exercise to keep a healthy body, and when done right is a time of meditation. I, myself, have taken to saying the rosary during my morning exercises." It was true. He'd discovered how to keep count of his Hail Marys and Our Fathers without fingering the beads, relating them to the rhythms of his warm-up exercises. For the sake of variation, because his former Protestant sensibilities demanded he not fall into too rote a habit, he alternated Latin, English, and Gaelic in his recitation. Once finished with the rosary/warm-up, he would then begin the intense weapons/fight exercises. He found the combined disciplines strengthened his concentration.

He told the priest, "I would do those exercises, even if I never expected to fight again as long as I lived." Also true. He'd once dedicated his life to teaching the techniques, knowing that in the relatively nonviolent Tennessee suburbs he would never need them outside the dojo or sport competition.

"I'm appalled," said Turnbull, and at the tone of his voice Dylan had to stop walking and turn. Turnbull's expression was horrified. "The rosary is a sacred thing and should be done with reverence, on one's knees!"

"Father Buchanan never felt that way. He always said prayer shouldn't be set aside for certain moments of the day, but should be done at every opportunity. He never had a prob . . . he never objected to people keeping their beads at hand to say the rosary at any time."

He sighed, a little surprised to be having this argument with anyone, let alone a priest, given his origins as a Methodist. "In any case," he continued, "Sunday evening is the only time the men can come together for something that isn't work. I am going to continue my own workouts, and will teach anyone who wishes to learn." He returned his attention to the job at hand, wishing the priest would give it up. "I don't think you'll be able to make the men quit coming."

"There is excommunication."

Dylan turned again to peer at the priest. The man's mouth was a straight line, turned down at the corners, and his eyes glowered from beneath a lowered brow. It occurred to Dylan he'd never seen Turnbull smile in any convincing manner. Though the priest smiled often, there never seemed anything the least sincere in it. Again Dylan missed Father Buchanan's hearty laugh. "You would excommunicate them? Just because they want to learn how to keep a healthy body?"

Turnbull raised his chin. "It's in defiance of God's law."

"It's counter to your personal interpretation of God's law, you mean."

The priest's eyes closed for a moment and a smug expression turned up the corners of his mouth. "In Exodus 20:8–11, we are given, *Remember that thou keep holy the Sabbath day. Six days shalt thou labor, and shalt do all thy works. But on the seventh day is the Sabbath of the Lord thy God: thou shalt do no work on it, thou nor thy son, nor thy daughter, nor thy manservant, nor thy maidservant, nor thy beast, nor the stranger that is within thy gates.*" Dylan looked at the ground and waited for the priest to finish. "*For in six days the Lord made heaven and earth, and the sea, and all things that are in them, and rested on the seventh day: therefore the Lord blessed the seventh day, and sanctified it.*" Turnbull inclined his head as if he'd just imparted something Dylan didn't already know.

Dylan sighed, and Turnbull's lips pressed even tighter. But Dylan said, "How about if I instruct the men to contemplate God while practicing of a morning? I mean, they probably are anyway, but would it make you feel better if prayer were part of the instruction?"

Turnbull's face was impassive, and Dylan knew the man was disinclined to compromise. But a struggle was going on behind the priest's eyes, so Dylan added, "On Sunday in weeks when you are here for Mass, how about you come give us a prayer?"

That did it. Turnbull didn't like compromise, but also couldn't resist a chance to stick his nose into things. He nodded. "Very well. Instruct the men to meditate on God, and I shall make myself available for a prayer when in Ciorram. Also, I must insist there be no weapons used during these lessons."

Dylan opened his mouth to object, but shut it when he realized further argument would be fruitless and the weapons issue could be skirted. He nodded.

When Turnbull also nodded and bade Dylan good day, as he turned to leave, his collar popped open to flap about his neck like a broken spring. He fixed it as he walked between the tenancies, but then it popped open again.

Dylan waited until the priest was quite gone before muttering, "You couldn't have done that a little sooner, Tink?"

"I was under the impression you nae longer wished my help."

He only grunted and proceeded on his patrol of the oat field.

During the harvest in late September, Dylan noticed a sudden weight gain in Cait, more sudden and more weight than she'd gained after the wedding. At night in bed she was softer pressed against him, and during the day the laces of her dress were far wider at her breasts than before. A private smile curled the corners of his mouth, and stuck there for days. He said nothing, waiting for her to tell him. But October arrived, and there was no murmur about the baby. He began to wonder when she would tell him.

"Cait's pregnant," he said to Sinann as he stacked oat sheaves on a slight rise out back of his house. The harvest had been a good one, which meant he could proceed with his plans for the barley. Sinann was directing the work, teaching him how to stack the sheaves so they wouldn't rot in the rain.

"Indeed, she is," she said in her "duh" voice.

He narrowed his eyes at her for a moment, but then shrugged. "I figured it out a month ago, but she hasn't mentioned it to me yet. I was just wondering if she was ever going to get around to it."

"When her belly is big, she'll tell. Until then, if she loses the bairn, it'll be her burden only and the pain quickly gone. Just as she did in June."

Dylan stopped work and stared. "Excuse me?"

"*Och*, ye dinnae need my pardon. . . ."

"No. Did you just tell me Cait lost a baby in June?"

Sinann nodded. "Ye'll recall she felt poorly for a brief time after ye returned from the shielings. When you saw the rags were in use, she let you think her cycle was the cause of the trouble, for there was nae point in putting you through the grief of knowing 'twas a lost child. For it was but a few weeks along, and even Herself hadnae been certain of it yet."

Dylan was appalled. "No *point* in telling me? You're joking."

She shrugged. "Nae, I'm not."

He turned and headed for the house. Cait had some explaining to do, keeping this from him, and didn't he have a right to . . .

Sinann's voice stopped him. "And if ye're smart, ye'll refrain from mentioning to Herself you know. This one is well past the time she lost the other, and so she's begun to hope. When the child is strong enough to make itself known, growing and a-moving in her, then will be the time for gladness. And even then it's best not to get yer hopes up. Even Ciaran isnae yet old enough for you to count on him living through the winter."

Dylan turned back to Sinann, suddenly at a loss. Powerless. He had to sit down for a moment, and lowered himself onto the ground where he was. His mind spun with horrible realization. Though he'd always known about the mortality rate of children in this century, he'd never brought himself to consider the possibility of losing his own son. And now his unborn child, and even Cait. Now he was forced to understand how little control he had over the well-being of his family. There were no real doctors here. He certainly had brought no more knowledge from the future than the basic concepts of killing germs with hot water and quarantining sick people. Even if things weren't kept from him, there would be nothing he could do about them. He looked up at the faerie. "But I'm her husband. Why . . . ?"

She said, "You're a man. These things arenae for you to know."

He sighed and ran his fingers through his hair. Sinann was silent as he said a quick prayer, then he blew out his cheeks, climbed to his feet, and returned to work.

October 31 came, which many still thought of as the beginning of the new year in the same way they thought of sunset as the beginning of the new day. Following the tradition as he had seen it practiced in this century, Dylan built a small fire outside his house, and from it he and Cait lit torches of dried heather. Then in procession—slowly, because Ciaran was very little and still unsteady on his feet—they circled the house three times—deiseil, of course. Then Dylan picked up the toddler and they all went down to the village with their torches.

As Dylan descended the trail with Cait, Ciaran on his shoulders—for he wouldn't allow Cait to carry the growing boy anymore—they looked out over the glen dotted with little bonfires. The distant lights in the dusk of sunset made him think of Halloween jack-o'-lanterns and trick-or-treating. The air was far nippier and wilder than the moderate fall weather of his childhood, giving an intense atmosphere of dead things abroad. Many of the clan were about, bringing their own torches to the large bonfire at the center of the village near the castle. As he drew near to the gathering, he could see many people wore masks and that made him smile.

As Dylan set Ciaran on the ground and threw his torch onto the bonfire to join the others, Marc Hewitt addressed him from behind a white cloth with eyeholes that was painted with the black nostrils and toothy grin of a skull. "Dylan, where's yer mask? The spirits of the dead are liable to recognize ye."

Dylan grinned. "I fear no man, living or dead." That made Marc smile behind his linen mask.

As at most celebrations in Glen Ciorram, there was food, and singing and dancing that went well into the night. The old man who was the best storyteller in the glen thrilled the children, and many of the adults, with spooky tales of ghosts and witches.

Ciaran fell asleep on Cait's shoulder, and she sat on a stool from one of the houses as she rocked him and listened to the stories and songs.

As Dylan stood listening, a quaiche of ale in his hand, he noticed a man standing at the very edge of the bonfire's circle of light. A shiver ran down his spine and out his arms, for his mind was already on ghosts and this man was obviously not of the glen. The stranger wore breeches and had an eerily still demeanor. But at second glance Dylan recognized the out-of-uniform Lieutenant from the garrison—the round-faced fellow from

Skye—whose name Dylan had learned was Niall MacCorkindale. The eerie thrill turned to anger, and Dylan passed the quaiche then faded into the darkness to approach the intruder.

"Are you nuts?" he said in English, his voice a low hiss.

MacCorkindale blinked, taken aback. He replied in Gaelic, "Nuts?"

Dylan continued in English, "Insane. Showing up here, like you're not one of the enemy."

The Lieutenant reddened and shifted to English, his voice pointed. "Only a traitor would consider me the enemy."

"You're a Scot and you're Catholic." There was a sharp glance from MacCorkindale, and Dylan said, "I've seen you cross yourself when you thought nobody was looking." The round face reddened. Dylan continued, "So you know better than that. You can come here out of uniform—you could even wear a kilt—but to these folks here you're still a Redcoat, and that makes you one of the occupation forces who have killed their kin and stolen their horses, their kine, and their land. I suggest you turn yourself around and go on back to the garrison before you get hurt."

MacCorkindale gave him a bland look. "Generous advice."

"Take it."

There was a long silence, then the Lieutenant turned his gaze to the bonfire. Orange flames reflected in his eyes. He said, "When I was a boy, I often leapt the flames at Samhain. No matter how far into the drink I might have been, I would try the fire. I landed on my behind more than once and was forced to roll in the dirt." A tiny smile curled the corners of his mouth.

"I'm dead sorry for your cultural loss, but you chose your uniform. You can't pretend the reason you're here is not to hold a gun on us. Leave, now."

The Lieutenant's shoulders sagged. "I'm sorry to hear you say that. I'd hoped you might not object to having another student on Sunday nights."

Red anger rose, and Dylan spat on the ground at MacCorkindale's feet. "Don't *even* . . . not *even* . . ." He took a moment to calm himself and to quit sputtering. Then he continued in a low voice, pointing a finger hard into the round face. "I hate the English Army as much as anyone around here, and I won't be party to training one of George's men. Bloody well go to China if you really want to know the things I could teach you. You won't learn them from me."

MacCorkindale's face darkened. "And if I should have you arrested?"

Dylan spread his hands. "Feel free. Let's go. But I'm not going to teach you how I fight. In fact, I think you should go now, before someone takes an interest in you and decides your lack of uniform makes you fair game for stoning. Or even shooting. Wouldn't that be lovely? Followed by a bloody massacre in retribution, all because you felt like jumping a fucking bonfire."

The Lieutenant's mouth pressed together in a white line. Without another word he turned and walked away into the windy darkness.

Then Artair's voice came from the midst of the villagers. "Dylan! Having a chat with yer Redcoat friend, there, are ye?"

Dylan groaned and closed his eyes.

CHAPTER 20

There was a great deal of resistance to Dylan's ideas regarding his sheep. While other farmers were smearing their sheep with tar and butter, Dylan argued with his wife, who insisted the sheep would die without protection from parasites and cold. She stood with her cloak wrapped around her while he stacked rocks to make an enclosure directly behind the house. It was a long, exhausting job, and he was getting no help from anyone, for they all thought he'd gone daft.

"They'll die. All the sheep my father gave us will die, and we'll be without clothing." The terror in her voice cut him, but he couldn't give in. He knew what was coming after the next two uprisings, and knew if his children and grandchildren were to prosper, they would have to succeed at something besides farming oats and running cattle. Another goal of improving the wool yield in his sheep was to produce extra cloth for sale in Glasgow or Inverness in the fall. Ramsay had been an asshole, but he was right about Highlanders needing things to trade for food, and Dylan knew manufacturing was an efficient way to raise the value of raw materials.

"The sheep won't die."

"They will. They'll freeze to death just outside our door. And they'll be eaten up by nits."

"The cold will kill the bugs. That tar stuff only makes more work for you to clean the wool. Also, the cold will make the fleeces thicker."

"More work for me, to spin and weave the wool.

Dylan paused in the stacking, and peered at her. "I thought you would like to have a new dress." He shrugged and went back to work. "I want my wife to have a new dress, so shoot me." He took the last rock from the cart, set it on the dike he was building, and went to lead his garrons back to the burn where he'd obtained the others he'd just set.

The enclosure was nearly finished, most of the stones having come from his field, some from dikes in Glen Ciorram that were no longer needed, and a few, but not many, from the ruined wall surrounding the castle. Now he was pulling stones from his burn, but he hated doing that, for the water downstream would be murky for a long time and the course of the bed would be changed. Besides, the rounded water stones didn't stack very well. But he'd run out of other sources that wouldn't cost him an arm and a leg, so now he was widening his burn to finish off the top of his dike.

Cait followed him to the burn, where he waded into the freezing water to pick a stone from the bottom. He said, "I won't let the animals die. They'll be right outside, where I can see them from the window." He waded from the water and set the stone in the cart, then waded back. His leggings were soaked, and his coat sleeves dripping. He was beginning to feel the cold, and knew if it was cold enough for *him* to feel it, he was in danger of a serious chill. He'd never had a cold in his life, but was keenly aware that in this place his first might kill him.

He patiently explained to Cait, "If the weather gets too bad, there's always the byre where they can wait out a blizzard. Another thing is that I can let them graze on the slopes if the snow is light. Sometimes on the fields." His herd was small enough yet to not deplete the soil with grazing, but he wouldn't be able to let them graze too much on the fields once the herd grew to a good size, any more than he could put his cattle out on them longer than it took to graze down the oat stubble after the harvest. He reached into the water and pried up another rock to lift it out. "Letting them graze in the winter will make them fatter, come spring." Well, less skinny, anyway. There was never enough fodder to keep the stock more than barely alive during winter. He stood knee-deep in water, the hem of his kilt trailing in the flow, with a ten-pound rock in his hands and his head tilted to one side. "It'll be all right, Cait. Trust me."

She sighed, and he thought he saw a softening in her eyes.

He pressed the advantage. "I'm your husband. I won't let anything happen to you, or your sheep."

There was a long moment of silence, and she stared at him with worried eyes. But then she uncrossed her arms and stepped to the edge of the burn to take the rock from his hands.

Dylan shook his head and stepped from the burn with his rock. "No, I don't want you lifting. It's enough that you would have." Then she kissed him, and he set the rock in the cart.

Sinann hovered over the peat bog as Dylan dug with the L-shaped spade. "Ye've been neglectful of your studies, lad. There's much left to learn."

"I've been busy." Dylan was still busy. Over the growing season, he'd discovered that his new pastoral existence was at least as labor-intensive as his former life as a martial arts instructor. What with hauling water, whittling household utensils, milking, feeding, monitoring rutting, and shoveling out the sheep pen for the sake of his fertilizer pile, plus repairs on the house and accoutrements, constructing new furniture, guarding the crops, maintaining tools, negotiating with buyers of stock and sellers of necessities, there was little time for studying the craft of the *Sidhe*. At that moment, he was cutting peats from the bog to dry for the winter.

"Come."

Dylan threw another peat to plop on top of the others. He muttered in English, "Are you high?"

Sinann blinked. "I could fly as high as ye wish. Whatever that has . . ."

"It means crazy. Literally, it means *Are you on drugs?* Mind-altering substances, that is. Like whiskey. You must be crazy or drunk if you think I can leave my work to go play faerie games." Another peat plopped onto the pile.

"It isnae a game."

Dylan sighed. "Yeah, I know. It comes in handy; I've seen it work. You don't need to convince me."

"Ye need more knowing. There's much you could do to help yer family, were you to have the power and use it wisely."

He snorted. "So Father Turnbull can find out about it and accuse me of heresy? You know he asks people about me."

Sinann crossed her arms in front of her and glowered. "And what power does *that* one have over you?"

"Come on, Tink. You know they're still hanging witches around here. They'll be stopping after a few more years, but for the next twenty years or so, practicing the craft will still be a capital crime." He chuckled. "Then they'll make smuggling a capital crime, just so they'll have someone to hang every once in a while."

The faerie's eyes went wide. "Ye dinnae say!"

He shrugged. "Well, not for that reason, but yeah. The Crown is going to get pretty ugly about smuggling in another generation or so."

She thought about that for a moment, then shook her head and said, "Be that as it may, you should learn the craft for the sake of the knowing. What ye do with the power is your own affair."

He thought about that for a moment, then said, "All right." The sun was well overhead, and hadn't begun to dip yet. He threw his cut peats into the baskets across the back of his garron, then led the horse home. After setting his fuel to dry, he removed the horse's tack and the baskets, then hobbled him in the dooryard to graze. Only then was he free to follow Sinann for the rest of the day.

They went to the old tower, to the north of Glen Ciorram, which was a known haunt of the "wee folk," namely Sinann, and therefore avoided by humans. Dylan had taken advantage of the privacy here more than once, on occasions years before when he'd learned some aspects of the craft or had wanted to be alone with Cait. He sat on the large stone block in the middle of the tower floor. "So, Sinann, when are you going to tell me how you knew about the English patrol that passed us on the way to Edinburgh?"

Sinann blinked. "Patrol?"

"Yeah. You remember, when I told you my nativity and you worked out my astrological chart, you knew a patrol of English soldiers was about to catch up with us, and you told me to get off the trail. I've been wanting to know how you did that. I didn't know astrology could predict stuff quite that specific."

The faerie flew to sit on the steps, eye-level with Dylan. "It cannae." She hugged her knees, and only Dylan might have known it meant she felt guilty of something.

He frowned. "Then how. . ?"

"I wanted you off the trail. It was a quick, easy way to convince you."

His eyes narrowed at her. "You lied."

She spread her palms. "Ye should know better than to think I hadn't. I had to do what it took to get you into hiding."

"But the patrol . . ."

"It wasnae the English, neither. 'Twas the faerie Morrighan and her retinue."

That stunned Dylan. It took a moment to sink in. "Morrighan? The goddess of war?" Morrighan of the *Tuatha De Danann*. Also known as Morgana, the Morrighu, Fata Morgana, Morgan La Fey, and the Lady of the Lake. Her reputation for trouble was already centuries old, and would echo beyond even the twentieth century. She was a great deal more famous than Cuchulain.

Sinann nodded.

"She had been at the battle the day before. We saw her on top of a faerie knoll."

The faerie nodded again.

"Where was she going that night?"

She shrugged. "I heard her a-coming from far off. 'Tis nae good to encounter her. She'll bewitch the strongest man and turn him to her own ends. Even the great Cuchulain was taken in by her, and tricked into healing by magic a wound on her he'd inflicted himself. For only the blessing of Cuchulain could do such as that."

Dylan said, "After the battle, do you think she was looking for another fight? She surely wasn't looking for *me*."

Sinann shrugged. "I cannae say. But I do know you did well to hide as she passed."

"So I take it we're not going to learn astrology today."

The faerie snorted. " 'Tis but a parlor game, as ye said. No, today we turn to dance for raising the *maucht*."

"I know how to dance. I picked it up—"

"So much the better you know a few steps. In this dance, you will learn to raise power and bring yerself to ecstasy."

Dylan grinned. "Like sex."

She nodded, serious. "Very much like it. The dance will transport ye to a higher state." Her hands came together, and she began clapping out a rhythm. "Show me what ye know so far."

He nodded to the rhythm, then picked up his feet in a step like the ones he'd been shown during the Beltane celebration several years before.

Sort of like a cross between clogging and soft shoe, he found it simpler than many of the Asian fighting moves he'd learned over the years.

The faerie quit clapping, but said, "Keep it up." She flew to the ground and pointed to the grass in front of him. Suddenly a picture came clear in it. The grass was removed in a pattern, showing the ground beneath, which had been stained blood red by the death of Fearghas MacMhathain centuries before. The red drawing was of two circles, one with a small dent in one side, connected by two curved lines. "This sigil is your *Sùil Dhé Mhór*, the Eye of the Great God. Focus on it. This particular sigil denotes power. Dance around it."

Dylan obeyed, continuing the dance, hopping on one foot, then springing to the other foot and back again, over and over.

"Dance with nae thought. If ye become tired, continue the dance. Look only at the sigil." Around and around the sigil he danced. "As the energy increases, dance closer."

He felt something, but wasn't sure if it was *maucht* or fatigue. Sweat began to trickle from his hair and into his beard. His sark clung to his back, and the linen and wool just over his belt were quickly soaked. His breathing quickened.

The world spun, suddenly out of control. Dylan nearly fell to the ground, but caught himself and stood, panting, over the sigil. "What was that?" Then he saw a figure sitting on the stone block in the center of the tower.

"Cody?"

She turned to him. "Dylan . . ."

Then she disappeared.

"Sinann, what was that?" Dylan went to the stone, gulping breath, and he waved his hand through the spot where he'd seen Cody.

The faerie was wide-eyed with surprise. "I dinnae ken what it could be. You called her by a name. Do you know the lass?"

Dylan stared hard at the stone, as if he could still see her if he tried hard enough. "Yes. She was my friend in the future. I don't think she was trying to contact me. She was as surprised as I was."

Sinann chuckled. "*Och*, the lass should be a witch, for having so much ability. Were she to learn control, there would be no end to her power."

Dylan had to smile at the thought of Cody learning control. "She's a unique woman, all right. But what was she doing here? I mean, she was sitting on the stone. How come she came to *Scotland*?"

The faerie shrugged. "I surely dinnae ken. As she seems to have failed in her communication, more than likely we'll never know."

As winter approached, Dylan's tooth worsened quickly, growing into a constant ache. By November his entire jaw throbbed, and tendrils of pain had made their way along it and into his skull. He'd had far worse pain than this before, but he figured being run through with a cavalry sword would have been more merciful a death than this. The bad tooth was half gone now, and a swelling had risen beneath it. He'd used all his aspirin trying to put off the inevitable. The thing he'd dreaded for months had to be done now. The tooth had to be pulled for the infection to begin healing.

Local tradition was for the blacksmith to perform the miscellaneous functions of medicine that were not the jobs of a midwife or physician. Midwives delivered babies and physicians looked mostly toward the balance of humors: black bile, yellow bile, blood, and phlegm. Since nobody in this century had much of a clue about human anatomy, Dylan regarded all of them as persons to be avoided.

However, by virtue of the fact that Tormod Matheson, Ciorram's blacksmith, was the only man in the village who owned a pair of pliers, and Dylan certainly wasn't likely to pull the tooth himself, there was nothing for it but to resign himself to letting the blacksmith pull his infected tooth. Now that winter was setting in, there were no more excuses to put it off.

"Here, take this with ye." Cait handed over a corked ceramic jug as he was about to leave the house.

Dylan pulled the cork and sniffed. Whiskey. About half a gallon of it, by estimation. "Where'd you get this?"

"I sewed and embroidered a new sark for Keith Rómach." Dylan raised his eyebrows and Cait added, "He's courting Owen Brodie's daughter, you know."

Dylan laughed. "No, I didn't. I'm always the last to know that sort of thing. So Keith has his eye on a lass, does he?"

"Dinnae try to change the subject, and ye're nae going to dally on your way to Tormod's house until it's too late and the sun has gone." She nodded toward the jug. "Ye'll need this for the pain. Take as much of it as you can, and dinnae let Tormod have a drop until he's done what you came for. If luck is with you, ye'll pass out before he begins. Here. Go. And tell him for me I'll take it out of his hide if he breaks your jaw."

Dylan groaned and felt of the swelling in his face, then corked the jug. "Thanks." He gave her a quick kiss with the side of his mouth that wasn't sore, then set out for Tormod's house.

On the walk into the lower glen he took a good many slugs of the whiskey, so by the time he arrived at Tormod's house, the pain was beginning to mellow. Because he felt better, he had half a mind to go home, but decided against it at the prospect of facing Cait's wrath when he got there.

Tormod greeted him from under the tree by the stone shed that sheltered his forge. Though the blacksmith's house was peat, the outbuilding was of stone to reduce the risk of fire. The thatching on it burned occasionally, but never caused much damage when it did. Today Tormod was making cattle shoes and had a small pile of iron crescents next to his anvil. "Dylan Dubh! Wanting that tooth out now, are ye?"

Dylan nodded, and took another drink from the jug.

Tormod nodded toward his house. "There's a chair just inside the door. Bring it out here where the light is good." It was an overcast day, but daylight of any sort was better than a candle for seeing inside a man's mouth. Dylan obeyed, then swallowed some more whiskey as he waited for Tormod to finish the shoe on his anvil, douse it in a water bucket, and throw it on the pile.

"Donnchadh!" Tormod shouted to his apprentice, who was Ailis's little brother. "Fetch me a bit of linen!" The boy hurried from the shadows of the shed and into the house.

Dylan sat in the chair and took another drink.

Tormod went to a wooden box nearby and began rummaging through tools with much clanking and thumping. "Are ye well into the whiskey yet, there, Dylan?"

Dylan looked at the jug and shook it, estimating he'd drunk about a pint of the stuff. He could feel it in his joints, and the day felt warmer than it should have. "Pr'aps." He took another mouthful and swished it around his tooth before swallowing. The pain surged then mellowed.

"Might ye spare me a drop?"

"You can have the res' of it as a bonus if you don' break my jaw. But if you do break it, you gotta face my wife."

Tormod grinned and his eyes widened. "*Och!* You know how to threaten a man, Dylan!"

Donnchadh came with a linen rag, from which Tormod tore a square the size of his palm. Then he pulled a pair of long-handled pliers from his toolbox and slipped them into his belt. "Now, Dylan. Do you wish Donnchadh here to hold yer arms?"

Dylan flexed his hands and considered. "Nah." He set the whiskey jug on the ground and gripped the seat of his chair.

"Tilt back yer head."

Dylan obeyed, and opened his mouth. The air on his tooth renewed the ache. Tormod stuck his finger in to pull back Dylan's cheek for a look, and the finger tasted like iron, carbon, and oil. "Good. We've enough there to grip." Then from his sark pocket he took a small piece of wood. He pulled back Dylan's cheek again, checked the piece against the tooth, then drew a dirk from his belt to whittle the wood down some. This time when he checked it for size, he went ahead and stuffed it into the cavity. A jolt of pain shot through Dylan's jaw, but he only blinked. Tormod said, "This'll help keep it from breaking apart while I pull it."

Now Tormod took the linen square and folded it in half. He placed it over the bad tooth, and with his other hand pressed Dylan's head back to brace against the back of the chair. Still holding the linen, he then took his pliers from his belt. Dylan closed his eyes and drew a deep breath as the pliers went into his mouth and were positioned on the tooth over the linen. Tormod held Dylan's chin tight, bore down on the pliers, then twisted the tooth hard back and forth. There were two loud cracks. Blinding pain made Dylan grunt as it filled his head. He gripped the chair tight, to keep his hands away from Tormod and his mouth. Then Tormod yanked once and the tooth was pulled free. The blacksmith backed away as Dylan leaned forward, panting through his nose with the pain. Blood filled his mouth, and a trickle escaped from between his lips.

"Spit."

Dylan spat on the ground, a large glob of blood and saliva. The pain was now a dull thudding in his jaw that radiated into his skull. Tormod tore another piece from the large linen rag, and ordered Dylan to open his mouth. Then he stuffed a wad of cloth into the space where the tooth had been, and Dylan bit down on it. It was soaked almost instantly, showing blood on the ends dangling from his mouth.

"Can ye move yer jaw?"

Dylan checked to see if his jaw was broken, then reached down for the whiskey jug and handed it to Tormod with a nod of approval. He took two shillings from the purse in his sporran and handed them over as well. Then he stood, nodded good day, and headed home.

If it hadn't been such a cold day, he would have liked to curl up under a bush to sleep off the whiskey and pain. But Cait and a warm hearth awaited at home, so that was where he was headed. He cut through the village on his way to the bog trail.

The luck of not having his jaw broken seemed to be all that was allotted to him that day, for as he passed Nana Pettigrew's house, three Redcoats stepped out. One was Niall MacCorkindale, and one of the other two was still buttoning his breeches.

Dylan, staggering drunk and his entire head throbbing, had no wish even to be seen by these men. But it was too late. MacCorkindale spotted him, and muttered something to the other soldiers. The Redcoats readied their muskets, and one of them shouted, "Halt!"

Crap. Dylan stopped walking and the two dragoons approached. One of them, a Cockney Londoner by his speech, said, "Where are you going?"

With his mouth stuffed with a bloodied linen rag, Dylan declined to speak but pointed toward the hill behind which was his property.

"Are ye dumb, then? Or is it you refuse to speak? I'll have no insolence from you. Dirty rebel, is what you are." The two muskets trained at Dylan's face. He looked over at MacCorkindale, whose face was dark with fury.

"Speak, Matheson!" It was plain Dylan was in for a beating at least, or perhaps even an arrest. Fighting wasn't an option, and he was too drunk and too pissed off to talk his way out of this one. So he began to retch.

The soldiers took a step back. Dylan made his gut heave, and let a trickle of blood from between his lips. The surprised soldiers gaped as more blood dribbled out and over Dylan's bearded chin. His gut heaved some more, and there were gargling noises as he forced blood through his nose. He coughed, and it sprayed over the shiny, well-kept muskets. MacCorkindale's eyes were wide now.

The retching worsened, and Dylan bent as if in a paroxysm of stomach pain. His mouth opened, and he let the bloodied linen drop to the ground, where it lay there, looking just like an internal organ of some sort. Thereupon, he collapsed on top of it and lay as still as he could.

A dark, horrified silence followed. Finally, one of the soldiers muttered, "He's dead."

"He inn't. Still breathing, ye see."

"He'll be dead soon enough, what with his insides all coming out like that."

MacCorkindale called to his men, "Let's go, the two of you. Let his kinsmen sort him out."

Dylan heard footsteps leave him, then the clatter of galloping hooves dwindled in the distance. He waited, to be sure they were truly gone, then climbed to his feet. Staggering and wobbling, he regained his bearings, then struck out for the bog trail and home.

The harvest was in, the sheep enclosure finished and filled with sheep, the cattle in the byre, and peats were stacked and dried for the winter. It was time for Dylan to set out for Inverness, to find a whiskey still, some Cheviot sheep, and a lawyer to change Ciaran's name. He hitched one of his garrons to the cart; donned both his shirts, both pairs of woolen stockings, his leggings, coat, and gloves against the weather; and slipped his royal pardon, wrapped in oilcloth, into his sporran. He would need the pardon if stopped and questioned by anyone in His Majesty's service along the way. He set out, leading the garron and the empty cart.

The walk to Inverness was uneventful. In the muddy, smelly city between Loch Ness and the Moray Firth, Dylan located a man of law with more or less a good reputation, who was affordable. Dylan's need was a simple one, and in short order the paper was drawn up for signing and shillings were paid. Dylan slipped the adoption document into the oilcloth with his pardon.

The sheep were easily found, though a mite expensive because they were young, large, and healthy. Dylan bought a ewe and a ram, both born just that year. Since he wanted to cross them both with his own sheep, he hoped the ewe wouldn't come into her first heat before he could make it home.

The still was even more expensive than the sheep, and harder to find, but Dylan succeeded in locating and loading into the cart a contraption that would be a good start in the local whiskey business in Ciorram.

All these things accomplished, Dylan headed home, making the trip over the mountains with as much speed as he could manage at a walk with a cart full of iron pot and copper tubing, and two young sheep tied to it.

While making his way along the shore of a small loch he couldn't put a name to, he came upon a young girl who was weeping. With one hand pressed to her face, she sobbed inconsolably, crouched at the water's edge. It was a cold day, and she shivered under a red cloak.

He slowed in his walk. She was a beautiful girl, looking to be in her early teens. Her hair was even darker than his, and shone blue in the patchy sun. As he approached, he said, "What's the matter, Miss?" He looked around for brothers or a father who might be responsible for her, but there was nobody at all. "Can I help you?"

She looked up at him, and he flinched. Her right eye was gone, her face having been slashed with what must have been a dirk, or perhaps a sword. It was an old, scarred-over injury, but was apparently cause for a great deal of heartache.

He repeated, "Is there something I can do for you?"

Her one eye seemed distrustful. "I need naught from any man."

He crouched on his heels to be at eye level with her. "Well, if you get to know me, you might find I'm not just any man."

That didn't bring the expected laugh. Instead, she said, "Would a handsome man such as yourself even so much as give an ugly girl a drink from the loch?"

Her attitude was irritating, but Dylan was not one to treat a girl or a woman disrespectfully. Even a small misstep would be a good way to incur the ire of a male relative. So he replied, "Of course I would." He took the quaiche hung on his belt for traveling, and went to the loch where it lapped at the rocky shore. He filled the cup and brought it to the girl.

She shook her head at his offer, saying, "You drink first."

Dylan was nonplussed at that, but figured he could use a sip himself, and drew the cup to his own mouth. But before he could drink, the girl said sharply, "Did your mother not teach you to say grace over your food and drink?"

Irritation became anger, but he held his temper and obliged. "Father, we give thanks for the bounty of the earth. Bless this water and those who receive it. Amen." Then he drank, and the girl eagerly drank after him and handed back the cup.

In an instant, the horrible gash in her face was gone and her eye restored. A wide, cold smile lit her face, and then she was gone. All there was to show she'd even been there was the wet mark of her lip on the quaiche.

Dylan broke out in a cold sweat and stood, looking around, shivering in the cold wind off the loch. Slowly, he realized what had just happened. He remembered the wolf whose eye he'd put out, and he remembered the story of Cuchulain. As the wind blew locks of his hair around his face, he whispered to nobody there, "Morrighan, what do you want with me?"

There was no reply.

He pressed on toward home, and approached the glen the following day. Taking the cart past the garrison would be dodgy, since his still presented a potential problem with tax collectors and it would be best if Major Bedford and his minions didn't know of it. However, there was no way into the glen that would accommodate the cart, that didn't pass within sight of the garrison. Dylan decided to bluff it through and hope his still wouldn't be recognized as such. To aid in that, he cut several pine branches to cover the pot and tubing. Now all he needed was to not be stopped.

It was nearly sunset when he made the casual stroll past the garrison. He even waved at the two Redcoats who stood outside the barracks; they appeared to be Lieut. MacCorkindale and a lower-ranked sentry. No other soldiers were in sight, and Dylan figured they were all inside eating.

Dylan's heart skipped when the sentry unslung his musket and stepped to approach and challenge. Dylan stood to wait, patient and oh, so co-operative, so as to convince the soldiers there would be no untaxed whiskey sold by Dylan Matheson, nosirree.

But the sentry made only one step, for MacCorkindale reached out a hand to stay him. There was a short exchange, then the sentry stepped back to his post. Then, to Dylan's surprise, MacCorkindale pointed with his chin toward the trail that led to Sinann's tower. Dylan looked, then peered into the gathering dusk toward the church. Could he trust the Redcoat from Skye? Were there soldiers ahead? Or would he be stopped at the tower?

Dylan decided that if MacCorkindale wanted him arrested, he could have let the sentry do it. So Dylan nodded and clucked to his garron. He would take his cart up past the tower, then along the trail down the burn. If there were Redcoats in the glen, he could minimize exposure to them with a straight shot across to his own land.

As he turned his garron, he glanced back at the barracks. Mac-Corkindale had gone inside.

When Dylan arrived at his dooryard, Eóin, his brother Gregor, and Ciaran all gathered to see what Dylan had brought from Inverness. Siggy came to sniff the large, fluffy newcomers, who bleated indignation at his probing nose.

Dylan showed the boys the pieces of his still, which in its disassembled state looked like a pile of junk. Cait and Sarah came from the house to greet him.

When Cait saw the still, she stood with her arms crossed and a crease between her eyebrows. "The English will arrest you again." Sarah, who was peering curiously into the cart, cut a *bite your tongue* glance at Cait.

"No, they won't." He untangled the copper tubing, careful not to bend it and put a kink in it. "Nobody will even see the whiskey for three years. And when they do, I'll be paying my taxes on it. Legal as can be."

"Are ye insane?"

He looked up at her. "No, I'm not."

"The barley is going to whiskey, and will be set aside for three years? Whatever for, when the whiskey can be sold now? And have you any idea what the tax is on the stuff? Won't nobody buy it from ye for what it'll cost you. Not with two other stills in Ciorram."

Dylan smiled. "Yeah, they will." Nobody in Scotland had yet tasted whiskey aged more than a few months, and his product would certainly be in demand once it was ready and sampled.

But he lost his smile when he remembered his father, and the bottle in the old man's living room bearing a label that had said *Glenciorram*. He shrugged one shoulder and reminded himself that nobody had ever held a gun to the old bastard's head to make him drink. And certainly the presence of one more distillery in Scotland hadn't caused his alcoholism.

With a fresh smile, Dylan stood to show Cait the paper from Inverness. He pulled the oilcloth from his sporran. "Look," he said, eager to take her mind from the still and get her to smile, "I got the adoption. Once you've signed this, Ciaran will be a Matheson by name and I can call him my son."

That did bring a smile to her face, and she glanced over the page. "I write my name here?" Her finger tapped the spot under Dylan's signature as she turned toward the house. He picked up Ciaran to follow, and Sarah accompanied with her boys. It occurred to him there were no writing implements in the house, but that didn't stop Cait.

She went to the fire, where yet another rank-smelling concoction was boiling in a small pot. It smelled metallic, and Dylan looked for the bucket in which Cait had put pulverized oak galls and a few rusty nails to soak. A great many of the little round balls of bark had been gathered last month, and most of them would be used for tanning hides, but these that had been soaked with the nails would make black dye for the wool. The bucket was empty, so he figured it was the black dye she had on the fire. She was making the supply she would need for the weaving this winter.

The liquid in the pot was fairly thick and had bits of gall floating on top. Cait took a ceramic dish she used for a candle holder, and with her thumbnail scraped the melted wax residue from it, then dipped some dye from the pot. A fingerful of lard went into the dish, and she set it on the griddle she used for making bannocks, which she put on the fire. It didn't take long for the lard to melt into the already hot dye. Holding the dish with a rag, she set it on the table next to the paper Dylan had brought.

For a pen, she reached into Dylan's sark to take his *sgian dubh* and shaved a long sliver from a piece of scrap wood. Dipping the thin end into the ink like a brush, she painted her name beneath Dylan's on the paper. The ink went on grayish, but darkened after a few moments to a brownish black. The result resembled very sloppy calligraphy.

Then she turned the paper around to face Sarah, and handed her the pen. "You're our witness."

Sarah flushed, but smiled as she took the wood sliver to draw her name under Cait's.

She blew on the ink to dry it, as Cait stood and kissed Dylan. "He's yours now, and nae man can take him away, nor claim he's nae your rightful son."

Dylan took the paper from the table and his pardon from his sporran, and tucked them both inside the oilcloth. Then he set both precious documents inside the cabinet with his land deed and shut the door. There was an enervating sense of relief he would have denied, had he been asked, and he ran his hand over his son's fluffy, dark head. "Ciaran Robert Matheson," he murmured.

The still was set up in a clearing Dylan made at the thickest part of the forest on the south side of his property, for secrecy from gadgers would be necessary for the first three years of his enterprise. The hard part would be hiding the empty sherry casks he'd begged from Gracie, in which he would age the whiskey. A bracken-covered cave near the waterfall did the trick, in a spot accessible only by foot, and that with difficulty.

Dylan soaked the barley overnight in the burn, then spread it across a cloth inside his house for a week so the seeds would germinate in the warmth. Then the barley was dried in small batches over his hearth. The malting was a long, tedious process, but winter was upon them, so the family stayed indoors and were good company while the scent of toasted grain filled the house.

While Cait sewed cured rabbit hides together so Ciaran's bed would have a blanket warmer than an old kilt, Dylan read aloud to Ciaran and Cait from the Bible and from the poetry book he now knew almost by heart. Occasionally he told stories which were adaptations of films he'd seen, and enjoyed hamming it up with voices and sound effects. Ciaran's favorite was the one that began, "A long time ago, in a galaxy far, far away."

Cait giggled at his imitation of blaster fire sounds. "Guns dinnae sound like that at all."

Dylan grinned. "These do. See, they're not like our guns, they don't make explosions. They're machines that . . ."—he struggled for words she would understand—". . . that shoot little balls of light."

That made her laugh even more. "Balls of light to kill a man?"

"Oh, aye, and ships—big ships—that fly in the sky. They hop from star to star."

She dissolved into helpless giggles. "Oh, Dylan, you're the most fanciful man I've ever known. The things ye think of . . ." She shook her head.

The desire to open up and tell her of his world was almost overwhelming. But he kept shut. Even Cait, who loved him more than anyone ever had, might think him crazy if he claimed to be from the future. He wouldn't frighten her like that.

Then Cait said, "Of all the things I love about ye, Dylan Matheson, it's your imagination I love the best."

Dylan opened his mouth to reply, but shut it, then said it anyway. "So you don't mind when I have new ideas about raising sheep?"

Her grin waned, and she sighed. "You were right. I must have faith you wouldnae hurt us. And faith in myself that I wouldnae fall in love with a fool."

A wry smile curled Dylan's mouth. "All right, I'll call that a *yes*."

She giggled again, and he returned to the story.

As the pile of malted barley grew, Dylan began to wonder where he was going to store it for use.

One morning, he awoke to find a brand-new wooden bin in the middle of the sitting room floor. It was huge, large enough to hold his entire barley harvest, and the hinges and hasp were smooth, new iron. Not a scratch was on it, making it the only undamaged piece of wood in Ciorram.

Cait walked in from the bedroom and stopped to stare at it. "Look what the wee folk brought us." Dylan threw her a sharp glance, for he knew that was exactly what had happened. She continued as she walked around it to proceed with the making of breakfast, "Did Seumas steal it for ye, then?"

Dylan frowned and said, offended, "He didn't steal it. Seumas doesn't steal. Any more."

"Where did it come from, then? You dinnae buy it, for the lawyer's fee and the cost of the still have left us with not nearly enough for such a fine bin." She picked up the water bucket from the table and carried it to the door, where her coat and Dylan's hung on pegs. Her voice turned ominous. "If you've gone into debt with Owen Brodie for it . . ."

"I don't know where it came from." And that was all he could think of to say. He'd been lying to explain Sinann's antics for a long time, but this time his brain simply failed him for a convincing story. "I really don't know." He looked around for Sinann, but she wasn't visible. "Maybe it *was* the wee folk."

Cait threw her cloak over her shoulders, then picked up the water bucket for a trip to the burn. Once she was out the door, he hissed to the room, *"Sinann!"* There was no answer. "Sinann, I swear, if you don't quit this . . ."

The door opened again, and Cait came back in. "And who might this Sinann be?" Snowflakes dusted her cloak and cap, but they melted quickly and Dylan had a sense of her anger doing the melting.

He shut his eyes and sighed. *Busted.* His dread of the English paled, now, next to having to answer questions from his wife about a strange female. He went to his sporran for the Goddess Stone. One sweep of the room told him Sinann was perched atop the new bin, legs akimbo and one elbow leaning against a knee, her chin resting on her palm. She waved to him, a huge, evil grin plastered across her face. He said, "You won, Tinkerbell. Show yourself."

She shook her head, her grin never faltering.

A surge of alarm made his voice tense up. "Sinann, I mean it. You wanted her to know—you've been making yourself obvious for months—and now she knows."

The dratted faerie shook her head, leapt to her feet, and flew out the chimney hole.

Dylan groaned, then yelled, "Troll!"

Her voice came from the chimney. "I heard that!"

Cait, now more puzzled than angry, said, "Sinann? The faerie Sinann? You've made friends with the granddaughter of Lir?" She glanced around the room in search of the faerie.

That stopped Dylan cold, and he stared at his wife for a moment before he could speak. "You know her?"

"Of course, I've heard of her. But she's dead. Drowned. And she's Irish."

"I dinnae drown, ye sumph! I'm the granddaughter of the *Sea* God! Tell her that, lad!"

He wearily shook his head and said to Cait, "She wishes me to point out that her lineage makes her an unlikely candidate for drowning. I assure you, she's alive and kicking, and has been making my life miserable since I got here." He peered up at the ceiling.

Sinann shouted through the chimney hole, "Never mind I *saved* your life. More than once!"

He shouted back at her, "You wouldn't have needed to if you'd left me where I was!"

"There's gratitude for ye. Where I should have left ye was in the *Sassunach* dungeon!"

"If you'd been watching Cait like you were supposed to, I would never have been in the dungeon in the first place!"

Cait was peering up at the chimney hole at which Dylan was shouting, and she raised her voice herself, sounding like she wasn't entirely certain anyone was really there. "Sinann, might I have a word with you?"

There was a silence, and Cait looked at Dylan to know if the faerie had spoken. He shrugged and shook his head. "Sinann," Cait said, "will ye show yerself? Have ye the courage?"

The faerie peeked through the chimney hole, and Dylan said, "Come on down, Tink. The beans are done spilt." Finally, she dropped through the hole and flew back down to the lid of the bin, where she sat, facing

Cait, and waved her hand. When Cait's eyes went wide and she took a step back, Dylan knew the faerie had made herself visible to her.

"Och!" said Cait. "It's truly a faerie! I've not actually seen a faerie before!"

"Count your blessings." Dylan's eyes narrowed at the evil look Sinann threw him for that.

But Cait held out her hand to Sinann and said, a little wide-eyed but recovering from her surprise, "Pleased to meet you, Sinann." She nodded toward Dylan. "Dinnae mind him." She leaned down for a conspiratorial whisper. "He comes from the colonies and knows nae better."

They shared a giggle as Sinann took the hand, and Dylan groaned.

CHAPTER 21

The small amount of barley Dylan had planted yielded three casks of whiskey distilled over the course of the winter, which he put away in the cave after marking each, with a fingerful of ash, *1717*. From the yield he held out one jug for personal use, which he figured would last him the year. If the place were searched, the whiskey would be found, but the worst that could happen would be a fine from the excise authority and confiscation of the cask. Probably not even the fine, if the gadger in question were disinclined to report the confiscated whiskey. Dylan knew there were more illegal stills than legal ones in Scotland, and French brandy was coming ashore by the boatload without payment of tariff, so nobody was knocking down doors for the sake of a single jug of spirit.

In January, Ciaran turned two years old. The winter passed without incident other than the timely and gentle passing of the Widow Wilkie. Her property went unclaimed by her daughter, who had been banished to Inverness, and so was inherited by Nana Pettigrew, who was her niece. The Wilkie tenancy was turned over to Dùghlas Matheson, who was engaged to one of the kitchen servants from the castle. Keith Rómach Campbell had become engaged to the daughter of Owen Brodie the carpenter, and would marry her in May, though there was no land for them. They would most likely have to move to Inverness or Glasgow if Keith couldn't find a living in Ciorram.

Much to the surprise of the entire glen, Dylan's sheep survived the cold. Spring crept in on schedule, and the fleeces on the flock were the thickest anyone had ever seen. Cait's belly was now quite full, the child kicking and making its presence well known. She insisted the bairn would be a lad, for conception had been in early August and she was certain Dylan was wrong about the cause of gender. Dylan didn't argue with her, in case she did have another boy. Even if she was wrong about the cause, he knew the odds of the baby being male were slightly better than even. He decided not to force her to hope for a girl, and risk disappointment.

Cait's pregnancy fascinated him. At night in bed he measured it under his hand, and over the months felt her skin tighten until he thought it must split open. As the child grew heavy and lying down became uncomfortable, Cait took to using Dylan for a body pillow, resting the weight of her huge stomach against his side as he lay on his back. More than once he was awakened by a kick in the belly, and he reached into the front of Cait's nightdress to feel with his hand the baby moving. Sometimes he could make out the shape of a tiny foot pressed against his hand for several moments. He would push on it, then grin to feel it shove back in protest before finally retreating.

One afternoon Dylan fairly ran into the Great Hall of the castle, and found Gracie there at the fire. "Come quick! Cait's . . . she's . . ." Dang, the word was escaping him now. His Gaelic vocabulary gave him three or four ways to say "no," and he was deft with all of them, but now his English-speaking mind kept wanting to say *obair* even though it wasn't "work" Cait was doing. He took a deep breath. "The baby is coming."

The old woman's eyes lit up. *"Och!"* She scurried to the kitchen entrance and called, "Sarah! Come! Hurry! It's Cait!"

Sarah bolted from the kitchen, excited and rosy-cheeked, brushing flour from her skirt. "Cait's bairn?" When she saw Dylan, she brought up short and more of her face flushed, but she recovered quickly and said to Gracie, "You go with Dylan. I'll borrow some linens from the castle stock and be along directly." Then she hurried off to the North Tower.

Dylan watched her go, wondering how Sarah could stand living under Sinann's love spell. Though the faerie said it could be shaken off at any time, it was apparent Sarah hadn't done it, for she still had those hurt-puppy eyes every time she looked at him.

It was slower going to return to the house than it had been coming down, for Gracie was aging and had problems breathing besides. Finally they reached the house, and when Gracie entered the bedroom where Cait lay, she turned and closed the door in Dylan's face. He pushed it open, but she shoved it closed again. "Gracie, let me in!"

"You behave yerself, Dylan. This is nae thing for a man to see. Nor *want* to see, and I'm shocked you're even at the door. Go someplace where you're needed, for that wouldnae be here!"

He blew out his cheeks and turned to find something to occupy himself. He found Ciaran sitting on a chair, much more still than usual for the two-year-old. *"Thig, mac."* Dylan picked him up, then sat on the chair with the boy on his lap.

"Leugh mi," said Ciaran. Dylan didn't bother to correct grammar this time, but obeyed and reached behind him for the Bible on top of the cabinet. Ciaran preferred the Bible, probably because Dylan translated to Gaelic as he read, which he didn't do for the poetry. Except for the poetry reading, Ciaran hardly ever heard English around the house, and hadn't yet spoken any. Dylan figured he'd begin teaching it once the boy's Gaelic was more fluent and he would be old enough to tell the difference. And in the meantime Ciaran enjoyed the Bible stories filled with miracles, disasters, and sin.

A moan of pain came from the bedroom. Dylan looked up as cold sweat broke out.

Sarah came along shortly, laden with sheets and towels, and hardly glanced at him as she passed to the bedroom. The door was once again closed firmly.

Cait's parents arrived almost on Sarah's heels, and Una went directly to the bedroom while Iain claimed the other chair by the table. Ciaran slid from his father's lap and ran to his grandfather, who didn't let the boy onto his lap but did let him hug his knee. Iain chatted with him some in simple words while Dylan put more peat on the fire. It occurred to him he would be on his own for cooking supper, but he wasn't hungry yet and decided to cross that bridge when he came to it. *Drammach* would be enough for him on this day.

More groans came from the bedroom. Dylan and Iain both paused and waited for them to end, then resumed breathing when they did.

After a while, Seumas and Robin dropped in. The men chatted and Dylan passed his whiskey jug around. They'd probably wipe it out tonight, but that was all right. He could wait till next winter for another jug from the next harvest. Dylan was grateful for the talk, which distracted him from the sounds coming from the bedroom.

By sunset Seumas and Robin had taken their leave, and Ailis Hewitt came with a large basket of bridies on one hip and Aodán on the other. She handed Dylan the basket, saying, "Eat, man, ye look ill to fainting." Then she, too, disappeared into the bedroom.

Iain, Ciaran, and Dylan feasted on the pies of chicken, game bird, and oatmeal while listening to the sounds intensify in the next room. Dylan began to wonder when it was going to be over. The groans were cries now, and even Iain was starting to pale. Ailis didn't stay long, for her son was fussy. As she went, she promised to return in the morning. Nana Pettigrew passed her coming in, and in the bedroom the chatter picked up speed.

Ciaran fell asleep in Dylan's arms while Dylan and Iain talked in low voices, during the quiet moments, of everything except babies and birth. It was quite late when Iain finally called for his wife to return to the castle.

"Iain," said Dylan as his father-in-law stood, "would you and Una take Ciaran for tonight? I'd like it better if he weren't hearing his mother."

Iain nodded, and reached for the sleeping boy. Ciaran barely stirred, and looked even smaller than he was, curled up against the massive shoulder of the Laird. They left, and Dylan was alone by the fire while four women murmured to each other in the next room. Screams came more frequently now, and rattled Dylan's spine each time they did. Sleep for him was out of the question.

Hours dragged by. Dylan put more peat on the fire and tried to read from the poetry book, but it was useless. Why was this taking so long? How much pain was required to have a baby? He went to the bedroom door and put his hand on it. "Sinann," he whispered, "can you do something?"

There was no reply from the faerie, and he trembled. Cait went on screaming.

More hours passed. The cries were constant now. Dylan sat by the fire, trying not to think of what could happen to Cait. It was nearly dawn, and she'd been in labor since about noon the day before. Was this normal? Was the baby still alive? How could those women in there even tell? And if they could, would it matter? What if the baby strangled on the umbilical cord? What if Cait started bleeding and didn't stop? What if the baby just wouldn't come out? The screams went on, and he pulled his crucifix from his sark. He leaned over on his elbows and held the cross tightly in both hands. Pressing his forehead to his balled-up hands, he prayed for the lives of his wife and child.

He didn't know how long he was there, feverishly whispering the same words over and over, but the sky was purple turning to pink out the front window when an exultant cry went up in the bedroom, followed by the thin wail of an infant. He leapt up, went to the bedroom door, and pressed his face against the rope wattle. "Cait? Cait, are you all right?"

"Get away, Dylan Matheson!" Cait's voice was weak, but her attitude brought him relief. "Dinnae dare come in here!"

He lowered his voice. "How is the bairn?"

"She's well. Healthy and pink."

Dylan smiled and returned to the chair, for his legs would no longer hold him. Relief made him laugh softly to himself, then realization crept in and he looked toward the bedroom again. Cait had gotten her wish: a daughter. He called out, "See, Cait, I told you it didn't matter who was on top."

A titter of giggling came from the other women, and she called back, "It was the time before. I'm sure of it!" There were more giggles.

He laughed, good and hard, then was quite surprised when a tear showed up in the corner of one eye. Quickly he brushed it away with the heel of his hand, lest someone come in and see it. Sinann popped in, just in time to catch him at it. "*Och,* I cannae bear to see a man weep."

"Where have you been? She needed help."

"I was helping, laddie. I was holding her hand and telling stories about ye. She was especially amused by the one about the whore who put her hand up yer kilt . . ."

Dylan groaned.

". . . and how you put her off. I was telling her how much ye love her, and I was keeping your crew of midwives from yanking the bairn out of her like a pudding from a pot."

Dylan sat up. "What? Did they hurt her?"

The faerie pressed him back into his seat with a hand to his chest. "Nae. But some are known to hurry a birthing along, and I wouldnae have let them." He frowned, puzzled, but nodded stupidly. She continued, "Get some rest, lad. For a certainty, your wife is near to sleeping."

"Nuh-uh." He leapt from his chair and went to the bedroom door. "Let me see her." A chorus of women denied his request. Fed up with this treatment, he grabbed the top of the wall, shook it, and bellowed, "Let me see my daughter, or I'll come in and get her! Bring her out, now!"

There was a hushed but urgent murmuring, but no more denial, so he waited. Presently Gracie appeared at the door with a linen-wrapped bundle in her arms. At sight of the tiny creature, Dylan was so floored he almost forgot to reach for her. But Gracie handed her over. He took the baby awkwardly, afraid of crushing her but even more afraid of dropping her. He'd never in his life held a person this small.

Gracie helped him find a place in his arms where he could cradle the child. He went to the window to see his daughter by the light of the rising sun, squatted on his heels to be at a level with the window, and rested his arms on one knee. His little girl was so "pink" as to be almost red, and her eyes were open, looking around. He wondered what she could see— whether she saw his face at all, or just colors and shapes. The fuzz on her head was dark, like Ciaran's. Her mouth was the tiniest little pucker imaginable, every line perfect and new.

He leaned down to kiss her soft forehead and murmured, "Welcome to the world, sweetheart." His heart ached with pride.

The baby was named Sìle, baptized three days later by Father Turnbull, with Sarah standing godmother. Dylan never heard a word that was said in the ceremony; he couldn't take his eyes from his daughter.

Over the next year Dylan watched his children grow and his sheep herd increase. Each sheep produced more wool, now that he was allowing them to grow a winter fleece, and the lambs born that year with mixed Highland and Cheviot blood were large and had thick, soft fleeces. The following spring, of 1718, he culled a coarse-haired lamb from the herd and contributed a stew to the May Day feast. As his sheep herd increased, his cattle herd was maintained at a steady head count. As new calves were born, like other Highland farmers, he butchered or sold off the older animals. That winter, he'd been able to hold out two jugs of whiskey from the casks he put away, and now had six filled casks stored in his cave, three of them marked *1718*.

Father Turnbull continued to annoy, and as the priest became familiar with his parishioners, he pressed his rigid authority harder and Dylan's tolerance threshold diminished. The confessional was the most difficult aspect of Catholicism for Dylan to accept, since he'd not been raised to expect to blurt his innermost secrets to another man every few weeks. When Father Buchanan had been the parish priest, the exercise had been tolerable and Dylan had learned there could be value to talking things out in a safe place.

However, talking things out with Father Turnbull was never what Dylan considered "safe," and over time the priest began digging for things he thought Dylan might be hiding. Of course, there *were* things he was hiding. Sinann, for one, and his origins in the twentieth century for another. But he wasn't in much danger of Turnbull finding out those things, for the priest would have refused to believe. It was things about Dylan which weren't true that had the priest prying.

Having just come from the church one Wednesday, Dylan sought to vent his anger by chopping up a deadfall tree for the fire. Deep in the woods, chips flew and wood cracked under his ax, and soon a heavy sweat was running from his hair and down his back.

"I'm glad it isnae myself that's got ye angry, lad." Sinann perched in a tree nearby.

He didn't reply, but continued whacking the deadfall, now more interested in damaging it than cutting it into anything usable.

"What did the man of God say this time?"

Dylan finally paused in his work and leaned on the ax. "I talked to him about honoring my father. I mean, you know how I am with that. The guy was a worthless alcoholic."

"Did he defend your father, then?"

"Nope. That's not it." Dylan took another couple of whacks from the tree, then continued, panting. "He said, 'Yes, I know you hated your father....' I didn't *hate* him. But anyway, that's not even what he was after." Dylan's anger rose and his chest tightened. "Then he says, 'You have the same thing to confess each time. Could it be you have other sins to confess you're not bringing to light?' I said, 'Such as?' " Dylan whacked the dead tree again, and it fell into two pieces. "Well, then he starts in with 'You're the only man in Ciorram who never confesses to lustful thoughts.' I said, 'You're joking.' No, he was serious. He thinks I'm daydreaming about women other than my wife. I mean, has he *seen* my wife? And I asked him that. 'Have you *seen* my wife?' I said. And he says, like he's *forgiving* me of something, 'After more than two years of marriage, it's natural for a man's eye to wander.' Sinann, look around. Where's my eye going to wander? I just blinked at him. I said, 'My eye likes it at home just fine.' I mean, Sinann, I'm married to the only woman I've ever wanted to marry, and trust me, I've seen a lot of gorgeous women in my life and not many of them in Glen Ciorram. But then he says, 'Lying is a sin, my son.' Can you *believe* that? Now he's not only assuming I'm hot for other women, but that I'm lying about it when I say I'm not!"

"*Och!*" said the faerie. "I suppose it's a good thing ye care not what the man thinks."

Dylan blinked. She was right. He didn't give a damn what that narrow-minded nitwit thought. He took a deep breath, and much of his anger blew out of him with a huge sigh. "Yeah. It's a good thing." It took him a moment to gather himself, then he returned to the job of cutting fire-wood. He said, "You know what, Tink? You make a better confessor than he does."

Sinann giggled.

Dylan paused in his work again and said, "I don't know why he's even in Glen Ciorram. He's been here nearly two years, and his Gaelic is still barely understandable. I can't imagine what confession must be like for those who don't speak English."

"It's not a pretty thing to see, I assure ye."

He chuckled. "Been looking in on the confessional, have you? Shame on you."

"And what else would I be doing with my time, since you have nae further need of me?"

Dylan hefted the ax and returned to work. Between swings, he said, "Be glad of the peace, Tinkerbell, because it won't last."

Artair, Iain's heir apparent, was no longer a teenager, but had not gained any maturity and was proving to be a flaming Jacobite and belligerent toward the local soldiery. His conversation at *céilidh* that spring seemed geared toward stirring the Mathesons of Glen Ciorram into an uprising of their very own against the local garrison. One rainy night, while the women gossiped and spun wool near the hearth, the men gathered in a companionable group at the other end of the room.

Iain had of late taken to smoking a pipe, though tobacco was still expensive enough in Scotland that nobody else in the glen could afford to smoke. He made a fussy business of filling and lighting the ceramic pipe, then of keeping it lit over the course of the evening. It seemed every few minutes he was reaching for a candle to relight his dead tobacco. Dylan was glad for it, since the tobacco spent more time dead than lit, which cut down on the secondhand smoke.

"James intends to return," insisted Artair.

"Big deal," replied Dylan. He had whittling in his hands, a comb for Cait, of oak. To finish it, he would need to borrow a wire saw from Tormod, to make the teeth straight, thin and close together, but for now he was still working on the basic shape of it and thought he might carve a Celtic knot along the spine. He continued, "James was here before. It takes more than that for an uprising to succeed."

Iain peered at him through a wreath of smoke, looking enough like Clement Moore's Santa Claus to make Dylan smile. But the old man said, "Have ye abandoned the cause you fought so hard for, lad?" From his tone it was apparent he would be disappointed if Dylan had.

Dylan didn't wish to get into the real reasons he'd fought for that cause, for it had been circumstance rather than religious conviction or belief in James as the true king that had motivated him. Also, he knew there were better ways to beat the English than to kill them. But he said, to satisfy Iain, "I've abandoned nothing. I hate the English as much as I ever did, and will fight anyone who threatens my family, whether they're English, Americans, or Martians." That brought a chuckle. "But there's a time to fight, and a time to wait and see. This year is one for waiting and seeing."

Artair snorted. "You'll wait until the *Sassunaich* decide to search your house for whiskey, then when they take it and murder your family while they're doing it, you'll then decide it's time to fight."

"If you think I've placed my family in danger for a jug of whiskey, say so. Perhaps it would be best to pour it out than to risk the ire of His Majesty. I know I can do without the stuff if I have to."

"Coward."

"The point is, Artair, that my whiskey is *not* putting my family at risk. The *Sassunaich* are not in a mood to destroy me for a jug or two, and I have no reason to get ugly with them just now."

"And does the Major come a-buggering ye of an evening, laddie?"

"Artair!" Iain shouted, as he reached for Dylan's hand in which he held his *sgian dubh*.

Dylan gripped hard the knife in his fist, and the urge to slice Artair's face with it was nearly irresistible. But he resisted, and only glared at him.

Iain continued, "Artair, take that back or *I'll* kill ye!"

There was a long, tense silence as the men all watched Artair to see what he would do. The young man glared at Dylan, who gazed back as blandly as he could. It was up to Artair, now, whether there would be blood, and it was apparent he didn't have the support of anyone in the room on this one. He muttered, "I apologize."

Dylan nodded acceptance, and returned to his whittling.

Malcolm, quiet during the talk, said, "I think our colonial cousin has learned some maturity during his time on His Majesty's bad side. Perhaps it would be wise to listen to him rather than a boy who has never fought in a battle."

Dylan's eyes narrowed even more at Artair. He'd thought Iain had sent men to fight in the uprising. He looked askance at Iain.

The Laird said, "We sent some men, but not Artair, for we sent only those who wished to go under the authority of MacDonald."

In other words, Artair didn't go because he was too young at the time to lead the Matheson men and too spoiled to follow under the MacDonalds. Dylan grunted. On one hand, that was good, for it kept Clan Matheson away from the baleful eye of the Crown and increased their chances of not being decimated after the next rising. On the other hand, it meant the next clan Laird would be a bloodthirsty yahoo who would most likely lead the Glen Ciorram Mathesons to destruction, if not in 1719, then in 1745.

CHAPTER 22

Summer came, the cattle went to the shielings, and the Glen Ciorram crop grew healthy for another season.

Artair continued to grouse about the English soldiers, and in mid-July, Dylan heard from Cait, who had heard from Ailis, who had heard from Marc there had been an altercation between Artair and one of the dragoons earlier in the day. It seemed a rock had been thrown at the soldier's horse as he rode through the cluster of houses near the castle. The soldier brought his mount under control, then began questioning people in the vicinity. Ten or fifteen people had witnessed the act, and though nobody could identify the thrower, even the dragoon knew it had been Artair.

The young man was lucky the soldier didn't arrest him on principle and hold him indefinitely for questioning. Instead, the dragoon went on his way with a warning that the English wouldn't put up with that sort of behavior. The consensus among the witnesses was that Artair should watch his back from now on, lest a stray dragoon musket ball find his head one day. When Dylan heard this, he sighed and shook his head. Artair was going to get the entire glen burned out if he didn't quit this nonsense.

Not long after, Siggy disappeared.

"Siggy! Yo! Siggy!" Sigurd was not with the sheep, which had scattered. It took till sunset to find them all, and it was well dark by the time Dylan managed to get all sixteen head into the enclosure. He secured the gate, then turned to call his dog again. "Siggy!"

Cait came from the house, her cloak around her shoulders. "Something has happened to Sigurd?"

Peering into the darkness, straining to see into shadows, Dylan said, "I can't find him."

"He ran off?"

He shrugged. "This isn't like him."

"There would be nae point in having him for a shepherd if it were. Perhaps he's hurt. You'll want to find him if you can." She kissed her husband. "Go. There's a moon for ye to see by, and listen between calls. If he's alive, you'll hear him."

Dylan went to look, but the collie was nowhere to be found. The moon had nearly set by the time Dylan gave up and returned to the house for his supper. The dog had probably lost a fight with a wildcat, in which case it would be better if the body weren't found.

Nevertheless, he spent a good portion of the next day looking, but hope wore thin and finally died. Dylan stopped at Marc and Ailis's house to refresh himself with a quaiche of water before starting home, taking the shortcut up the crevice that would take him to the east end of his property, near where it made the jog. The shortcut was steep, but a far shorter walk than trudging the length of Glen Ciorram and doubling back past the peat bog.

Dylan climbed, mourning the loss of the only dog he'd ever had. Siggy had been a smart, hardworking shepherd and the most loyal creature Dylan had ever known. Another dog would be needed for the sheep, and training a puppy would be difficult. He would need help. Maybe someone in the glen could spare a trained dog, at least for a while. He cursed himself for neglecting to train a puppy while Siggy was still around.

"Dylan!" Cody again, sobbing now. Dylan turned to look. In the dim light of the waning day, there was a vague outline of a woman sitting on a boulder. Cody was dressed as he'd seen her at the Highland Games in Tennessee, wearing a traditional overdress and a white blouse, but no kerchief. He blinked, expecting the apparition to disappear, but it stayed. "Dylan," she said, "don't leave Cait tomorrow."

A chill skittered up his spine. He addressed the vision as it wavered in and out, less and less opaque. "Why?"

The sobbing echoed, as if she were calling to him through a tunnel. Tears glistened on her face. "Don't let her out of your sight. She's going to be killed. Tomorrow."

"How do you know?"

"Trust me." She pressed a hand to her mouth as the weeping overtook her and the image of her faded to almost nothing. "Just trust me, Dylan. Please trust . . ." Then she was gone.

Dylan stared at the boulder on which she'd sat, stunned into inaction. Cait killed? Tomorrow? He hurried up the hill and ran along his field to the house.

Bursting through the door, he looked around the candlelit room. Cait looked up from her carding and frowned. "What's wrong?" Dylan was panting, looking around the room, and Cait rose to see what was the matter. "Did you find him?"

For a moment he couldn't think of what she was talking about. Oh, yeah, Siggy. He took a deep breath and let it out slowly. "No. I've searched the property, and the entire lower glen. He's nowhere to be found. Nobody in Ciorram has seen him." Now he felt foolish. Cait wasn't going to die. Not with him around.

Cait sighed and returned to her work. "He was a good dog."

Dylan nodded. He found himself unable to take his eyes off Cait. The vision of Cody had rattled him so that his fingers were slippery on the door as he closed it. He told himself again that Cait wasn't going to die, but found himself less convincing than before. Was Morrighan playing another trick on him? Was it safe to assume she was? He longed to call Sinann to ask, but that would be a conversation he couldn't have in front of Cait, no matter how chummy the faerie might be with his wife. He sat in his chair near the fire, and felt of Brigid's silver hilt at his legging. Nobody would hurt Cait. Not as long as he was there.

Later, in bed, Cait lay with her head on his shoulder as she drifted off to sleep. He rolled toward her, and she adjusted to wrap an arm around him. In the darkness he whispered, "Are you happy?"

She made a clucking noise with her tongue. "For what would I be unhappy?"

He made a noncommittal grunt. "I wonder if you've ever regretted anything."

"*Och,* nae. And it's a silly question yer asking. I want for naught, and I love my husband more dearly than is given to most women. I'm blessed, and now I only wonder at why you're asking such outlandish things." She raised onto an elbow. "Is it yourself who has regrets?"

"No." He tried to think of what else to say, but nothing coherent rose to be said. It all bottlenecked in his chest so he was unable to put anything into words. Finally he was able to clear his throat and said, "No. I love you. That is the long and the short of it."

She snuggled happily into his arms. "Good. Then sleep."

It took long hours of trying before he was finally able to obey.

The next morning Dylan informed Cait he was going to let the sheep graze the dooryard because there were things he needed to do around the house.

"They'll be at the oats without the dog there." Cait had Sìle on her hip and the water bucket in her hand.

Dylan shrugged. "It can't be helped. Maybe Iain could spare Dìleas for a while, but until I ask him about it, the sheep will be hard to handle and we don't have the fodder to just keep them penned."

"But why . . . ?"

"Cait, don't argue. Please."

She closed her mouth and frowned at him. "Please" had become his signal that an issue was not negotiable. She knew he would never hit her, but she also knew he wouldn't discuss anything further once he'd asked her politely to stop arguing. "Very well," she said. "Take yer daughter, then, if ye're to be about all day. I'm off to the burn." She handed over Sìle and went out the door with the bucket.

He picked up his staff and followed her out, calling to Ciaran to come with him. The three-year-old ran after, and Dylan set Sìle down on the sod to play with her brother. Following Cait at a distance, he watched her take the bucket to the burn as he went around to the sheep enclosure to let them out. His glance took in the surrounding countryside, and he wished Cody had been more specific in her warning. Would a musket ball find Cait? An arrow? Would it be an accident?

The sheep were at the gate, waiting to be let out for breakfast. Dylan opened the gate and with his staff encouraged the herd toward the front of the house. They would spread thin without the dog there, but wouldn't go far enough to become lost. Not with the glen floor covered with young oats.

He called to his son, "Hey, Ciaran. Want to play a game? See if you can keep the sheep away from the oat field." So far they seemed happy with the grazing in the dooryard, and might be easy to discourage from the field.

Ciaran was delighted for an excuse to chase sheep, and he hurried to comply, positioning himself between the herd and the oats. None of the sheep seemed to take notice of the oats or Ciaran. Cait was on her way back to the house with the water for breakfast.

A thud of horses' hooves came up the trail from Ciorram, and the Mathesons both turned to see five dragoons ride into the glen. Lieutenant MacCorkindale from Skye was in the lead, his face stern and his cheeks flushed. As the five pulled up in front of Dylan, the Lieutenant said in English, "Come with us, Dylan Matheson."

Dylan's heart leapt into his throat and he set his jaw. His knuckles were white around his quarterstaff. He replied in English so the children wouldn't hear what was happening. "I cannot."

The Lieutenant snorted. "You will." A cold chill skittered up Dylan's spine as he remembered his first arrest.

"What is the purpose of this? I haven't done anything—"

"Take him." The Lieutenant gestured to two of his men, who dismounted and readied their loaded and primed weapons.

Dylan backed away as the dragoons approached. "Wait. Maybe we can clear up whatever this is." One dragoon raised his musket. Dylan reached for Brigid, though she was no match for the firearm. He couldn't let himself be arrested. Not today. "There's no need—"

"*A Dhilein!*" Cait's voice was hard. Alarmed. "Ye've done naught for which to be arrested. Keep it so."

Cold sweat covered him. No matter what he did, it would be wrong. On the chance that he could talk his way out of whatever problem concerned the Lieutenant, he straightened without drawing Brigid. "Don't do this, MacCorkindale."

The Lieutenant told his men, "Take him, I said."

Dylan took a step back and held out the staff to Cait at arm's length. "Cait, take this. And my dirks."

Cait came to take the quarterstaff and slipped Brigid from the scabbard in his legging, then reached into his sark for the *sgian dubh*. She kissed him, then stepped away from him. The dragoons lowered their weapons to take him and shackle his wrists. "Is this necessary?"

The Lieutenant declined to reply. The two dragoons remounted, one of them holding the chain attached to the shackles. Dylan walked behind the horse as they made their way from the glen.

He looked behind to Cait, and said, "Go to the castle, Cait. Take the children and go to your father. Don't leave the castle."

"It will be well, Dylan. My father will plead your case. You'll be freed." She watched him leave, and he kept his eye on her until he was too far down the trail to see her any more.

Dylan addressed the Lieutenant in a loud voice, for he was several yards behind him on the trail. "What is going on here, Lieutenant?"

Still, there was no reply from any of the soldiers.

Dylan was taken to the Queen Anne Garrison, through the village where not a soul was to be seen. All the young, unmarried men were in the shielings with the cattle, leaving the glen more fearful of the English soldiers. Even those few clansmen who weren't in the shielings or at breakfast just then would be reluctant to show themselves with the dragoons out and about. Dylan walked behind the English horse, wishing there were someone he could call to and send to protect Cait. He saw nobody.

As they approached the garrison, Dylan could see what had happened to antagonize the soldiers. Four horses, the ones that had been commandeered from the castle during the uprising, had been slaughtered, their necks cut neatly with a dirk. The carcasses lay in front of the two-story stone building, in a huge pool of blood that was beginning to trickle down the slope. This couldn't have happened much before dawn. Dylan had no clue why he was MacCorkindale's first suspect; this moronic stunt had Artair written all over it.

The soldiers escorted Dylan into the building, through the common room where mess tables had recently been scrubbed, into an office at the far end of the first floor. A wooden table dominated the room. The chair behind the table was upholstered in red silk, and a wide bunk with clean linen and silk coverlet stood at the other end of the room, so Dylan knew this was the commander's quarters. He said to the Lieutenant, who stood at the center of the room, "Where's Bedford?" The Major's absence was at least as alarming as anything that had happened that morning.

There was no reply. The Lieutenant, thin-lipped in his anger, gestured to the wall opposite, and Dylan turned to see another pair of shackles set into the wall. Panic clenched his gut, and on reflex he took a step back. His two escorts grabbed him by the arms. He was then released from his shackles and immediately chained to the wall, facing it. Dylan yanked at the shackles, though he knew it would accomplish nothing but sores and bruises on his wrists. "No, don't do this." It was a struggle to keep his voice even. He pressed his face to the stone and squeezed his eyes shut.

The soldiers were ordered out of the room and they obeyed, closing the door on Dylan and the Lieutenant. There was a dark silence. Dylan could hear the Lieutenant breathing; otherwise he wouldn't have known he wasn't alone. His own breathing became heavy as the fear rose in him. He pressed his face to the stone and whispered prayers under his breath, quickly, over and over. Finally, Dylan said aloud in Gaelic, "I didn't have anything to do with those horses."

The Lieutenant said in English, "Did ye not?"

Continuing in Gaelic. "I did not."

In English: "Then who did?"

"You know better than to ask such a question. If I knew, I wouldn't say. But the fact is, I don't know and won't guess. I don't have it in me to mention the name of a kinsman to the *Sassunaich*." He turned his head to peer at MacCorkindale from the corner of his eye. "And you already know that." He yanked on the irons at his wrists. An unwelcome tone of pleading crept into his voice, though he fought it. "So how about letting me out of these so I can go back to my family?"

"Are you a Jacobite still? We know who killed those horses; who told him to do it?"

Dylan grabbed the chains in his fists as red anger filled his head. "Fucking *Sassunach*. Traitor. You've turned into one of them. You'd destroy your own people for the sake of a job. If you're going to whip me, then do it. But know before you do, it won't get you any sort of information. Take a look at my back. You people think I'm the weak link in this clan because I was born in America, but the truth is I'll let you kill me before I'll betray a kinsman. So kill me and get it done with." He twisted himself around to see MacCorkindale's face again. "But before you do—now—right now—send someone to my wife. Send one of your men. Don't let my wife be alone today." Panic crept into his voice and he fought it down. "Not today."

A frown creased the Lieutenant's brow. "What is it ye know beyond the ordinary, Matheson?"

Dylan held the chains in his fists and stared at the floor covered with dried reeds. He said nothing.

The Lieutenant went to Dylan and pulled the neck of his sark back and down to expose part of his back. MacCorkindale's voice was soft as he muttered, "Good God." He finally switched to Gaelic. "What is it that's about to happen, Matheson? Has yer faerie told ye something you would do well to tell me?"

Dylan blinked, surprised. Did MacCorkindale know about Sinann? Or had he merely been talking to Father Turnbull? Dylan said, "No. It's my wife. There's been a threat against my wife. I swear I know nothing about the dead horses. But the longer I stay here, the better the chance something will happen to Cait."

The Lieutenant considered that. He said thoughtfully, "You let yerself be arrested, knowing this?"

"Did I have a choice? I'm no good to her dead, am I?"

"You swear ye werenae involved with the slaughter of the horses?"

"You heard me." He knew the common belief was that breaking such an oath would condemn a man to eternal damnation. He'd been part of this culture long enough, and seen enough truth in legend, not to be far from believing it himself. "I swear it."

The Lieutenant considered that for another long moment, while Dylan felt time speeding past. Finally, the Lieutenant sighed and freed Dylan's wrists with a key from a jangling jailer's ring. He said, "Take one of the horses tied outside. I expect it will be returned by tomorrow. I pray you find your wife well."

Stunned beyond words, Dylan rubbed his wrists and stretched his aching shoulder and back muscles, then stared at the Redcoat for a moment. He'd not dreamed of simply being released. "Thank you." The words, said to an officer of the English Army, nearly stuck in his throat. He swallowed an angry comment that the arrest had been unnecessary to begin with.

"Get out," said the Lieutenant.

Dylan hurried from the room and through the barracks filled with soldiers. A shout went up behind him as he fled through the front door, and men scrambled for their muskets. Outside, a row of horses stood at a rail, all with bridles but no saddles. Dylan leapt onto the nearest one, which reared as he hauled its head around. The sentry raised his musket and shouted an alarm and several men hurried from the barracks to take aim at Dylan. But the Lieutenant ordered them all to stand down. Dylan kicked the horse into a gallop and sped down the track to Glen Ciorram.

At a full gallop the entire way, he was nearing the castle when he saw Sarah running across the drawbridge toward the gatehouse, crying at full voice. She carried Sile, and Ciaran ran behind, the children also wailing. Dylan pulled up, the dragoon horse dancing with impatience and confusion. His heart stood still, then it began to pound, and he kicked his mount into a gallop toward his house. "Oh, God."

He tore into his dooryard, scattering sheep, and leapt from the horse. Sinann appeared, hovering before him, waving her hands. "Dinnae go. Stay here, dinnae go in there."

He batted her away. She flew behind him and grabbed the back of his sark. "I beg you! Dinnae go!" He shook her off. But when he burst through the door of his house, he wished he'd listened. The smell hit him first as his eyes adjusted to the dimness, then his knees tried to go out from under him at the sight. He moaned denial and gasped for breath. "Nnno. Nnnuh . . ."

Cait lay on the table by the window, where bright morning sun from outside lit the scene in relentless detail. Her legs were spread wide, dangling at her thighs from the edge of the table so her toes almost touched the floor. Her skirts were pulled up, leaving her exposed from the waist down. A long knife pinned her neck to the table, and a thick stream of blood ran from it onto the floor. Spatters covered her entirely in tiny dots, like a schoolchild's art project. A pile of clothing lay on the floor, silk fabrics and soft leather that were luxuries alien to the peat house. The smell of ejaculate was strong, and Dylan's gorge rose. He coughed and swallowed so as not to vomit.

"No!" He shook his head and gasped, unable to accept this. He turned, searching for the faerie. "*Nooooo!* Sinann! Do something! Take it back! Make it change!" His head spun, and he looked around the room that no longer seemed like his home. It had been invaded and defiled, its sanctity destroyed.

The faerie wept as she said, "He came the very moment ye left. He surely was watching the house."

Dylan spun on her and spoke through clenched teeth. "Sinann, send me back! Send me back to this morning! Now!" The faerie lit on top of the malt bin, tears running down her face. She hugged her knees and rocked back and forth. Dylan's voice cracked, pleading. "Sinann, send me back to this morning so I can catch the sonofabitch who did this before he does it. Please!" She shook her head, and he choked on the desperation surging in him. He could barely speak. "*Yes!* You've got to do this for me! I've got to save her. I've got . . ." He looked over at the body and moaned, "*Oh, God.*" Trembling took him, and he wiped sweat from his forehead with a shaking hand.

"I dinnae think I can."

"Try! You've got to try! Please!" He gasped for breath, panicked at the evil he might have to accept. His teeth clenched. "*Do it!*"

Sinann raised her hand, and Dylan stood still to accept the magic. There was a slight buzzing sound in his head, but no darkness came. He remained where he was.

"*Please, Sinann!*" He fidgeted, impatient. It had to work.

She tried again, but nothing happened. Sobbing, she said, "It's nae good. I cannae send you to another time when ye already exist. There cannae be two of ye at one time."

"*No!*"

"Aye."

"*No!*" He grabbed Sinann by the front of her dress, slammed her against the wooden wall of the byre, and held her there. "*No!*" But the stunning horror crashed in on him. Sinann wept as she held his wrist in both her hands. He let her go, and she slumped onto the bin again, her face buried in her arms, sobbing.

As he turned to stare at his dead, violated wife, he thought he might pass out. *Wished* he might pass out. Wished he might die. There was a glow in the room, and Dylan's battered mind wished it could be a fire to burn the place down, and himself with it. Anything, rather than accept this. He picked up a chair to hurl it against a wall, but stopped when he heard a voice.

It was a woman's voice, one that seemed impossibly familiar. "Oh, God," she said. "This is a really bad time."

Dylan turned, baffled, to see a woman in jeans and a blouse. The world, which had just been turned on its head, now also blew inside-out. "Cody?"

CHAPTER 23

"Cody ..." Dylan stared stupidly at her as she stared at the body, horrified. He dropped the chair and hurried to pull Cait's skirts down over her legs, then yanked the knife from her throat. Gently, he laid two trembling fingers on her eyes and closed them.

"Oh, Dylan ..." Cody began to cry, holding both hands over her mouth as if she might vomit. "Who did this?"

He spun on her with the knife in his hand and scowled. "If I knew who did this, he'd be dead on the floor now." Cody flinched, and he turned away, turned back to look at Cait, then turned away again as his stomach hitched.

Then he looked over at Cody. "Why are you here?" A thought occurred, and he said, "If you've come to prevent this, you're too damn late." He looked over the knife he held in his hand, covered with Cait's blood, and for one fleeting moment wanted to stick it in his own neck. But that passed. Surely there was someone else more deserving to die over this. He began to look more closely at the knife.

She shook her head. "No, I didn't know. It's ..." She reached into her jeans pocket, but then stopped, as if she'd changed her mind. "I ... oh, Dylan, I'm so sorry."

Dylan barely heard her; he was busy figuring out whom to kill. The knife in his hand was not a dirk, but an English plug bayonet. The handle was plain wood, and the brass mount at the pommel was threaded for insertion in the barrel of a musket after the first volley of a battle. It was a weapon of the English infantry. *An Sassunaich.*

Rage surged, but at the same time he realized there were no true infantry in Glen Ciorram, only dragoons who, though they carried muskets, didn't generally use bayonets. Dragoons served more as reconnaissance and heavy cavalry than for close-in fighting any more. Particularly, they wouldn't use plug bayonets that hadn't been in use since the English defeat at Killiecrankie in 1689. The knife in Dylan's hand had been obsolete as English military gear for nearly thirty years.

This didn't scan, but surely the murderer was Bedford. It had to be Bedford. Dylan choked down his fury to think straight. He took deep breaths, and clenched his fists to stop the shaking.

Finally, he looked at Cody and frowned at the way she was dressed. "Get out of those jeans," he ordered.

"Huh?"

"Take off those jeans." He was terse, wanting no argument that might nudge him over into blind rage. "Sarah is at the castle, getting help. If anyone sees you in those, they'll freak out over a woman in breeches. They're even liable to blame you for this, just because you're a stranger. An obviously insane stranger who dresses like a man and might take it into her head to kill like one. Here . . ." He went to dig through a basket of rags, and came up with Cait's old dress, which was worn nearly to threads but would hang together well enough to serve. "Put this on over your blouse, and we'll hope nobody notices you're not wearing linen underneath."

"Dylan, I don't think . . ."

"Just do it!" He was within a hair of killing someone, and just then it didn't much matter who. "Dinnae argue with me, girl, for you don't know what you've stepped into. So take off the fucking jeans. Now." He turned toward the bin. "Sinann, help her."

Sinann snapped her fingers, and the jeans flew apart at all the seams. Belt loops, fly, and pockets went flying. Cody let out a scream as the denim dropped to the floor on all sides. Dylan tossed her the dress, and she caught it. "Hurry," he said, "it won't take long for them to come. They'll hurry and they'll be more than a few, and they'll be extremely pissed off. My wife was well-loved by many besides myself."

Cody stepped into the dress, and Dylan helped her with the laces. Once it was on, he bent to scrape dirt from the floor and rub it on her, over her dress, her face, her hair. "Wha . . . ?" She tried to brush his hands away.

He continued to cover her with dirt, saying, "You've come a long way. You've lost your kerchief and baggage, and your escort has been killed by a fall from a cliff. You've been traveling for days, coming from Glasgow, you're hungry as hell—but don't you dare say *hell*—and you're looking for me because you're my cousin. My mother's sister's daughter. Remember that; you know only my *mother's* family, and you don't remember my father at all. You say *nothing* about my father. You're from Virginia, and you are expected. I had a letter from you six months ago. Got that?"

She nodded, looking frightened. Like she might cry, but she swallowed it. Dylan stepped back, and realization struck him in the gut. Cody looked exactly as she had the day before, in the vision. He spun on Sinann, wanting to know what was going on, but the faerie was still sobbing into her arms. Cody blinked tears from her eyes.

He grabbed Cody by the arm and drew her outside. Standing in the dooryard, he pointed out over the waving field of oats gleaming green in the sun and said, "Go that way, down the side of the field, not through it, 'cause you don't want to make a path for someone to see. When you reach the end of this field, turn left and follow the crevice between those peaks there, all the way down to the larger glen . . . valley. Try not to fall, or get stuck. Find someone—anyone will do as long as it's not a Redcoat—and tell them what I just told you, and they will help you find me. You can trust with your life anyone who thinks you're my cousin. Okay?"

Cody nodded again, and the grief in her eyes made his own rise to choke him. He swallowed hard, and said, "Then go. I'll see you in a little while." She started walking, and as he watched her go, he wondered what in God's name she was doing there.

Then he went back into the house, and the stench of rape and violent death choked him again. The horror slammed into him anew, and he flinched, staring hard at the floor while he struggled to breathe. It was several moments before he could force himself to approach the table. Sinann still crouched on the malt bin, weeping, hugging her knees.

She spoke, a running babble of terror. "I tried to stop him. I did my best. Ye can see his clothing on the floor, and ye must know he dinnae seem to care how bare he was, nor how often he tripped over his toes, for ye ken he's a madman, and yer Cait put up a fight of her own but couldnae save herself, and I swear I dinnae know he was yet alive, ye must believe that, and when I saw I couldnae stop him, I flew to find you, but when I got there, I could see ye were surrounded by a hundred soldiers and indisposed to come nae matter how desperate ye might be to leave the garrison, and so when I returned here, the deed was done and he was gone and I've no idea where. *Och,* Dylan . . ."

Dylan still had the bayonet in his hand, and realized it only as he neared Cait's body. He stared at it a moment, then set it on a chair before stepping close to the table. "Cait . . ." Her pale face now had a transparent blueness, in stark contrast to the blackening blood spattered everywhere. He reached beneath and lifted her legs to lay her sideways on the table. He noted she was still warm, and not all the blood had dried yet, but there was no need to preserve forensic evidence. There would be no fingerprints taken, no blood splash analysis, no skin taken from beneath the victim's fingernails, no DNA analysis of the semen, no cloth fibers nor stray hairs collected. He said to the faerie, his voice low and choked, "What do you mean, you didn't know Bedford was still alive?"

"It wasnae Bedford."

He looked at the pile of clothing on the floor, and the sight of finely cut red velvet and doeskin bred horror. "Ramsay?"

Sinann nodded. "Aye. I dinnae ken how, but 'twas Ramsay. He's alive, and he's the one killed yer Cait."

Tears filled Cody's eyes so she could hardly see, and ran down her face to drip from her chin. She made her way down the valley to the spot where Dylan had told her to cut between two mountains. "I didn't know," she said, over and over. "I didn't know. It wasn't in the records." Why had that stupid faerie sent her to that very moment? What sadistic bent had caused Sinann to drop her in the midst of this horror? Where was she, anyway? She sobbed as she went on walking.

The crevice between the hills was steep in all directions, and she picked her way carefully among huge boulders, ferns, and dead trees, terrified of falling. It was a long way down, a long walk even without the rough terrain. A trickle of water ran here and there between rocks and under ferns, and if she stepped too close to it, her sneakers slipped on the mossy rocks. Soon her legs were trembling with exhaustion and she had to sit down on a boulder.

Sobs shook her. All that blood! Poor Dylan! She cried until she just couldn't cry anymore, then sat, gasping, on the rock. Poor Dylan. Now she knew why the faerie had kept saying, "One day earlier." Cody had been supposed to warn Dylan. But she had failed.

As Cody's mind settled and cleared, another thing the faerie had said came to the fore. Something about Cody being a natural witch. Witch? It had been right after she'd seen Dylan in the tower. She'd done that herself, it seemed. She'd contacted Dylan in the past.

Hope blossomed. Could she do it again? But only by one day. If she could glimpse him hundreds of years in the past, it should be easy to contact him only the day before. Her heart beat faster, and she gulped the air. What if she could save Dylan's wife?

She sat up and closed her eyes, concentrating the way she had in the tower. Using the meditation technique Dylan had taught her, she focused on him. Breathing slowed. Her mind focused on Dylan, then narrowed to Dylan the day before. *One day earlier.* Where had he been? Her mind explored the vicinity. Breathing slowed even more. She opened her eyes. The world seemed fuzzy. It was darker than a moment ago. For a second her attention wandered and it grew light again, but she focused and returned to where she'd been.

There was a movement nearby, a shifting of the air that resolved into a figure. A man, walking. It was Dylan. Cody began crying again. "Dylan!" He turned to look. The surprise on his face would have been comical in another situation. "Dylan," she said, "don't leave Cait tomorrow."

"Why?" There was apprehension in his voice. He was taking her seriously. That was good.

The sobbing took her again. Tears were cold on her face. "Don't let her out of your sight. She's going to be killed. Tomorrow."

"How do you know?"

"Trust me." She pressed a hand to her mouth. She couldn't control the weeping. The image of Dylan began to fade as she dissolved in tears again. "Just trust me, Dylan. Please trust . . ." Then he was gone.

She sighed, satisfied. He was warned. She'd succeeded. That gave her the strength to continue on down the crevice. She walked onto the glen floor, the tears slowing.

Ahead a house crouched, well into the valley, low and brown like

Dylan's, covered with vines and flowers and the roof a dirty brown thatching. A woman was at the window, and hurried out the door at sight of Cody. "*Och!*" said the woman. She was skinny and rawboned, and had an infant on her hip. A toddler followed her from the house. At first she struck Cody as ragged and impoverished, but on second glance Cody could see she and the children were clean and their clothes well-mended, and perhaps the woman was not as old as she had at first appeared. Cody recognized Gaelic but didn't understand it, and the voice was filled with concern.

"Help me," said Cody. New tears came. She struggled to remember the story Dylan had told her to give. "Help me, I'm lost." The woman didn't seem to understand. She frowned, but Cody persisted. "I need to find Dylan Matheson."

Then the woman's eyes lit up. "*Dilean? Dilean Dubh? Och, tha!*" She handed over the infant and picked up the toddler, then gestured for Cody to come with her. When Cody hesitated, the woman took her by the arm to guide her along the path from her door. As they walked between oat fields, Cody looked around and began to recognize where she was. This was Glen Ciorram, about halfway to where the castle sat at the edge of the lake. It looked a bit different without so many houses dotting the landscape, and the village seemed completely missing. Instead of sheep pastures, the valley floor was sectioned into plots where grain grew, divided in some spots by stone walls and in others by terraced levels. But, as much as the valley floor had changed over the centuries, she recognized the rocky hills to the south and the wooded ones to the north. Down the valley, the castle was visible and the lake beyond it glittered in the sun.

She tried to tell this woman the story Dylan had given her to tell, but the woman only shook her head and chattered on in Gaelic. She smiled, which was a relief, but Cody gathered she spoke no English and had understood only Dylan's name. So Cody let herself be guided to "Dylan Doo."

As they neared the castle, the woman began to veer to the left, toward a trail that led off to some woods near the lake. But some women came through the castle gatehouse, and Cody's escort called out to them. The reply was agitated and tearful, and the escort replied in a shocked tone. She took Cody's hand and drew her toward the castle. Cody guessed the news of Cait's death was spreading. Her heart sank. The place was in an uproar, women crying and men red-faced with anger and grief. It was plain her warning to Dylan had failed to prevent disaster, and now she feared something worse had happened. What of Ciaran? Or Dylan himself?

Approaching the castle, Cody couldn't help but stare around her at the stone rampart and towers of the structure. They were all so *old*. Many times older than the oldest building she'd ever seen at home. In the courtyard area of the castle just inside the gate, one large man with a long, dark blond beard was shouting at people. Some of the men were shouting back, and all were furious. In the structure to Cody's right there were some large doors, where people scurried in and out. Cody's guide let her toddler down so he could run and play with some other children in the courtyard, then relieved Cody of the infant. She said something to another woman walking by, who stopped and peered at Cody with deep curiosity.

"Who are ye that ye're in search of Dylan Dubh?" the second woman asked. She was as thin as the first woman, but taller and a mite older.

"My name is Cody Marshall. I'm . . ."—*the story, remember the story*—". . . I'm looking for my cousin, Dylan Matheson. He's expecting me. My . . ." she looked back toward the castle gates and wished Dylan were here, "My escort . . . he died. Fell." Tears rose again. Where was Dylan? Why hadn't her warning stopped the murder? Her heart stood still. "I need to find my cousin. Please, where is he?"

"Come with me." The tall woman guided her through those large doors, past a wall hung with well-used swords, dirks, and some firearms, then into a huge room echoing with voices. A fireplace at one end emitted smells of cooking, and there were several roasts on a spit over the fire. There were many tables around, some benches and a few stools. Two small children were sitting on a bench by a table near the hearth, crying. An older boy sat quietly with the little ones, looking like he would cry soon, too, but was struggling to be a grown-up.

The tall woman said, "Ye came at a bad time, Miss Marshall. We've just now discovered a kinswoman has been murdered. The wife of your cousin, in fact. It was a horrible . . . just horrible . . ." The woman welled up with tears, and Cody could see from her reddened eyes she'd been crying for a while. The woman went to the crying children and picked up the girl, who appeared about a year old, hugging and rocking her.

Then, as if coming to her senses, she turned and addressed Cody again. "I apologize, Miss Marshall. My name is Sarah Matheson. Have you eaten?"

Though she remembered her instruction from Dylan that she must appear hungry, she shook her head. "I couldn't possibly . . ."

"Nonsense. Here, take your cousin a spell, and I will be back shortly." She handed over the child, and hurried away through the door next to the fireplace.

Cousin? Cody looked at the girl, then at the boy, who might have been three or four, and knelt by him. "Ciaran?" He perked and said something in Gaelic, wiping his eyes and looking into hers. This was certainly Dylan's little boy, and the baby most likely a daughter, though she resembled their father less. The baby's hair was dark like Ciaran's, though it was a mass of curls, and two small dimples decorated her cheeks.

Cody held out her hand to the boy and said, "Hi, my name is Cody." He took the hand but said nothing further, and only regarded her with wide, blue eyes.

The argument outside became louder and more intense, and Cody's heart leapt as she recognized Dylan's voice in the mix. She stood, searching for him. He was shouting in Gaelic, which seemed odd to Cody, for she'd never known him to speak more than a few awkward sentences of it. But even more odd was his bearing when he entered the huge room with the large blond man, followed by a much younger man with more reddish coloring, who was also shouting to be heard over the din. Cody had seen Dylan in a kilt before, of course, but now he wore it as if he'd been born in it. He spoke rapid-fire Gaelic, angry and red-faced like the other men, and succeeding better than most at shouting down the larger man.

Dylan turned to another man standing quietly nearby, and reached out for the sword the other man held. The quiet one relinquished the weapon, and Dylan hung it across his chest from its cloth baldric. Then he returned to arguing with the big man and his young ally.

Sarah returned from the other room with a wooden plate containing a sandwich-looking thing stuffed with cheese, and a napkin folded under the plate. Cody set the baby on the bench next to Ciaran and accepted the food, though she truly couldn't imagine eating. She looked toward Dylan and said to Sarah, "What are they fighting over?" She sat on a nearby stool.

Sarah picked up the baby and sat on a bench near Cody. "They all want to kill Major Bedford, for he's the one as done the deed."

Cody frowned, uncomprehending. "Deed? You mean the murder? You're sure?" She knew who Bedford was, for Dylan had told her about the Englishman who was responsible for the scars on his back.

"Aye." Sarah spoke as she continued to listen to the argument. "Dylan says it was an English bayonet killed Cait. Bedford has threatened him, and the entire clan as well, for years. He's killed other Mathesons in the past, including my own husband. The entire glen would like to see the Major's throat cut. Iain Mór is arguing now that the clan should rise against the garrison. Artair, there, is his younger brother and would lead the rising. Dylan wishes to kill the murderer himself, without assistance."

"Iain is the big guy . . . uh, man?"

"Aye. He's the Laird and he's Cait's father. A number of years ago Bedford killed Iain's father, as well, and the Laird has been of a mind for vengeance since then. But Dylan is telling them both there is nae need to jeopardize the entire clan for the sake of ridding the world of one *Sassunach*. Dylan is telling Iain and Artair to not give the English an excuse to confiscate the entire glen. Dylan wishes to take personal revenge, as well."

Cody nibbled on her sandwich and watched the argument. She'd never seen Dylan like this. The man she'd known, and the boy before that, had always had a quick temper, but it subsided just as quickly. This unrelenting rage just wasn't him. The poor guy was surely upset about his wife. She said, "Dylan will calm down after a while. He doesn't mean what he says."

Sarah gave her a glance she thought looked like pity, but Cody didn't know why.

Cody's heart lifted when it seemed Iain and Artair were backing down. Voices were lowered, and the three men began to sound more reasonable.

Ciaran stood up on his bench and shouted out to his father, which caught Dylan's ear and cut short his argument. Without another word to the Laird or the brother, he strode across the room to pick up his son and murmur something to him Cody didn't understand, but from his voice she could tell he was saying everything would be all right, hugging him and pressing his face to the boy's head. Then Dylan sat him on the bench and squatted on his heels to be at eye level with the child. He spoke in a level, careful voice, stroking his son's head and brushing the hair from his eyes. The boy replied something that sounded like *cota cherk*. The next thing he said, though, Cody understood fully: *"An Sassunach."*

Dylan stood, one hand on the hilt of his borrowed sword, and muttered, as if to himself, "He's dead meat."

Cody stood, put her hand on his and said, "Dylan, you can't kill him; you would never kill anyone. I know you; you don't have it *in* you to kill."

But Cody's childhood friend frowned at her, his blue eyes smoldering in an unfamiliar, bearded face. There was a bitter edge to Dylan's voice, and his gaze chilled her to her spine, as he told her, "There are no fewer than eight souls in hell who would assure you I *do* have it in me."

Cody was speechless. Horrified.

He turned to leave, but she kept her hold on his hand and confronted him. "*Dylan!* You can't!" Had he really killed people? "You're not a murderer!"

"No. I'm not." He was impatient and puzzled now, as if she'd stated the obvious. She was confused.

Regardless, she couldn't let him go out and kill that Bedford guy. "Sarah, tell him he needs to stay."

Sarah nodded, and came to take Dylan's other hand. She spoke to him in Gaelic, softly but quickly so he would listen.

He replied in English—a relief to Cody, whose head was beginning to hurt trying to figure out what everyone was saying. "I can't let him live. Not now."

"Then wait. Give Cait the respect of a proper burial. Be there for her tonight." Sarah also spoke English for Cody's benefit now. "Keep watch with her."

Dylan's body seemed to sag at mention of his wife's last night above ground. The struggle in his eyes was a long one, but finally he said, "Aye. Aye, you're right. After she's . . . after the funeral. I'll wait that long." He lifted the baldric from his shoulder and laid the sword on a table, then picked up his daughter to hold her and murmur softly to her in Gaelic.

CHAPTER 24

Dylan had no intention of killing Bedford. But he couldn't tell the clan why he knew Bedford had not killed Cait, and furthermore couldn't let them know Ramsay was still alive. With Ramsay alive, Dylan's marriage to Cait and the legitimacy of their daughter would come into question, not to mention the several complex issues regarding Ciaran's birth. Dylan had to talk Iain and the rest of the clansmen into letting him take vengeance alone. Then, once the anger of the clan was defused, he would figure out how to justify not killing the Major at all. It was a difficult thing to hold his hand, for Bedford certainly deserved to die for other reasons, but it was best for everyone if his death weren't attributable to a Matheson.

The wake was a nightmare for Dylan. He returned home with his kids, Sarah and her sons, and Cody, to find Una and Gracie had cleaned Cait's body, scrubbed the table and swept the floor of blood, and laid the body out on a clean linen sheet. The bloodied clothes had been stuffed into the rag basket, along with Ramsay's silks and Cody's jean pieces he'd left on the floor.

Una sat by the fire, weeping, inconsolable. Several women around her spoke in low, soft tones as Una covered her face with her hands. Father Turnbull was beside the body, murmuring in Latin. Dylan set Ciaran on the floor and went to the table to see his wife, his heart hammering his chest. The priest stepped aside as Dylan leaned over the body.

Cait didn't look asleep. She looked murdered. Pale and mottled, she had two deep purple gashes in her neck and the bottoms of her feet were unnaturally clean. There were deep cuts on her hands that bespoke a struggle with the bayonet as she had died. The awful smells were gone, washed away, replaced with fragrant herbs and oil, and Dylan hoped the women had washed away all the murderer had left behind.

They hadn't yet finished winding the body, so he lifted the edges of the sheet to cover her, tucking it gently around her legs, then around her arms and chest, leaving only her face visible. He could feel the stiffness of rigor now in her arms, though it hadn't yet reached her legs. The women would sew the shroud closed, but for now he didn't want the children to see their mother naked and violated. He tucked the linen up around her neck, then smoothed her hair from her face.

He kept expecting her to open her eyes and smile up at him, and on only the most superficial level he knew she wouldn't. His heart insisted she was still alive—couldn't be dead, for if she were really dead, his heart would die right along with her. The time had been too short. He'd waited so long for her and had come so far, they should have had a lifetime together. Two years was impossibly short.

He half-crouched to lay one arm over her, the other circled her head, and he laid his mouth aside her ear as he said slowly, carefully, "*A Chait, m'annsachd*, I'm sorry. I'm so sorry." He'd failed to protect her. The crushing knowledge that he'd failed in his most important responsibility stopped his breath. He closed his eyes and cleared his throat, then forced several deep breaths before continuing. "Thank you for being my wife." He paused as he caught a last remnant of the scent of her in her hair, and it filled his head. He went on, "Thank you for giving me children." His heart began to realize he was saying good-bye, and the pain approached like an avalanche rumbling in the distance. He took a deep breath. "Thank you for the most pure happiness I could ever have known." He kissed her cheek, stood to kiss her lips, then straightened and went to sit in the chair by the cabinet.

His jaw clenched against the agony that slammed into him, and he concentrated on breathing. His thumb rubbed hard against the arm of his chair, back and forth in a steady rhythm. Nobody would see him break down. He required a stoic demeanor, for the sake of all the other people around who had loved Cait, too. Una could weep, the children could cry, but it was for him to bear his pain like a man, so the others would know stability was not lost.

Sarah came to him, picked up his hand, and pressed something into it, closing his fingers around it. He looked, and found Cait's wedding ring. "No," he said, and caught Sarah's hand as she turned away. "No, I want her to be buried with it."

Sarah took his hand again, and pressed it closed around the ring. "She cannae. Unless ye would have her dug up as soon as news of it left the glen. Especially with the soldiers in the garrison so nearby. Ye cannae let her wear gold in her grave with strange men about. In particular *English* men, who have nae respect for us."

His lips pressed together, he nodded, then took his crucifix from under his sark to return the ring to the linen cord where he'd kept it so long. Once more inside his sark, the ring felt cold against his skin.

Ciaran climbed into Dylan's lap while Sìle played on the floor at his feet. She had a rag doll her mother had sewn from the remnants of one of Dylan's old sarks, and was beating it against the floor to watch the dust rise from under the dried reeds. Ciaran curled up against his father's chest, his thumb in his mouth. Dylan hooked a finger around the boy's wrist and pulled out the thumb with a tiny, smacking sound. "No." Ciaran put it back in, and Dylan pulled it out again. "No, I said," and he held his son's hand completely inside his own.

Dylan said, "You're afraid." Ciaran nodded. Dylan was horrified the children had witnessed the assault, and wished he knew how to deal with that sort of emotional trauma. He said, "Today when you saw the bad man, did he see you?" Ciaran shook his head. "You hid." Ciaran nodded. "How?"

"Mother said. She said to get in the box." He pointed to the malt bin. "Were you afraid?"

Ciaran nodded. "She had the bucket and it spilled."

"You all were outside the house and she took you inside?"

The boy nodded again. "The water spilled. She said to go inside to wait for breakfast, and we went inside. She put us in the box. She said, *Don't look and be quiet.*"

"But you looked." When Ciaran wouldn't answer that, he said, "It's all right, son. If you looked, it's all right. I only want to know what you saw. You told me you saw a man in a red coat."

"I looked like this." Ciaran put a thumb and forefinger up to each eye to show how narrow the gap was through which he'd looked from under the box lid.

"Good boy, he didn't see you. Were you looking the whole time?" *Please say no.*

Ciaran shook his head, and that brought some relief to his father. "Mother started to go outside again, but the man came inside. The man was talking, but I didn't know what he said. They both talked." Dylan nodded. Ramsay would have been speaking English. "Then Mother shouted at the man in the red coat. I put my hand over Sìle's mouth, and she was quiet. We stayed quiet." His lip quivered. "And then there were noises."

"Don't think about the noises, Ciaran." Dylan adjusted the boy's weight on his lap. "You're a brave boy. You protected your sister." But Ciaran buried his face against his father's chest and began to cry, and Dylan knew why. "Ciaran," he said, hoping he could make the three-and-a-half-year-old understand, "it's good that you hid. You're too little to save your mother. You did what was right. You saved yourself and your sister, and that's what your mother wanted. You did well, son. I'm proud of you, and your mother up in heaven is proud of you."

The crying faltered, but didn't stop. Dylan reached behind to the cabinet for his sporran, and dug into it with one hand for the talisman, which he showed to Ciaran. "Here, look at this." The boy looked, snuffling. "This here is a magic brooch. It's a talisman of protection. See, it's a symbol of the Clan Matheson. That's your people. It protects you like your clan, but for it to work, you must keep still. When you wear it, nobody can see you if you keep still. That way your enemies can't find you." He handed it to his son. "I want you to wear it whenever you feel afraid. Then nobody can find you to hurt you. Just remember you must be still and not move for it to work."

Ciaran took the talisman and pinned it to his sark, then laid his head against Dylan's chest. He disappeared immediately.

Dylan groaned and felt the boy's invisible chest to remove the invisible talisman. Ciaran reappeared. "I can't see you, either. Keep it inside your sark until you need it." He pinned it to the inside, and Ciaran curled up to sleep against his father's chest. Dylan reached back to the cabinet to put the sporran away, and lying on the shelf was a piece of paper that was the whitest he'd seen since . . .

He snatched it up. Photocopy paper, it was, folded in quarters. He slipped his thumb inside the fold for a look, confirmed it was a photocopy of something, then put it inside his sark.

Iain arrived at the wake, accompanied by Malcolm, Seumas, and Robin. Marc was close behind, with Ailis and their two sons. The men paid their respects to Cait, then went outside for an angry discussion of their many grievances against the English. More mourners came, some with food and some with whiskey and ale. With so many people milling around, many went outside to talk and eat.

When darkness fell, Dylan put the kids in their beds to sleep, then claimed a spot to sit on the floor near the closed bedroom door. But that proved too much in the line of traffic, so he wandered outside where people stood around or sat on the sod to talk. Some boys—Eóin, Gregor, and Coinneach—wrestled near the edge of the oat field.

Dylan wondered for a moment why the world hadn't come to a standstill. Surely existence must have ended, but it seemed he was the only one who knew it yet. He went around back to the sheep pen and sat on the stone dike.

Cody helped Sarah sew up the edges of the shroud Dylan had tucked around his wife's body. Sarah twisted the end of her thread around her finger to put a knot in it, and started at the feet. Cody, with the needle and thread she'd been handed by Sarah, went to the head. She paused for a moment, gazing at Cait's pale face. The woman had surely been beautiful. It was evident even in the discolored, lifeless face. Cody could see why Dylan had been so attracted to her.

She'd not known Cait, but she knew what Cait meant to Dylan. She remembered his voice when he'd talked on the phone about the woman he'd fallen so deeply in love with back in the past. At the time he'd been in awe of the strength of his own passion, awash in the enormous changes Cait had made in him. Her death was unthinkable. Cody knew what horrible pain this must be for Dylan. Tears stung her eyes as she folded the linen over Cait's face and pulled the thread between her fingers once to straighten the kinks, before pushing the needle through the shroud cloth.

It seemed to take forever to stitch the shroud closed. Sarah's work was careful and close, so Cody made her stitches the same. At least, she tried to. Sewing on buttons and repairing burst seams wasn't much experience at sewing, and inevitably her stitches were less neat than Sarah's. It didn't help, either, that her fingers were trembling.

When the job was done and the thread bitten off, she gave the needle back to Sarah and went to the window for some fresh air. This tiny, dirt house was awfully stuffy, and there were people everywhere, talking and drinking. Someone outside began singing melancholy songs to the accompaniment of a little wooden flute. A chilly breeze wafted through the window, and Cody leaned out for some relatively fresh air, marred by a whiff of sheep at the far end of the pen.

Dylan was out there, sitting in the moonlight on the stone wall. The breeze tossed small locks of his hair around his face, but he wasn't wearing a coat. She retreated from the window and turned to look for one, peering through the candlelit dimness into dark corners where belongings sat or hung on furniture or on pegs on the walls. There, that must be it, hanging on a peg by the door. She folded it over her arm and went outside, around to the rear of the house where Dylan sat.

He stood when he saw her, a gesture that struck her as formal and un-Dylan-like. "Here," she said, "you looked cold, so I brought your coat."

A smile touched his mouth, mostly hidden by his ragged beard. "I'm fine, thanks." So much about him had changed, it seemed. Even his voice was different. Deeper, somehow. He spoke more slowly than he used to, as if careful of choosing his words in even so simple a statement as "I'm fine."

"Oh, good, then could I wear it? I'm freezing." He nodded, and helped her slip her arms into the sleeves. Her teeth were chattering, and she was shivering, she was so cold. How he could be comfortable was a mystery. She huddled inside the heavy, dark wool, engulfed by the too-large garment.

There was a silence as they stood, staring at each other, then he said, carefully, "I'm sorry about the crappy welcome. I guess I should say Hello. How have you been?"

Cody's throat closed, and tears sprang to her eyes. She pressed her fingers to her lips for a moment, then put out her arms to embrace him. "Oh, Dylan . . ."

He thwarted the hug by taking both her hands in his and holding them together inside the two of his. "No." Her mortification must have shown on her face, for he continued, "No, it's not that. You must understand that any touching would be misinterpreted by anyone who saw." He glanced at the back window of the house. "Even if you're my cousin, they'd still take it wrong if you hugged me. They would be shocked beyond belief if I were to prove too chummy with my female cousin just now." He shook his head. "I won't let that happen to Cait's memory. I care for these people, and they've accepted me as one of their own. This is the way they are, and I'll live by their standards if I'm going to live among them."

"I'm sorry."

He sat back down on the stone wall. "Don't be. You couldn't know." Cody perched on the wall to his left as he continued. "When I first got here, I was lucky to have Sinann whispering in my ear every time I was about to . . ." He looked to his right, made a disgusted noise, then returned his attention to Cody. "Anyway, as I was saying before I was so *rudely* interrupted"—he glanced to his right again, then continued—"this is a different world."

The moon was full and throwing a silvery pall over the glen, and the oat crop hissed in the breeze down the glen. The sheep huddled at the far end of the enclosure, asleep. Cody regarded him, her head tilted. "You've changed, Dylan."

He snorted. "I hope to God I've changed. Four years ago I didn't know what the world was about. I'd never been truly hurt or injured, never been hungry, never been in love, never had a real family. I knew nothing."

"Now you know everything?"

He peered at her and frowned. "What I do know now is that I haven't got the answers to anything, where before I thought I had them for everything."

"You think you couldn't have found answers in the twentieth century?"

He shrugged. "Maybe." He started to say something else, then shut his mouth.

"Don't you miss it? Any of it?"

"Of course, I do. I miss my mother. And, to be perfectly honest, I miss you." She couldn't help smiling at that, and a smile touched his lips. He continued, "I miss toilet paper, indoor plumbing, barbecue sauce, telephones, painless modern dentistry, and thong bikinis on girls." He paused, thinking for a moment, then he said, "You know what else I miss?"

"What?"

"Listening to rock music while watching cartoons with the sound down."

Cody laughed. "Oh, man, I haven't done that in years."

He threw his head back and took a deep breath, a wide smile on his face. "It was so cool the way the action always matched the music. Didn't matter what it was, it always looked synchronous." The lines in his face seemed to smooth out, and the light of nostalgia in his eyes was almost youthful. For a moment, the old Dylan was back.

"Quite a change from that, to be living in abject poverty." She indicated with a tilt of her head the tiny mud hut overgrown with moss and flowering vines.

A laugh came from him, sounding almost like a burp. "Cody, by local standards I'm a wealthy man, which, besides being cousin to the Laird *and* the father of his grandchildren, makes me influential in Ciorram. I'm dead certain Major Bedford had no idea how much this land was worth when he arranged for the Crown to award it to me. Or possibly he'd expected to simply take back the deed and sign it over to himself after I died at the hands of the assassins he sent after me in Edinburgh. This piece of land is huge compared to the individual tenancies in the glen below. My family eats every day, even in winter, and I have surplus crop to trade in the village. I own a still that produces over a hundred gallons of whiskey a year. My sheep herd is the largest in Ciorram, and each animal produces more wool every spring than any other sheep in the glen."

"You're happy here?"

He thought for a moment, then said, "I've gotten used to it here. I've learned that electricity is not essential to happiness. That there's a value to doing some things the slow way. Quality of life depends less on how fast you travel than on who you're traveling to meet. I have friends and family here. I belong here. I came back because I don't belong in the future any more. I'm not sure I ever did. I believe I was sent here for a reason."

"What reason?"

"Don't know yet." He shrugged. "All I know is that I can't go back. It wouldn't be right."

"But it's so dirty and smelly here."

He sighed and looked around, at his sheep, his pasture, the stream that burbled over rocks nearby. "The smells aren't so bad. You get used to them after a while and tune them out so they become baseline. You know,

I bet you can't smell car exhaust unless you stick your nose up the tailpipe of a running car. But I sure could smell it when I went back for those six weeks. I can't smell cow manure anymore to save my life, but I can smell rain on the wind. And I can smell the barley when it's become malted. I can smell the earth warming in the springtime and the new grass as it grows. Nothing, except bad meat, really stinks to me anymore."

"Even that pot you've got sitting under your table?"

"What, the ammonia? You can smell that? Well, shoot, Cait tied an oilcloth over the top, but I guess I should get her to . . ."

He blinked, then looked away, his head bent forward. *"Oh, Jesus."* His voice was barely a whisper. "I don't believe I just did that."

There was a long silence. Cody waited, wishing she could put an arm around him. She said softly, "It's all right, Dylan. It just means there are places deep inside that haven't accepted it yet."

After a minute or so, Dylan appeared to breathe again and looked up at the moon. Finally, he said, "So, how's old Raymond?"

Cody took a deep breath to loosen her unbearably tight chest, then said, "Raymond won't be born for another two hundred and fifty years."

That brought a wry smile. "Ah. Then how *will* he be when one day you go all the way to Scotland, looking for a faerie to transport you back in time?"

She shrugged. "For what it's worth, we're still married."

He lowered his chin to peer into her eyes and read them as he urged her to continue, "But . . ."

Another shrug. "He's being a butthead."

Dylan flashed a white grin, another glimpse of the old Dylan—the one who had been her best friend for thirty years. "But you love him anyway."

She sighed and stared hard at the ground. "I don't know, Dyl. I've been doing a lot of thinking."

"What's there to think about? He's your husband."

She looked up at him and once again found the hard eyes of the new Dylan. This was not what she'd hoped to hear. "Is this still you adjusting to the people around you?"

He shook his head. "I've always felt that way. Marriage is sacred."

"You wanted your mother to leave your father."

"Does Raymond beat you?"

"No."

"Then it's not the same thing. Has Raymond broken any other vows to you?"

She shook her head.

Dylan opened his mouth to speak, but hesitated. There was a brief silence as he considered his words, then, "Cait and I had disagreements. There was a time when I began to have doubts. I wondered whether she regretted the marriage. But when I asked her about it, she said she would never have allowed herself to fall in love with a fool. Cody, I think you're nuts about Raymond. That can't have changed. I've known you all our lives, and I don't think you could ever have fallen in love with a fool or a bad man. Trust me on this, there is *nothing* more important on earth than your family. Ray is your family. You love him, he loves you, it's that simple."

"Dylan, he wasn't always this way."

"And what changed?"

"He's been awfully cranky since you . . . well, left."

Dylan snorted. "He misses me that much?"

"No, I do."

Dylan's eyebrows went up. "Ah. You're in mourning, and he can't handle it."

"Exactly."

He chuckled. The carefulness returned to his voice and he glanced around. "I was kidding, Cody. I mean, it's been damn near three years . . ."

"It's been six months since you left. I mean, for me. I went looking for Sinann in the summer of 2001."

That silenced him for a moment. Then he took a deep breath. "Why did she send you to this date?" His voice took on an ominous edge, and he glanced over to where the faerie must have been sitting. "I know it wasn't to warn me."

With a start, Cody suddenly remembered Sinann's letter. "Wait. She gave me something to give to herself when I got here. I forgot all about it." Cody reached under the wool dress and into her blouse pocket to pull out the yellowed paper Sinann had given her, and opened it. No sooner did she have it unfolded than it was snatched into thin air, and disappeared.

"Tink!" Dylan's voice was hard. "What did you do?" There was a silence, and he appeared to be listening. Then the lines of his face hardened. "Oh, God."

Cody looked around, but saw nothing. "What did she do?"

His eyes danced with fury. "She says it was a letter to herself. The letter says she'd tried to send you back to yesterday, but couldn't. In the letter, she guesses it was because of her attempt this afternoon to send *me* back." He paused for a moment, then went on, as his voice tightened and he gestured in an effort to describe a process he didn't seem to fully understand. "She thinks the magical forces attracted each other, or something, and that caused you to arrive a day later than you were supposed to. She thinks that in each of the three instances I was sent through time, my exact destination was determined by the presence of magic near the destination moment; each time I arrived at a time and place where magical energy was present." His voice was shaking now, and he'd gone pale. Cody wasn't sure why.

She gasped as she realized something. "But, Dylan, if Sinann knew in the future that Cait would be murdered, why didn't she tell you when she sent you back last November?"

He sighed. His eyes were more haunted than she'd ever seen them before. He shook his head. "Because I *was* forewarned. Yesterday I saw you in the hills, and you told me this would happen. Even though I knew it was going to happen, I couldn't prevent it. I was being interrogated by the Redcoats. There was nothing I could do."

"And so she tried to send me back to the day before, so Cait wouldn't be alone while you were detained." An idea struck, and she addressed the spot where Sinann was sitting. "Hey, what if you tried again? Send me back to the day before."

Dylan listened for a moment, then said, "She says no. The presence of the magic this afternoon would still interfere, and you would arrive at or near the same moment you did last time, too late to prevent the murder. Also, there's the fact that you can't exist in two places at the same time. Best case scenario, she would fail to send you back at all. Worst case, you would arrive a few seconds before your other arrival. That would be fine, until the moment when you arrive from the future. Once that happened, the you that had arrived from this evening would cease to exist. You would be dead. History can't be changed. Sinann knows that." He glanced around for the faerie, but didn't seem to see her. "I've tried to change things, but have never been able to."

"But history *can* be changed! I can prove it! See, I read in a history book about Ciaran!"

That brought a blink and a snort of surprise. "My son Ciaran? Ciaran

Robert Matheson? How can you be sure?" In spite of his surprise, there was a note of pride in his voice that his son's name would go down in history.

She shrugged. "Well, I think it was him. At Culloden." Dylan paled, and she hurried to continue. "It didn't say he died there. But in any case, I also found something else." She reached for her jeans pocket, which was no longer there. "Oh. What happened . . . I had a photocopy. . . ."

"This?" Dylan pulled the paper from his shirt.

"There it is." She reached for it, and unfolded it to show him. "It's why I came. It's the church records of deaths in Glen Ciorram. Ciaran's name is in it. But if he was at Culloden, this couldn't be right. Something changed, somewhere." She held the page up to the moonlight to see.

He looked over her shoulder. "Are you sure it's the right church?"

"Our Lady of the Lake in Glen Ciorram. That's the one up near the garrison, right?"

"Yeah." He took the paper to read it himself. "Cait's not here. But Marsaili is. Sarah's youngest son and Marsaili's mother. Miles Wilkie. They all died in 1714. Seonag died the year after. Miles's widow isn't here, though, nor anyone else who died. . . ."

Then he put his finger on Ciaran's name. It stood out from the others, in careful, block lettering: Ciaran Robert Matheson. The date was . . .

"Day after tomorrow."

Cody nodded. Dylan began to tremble. He whispered, as a prayer, *"Not my son, too. Please, God, don't take my son. Please let this be a lie."* Then he ran his finger along the page. "The Widow Wilkie isn't here. And Cait. Cait isn't here. In fact, look at these dates. Before Ciaran, the last death was Seonag in 1715. No other deaths were recorded for seven years. After, they pick back up in 1722, when . . ." He folded the paper in a hurry. "Oh, God, I didn't want to see that. Not Malcolm." He looked sick, overwhelmed.

Cody reached for the paper. "Maybe you shouldn't read any more." He relinquished the paper, like an evil thing, and she said, "We've got to keep a close eye on Ciaran for the next couple of days."

Dylan nodded, deep in thought.

CHAPTER 25

Dylan sat up with Cait most of the night, along with fifteen other kinsmen. Near dawn, he wandered into the bedroom and found Cody and Sarah asleep in his bed. He returned to the sitting room and found a spot on the floor near the fire, between Seumas and Robin. He wrapped himself in his plaid and closed his eyes, expecting to drop off immediately. Dylan had learned long ago to sleep wherever he could lay his head, but now he did no better than a light doze that didn't feel like sleep at all. He lay there, listening to the snoring of his friends and family, marking each moment until he would have to put his wife under the earth.

Cody and Sarah awakened in the small hours to watch over Cait as Dylan pretended to sleep. Once the sun was well up on a gray day, the smell of boiling parritch stirred him, and his children's voices urged him to join them. He sat up, groggy and aching, and pulled Sìle onto his lap, where she poked and played with her rag doll. Today the funeral awaited him, like a sphinx that would test him as he passed.

The clan buried Cait in the churchyard, amid the skirl of bagpipes, the wails of women, the tight-jawed faces of men, and a long, tedious speech from Father Turnbull. It seemed to Dylan the priest dwelt unnecessarily on the shocking circumstance of Cait's death.

The body was interred in the winding sheet, laid carefully at the bottom of the grave by Artair and Robin. Dylan hated there was no coffin, but even if he'd had the cash for it, there wasn't one to be found between here and Inverness. Above the Highland line, coffins weren't just for the rich, they were for the *wasteful* rich. He looked away as earth was shoveled on top of her.

And the thing was done. The clan returned to their homes and their work, and Dylan took his children with him to the high glen.

He had no heart for chores, but things needed doing. He milked the goat, pastured the sheep, and repaired one of the horse collars. Cody and Sarah were there to prepare food and watch the kids, and that was a relief. Cody's photocopy made Dylan terrified for Ciaran, and so he was glad for two more sets of eyes.

It was late afternoon when Bedford and a contingent of his dragoons rode into the dooryard. Dylan looked up from closing the gate behind his sheep, and the sight of five red coats made him grip his staff hard with both hands to keep from drawing Brigid. The Lieutenant accompanied Bedford. Dylan said, "May I help you?" Cold formality was his only choice of action.

The Major pulled up and the Lieutenant gave the order to halt. Bedford said to Dylan, "We've come to investigate the murder of your wife."

"You needn't bother. I know who did it." From the corner of his eye he saw Cody and Sarah peeking around the corner of the house, keeping close to it where they were partially hidden.

Bedford only glanced at them, then dismounted and addressed Dylan again. "Good, then you can identify the culprit and we shall take proper action."

Dylan shrugged. "Never mind. It will be handled." He bit back an ugly comment about English justice. Sending Bedford to arrest Ramsay would be a monumental waste of breath at best.

Bedford shifted his weight and lifted his chin. "If you think an unsanctioned hanging will be tolerated in my jurisdiction . . ."

Dylan set the end of his staff into the ground and shifted his weight with an insouciant air. "Last I heard, Major, the Laird's jurisdiction still holds. I think it's Iain Mór you need to harass on the subject of unsanctioned punishments." Dylan stepped close and lowered his voice. "In any case, I've nothing to say to you."

His eyes narrowed at the Lieutenant and he raised his voice. "Perhaps you want to arrest me again just for the fun of it, thereby giving the murderer a shot at the rest of my family." The Lieutenant looked away, and his cheeks reddened.

Bedford's voice had an angry edge. "You would do well not to withhold information of this crime. You could very well be held as culpable as the criminal himself. For instance, I would be very curious to know where your MacGregor and Campbell friends were yesterday morning."

Dylan blinked. *Seumas and Keith? Oh, for Pete's* . . . "If you're looking for someone to torture for information, then how about you chain yourself to your barracks wall? I'm sure you know at least as much about this as I do. Maybe more."

Blank surprise crossed Bedford's face, and Dylan suddenly wasn't sure of what Bedford knew or didn't know. He was certain Bedford knew Ramsay was still alive, for Bedford must have arranged for the escape from the Tolbooth. But perhaps he didn't know Ramsay was nearby. The Major said, "I can't imagine what you could possibly mean by that."

"You will. Think on it, and you'll figure it out." He raised his voice for the benefit of the rest of the soldiers. "So, if y'all are not going to haul me in again, I believe my supper awaits me. My wife is dead, my children need tending, and I have a life ahead of me to sort out. I bid you all good day." With that, he turned his back on the Redcoats to go inside. Cody and Sarah scurried in before him.

Just inside the door, he gripped his staff and waited. There was a long silence outside before he finally heard the sound of the soldiers riding away. Then he let his breath out with relief. It wouldn't have taken much justification for Bedford to have arrested him.

At sunset Dylan sent Cody with Sarah to stay at the castle, for it would be unseemly for her to stay overnight with Dylan. She promised to return early to make him breakfast, and he smiled, knowing it would be more like him teaching her how to do it without a stove.

He put the kids to bed very shortly after supper, for they were exhausted and cranky from the emotional two days and the late night previous. "Off to bed with the two of you." He picked up Sìle, who talked to him in baby chatter, then laid her head on his shoulder. Ciaran followed quietly, and climbed onto the lower bunk. Dylan set Sìle into the lower bed, then lifted Ciaran onto his own bed above. Sìle curled up on her pillow with her thumb in her mouth and closed her eyes, but Ciaran kicked and fussed. "Hey," said Dylan. "No guff."

Ciaran shook his head and whined. Dylan was in a mood to order him into bed and just leave him there, but instead he gathered the boy into his arms and sat on the lower bunk. "You need to sleep."

Ciaran shook his head. "The man in the red coat will come."

Dylan stifled a groan, helpless in the face of his son's all too valid fear. The temptation was to lie, but instinct told him it was a bad idea, for Ciaran could not help but be aware the glen was crawling with men in red coats, men who did not like Mathesons. "If he comes, I won't let him hurt you."

"What if he kills you like he did Mother?"

Excellent question. But a bluff wasn't the same as a lie, so Dylan shook his head. "No, he won't. I can fight better than your mother could. I'm bigger and stronger. I'm stronger than the *Sassunach* in the red coat. I will kill him first."

"Why didn't you kill him before he killed Mother?"

Pain hit Dylan's gut like a cannonball. He opened his mouth to answer, but no sound would come. He swallowed hard, and finally was able to say, "I wasn't here."

"Why weren't you here?" The simplicity of the three-year-old's logic cut to the bone, and Dylan felt laid open. Though he'd tried to stay with Cait yesterday, in his heart he was certain it was his fault she was dead.

He took a deep breath to explain that he'd been taken to the garrison for questioning, but changed his mind. That threat still existed, and the likelihood of the English arresting him again in the future was a good one. Ciaran's fear was the enemy tonight, and making the boy even more afraid of the soldiers than he already was would defeat the purpose of saying anything at all. Instead, Dylan said, "Ciaran, I can't answer that. I don't know why things happen the way they do. What I can tell you is that I won't let you be alone. You can sleep in here, and I'll be right here in the house with you. And I won't leave without you."

"Do you promise?"

Dylan nodded. "I swear it."

Ciaran also nodded, and reached for the ladder to climb into bed.

With the kids tucked in, Dylan returned to the sitting room and found himself alone. Completely. He stood in the middle of the room and looked around. When had been the last time he'd been alone like this? There had been that time last fall he'd been in transit to Glasgow, and other times he'd traveled to do business, but he'd never felt alone then. He'd always known Cait would be here when he returned home.

But now he *was* home. And it was all wrong. He couldn't even sit down now, because there was no Cait to sit in the other chair. He looked around the room, at all the places she wasn't. There should have been more than one candle lit, but she wasn't there to light the others. The wool for spinning should be out, being spun as she talked to him and listened to him. If he sat in his chair by the fire, the silence would be unbearable. The darkness would engulf him. He turned toward the bedroom, but neither could he lie down to sleep. He'd never slept in that bed without Cait, but now he would never sleep in it with her. No matter where he went, for the rest of his life, she wouldn't be there.

The pain he'd kept at bay now swept in on him. His body clenched against it. Grief rose from his gut to choke him. Half of himself had been ripped away, and the remainder was a tight bundle of raw agony. "Cait," he whispered. He turned, searching. The irrational conviction crept in on him: she must be somewhere close, unseen in a dark corner or about to come through the door. But she wasn't. At that moment she was under the earth, cold and unprotected.

He hugged himself, and the pain kept on. His knees went wobbly, and he knelt to keep from falling. The pain continued. He realized he was holding his breath, but when he let it out, a sob came with it. Another one followed. "Cait." The remnants of his strength crumbled, and he collapsed on the dirt floor, huddled in an aching wad, sobbing by the light of one flickering candle.

Sinann's voice, softer than he'd ever heard it, came to him. "Sleep. Sleep the night, and when you awake, be rested." Mercifully, sleep took him.

When he awoke at dawn, a numbness had set in that left nothing but a knot of anger in his gut. He rose from the floor and pulled Brigid from her scabbard in his legging. It was time to go looking for Ramsay.

He said to Sinann, "Cody will be here soon. Probably before the children wake up." He spotted the bayonet on the cabinet and went to pick it up, leaving Brigid on the table. "But if not, you stay with them until Cody gets here." He hefted the bayonet, then tossed it and caught it. Good balance. Sharp, too, and the hilt had a good finger guard, which Brigid did not. These plug bayonets were meant to be used as knives when not screwed into a musket barrel. It would be fine justice to stick this thing into Ramsay's neck.

He went outside, and Sinann followed. There he slipped the bayonet into his belt and began to stretch. The weapon was new to him, so he needed to work out with it a little before going after Cait's murderer. The sun rose behind scattered clouds, sending pink and gold rays across the silver sky.

"Ramsay is two days gone. Do ye think there's hope of finding him?"

"It's not rained since then. I've followed colder trails."

"And when ye find him, what if he kills you instead?"

"Then he kills me. But I can't just let him go. I couldn't live, knowing he was out there. He's going to die, and I'm going to kill him. That's the long and the short of it." Dylan faced the rising sun. After a brief warm-up, he pulled the bayonet from his belt and began a deadly, aggressive form with it. He focused his anger, intent on the image of Ramsay's watery eyes, his thin mouth. The bayonet was less graceful than long, silver Brigid, but he quickly learned the feel of it. The blood in him began to sing. His heart thudded, steady and strong, and soon a fine sweat covered him.

The sun was just above the horizon when Sinann's voice alerted him. *"Och."* He looked up to see a man approach, descending the hill at the east end of the glen. The figure came slowly and purposefully, straight for Dylan, walking through the oat field. As the man neared, Dylan could see he was dressed like an Englishman, in velvet and ruffles that flapped in the breeze. The hair stood up on Dylan's neck as he waited, patient and silent, the bayonet at the ready. Many yards from the edge of the field, the man drew a rapier. Still Dylan waited, letting the intruder come to him. When the figure came close enough to recognize, there was no surprise.

"Ramsay."

The Lowlander stepped from the field, struck a pose, and saluted with his sword. "Mr. Mac a'Chlaidheimh. I mean, Matheson. What an odd thing it is to call you that. Change your name to your wife's, did you? I knew she was a selfish shrew, but I had no idea you were so spineless."

Dylan ignored the lame insult and backed, drawing Ramsay away from the field, then circled so the oats would be at his back, for that position also put the rising sun in Ramsay's face. Dylan kept Ramsay talking, to distract him from his intent. "I see you brought a change of clothing with you on your visit to the glen."

"Indeed, I did. A good thing, what with my coat and breeches flying apart on me the way they did. Strangest thing, that. Not that I gave a damn about having to return through the forest in my shirt."

"Bedford let you escape the Tolbooth."

Ramsay laughed and squinted into the sun. He tried to circle, but Dylan wouldn't allow it and they sidled along the edge of the field. Now it was Ramsay's turn to string out the conversation, which might give him a chance at a better position. "Better than that, he engineered it. Provided me with a weapon, horse, food, and money."

"All this time, he knew you were here."

"Don't be stupid. There is an abandoned house two miles south of here. I arrived by foot. Bedford has not the first notion of where I am, and I prefer it that way. After that whore who called herself my wife turned on me, he wished to preserve our business relationship, and therefore necessarily my life. Though I was no longer able to own property in my name, I still had the *Spirit*, for I'd never owned her to begin with. I was able to transfer ownership of one other ship to a fictional name, and thereby was also able to continue my covert dealings. Pirating and whatnot. My legitimate business was at an end, but the other was profitable enough for Bedford that he couldn't bear to see me hang. Furthermore, there was the matter that any gallows confession from me might prove embarrassing for him."

Dylan stood hip-shot, deceptively casual to invite an attack while his position was good. "Bedford was looking for evidence against you so he could blackmail. He must have been apoplectic when Cait went to his superiors with her evidence instead of to him."

Anger flushed Ramsay's face, and his voice thickened as he spoke through clenched teeth. Dylan's heart lightened, for it would be to his advantage if Ramsay struck in anger. "It was appalling how eager Bedford was to help me turn outlaw. He was making entirely too much money selling me all the extraneous people the army picked up here and there. He had to arrange for my continued existence, lest he come up for promotion and not be able to buy his rank or support the monstrously expensive manner of living required of a Colonel. Not much inheritance for the youngest son of a youngest son, you know. With the help of my dear, sweet wife, he had me at his mercy. The bastard still has me by the throat, which turns out to be what he had been after all along. Far from apoplexy, he should have danced for joy. That whore of a wife of mine gave him what he wanted."

Rage suffused Dylan and his heart thudded in his ears. "So you killed Cait."

"Of course, I did. And while I was at it, I exercised my husbandly right. To be sure, I'm far more predictable than you are." Ramsay closed in with his sword. Dylan held his ground as Ramsay asked, "Why haven't you killed Bedford yet? I fully expected you to march over to the garrison and dispatch him without blinking." He switched the tip of his blade back and forth a few times by way of warming up, then shrugged. "No matter. I'll simply kill you. That should shake up your kinsmen a bit, shouldn't it? It will be a miracle if the Major survives the resulting uproar. And if he does, again no matter. A dirk will end up in his back just the same. Your dirk, in fact." Ramsay made a foolish gesture of intent with his sword—a foppish flourish—before lunging.

Dylan parried and attacked with the bayonet, wishing mightily he had a sword. Ramsay parried and riposted. Dylan parried and retreated far enough barely in time. The speed of the rapier was blinding, and the edge sharp enough to slice him to the bone if he stayed too long within its reach. Ramsay lunged. Dylan parried and backed, but Ramsay caught him with a slash across the chest. It sliced through his sark on the right, but on the left was defeated by the wool plaid. Dylan gasped for breath and fury rose with the metallic pain.

Sinann's voice came. "Easy, lad. Dinnae let him cloud yer mind with anger."

Dylan took a deep, calming breath, for she was right. But he said, "Get in the house, Tink. The children." A confused frown crossed Ramsay's face, and he took tiny glances to his rear. Dylan took advantage and harassed, but Ramsay parried successfully and held his ground.

"But if Ramsay's breeches should suddenly fly apart . . ."

He said through clenched teeth, "He'd fight naked. Go. Now." Then he addressed Ramsay. "You raped her."

Ramsay blinked at Dylan's blunt language. "Nonsense. She was my wife. Furthermore, laddie, you might look to the legitimacy of your children. The law severely curtails the paternal rights of men who go about fucking the wives of other men."

"She was never your wife. That . . . *marriage* was never legal. And, as far as the law is concerned, you've been dead for over two years." He tilted his head and said matter-of-factly, "Which makes no difference anyway, for I'm about to kill you myself." He rose to a crane stance, more to confound his opponent than for any efficacy against the sword, then, when the puzzled look crossed Ramsay's face, Dylan feinted and fell back. The Lowlander parried air. Confusion showed in his fidgety engarde.

Dylan went into a series of misdirections, circling fists combined with a twirling mulinette of the bayonet. He feinted again, and Ramsay went for it. This time, instead of retreating, Dylan made a real attack elsewhere, which Ramsay barely parried. Dylan retreated in a hurry to get out of reach of the rapier's riposte. Ramsay made a flurry of thrusting attacks, which Dylan parried with the reflexes of hand-to-hand sparring. He barely deflected the blade enough that the point of the rapier missed its marks, but one miscalculation let the point catch his cheek.

Dylan let go a roar of outrage. He tasted blood, and with his tongue felt an exit hole inside his mouth. Blood ran down his face, then dribbled from his beard. Ramsay pressed his new advantage, and Dylan retreated in a hurry, backing into the oats.

Ramsay followed. "Ruining your crop, lad. What will your brats eat if you go stamping about in their meager food?"

"Shut up." Dylan could hardly see through the crimson rage. He slapped the rapier aside and rushed the Lowlander, roaring as he came, and Ramsay fled, out of the oats and onto the sod. Dylan charged then, trying for Ramsay's throat, but was knocked in the teeth with the rapier's hilt. Once again Dylan had to leap back far enough to be out of the rapier's reach. *Damn!* Ramsay grinned as he struck engarde again.

Dylan spat blood and sat back in a hanging guard now, waiting for Ramsay to come at him—a dangerous ploy, given the speed of Ramsay's sword. But Dylan needed to sucker him in on his own terms. He stepped back, inviting aggression.

Ramsay took the bait and lunged low for Dylan's vulnerability. Dylan stepped back and let him come, parried downward, then stepped on the lowered blade. The tip trapped against the sod, the hilt was snatched from Ramsay's hand to *whap* against the ground, and Dylan backhanded him with his closed left fist. Ramsay staggered back, disarmed, and Dylan followed to slam the bayonet into his gut.

The Lowlander cried out as he fell backward to the sod. Dylan pulled his weapon free, dropped to his knees, and buried it in Ramsay's throat. Then he yanked it out. Blood sprayed with Ramsay's last gasp. Dylan ignored it. He turned the bayonet and took it in both hands, then thrust it in again. And again. A fourth time he stabbed with all his strength, though Ramsay was dead now and his head nearly cut off.

Chest heaving, Dylan leaned over the body and spat a glob of his own blood into Ramsay's red, surprised face. Then he pulled up the bayonet, which was stuck more in the ground beneath than in Ramsay's flesh.

A pair of English cavalry boots stepped into view, a sword was pulled from its scabbard with a metallic *zing*, and Bedford's voice said, "That wasn't very nice."

Dylan, nearly spent, parried just in time the sword meant to take his head. He hauled himself to his feet, switched the bayonet to his left hand, and spun to pick up Ramsay's rapier. He spun again to face Bedford. Blood covered him, and the bayonet was slick with it. He wiped some onto his kilt, and Bedford took advantage of the distracted moment to attack. Dylan parried and retreated again. The rapier was awkward in his hand. He hadn't used a sword this light since the foils in his Tennessee fencing classes. The balance was strange. He tried a mulinette to get the feel, then parried as Bedford attacked and backed him along the side of the field.

With his fighting edge dulled by the fight with Ramsay, Dylan was now at a severe disadvantage. In addition, he didn't want to kill Bedford, for Crown reprisals would devastate Ciorram. Struggling for breath, he said, "Why kill me?"

Bedford rolled his eyes, took a hip-shot stance, and pointed his saber at Dylan's chest. "In the first place, you sheep-buggering bastard, you know things I would rather not have bandied about the countryside. In the second place, you damn near killed me four years ago. You murdered my sergeant and participated in a bloody uprising, then had the effrontery to send your whore to ask for pardon. The real question should be, why haven't I killed you before?"

Dylan raised his chin and said with the little breath to be had, his speech blurred by a swollen cheek that filled his mouth with blood, "The answer to that is that by the time you caught me, I *was* pardoned and beyond your reach." If he could keep this jerk talking, maybe there would be time to catch his breath. Sweat rolled from his forehead and trickled into his eyes. He blinked hard and tossed his head to throw it off, then spat pink foam onto the sod at his feet.

"Exactly." Bedford attacked, and there went Dylan's chance at recovery. Dylan parried furiously as he retreated, his arm aching under the shock of each blow. The curved cavalry sword was slightly heavier than the rapier, but in Bedford's hands negligibly slower. Dylan found himself over-controlling, and had to adjust his mind-set from slashing to stabbing, one thing for which the rapier was better than the saber. His speed improved. He got in a good poke at Bedford's thigh, but not deep enough. The *Sassunach* bellowed and attacked again, with added anger and force, but slightly less control.

A movement behind Bedford caught Dylan's eye. Cody rounded the corner of the house and gawked at the fight, flat-footed with surprise. Dylan focused on Bedford and made a series of feints and attacks, backing him toward the house and Cody, then retreated to give himself room. Bedford swore, panting. In the scant moments Dylan had bought himself, he bent to tap with the bayonet the empty scabbard at his legging. He dared a glance at Cody, tapped the scabbard again, then parried Bedford's next attack. From the corner of his eye he saw her scurry into the house.

But she left the door open. A few moments later, Ciaran came outside. Dylan's heart lurched. Sinann was tugging at the boy's sark, but he fought her and stepped farther into the yard. Dylan yelled, "*No!*" He waved his son back inside.

But Bedford turned and saw the boy. Dylan attacked and was parried, then Bedford, without another instant of hesitation, ran to catch Ciaran before Sinann could haul him back inside. Dylan followed, but Bedford had Ciaran by the collar, his sword to the tiny throat, before Dylan could catch up.

Dylan skidded to a stop on the sod, the rapier cocked like a baseball bat to slash Bedford's neck. "Let him go," he said through clenched teeth. "If you hurt him, by God I swear I'll have your balls on a platter." Ciaran stared wide-eyed at his father, his lip trembling. Dylan slipped his hand inside his sark. Ciaran reached inside his own sark for the talisman pinned inside. *Good boy.* Then he held out his palm to stay his son from using it yet. Ciaran held it in his hand.

"Put down the sword and the bayonet, or he dies." Bedford's voice was triumphant. He figured he'd won.

I nside the house Cody found the knife, the one Dylan usually kept in the scabbard strapped to his leg, on the table. She went to the window to look out, and nearly screamed at what she saw. But she put a hand over her mouth and swallowed her terror. The Redcoat, his back to her, had Ciaran. Bedford was demanding, "Put down the sword and bayonet, or he dies."

Dylan replied, "I swear it, Bedford, on my life, I'll kill you." Bedford was facing the door now, and Cody couldn't go through it again unseen, so she climbed through the window. Why had Dylan wanted her to get the knife? How was she supposed to give it to him without the Redcoat seeing?

Then it came to her: she was supposed to stab the Englishman.

Her stomach turned. She held the knife ready, but couldn't bring herself to do it. She shifted her weight from side to side, wishing Dylan would attack. But she knew it was up to her. She raised the knife. Taking deep breaths, she struggled to summon the courage to use it.

"Throw down your weapon, Matheson." Bedford's attention was on Dylan.

"No." Dylan stared straight at the Englishman, so as not to give away Cody and the knife behind.

"If he dies, it will be on your conscience." So smug! Cody adjusted her grip on the knife and thought she could stab him then, but her arm wouldn't move. Tears began to rise. She hated herself. Dammit, why couldn't she do it? Her grip tightened on the silver hilt, but no matter how she held the knife, she couldn't bring herself to stick it into another human being.

Finally, his mouth a hard line, Dylan dropped his weapons. They thudded to the sod.

Bedford said in a disgusted tone, "Imbecile." He shoved Dylan's son forward a couple of steps, just enough to make room to swing, and hauled back on his sword for a stroke at the little boy's neck.

"*No!*" Dylan made a dive for the rapier, but he was too far.

Cody's heart galvanized. She stabbed Bedford in the pit of his raised arm, and the saber clattered to the ground. Bedford bellowed in pain.

Dylan yelled, "Now, Ciaran!"

Cody yanked out the bloodied dirk and backed off, holding the knife at engarde like a sport foil, the only sort of fighting she knew.

"*Bloody hell!*" The Englishman turned on her, evil intent in his eyes.

D ylan's heart soared. "Now, Ciaran!" The boy dropped to the ground and put the talisman on his shirt. He disappeared immediately. Dylan snatched the rapier from the sod and rushed the *Sassunach*.

"*Bloody hell!*" Bedford held the wound under his arm and looked around, turning this way and that but finding no small boy. Then he turned on Cody.

Dylan held the rapier point to the Major's back, pressing just hard enough for the tip to pierce the wool. "Get out. Ciaran is gone, over the hills, and in a few minutes our nearest neighbor will know you tried to kill him. In half an hour most of the glen will know. In an hour, the church bell will ring for a meeting of the clansmen, including myself. The issue under discussion will be whether to make a complaint to your superiors about Ramsay and your dealings with him, or to keep quiet and hold this over you for the rest of your tenure in this glen. I, myself, will recommend leniency because"—he showed his teeth in a cold smile—"I wish to keep you where I can find you."

Bedford's face was dark red, a white line of pain around his mouth as he pressed his hand to his armpit. He said nothing.

Dylan continued. "You will have a career in the military only so long as you toe the line in this glen. You will have breath only so long as my children remain safe. And I assure you, should anything happen to either one of my children—should *lightning* strike—you will die for it." He dug the tip of the sword into the Major's coat. "Have we an understanding, *Sassunach?*"

Bedford nodded.

"Then you get your sorry ass off my land. And when you return, do it with proper respect, bearing in mind how much I and my clan *do* know about you."

Bedford stepped away from the blade. He nodded toward the sword on the ground and said, "My saber."

Dylan's lip curled. "No, you nitwit. *My* saber." He gave Bedford another poke to get him moving, and the Major lurched a few steps before leaving at a controlled, dignified pace.

Dylan waited till the dragoon was mounted and quite gone, then waited some more, before kneeling beside the spot Ciaran was hiding. He said in Gaelic, "Good lad. I'm proud of you."

Ciaran reappeared, the talisman in his hand, and leapt up to hug his father's neck. Dylan picked him up and stood, hugging him so tightly the boy squeaked. Ciaran came away covered with blood, which Dylan tried to wipe off the boy's cheek with his fingers but only succeeded in making a larger smear. Cody hurried to help, wiping Ciaran's face clean with the hem of her dress.

Then Dylan set his son on the ground and gave him a pat on the bottom. "Now, into the house with you. Go play with your sister and keep Sinann out of trouble." Ciaran clung to his father's knees. Dylan pried him off, knelt, and said, "It's all right, son. I'll be inside shortly. I must do something first." Finally, the boy obeyed.

Once Ciaran was inside, Dylan took Ramsay's rapier and Bedford's saber and slid them both into the thatching over the door to hide them. Then, dabbing tenderly at the gash in his face, he went around the end of the house to the chopping block and yanked his ax from it. Cody followed, saying, "Dylan, you're bleeding."

"No, I'm not." He touched the cut on his chest. "Not much, anyway." He then went back around to the front, where Ramsay lay.

"But you're covered with . . ." Finally Cody saw the body, and gasped. "Oh, my God."

"Cody, nobody can be allowed to see this body, or even know about it. As far as anyone is concerned, Major Bedford murdered Cait." He sauntered over to the nearly decapitated body. Several yards away, he unbuckled his kilt to drop it onto the sod.

"This guy did it? Not Bedford?" She picked up her skirts and went toward the body, leaning over for a good look out of curiosity, but hesitant to get too close. She picked up her feet, careful not to get blood on her sneakers.

Dylan nodded and approached the body in just his sark, taking care as he would with a snake he wasn't sure was entirely dead.

Cody's voice trembled. "Don't you want your clan to know who killed your wife and that he's been stopped?"

Dylan leaned over to get a good look at Ramsay's dead face. "Nope. This here is Connor Ramsay. Anyone finds out he was alive when Cait and I were married, the legitimacy of our children comes into question. Their marriage wasn't technically legal, but without Cait I could never prove that." He knelt and drew his *sgian dubh* to begin cutting the buttons from Ramsay's coat. "Where you and I come from, that might not be such a big deal. But here, producing illegitimate children is a criminal offense, and illegitimacy can damage a child's entire life. Only the extremely rich and powerful, or the abject poor, can live that way."

Cody's voice went soft, shocked. "You did this. You killed him." She was gagging, and Dylan wished she would either stop that or do it somewhere else.

He focused on his work. "Had to. I'd be dead otherwise. *Really* dead. Not just *let's pretend*, sparring dead. He was doing his level best to kill me."

"So it doesn't bother you?"

Now he looked up. "What would you have me feel, Cody? Grief? I've enough of that just now, thank you. Regret? He murdered my wife, and would have done the same to my children and myself if he could." Dylan returned to his job and continued stripping the body. The buttons and jewels, purse, and other things of value he set aside in a small pile for Tormod to melt down for him. The red silk, soft leather, and linen he put in another pile for burning. Then he scabbarded his dirk, turned to Cody, and said, "Go into the house. Make sure the children stay away from the window. You'll do well to keep away yourself." She nodded. He watched, until she closed the door behind her.

Then he turned to Ramsay's body, hefted the ax, and with one casual swing took the head off completely. Methodically, without emotion of any kind, he continued dismembering the body. Blood flooded the sod and a rain of gore, flesh, and bone fragments splattered over his sark.

Once the body was reduced to manageable pieces, he dropped the ax and went for his shovel, which leaned against the side of the house. With it, he dug a shallow hole in his compost heap. Then he began carrying the pieces to it, the soft flesh still warm in his hands. He felt nothing.

Dylan shoveled enough manure, garbage, beef bones, and leaves over Connor Ramsay to be certain nothing recognizable as human would surface before next spring. At the next plowing he would pound the rotted bones to dust and spread the pile over his fields as fertilizer. It would probably be the most useful Ramsay had ever been in his entire worthless life.

The ax and shovel were slimy with blood and excrement, so he took them to the burn, where he cleaned them, then waded into the water to clean himself. He crouched, and pulled his sark over his head to scrub blood from it in the cold, running water.

Clear water flowing around him, he ran wet fingers through his bloodied hair. For a moment he stared at his hand running red. Then he continued washing blood from himself, and felt absolutely nothing.

CHAPTER 26

Dylan wrung out his sark and pulled it back on as he returned to the house. The summer sun was high, and would dry him quickly. He put his head through the window and said to Cody, "Give me that photocopy." She pulled it from her blouse and handed it to him. He unfolded it and sat on the sill to read it in the sunlight, expecting to see Ciaran's name gone from it, but the name was still there. "This isn't right." He looked around for Sinann. "Tink, how is this supposed to work? What's going on here?" The faerie wasn't showing herself. He figured she was too embarrassed, as she should be.

Cody looked at the paper. "It should be gone. I came to keep Ciaran from dying, and so it should be gone because he didn't die." Her hand covered her mouth. "Oh, God, the day isn't over yet. You don't think, maybe . . ."

Dylan looked in the direction Bedford had taken. "I'll be damned if I'm going to sit around till sunset to see if my son dies. Go get Sìle, and Ciaran, and come."

He guided them all down the steep route Cody had taken from the house two days before, picking their way carefully through the crevice to Glen Ciorram. At Marc's house, which sat at the foot of the crevice, Dylan stopped and asked Ailis to let Ciaran and Sìle play with their sons for a little while; he and his cousin were headed to the church.

Ailis shook her head. "Dinnae be spending all yer days at Cait's grave now."

He translated the Gaelic to Cody, then told Ailis, "It's only for a moment. For the sake of my cousin, who never knew Cait but wishes she had." That brought a puzzled look from Ailis, but Dylan let it pass. He and Cody continued on their way to the church.

Father Turnbull was on his way to another church in the parish that day, so there was no resistance when Dylan and Cody entered the rectory next to the vestibule. The darkness inside was damp and heavily scented with incense and beeswax, murky in the depths of the stone church in spite of the day being only half over. Dylan searched the dimness for a candle, and when he found one, he lit it with the flint and steel next to it. A weak, flickering light revealed a dusty place that seemed to have been uninhabited for years.

The room was sparsely furnished with only a hard, narrow bed, a rough table, one chair, and several bookshelves stacked with a few ledgers. Not many, though, for keeping written records was an idea fairly new to the Highlands. One of those ledgers lay on top of the table, and Dylan set the candle down to open it.

"Death records. This is the current book—the back pages are empty." He paged through to find the last entry, and when he found it, pulled Cody's photocopy from his shirt to compare it. This was the page she'd been sent, all right. All the entries matched, right up to Seonag's death in 1715, except that everything afterward was blank. "Turnbull hasn't been keeping records. I bet he hasn't even cracked this book. Seonag was the last in the glen to die when Father Buchanan was alive. This is his hand-writing. The next name after Ciaran's is Malcolm's, in 1722. And it's a different handwriting than Seonag's or . . . *Ciaran's*. It's . . ."

Then it hit him. The block lettering was his own. "I wrote this."

Cody frowned. "Why?"

"So you would come. So you would save Ciaran's life."

"But why would you write Ciaran's *death* record to save his life? That's pretty creepy."

"I did it—*will* do it, because I already know what brought you here." He took the candle and looked around the room until he found a large bottle of ink and an old, dirty quill. He pulled the cork from the bottle and stuck in the quill; the ink was thick but not entirely dried out. He took them to the table and began to write in the book.

"Dylan, you don't have to . . ." But just then an accidental blob of ink smeared on the page. It matched exactly a small blob shown in the photocopy. "Oh . . ."

When he was finished, he stood and leaned over to blow on the wet ink. It was *very* creepy to see his son's death record, but at the same time he knew it was necessary. Now he could rest assured there was no other reason for it. "History can't be changed. Things happen for a reason, and sometimes the reason is that there is no other choice but to do what you must."

Cody stepped close and hugged him.

Sinann appeared, startling them both. "Shame on the both of ye. Now, young lady, are you ready to return to your husband?"

Cody hesitated. Dylan could see she was thinking about staying, and he waited for her to think it through. She said, "Ray will be really snarky when I get home." She looked at Dylan. "But I have to agree that marriage is sacred. You said I was 'nuts' about him, and I can't argue with that." She sighed. "Yes. I need to at least try to work things out with Ray."

Dylan smiled, and hugged her. "You'll make it, I know you will. When you get home, tell Mom hi for me." A shadow crossed her face, and he said, "Well, maybe not. Just make sure she knows I love . . . loved her."

Cody nodded, and Sinann raised her hand. "Are ye quite finished now?" Cody nodded again, Sinann snapped her fingers, and Cody was gone.

Dylan was alone the day he climbed the slope to the churchyard, carrying a wooden cross he'd hammered together out of scraps of lumber. Sunrise was well under way, the golden sunshine warming the ground where he walked. The woods behind the church were alive with birds, the cacophony of their calls almost distracting. He went straight to the newest grave, and shoved the cross into the ground at the head of it. He planned to replace it one day with stone, or even marble if he could manage it. Perhaps if Ramsay's gold and silver weren't needed next spring, he would use them to buy the stone then. A nice, white marble carved with an angel. She would like that.

He sat on the ground, cross-legged, near the head of the grave, and breathed deeply of the morning air. Summer flowers were in bloom, and the world smelled fresh and warm. Some roses nearby threw a rich scent. He began talking to Cait. He told about Ramsay coming, of the fight, and informed her that her murderer was dead. The sun rose a little higher. He told of Ciaran's close call, and assured her their son was none the worse for wear. "He's a strong one. Smart."

He continued, "Cody returned to her husband, and I think they're going to do all right." A wry smile lifted the corners of his mouth. "I think she's found a new appreciation for the boring, peaceful life. She wanted me to go with her, but I couldn't. I know I'm meant to stay here.

"When I came back, Cait, I came for you, and for Ciaran, but I think there's more to it than that. I was brought here for a reason, and I think that reason is that I know things about the future that can help the folks here in Ciorram. I don't know why I was chosen, or if the choice was accidental, but I do know there must be a purpose to this."

His chest tightened. He took a deep breath and let out a sigh. "There's a lot of work ahead. I've got to convince your father that bucking the Crown will only get him killed and his people transported, hanged, or imprisoned. I can't let Artair succeed him, or that fool will destroy us all. I've got to help the clan, our children, and our grandchildren make it through the hard times ahead." A dry laugh rose in him. "If I live long enough. Who knows, maybe I'll be joining you before too long."

He took a deep breath and said brightly, "So, how have you been? Bored? I can imagine. You were never one to be still for long."

He stayed a few minutes longer, warming himself in the sun and re-membering. Finally he kissed his fingers and pressed them to the freshly dug ground. "See you later, sweetheart." He stood and made his way back down the glen toward the castle, where his children waited for him.